WEST WYANDOTTE
KANSAS CITY KANSAS
PUBLIC LIBRARY

Ðisney
Olaf's
FROZEN
ADVENTURE

D1316786

Also From Joe Books

Disney Princess Comics Treasury
Disney Frozen Cinestory Comic
Disney Cinderella Cinestory Comic
Disney Frozen Fun Book
Disney Zootopia Cinestory Comic
Disney Winnie the Pooh Cinestory Comic
Disney Alice in Wonderland Cinestory Comic
Disney Star vs the Forces of Evil Cinestory Comic
Disney Princess Comic Strips Collection Volume One
Disney Princess Comic Strips Collection Volume Two
Disney Moana Comics Collection
Disney Elena of Avalor: Ready to Rule Cinestory Comic
Disney Tangled Cinestory Comic
Disney Beauty and the Beast Cinestory Comic
Disney Tangled Before Ever After Cinestory Comic

Disney
Olaf's
FROZEN
ADVENTURE
CINESTORY COMIC

JOE BOOKS LTD

Copyright © 2017 Disney Enterprises, Inc. All rights reserved.

Published simultaneously in the United States and Canada by Joe Books Ltd,
489 College Street, Suite 203, Toronto, ON M6G 1A5.

www.joebooks.com

No portion of this publication may be reproduced or transmitted,
in any form or by any means, without the express written
permission of the copyright holders.

First Joe Books edition: November 2017

Print ISBN: 978-1-77275-490-2
ePub ISBN: 978-1-77275-853-5

Names, characters, places, and incidents featured in this publication are
either the product of the author's imagination or are used fictitiously.
Any resemblance to actual persons (living or dead), events, institutions,
or locales, without satiric intent, is coincidental.

"When We're Together"
Words and Music by Kate Anderson and Elyssa Samsel
© 2017 Wonderland Music Company, Inc. (BMI)
Used By Permission. All Rights Reserved.

"That Time Of Year"
Words and Music by Kate Anderson and Elyssa Samsel
© 2017 Wonderland Music Company, Inc. (BMI)
Used By Permission. All Rights Reserved.

"Ring In The Season"
Words and Music by Kate Anderson and Elyssa Samsel
© 2017 Wonderland Music Company, Inc. (BMI)
Used By Permission. All Rights Reserved.

Joe Books™ is a trademark of Joe Books Ltd. Joe Books® and the
Joe Books logo are trademarks of Joe Books Ltd, registered in
various categories and countries. All rights reserved.

Library and Archives Canada Cataloguing in Publication
information is available upon request.

For information regarding the CPSIA on this printed material,
call: (203) 595-3636 and provide reference #RICH 767318
1 3 5 7 9 10 8 6 4 2

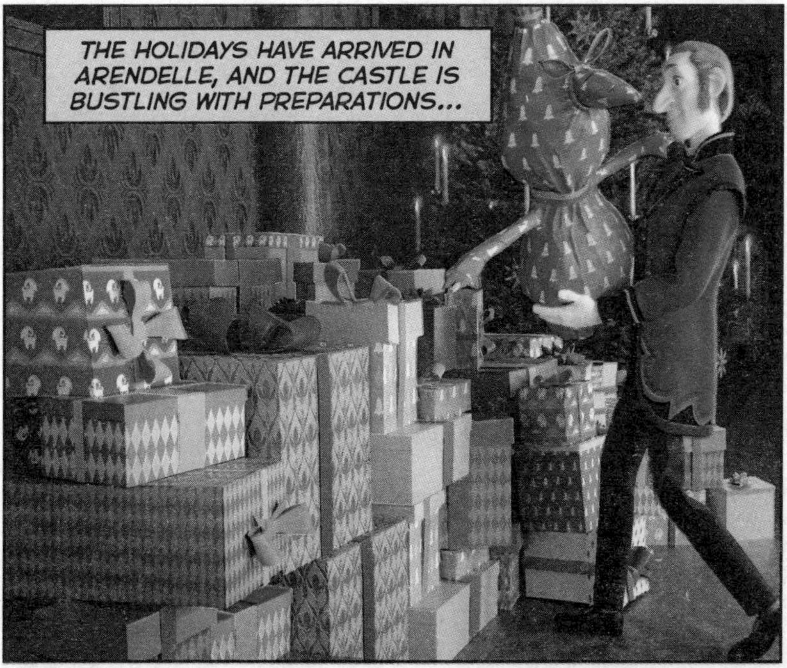
THE HOLIDAYS HAVE ARRIVED IN ARENDELLE, AND THE CASTLE IS BUSTLING WITH PREPARATIONS...

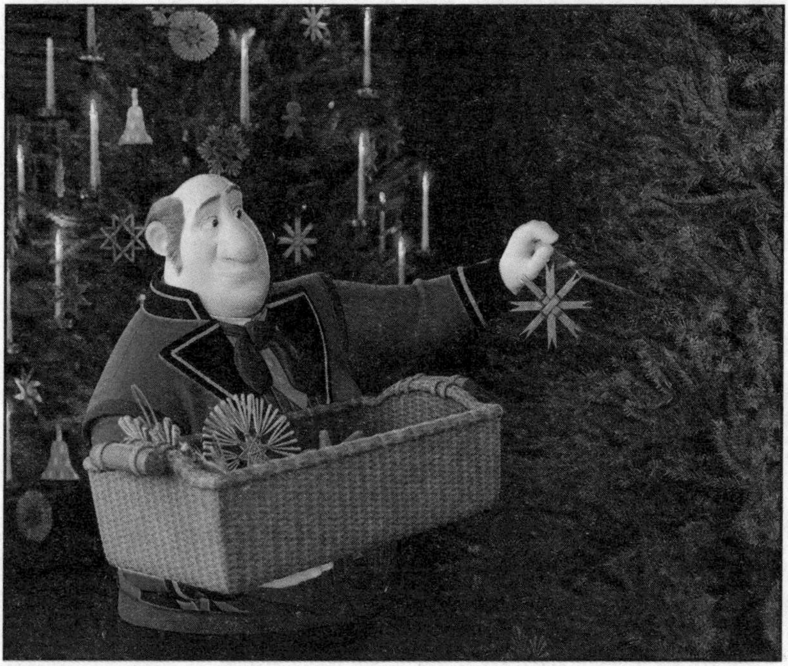

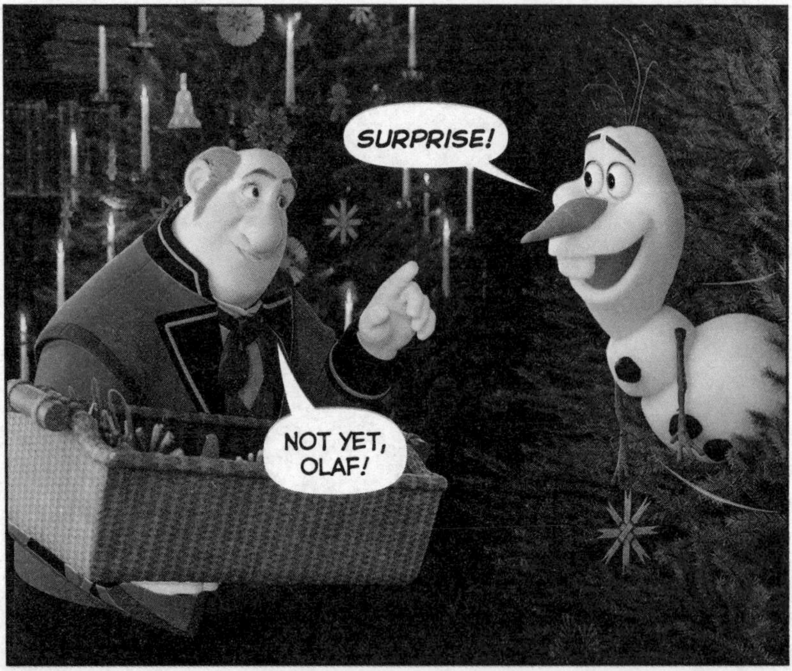
SURPRISE!
NOT YET, OLAF!

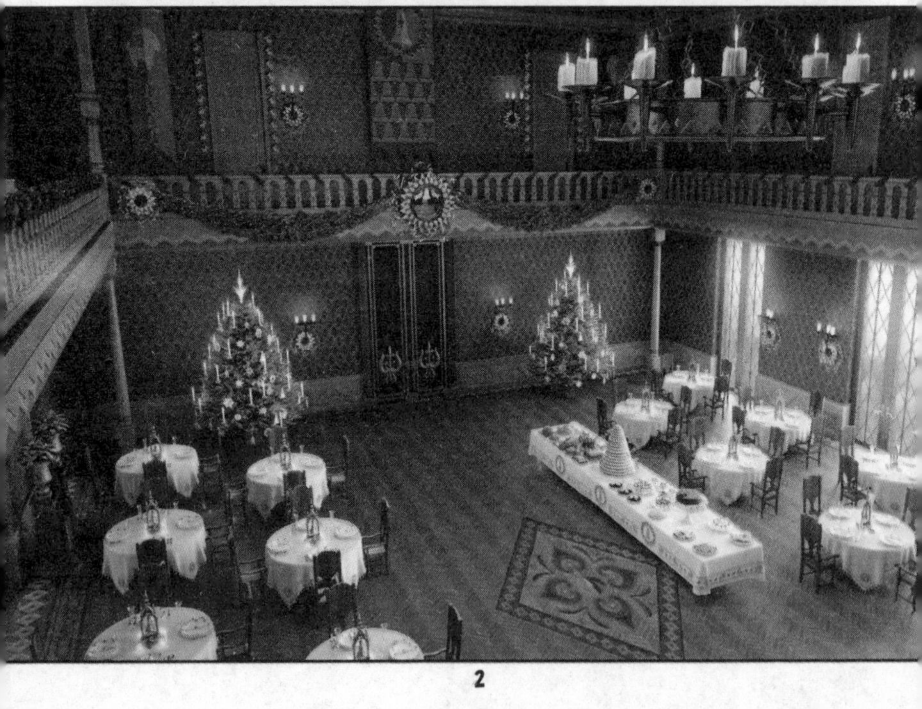

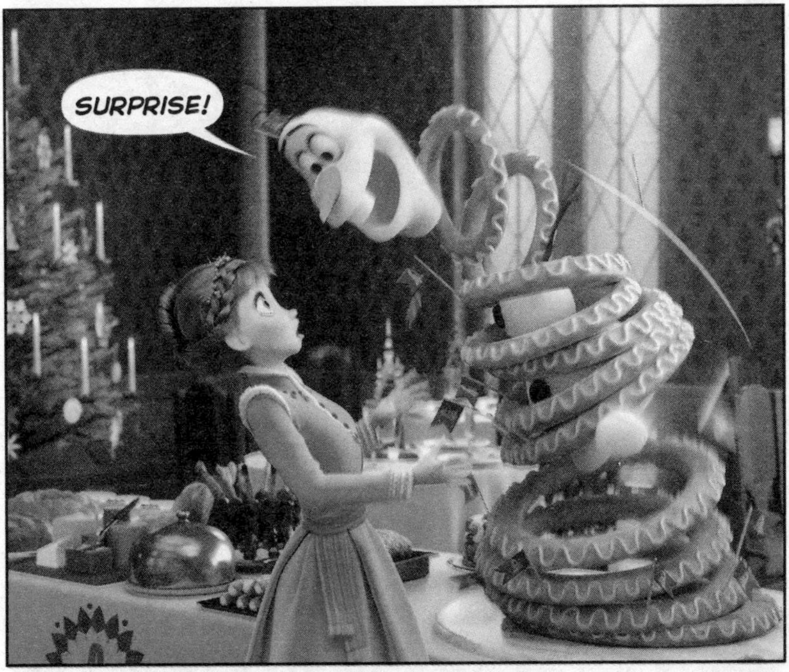
SURPRISE!

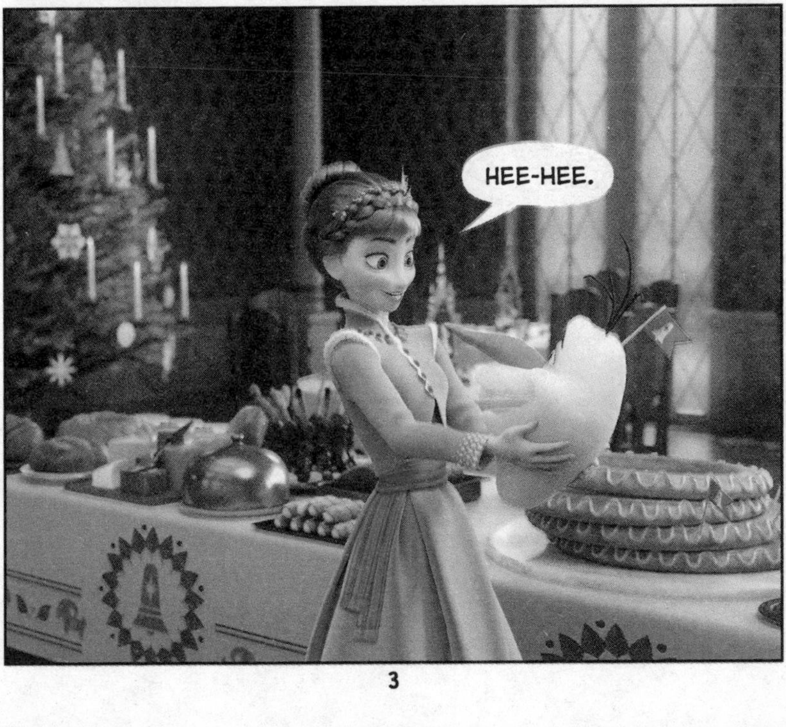
HEE-HEE.

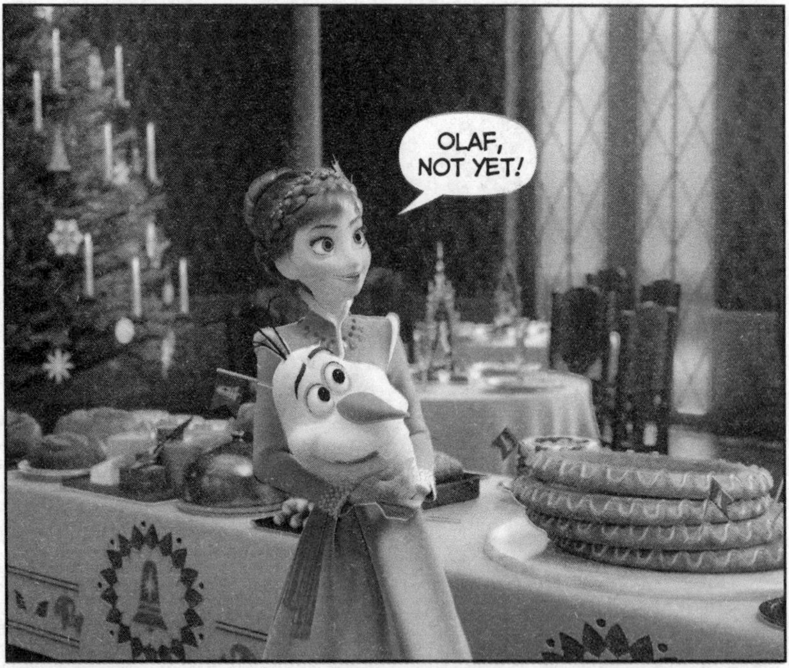
OLAF, NOT YET!

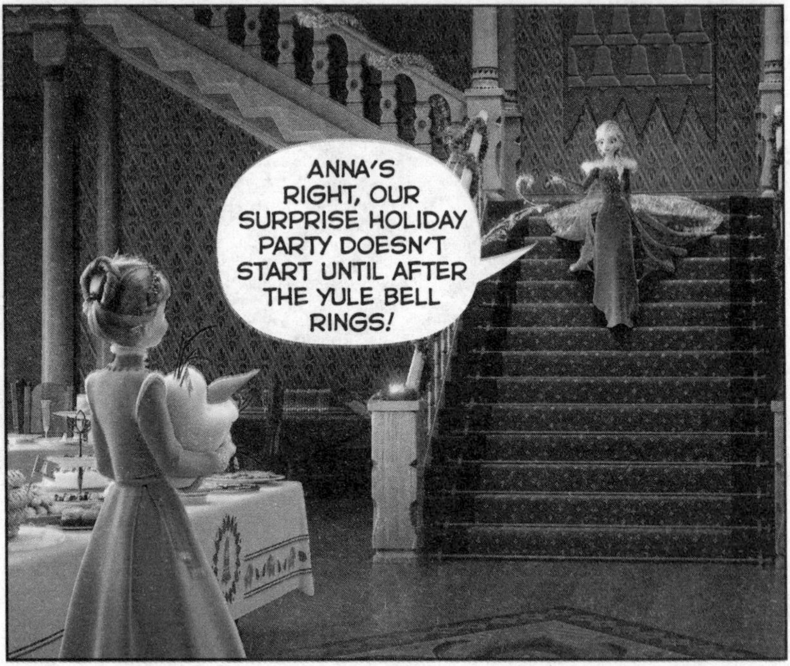
ANNA'S RIGHT, OUR SURPRISE HOLIDAY PARTY DOESN'T START UNTIL AFTER THE YULE BELL RINGS!

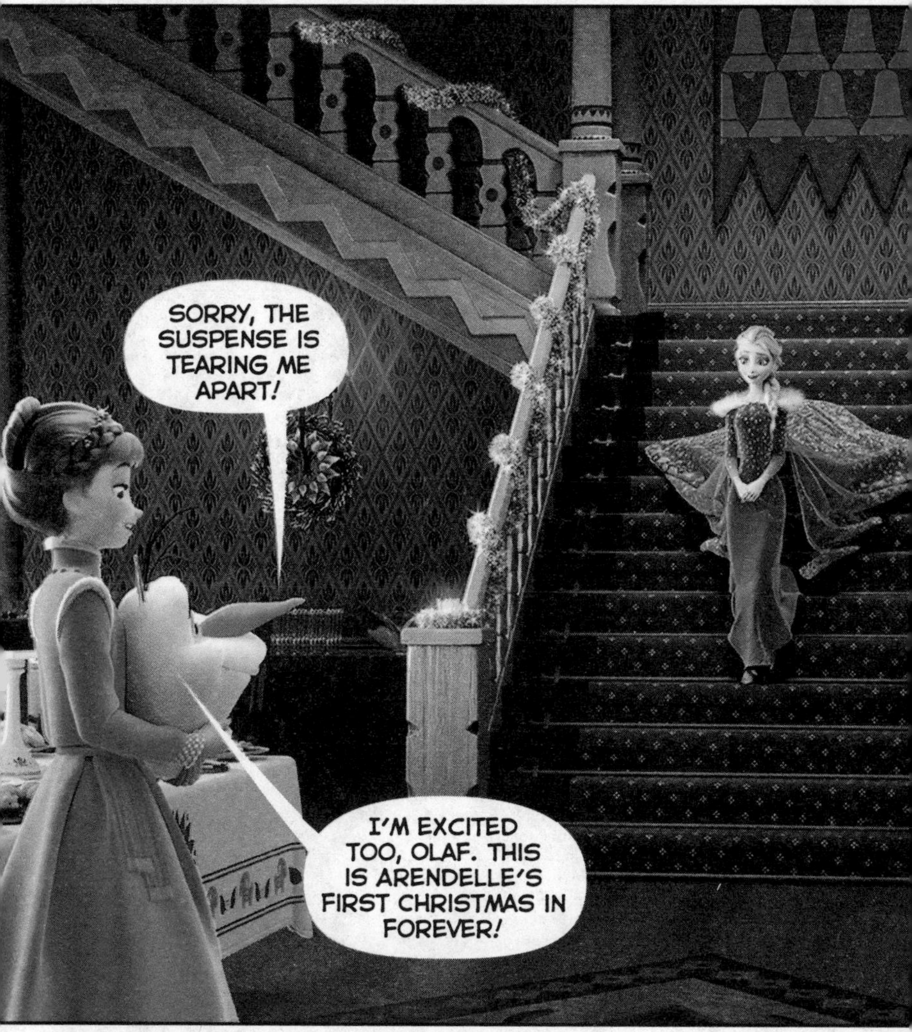
SORRY, THE SUSPENSE IS TEARING ME APART!
I'M EXCITED TOO, OLAF. THIS IS ARENDELLE'S FIRST CHRISTMAS IN FOREVER!

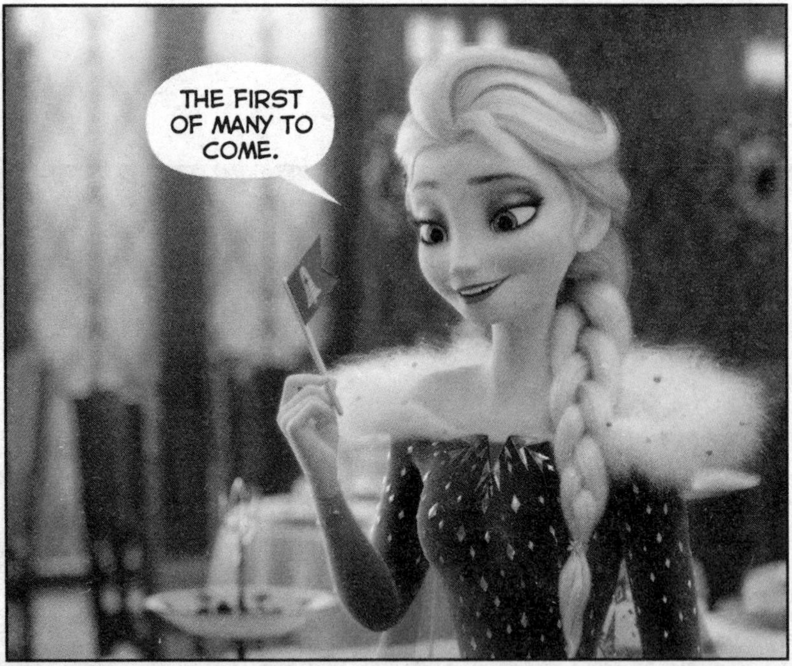
THE FIRST OF MANY TO COME.

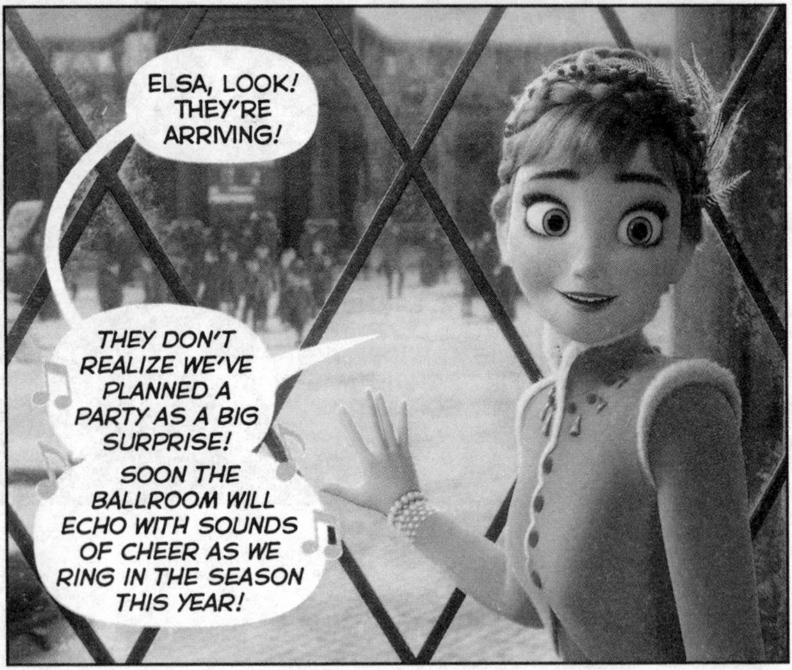
ELSA, LOOK! THEY'RE ARRIVING!
THEY DON'T REALIZE WE'VE PLANNED A PARTY AS A BIG SURPRISE!
SOON THE BALLROOM WILL ECHO WITH SOUNDS OF CHEER AS WE RING IN THE SEASON THIS YEAR!

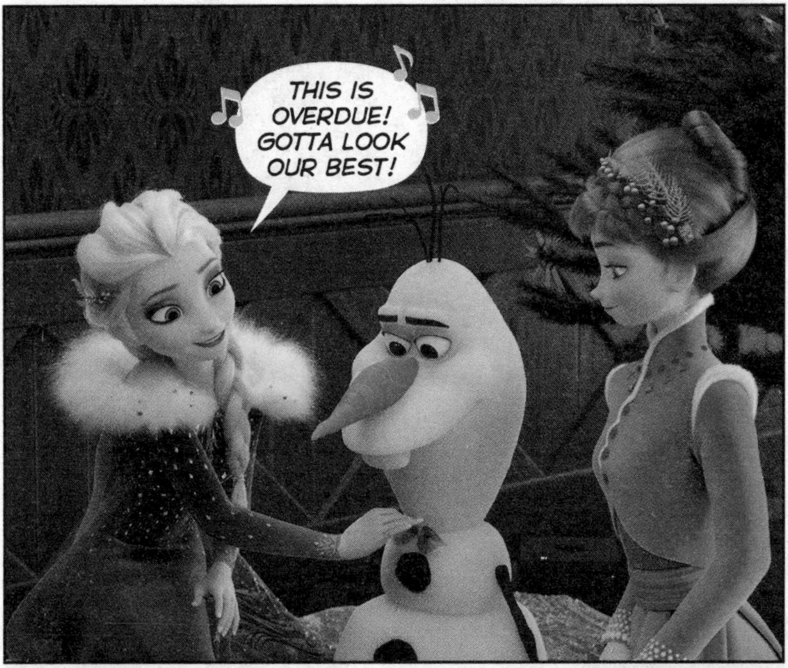
THIS IS OVERDUE! GOTTA LOOK OUR BEST!

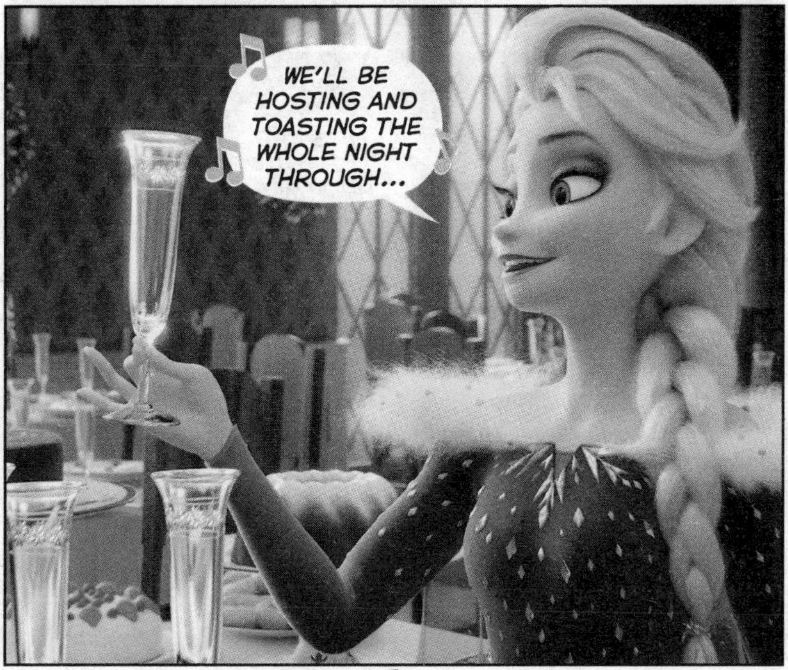
WE'LL BE HOSTING AND TOASTING THE WHOLE NIGHT THROUGH...

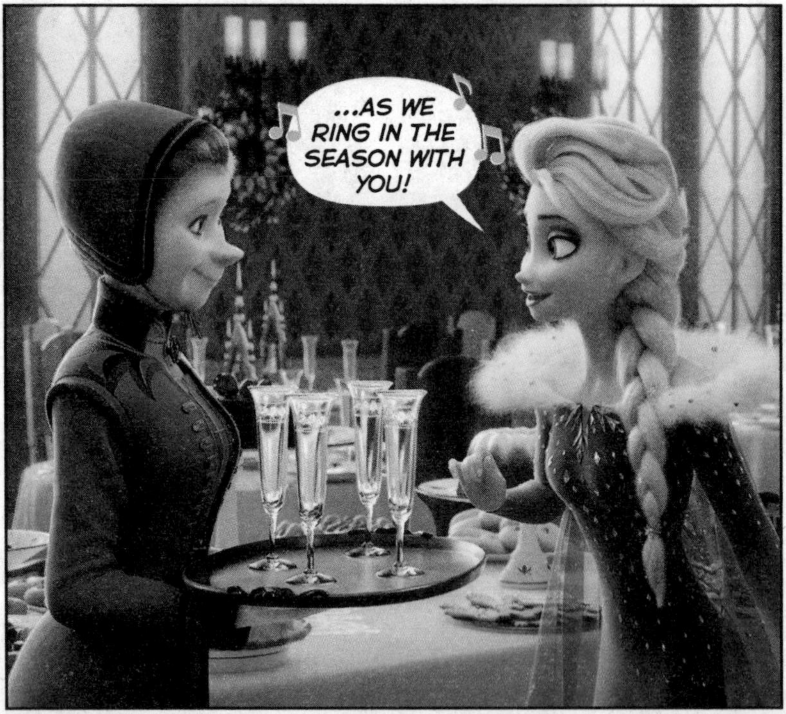
...AS WE RING IN THE SEASON WITH YOU!

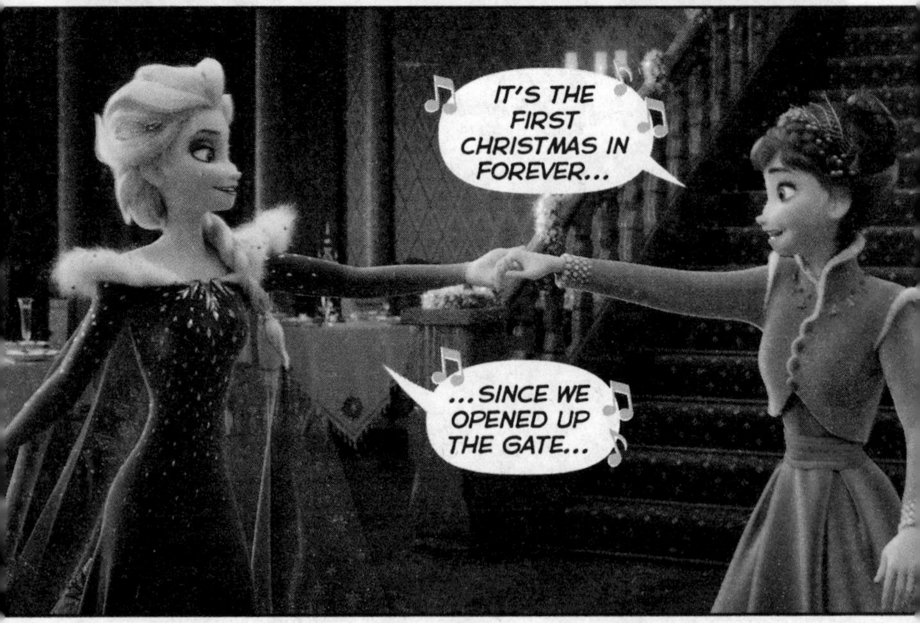
IT'S THE FIRST CHRISTMAS IN FOREVER...
...SINCE WE OPENED UP THE GATE...

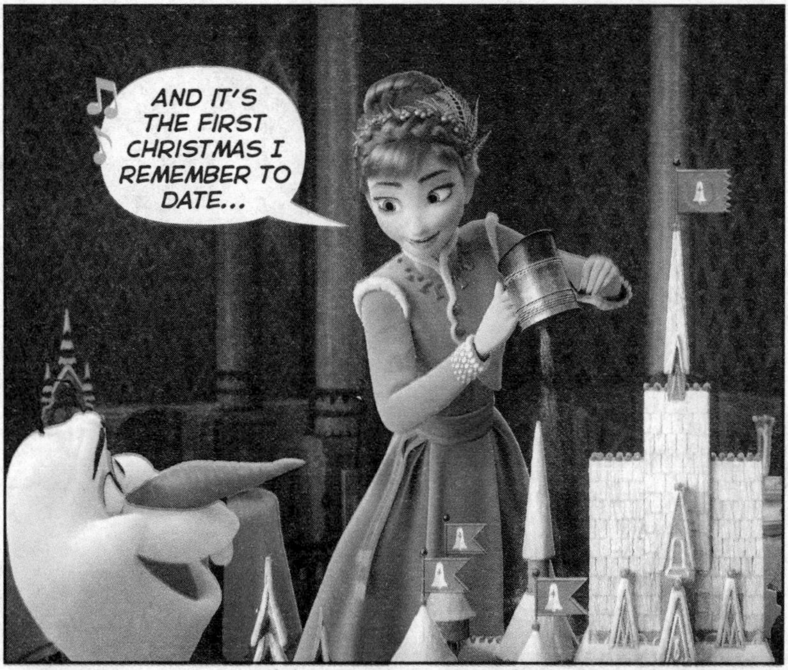
AND IT'S THE FIRST CHRISTMAS I REMEMBER TO DATE...

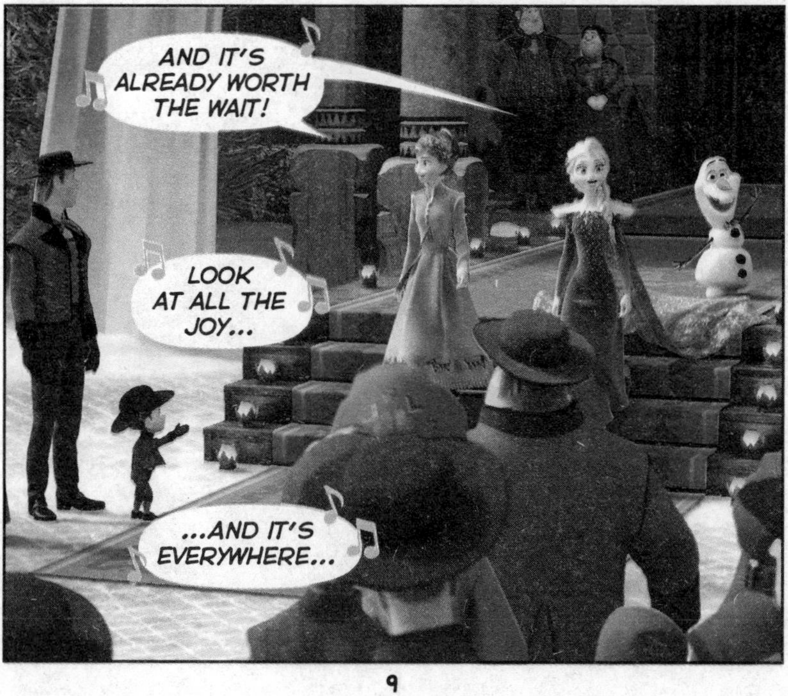
AND IT'S ALREADY WORTH THE WAIT!
LOOK AT ALL THE JOY...
...AND IT'S EVERYWHERE...

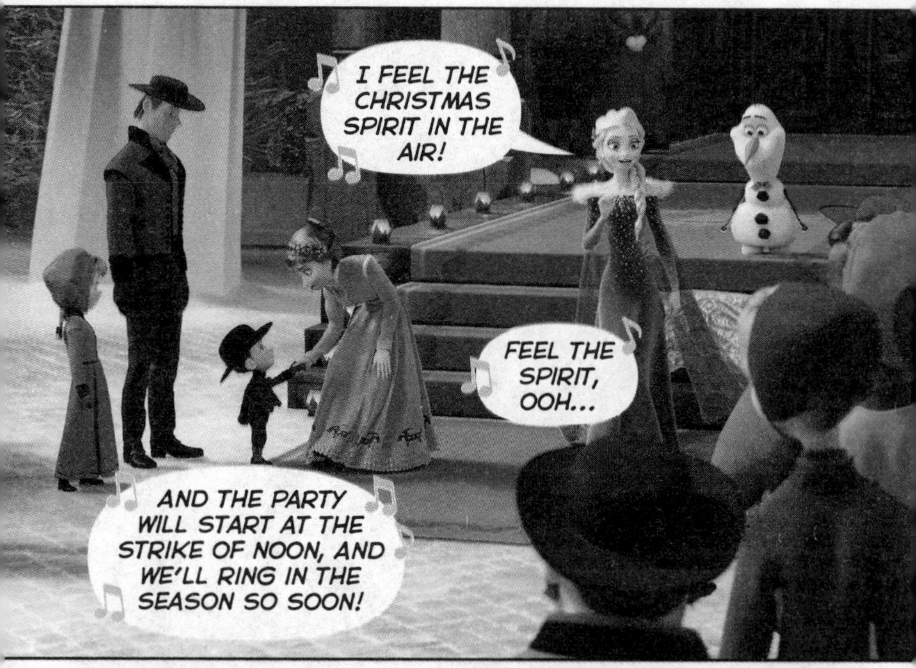
I FEEL THE CHRISTMAS SPIRIT IN THE AIR!
FEEL THE SPIRIT, OOH...
AND THE PARTY WILL START AT THE STRIKE OF NOON, AND WE'LL RING IN THE SEASON SO SOON!

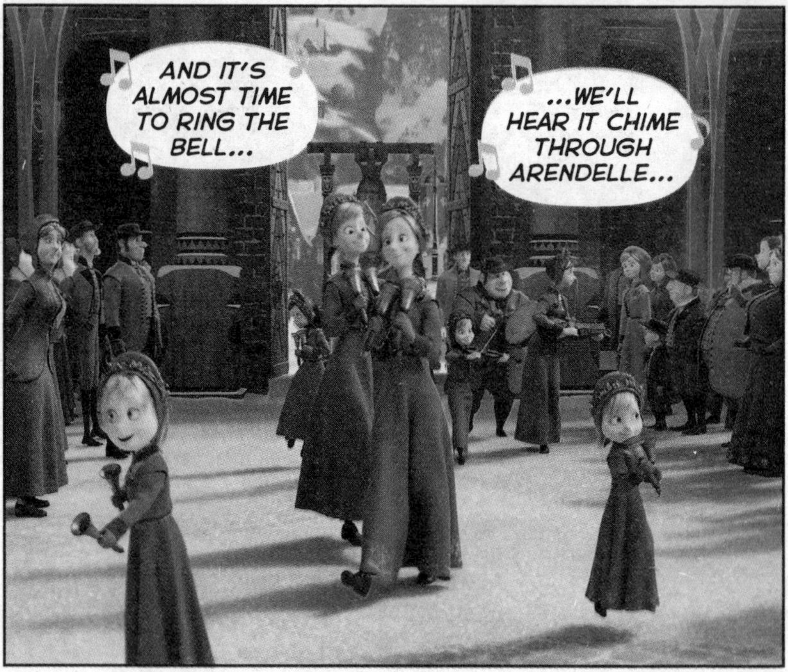
AND IT'S ALMOST TIME TO RING THE BELL...
...WE'LL HEAR IT CHIME THROUGH ARENDELLE...

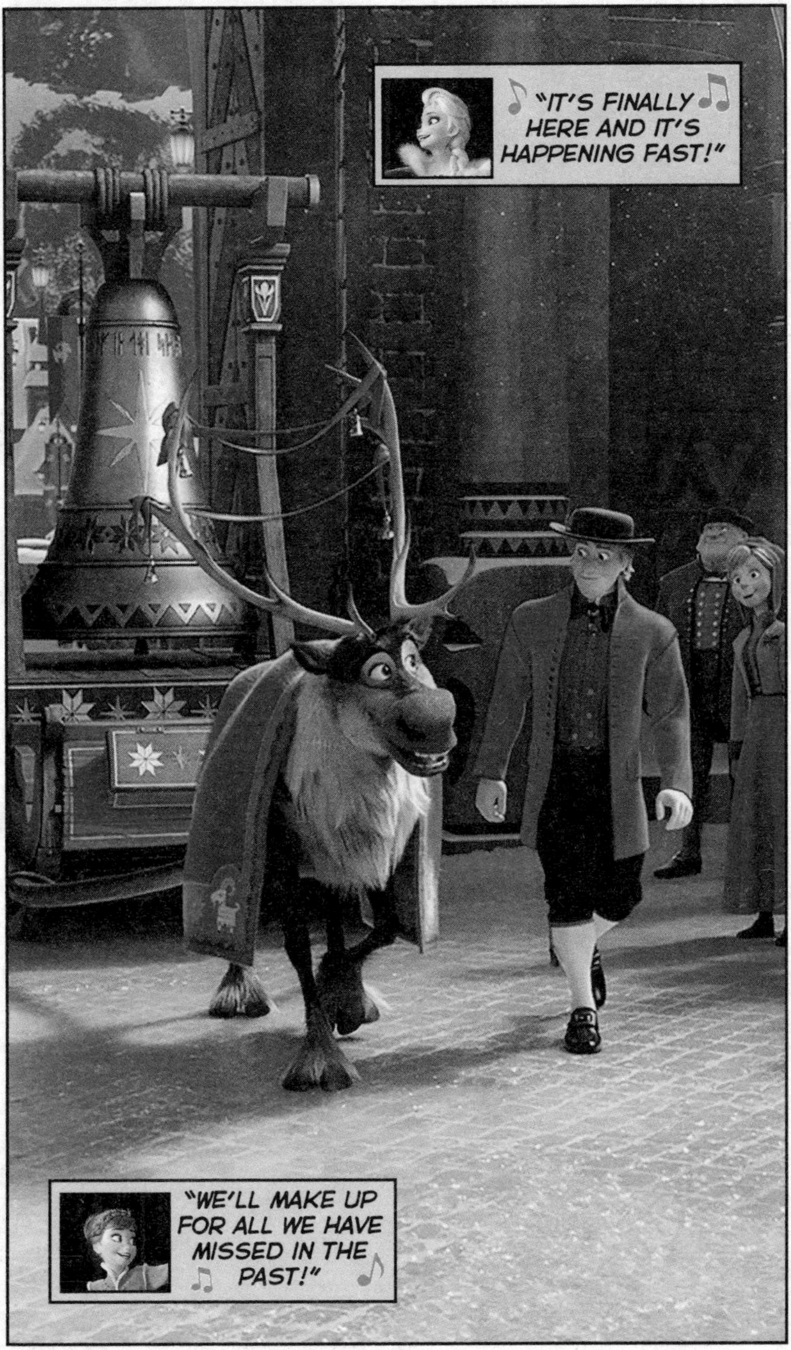
"IT'S FINALLY HERE AND IT'S HAPPENING FAST!"
"WE'LL MAKE UP FOR ALL WE HAVE MISSED IN THE PAST!"

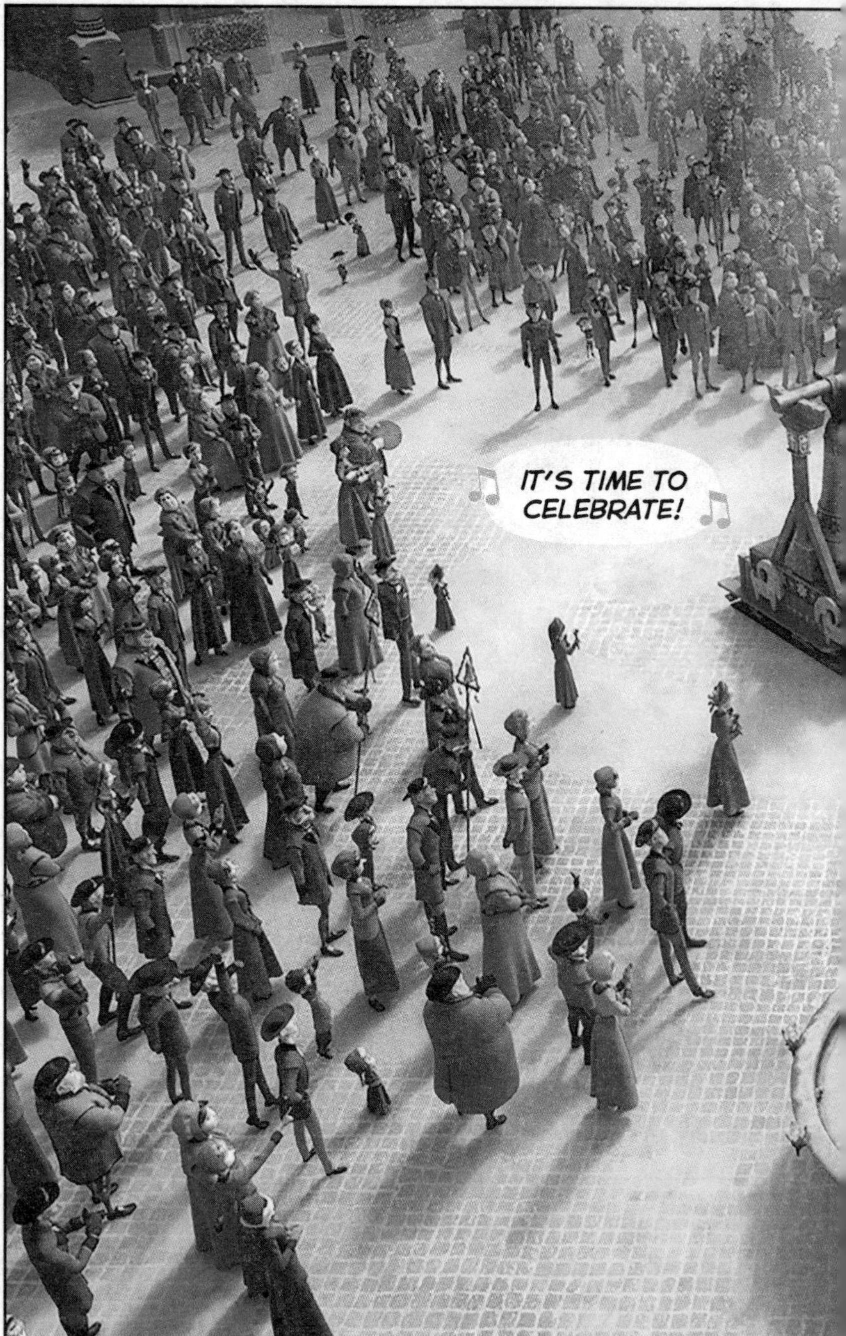
IT'S TIME TO CELEBRATE!

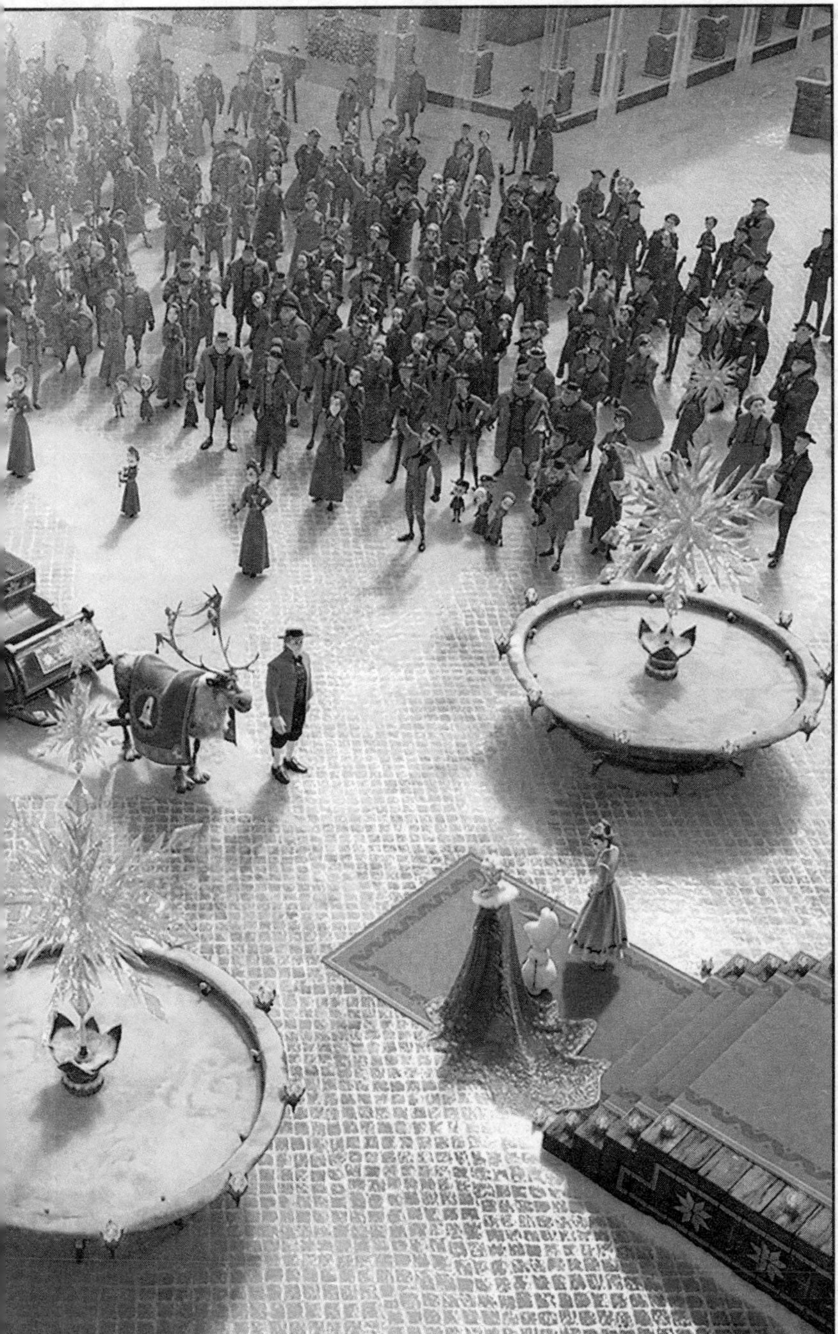

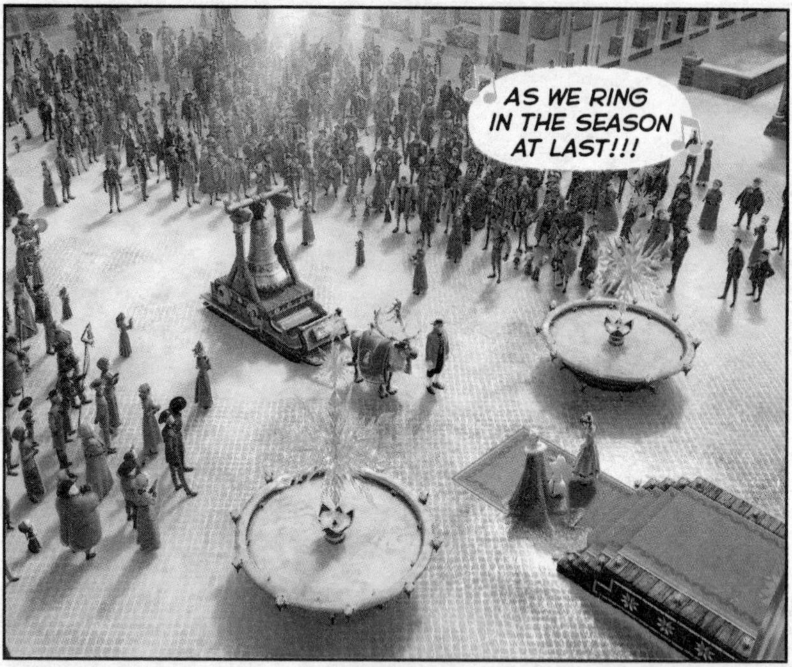
AS WE RING
IN THE SEASON
AT LAST!!!

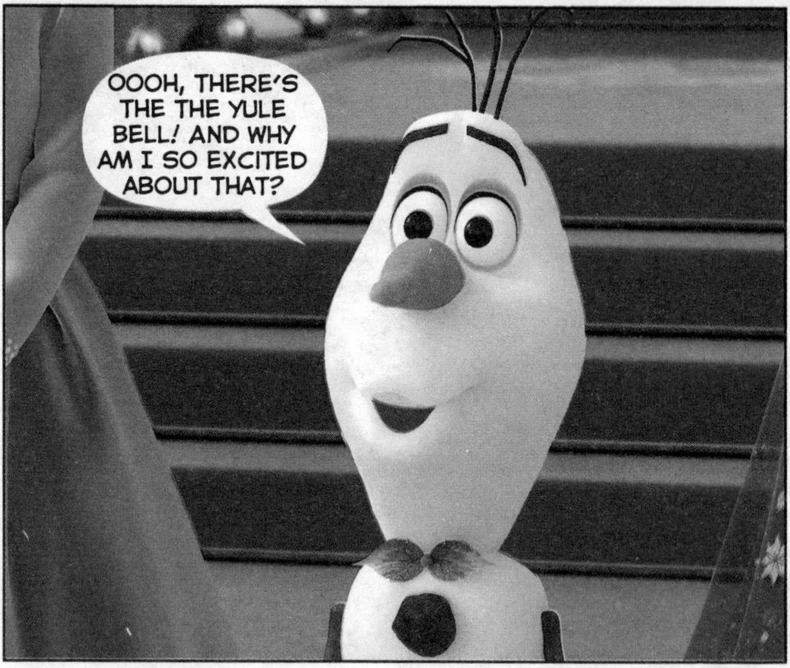
OOOH, THERE'S
THE THE YULE
BELL! AND WHY
AM I SO EXCITED
ABOUT THAT?

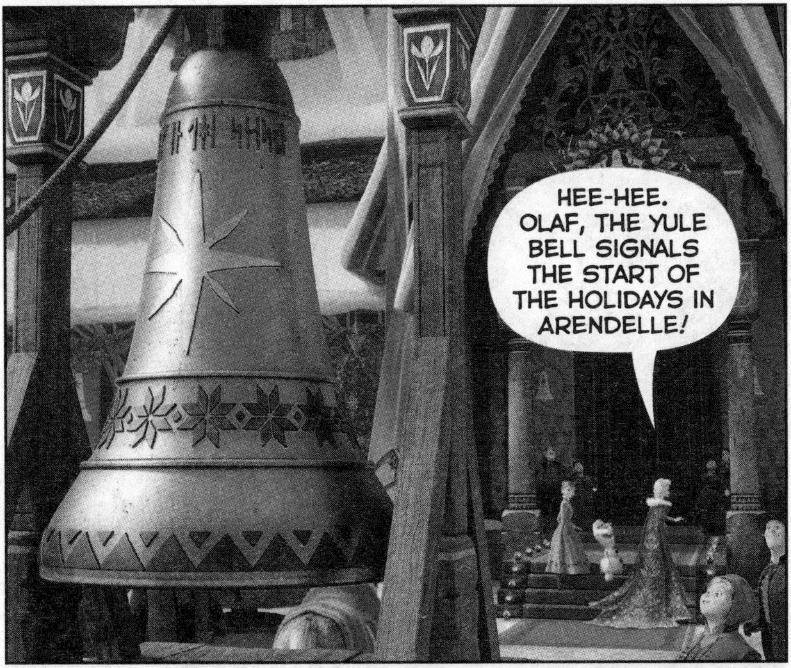
HEE-HEE. OLAF, THE YULE BELL SIGNALS THE START OF THE HOLIDAYS IN ARENDELLE!

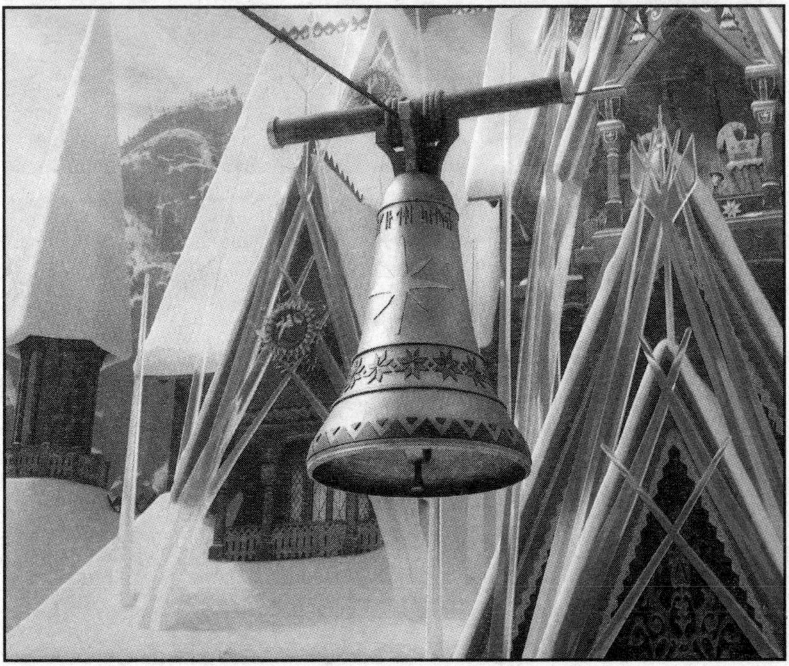

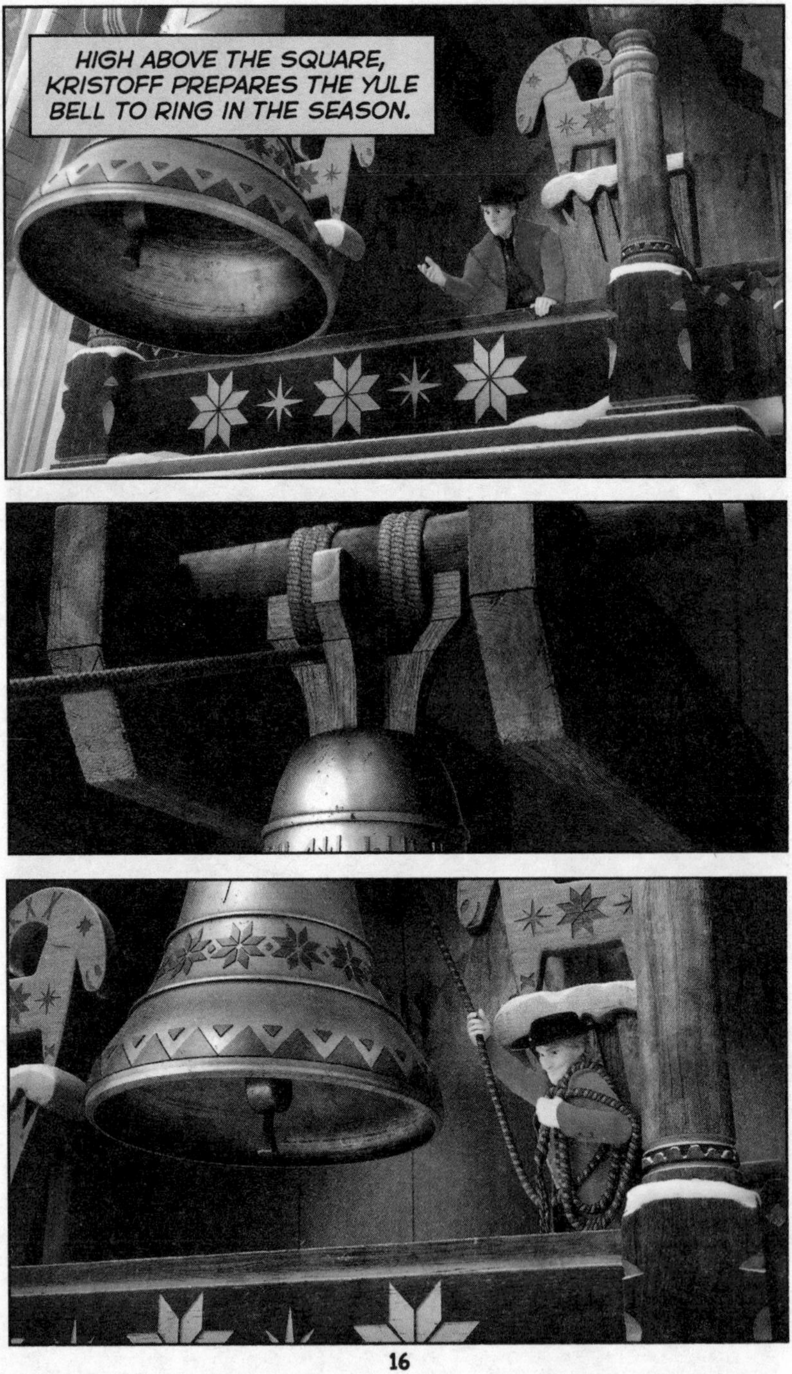
HIGH ABOVE THE SQUARE, KRISTOFF PREPARES THE YULE BELL TO RING IN THE SEASON.

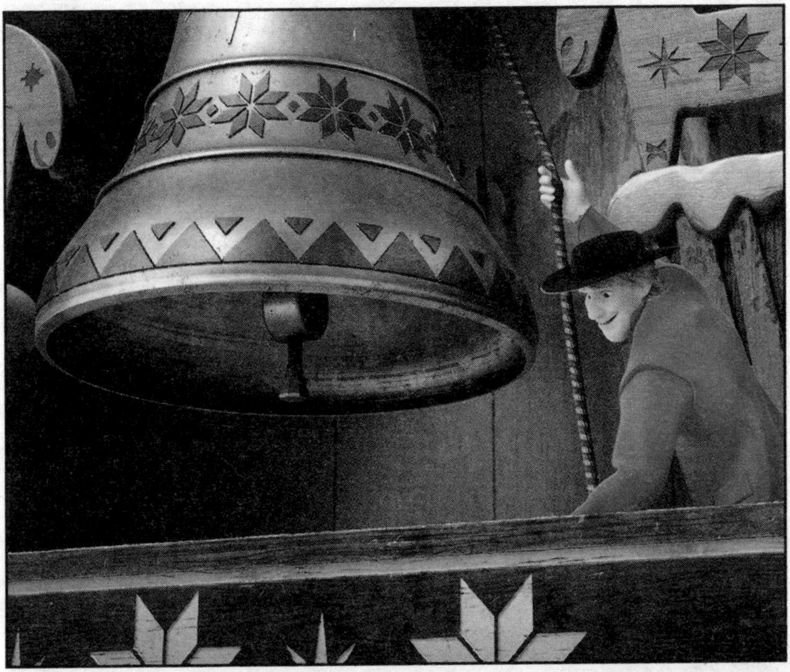

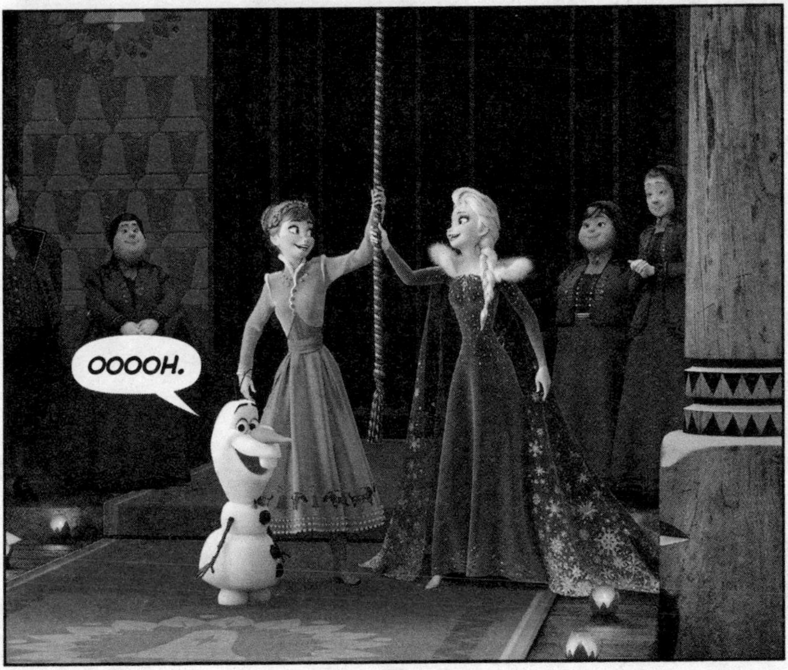
OOOOH.

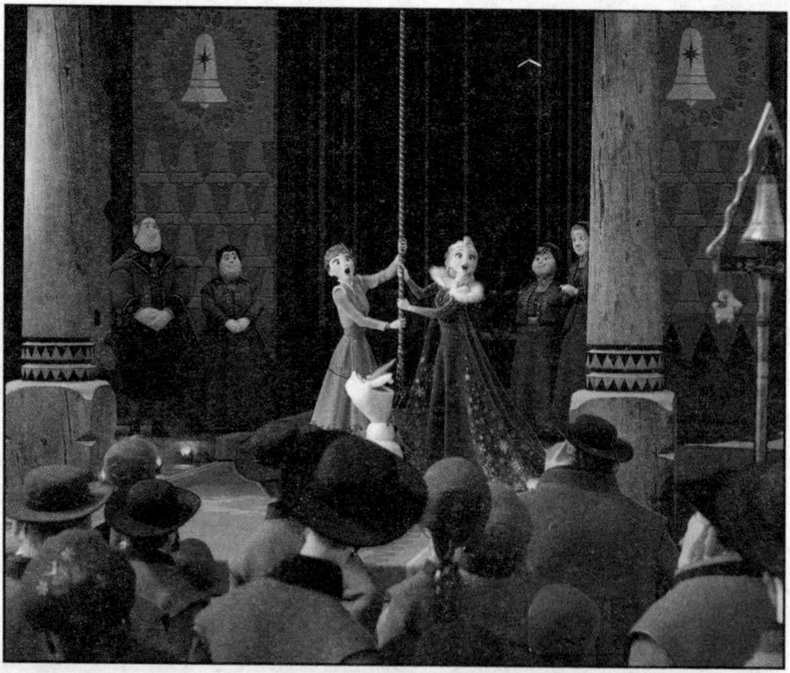

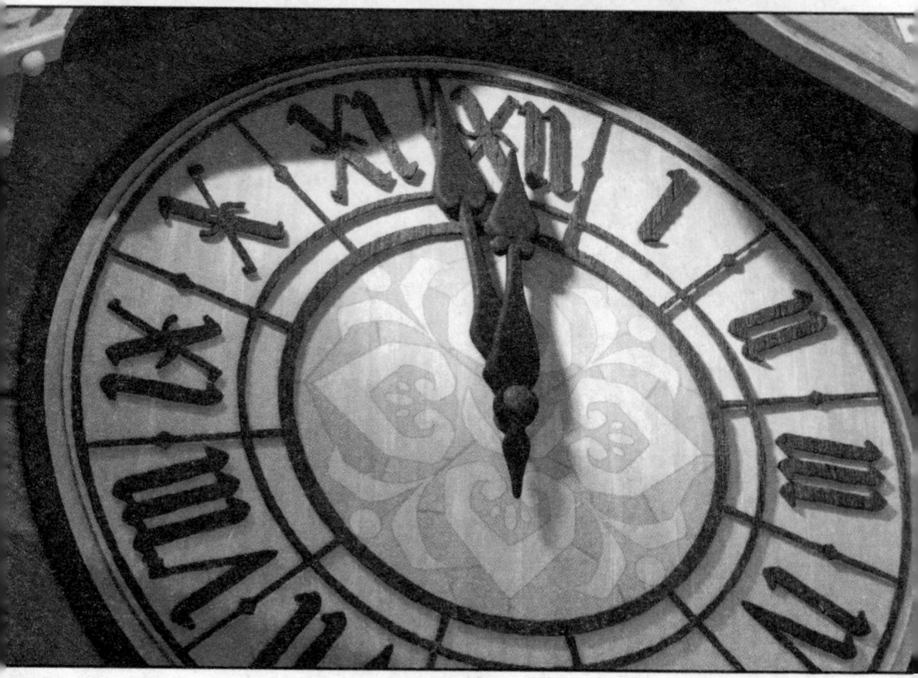

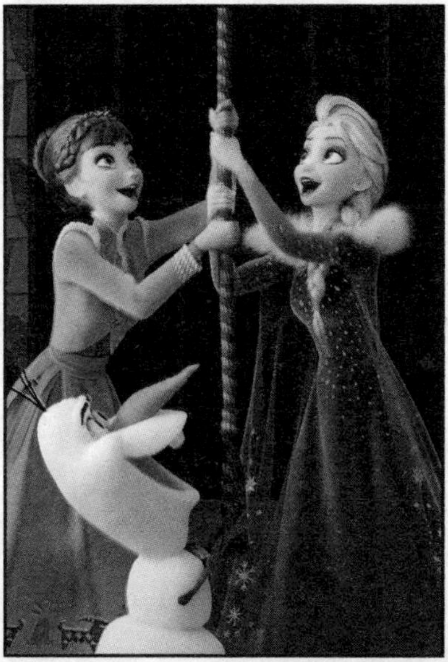

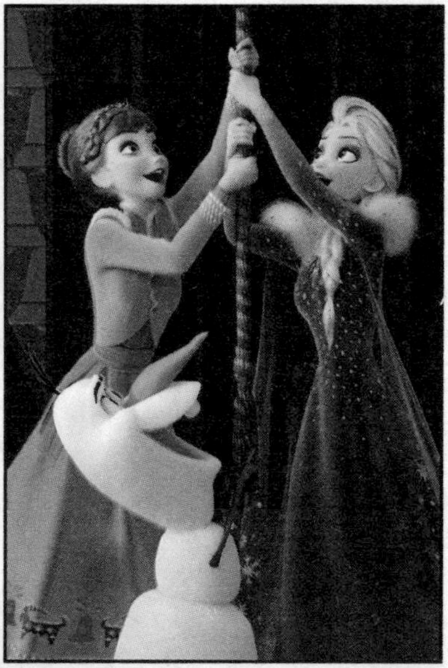

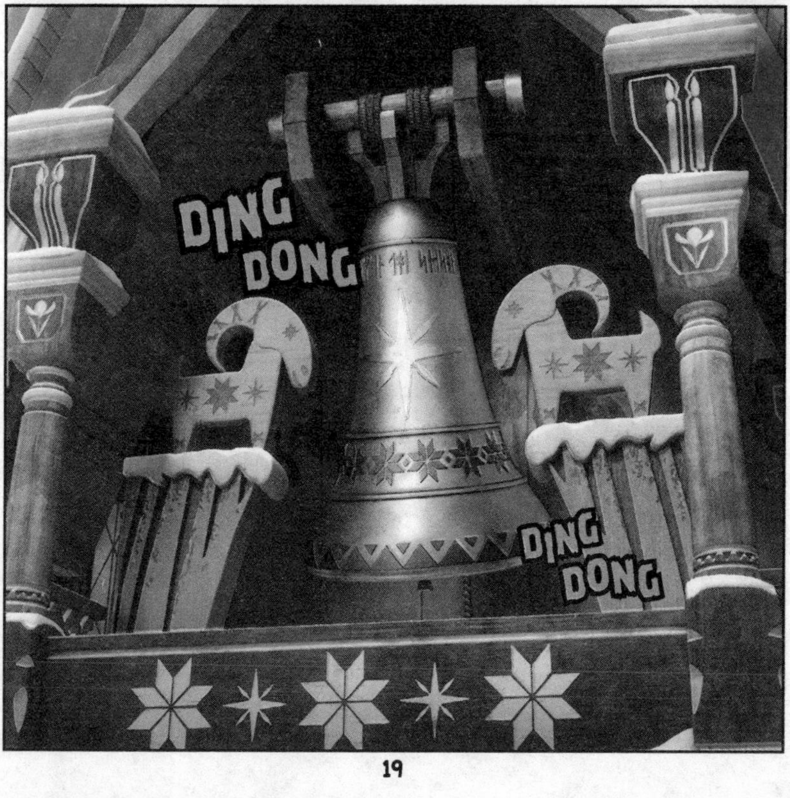
DING DONG
DING DONG

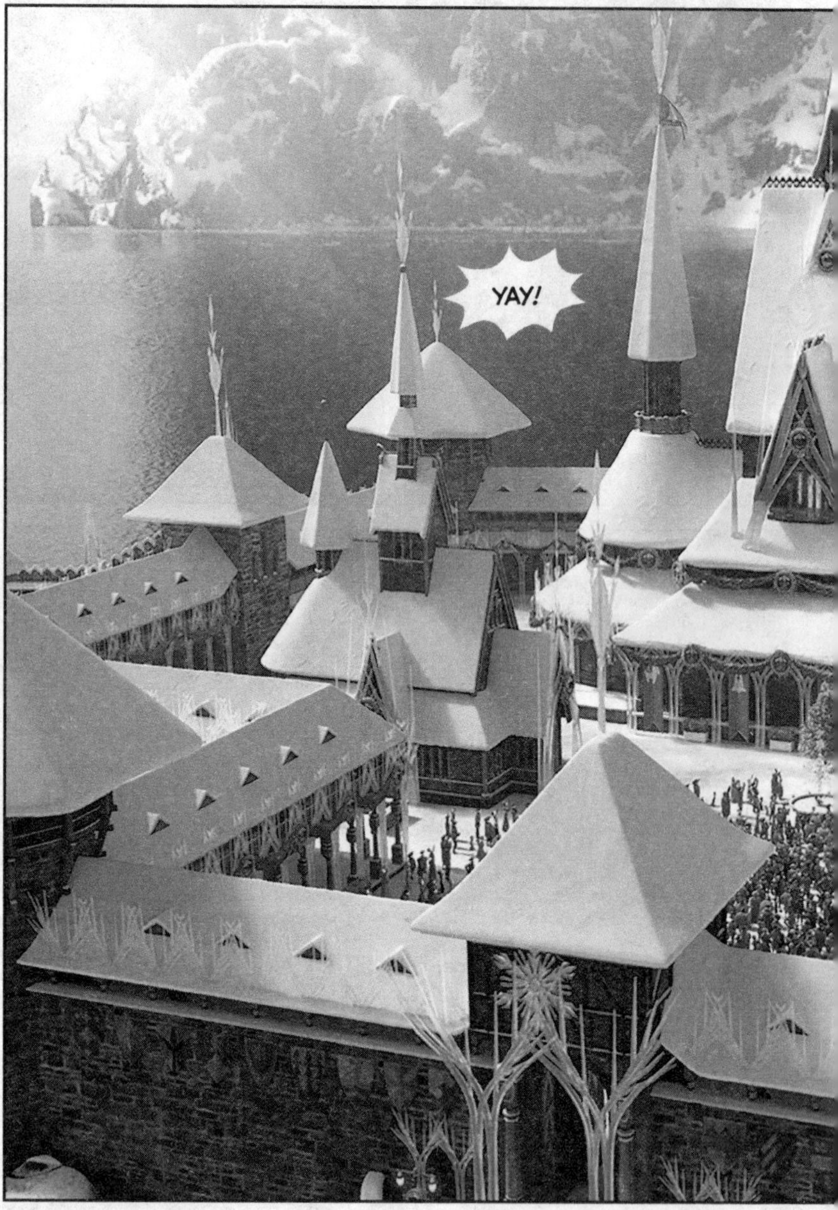
YAY!

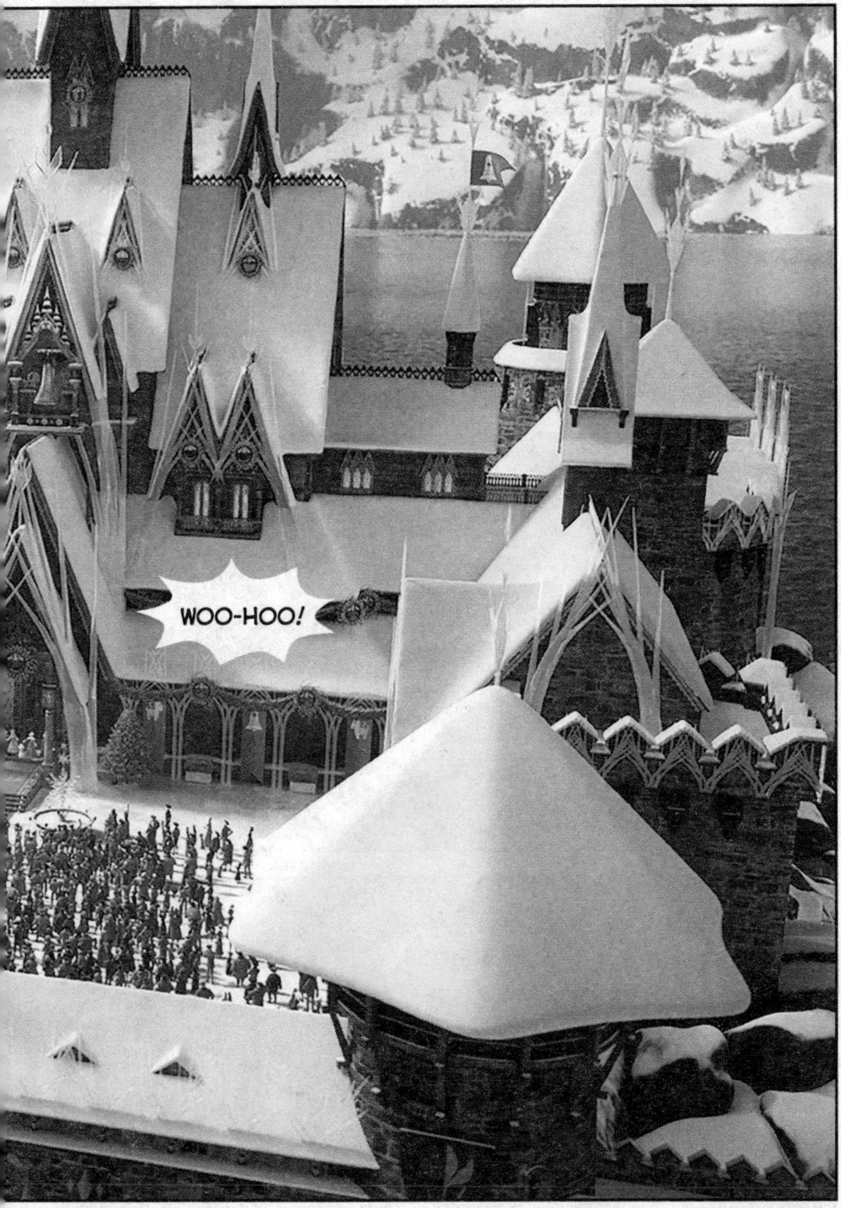
WOO-HOO!

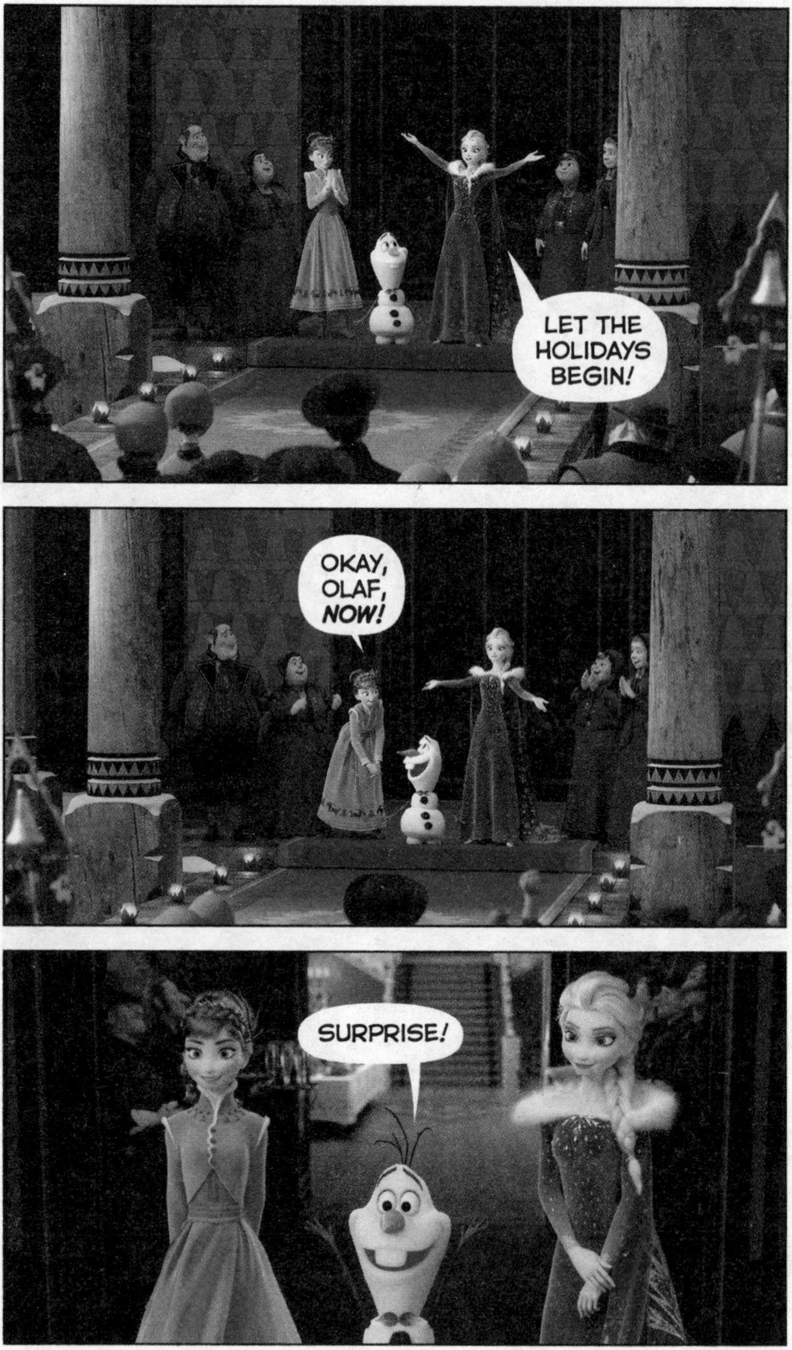
LET THE HOLIDAYS BEGIN!
OKAY, OLAF, NOW!
SURPRISE!

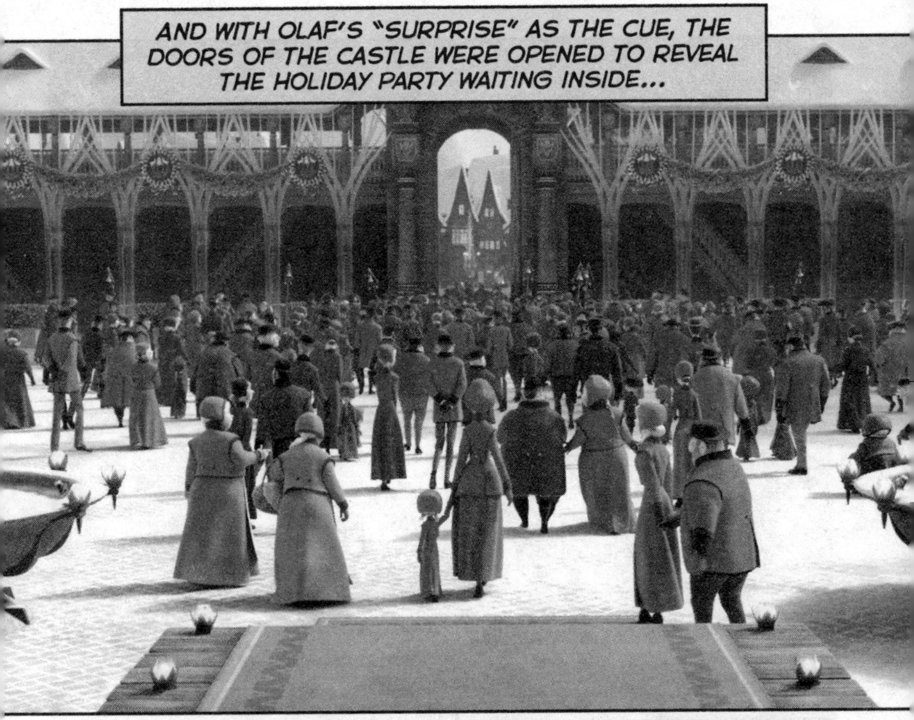
AND WITH OLAF'S "SURPRISE" AS THE CUE, THE DOORS OF THE CASTLE WERE OPENED TO REVEAL THE HOLIDAY PARTY WAITING INSIDE...

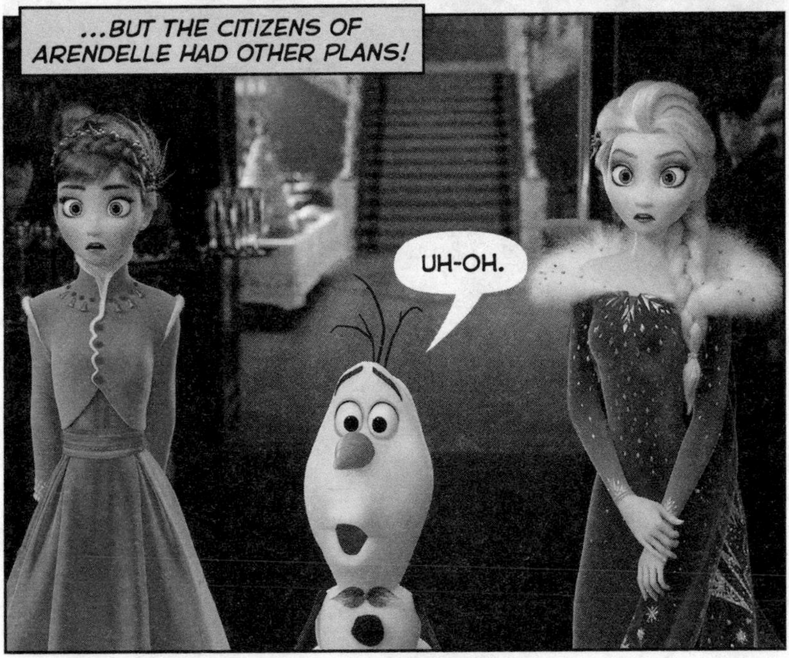
...BUT THE CITIZENS OF ARENDELLE HAD OTHER PLANS!
UH-OH.

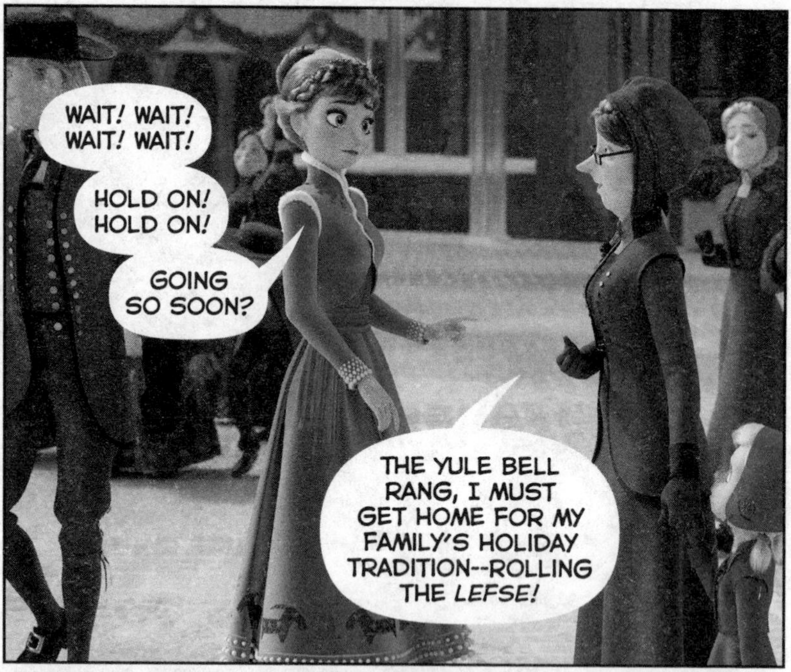
WAIT! WAIT! WAIT! WAIT!
HOLD ON! HOLD ON!
GOING SO SOON?
THE YULE BELL RANG, I MUST GET HOME FOR MY FAMILY'S HOLIDAY TRADITION--ROLLING THE *LEFSE!*

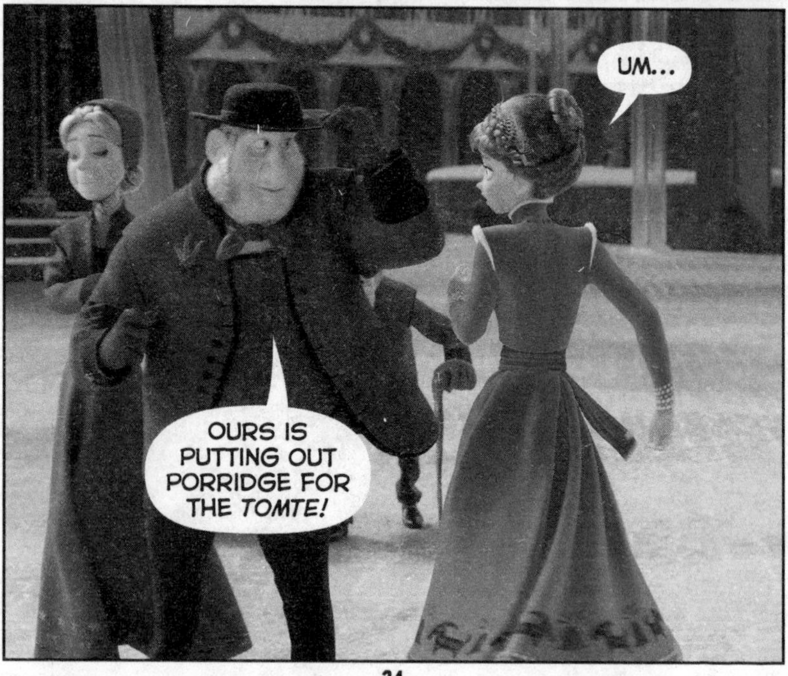
UM...
OURS IS PUTTING OUT PORRIDGE FOR THE *TOMTE!*

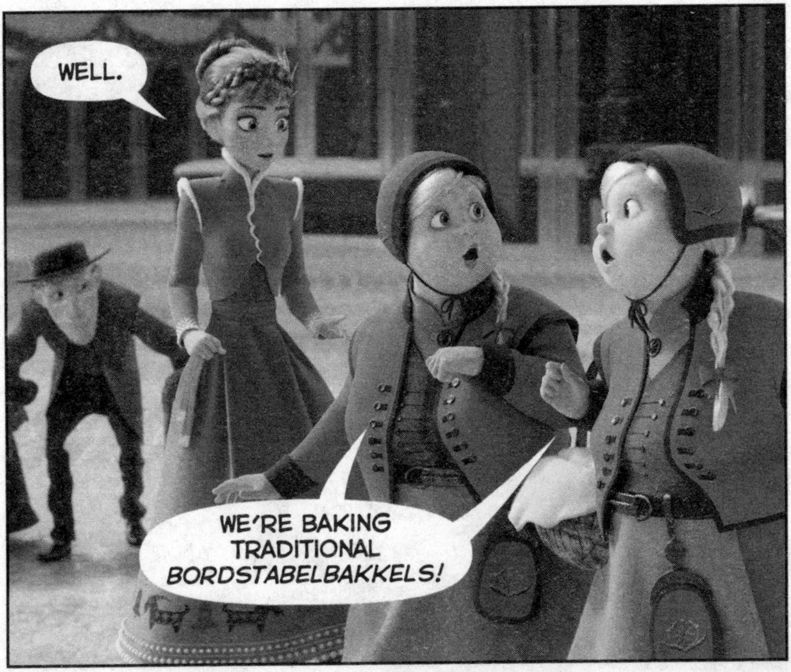
WELL.
WE'RE BAKING TRADITIONAL *BORDSTABELBAKKELS!*

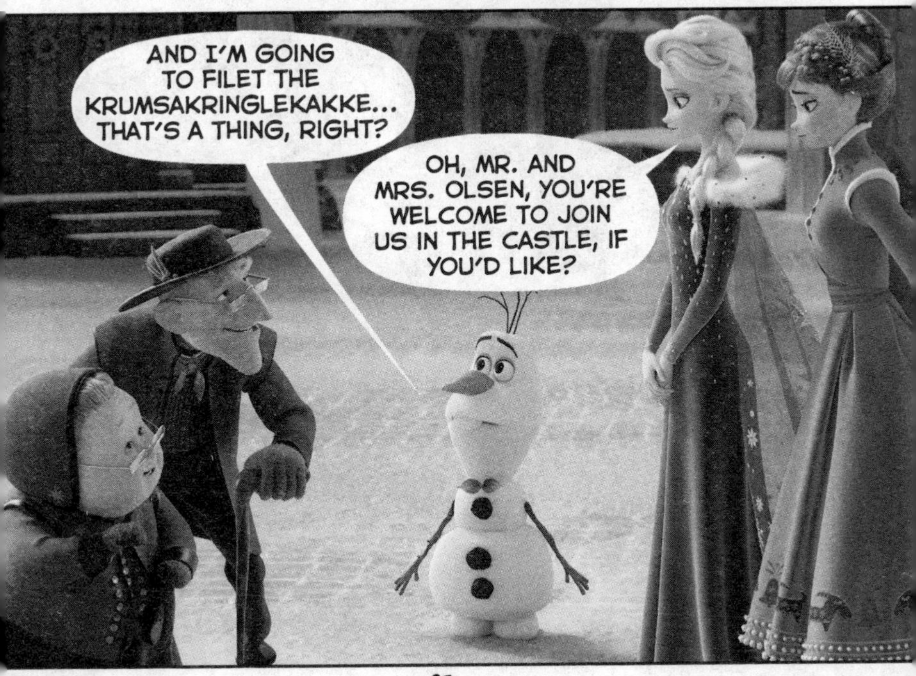
AND I'M GOING TO FILET THE KRUMSAKRINGLEKAKKE... THAT'S A THING, RIGHT?
OH, MR. AND MRS. OLSEN, YOU'RE WELCOME TO JOIN US IN THE CASTLE, IF YOU'D LIKE?

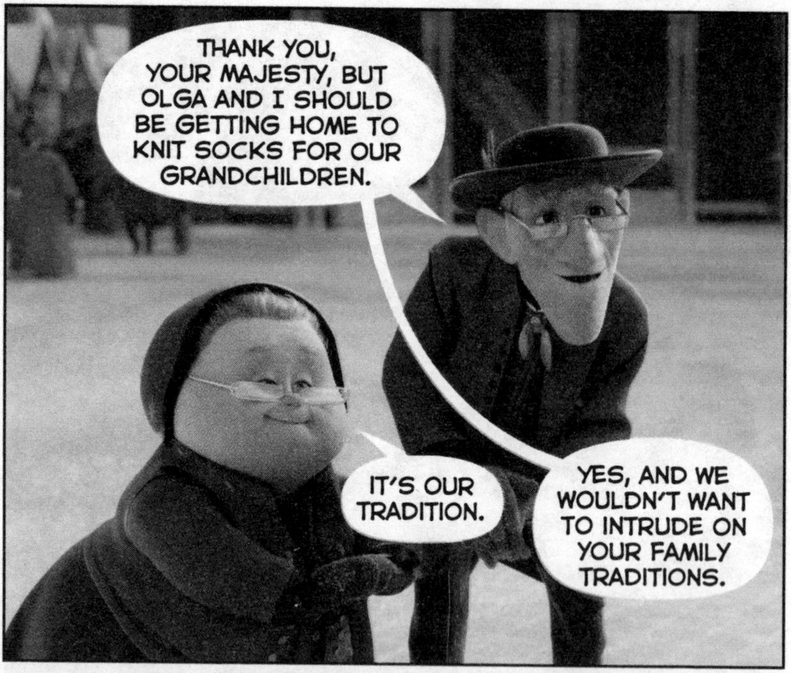
THANK YOU, YOUR MAJESTY, BUT OLGA AND I SHOULD BE GETTING HOME TO KNIT SOCKS FOR OUR GRANDCHILDREN.
IT'S OUR TRADITION.
YES, AND WE WOULDN'T WANT TO INTRUDE ON YOUR FAMILY TRADITIONS.

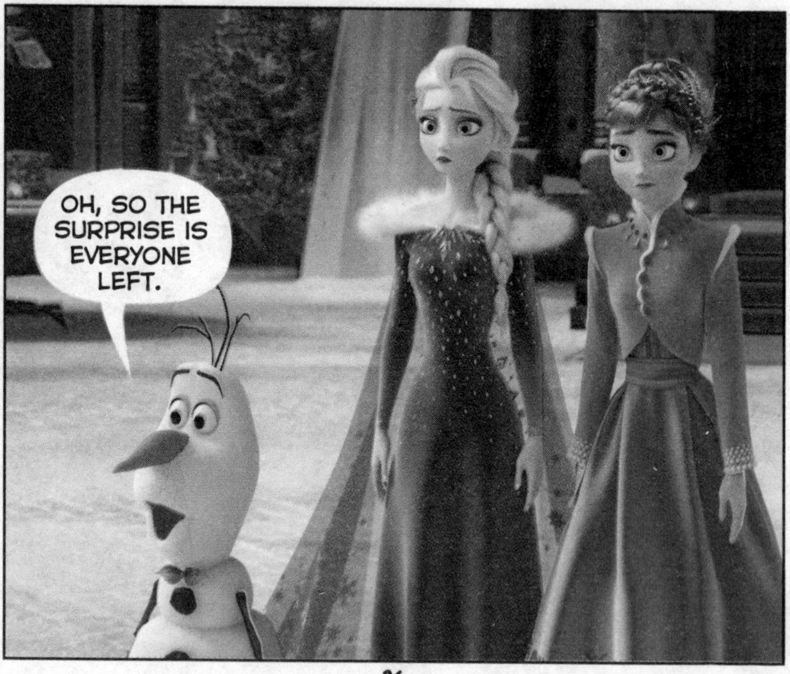
OH, SO THE SURPRISE IS EVERYONE LEFT.

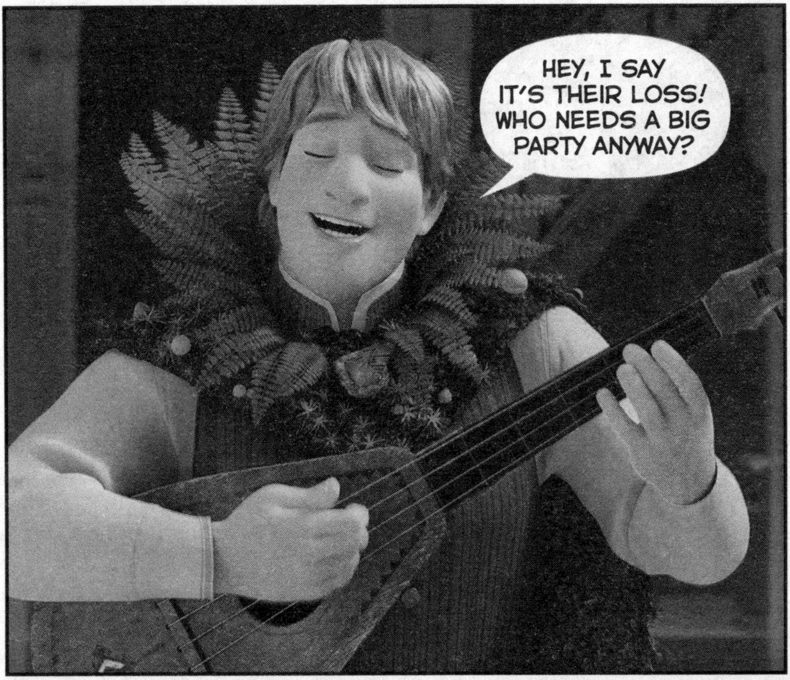
HEY, I SAY IT'S THEIR LOSS! WHO NEEDS A BIG PARTY ANYWAY?

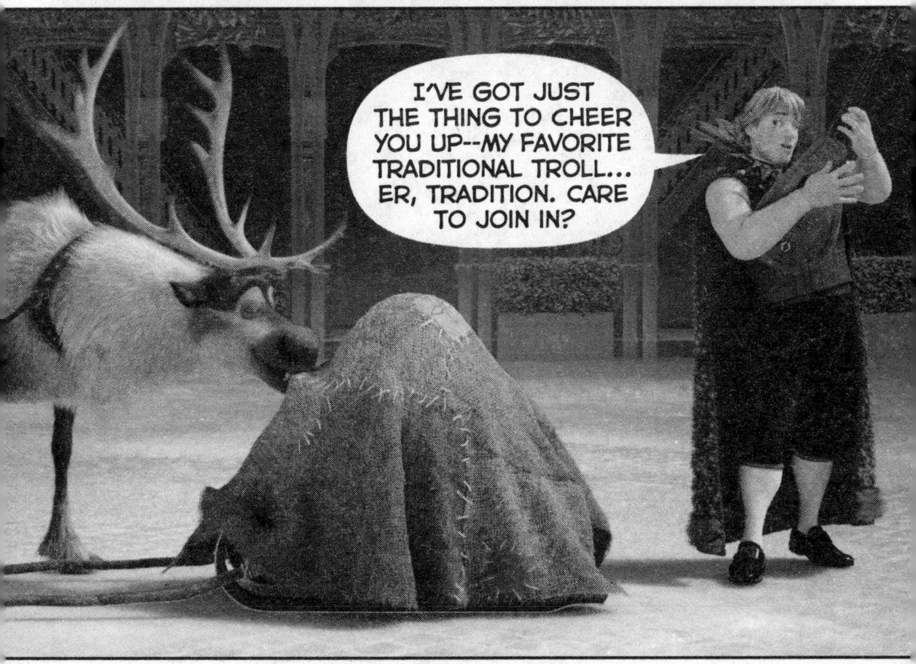
I'VE GOT JUST THE THING TO CHEER YOU UP--MY FAVORITE TRADITIONAL TROLL... ER, TRADITION. CARE TO JOIN IN?

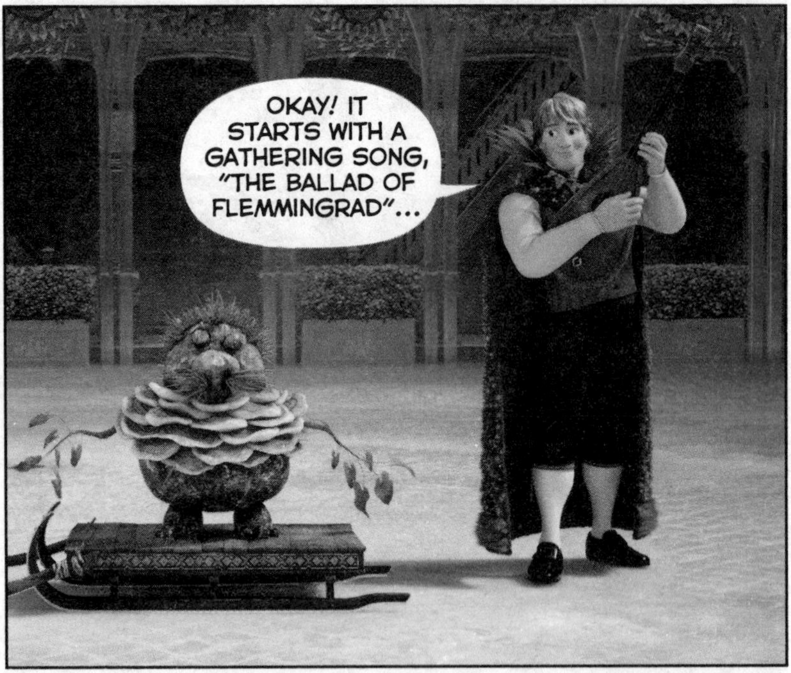
OKAY! IT STARTS WITH A GATHERING SONG, "THE BALLAD OF FLEMMINGRAD"...

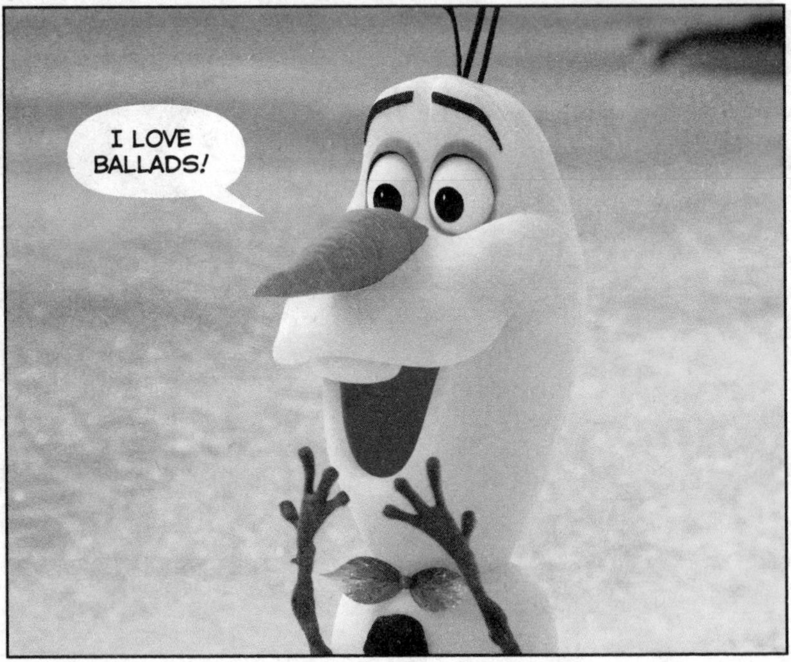
I LOVE BALLADS!

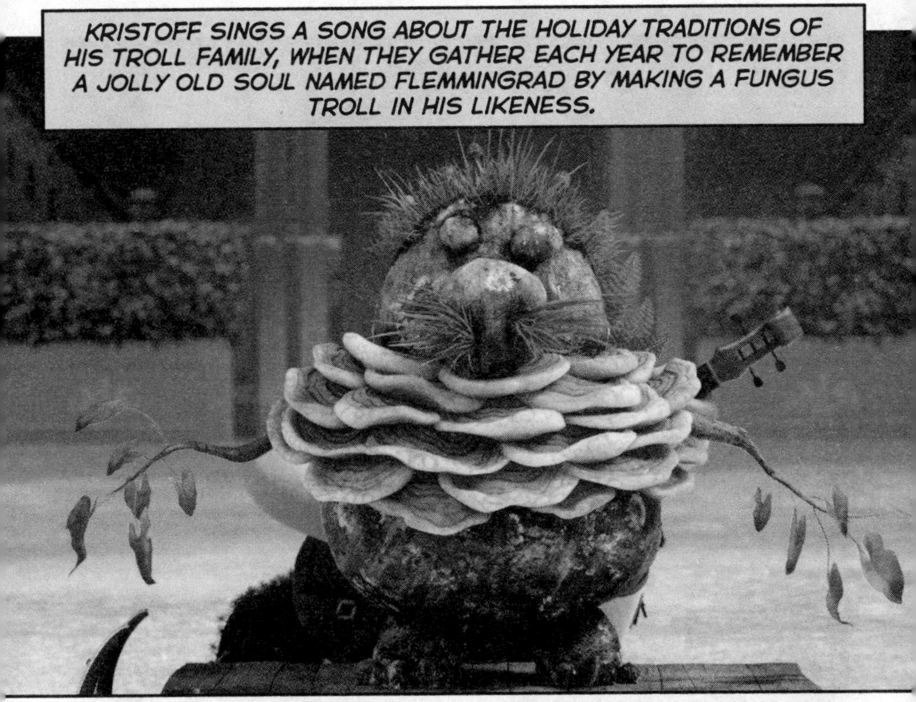
KRISTOFF SINGS A SONG ABOUT THE HOLIDAY TRADITIONS OF HIS TROLL FAMILY, WHEN THEY GATHER EACH YEAR TO REMEMBER A JOLLY OLD SOUL NAMED FLEMMINGRAD BY MAKING A FUNGUS TROLL IN HIS LIKENESS.

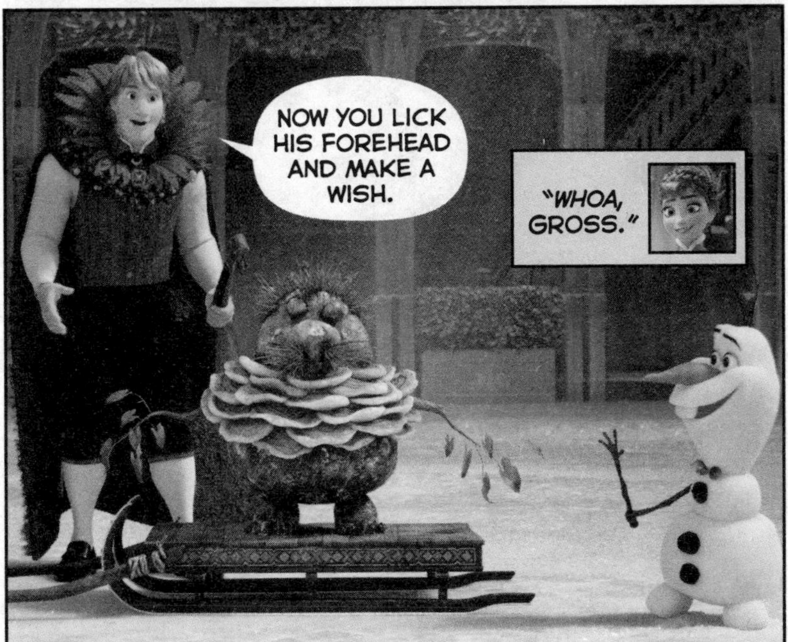
NOW YOU LICK HIS FOREHEAD AND MAKE A WISH.
"WHOA, GROSS."

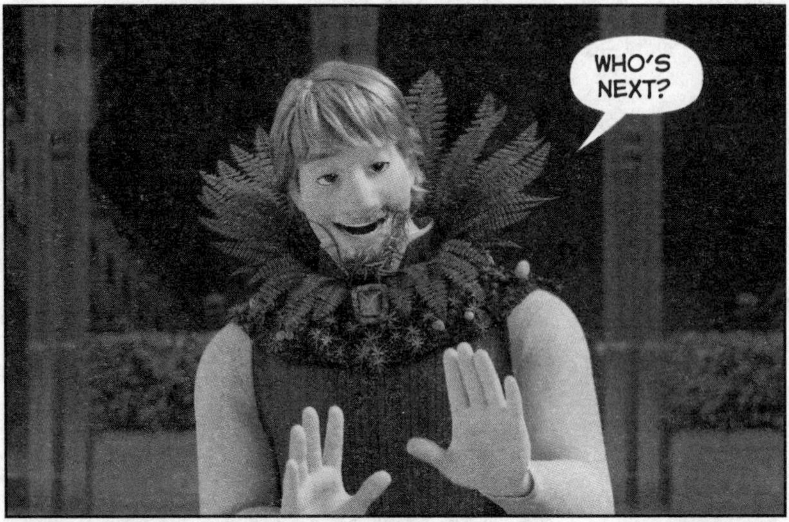
WHO'S NEXT?

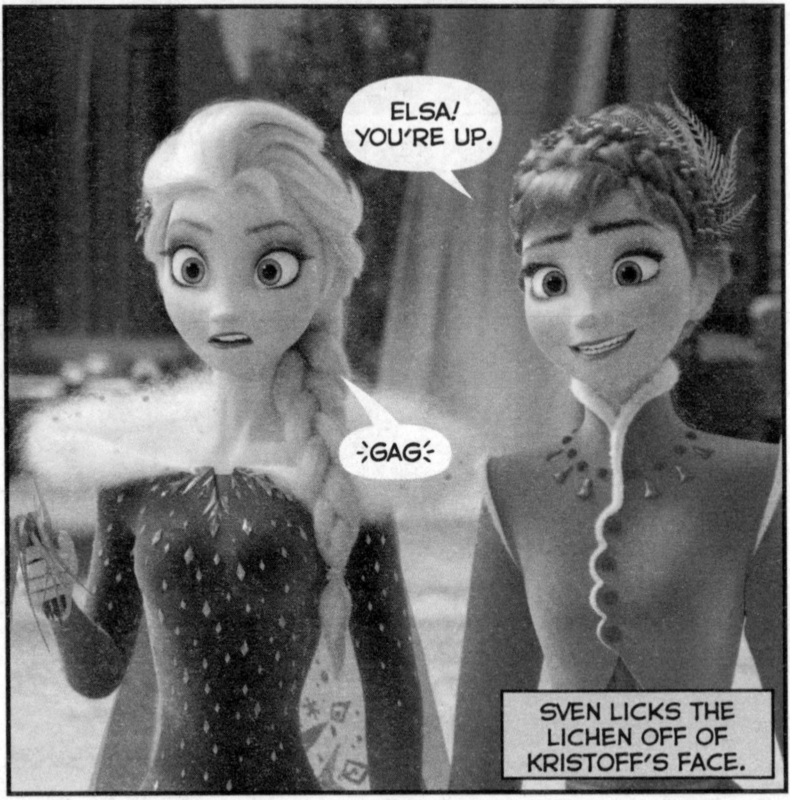
ELSA! YOU'RE UP.
GAG
SVEN LICKS THE LICHEN OFF OF KRISTOFF'S FACE.

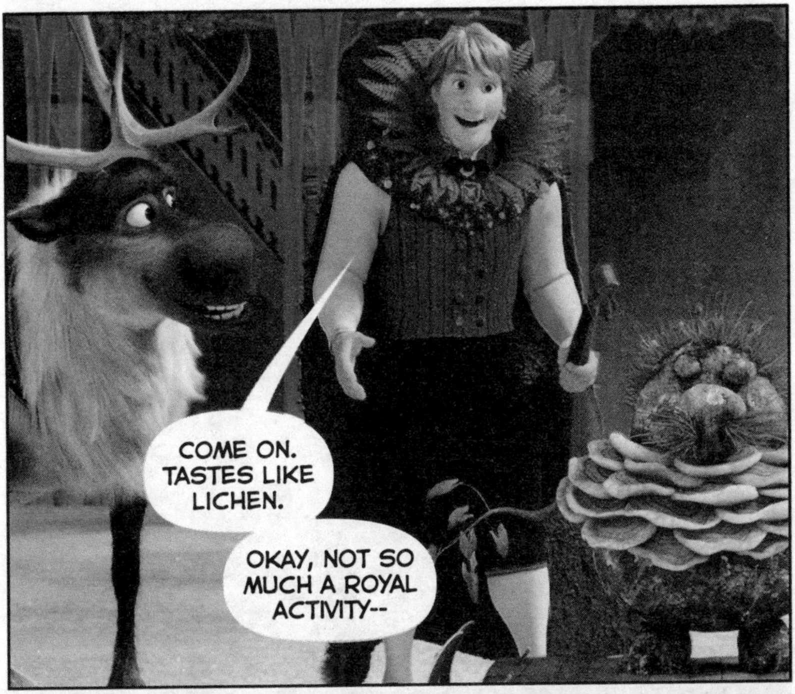
COME ON. TASTES LIKE LICHEN.
OKAY, NOT SO MUCH A ROYAL ACTIVITY--

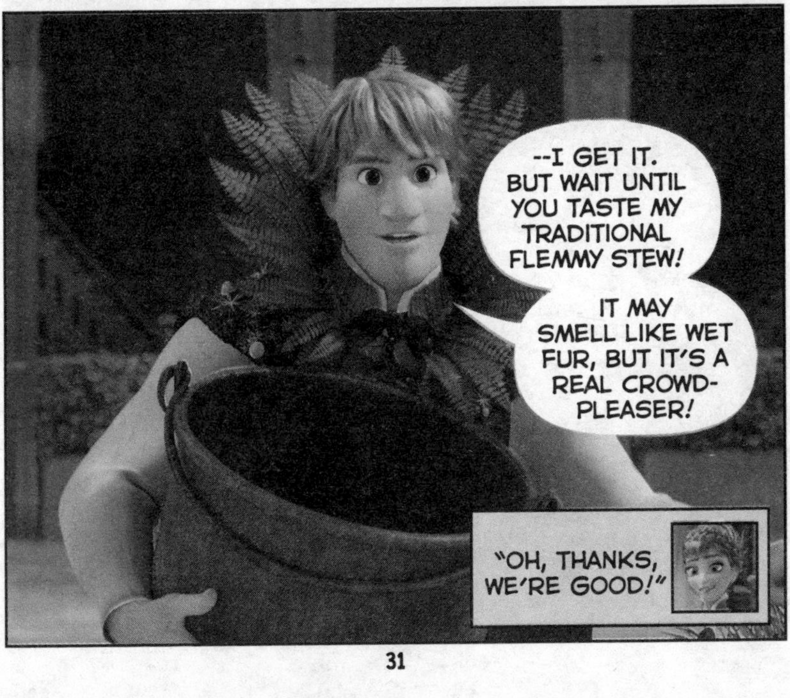
--I GET IT. BUT WAIT UNTIL YOU TASTE MY TRADITIONAL FLEMMY STEW!
IT MAY SMELL LIKE WET FUR, BUT IT'S A REAL CROWD-PLEASER!
"OH, THANKS, WE'RE GOOD!"

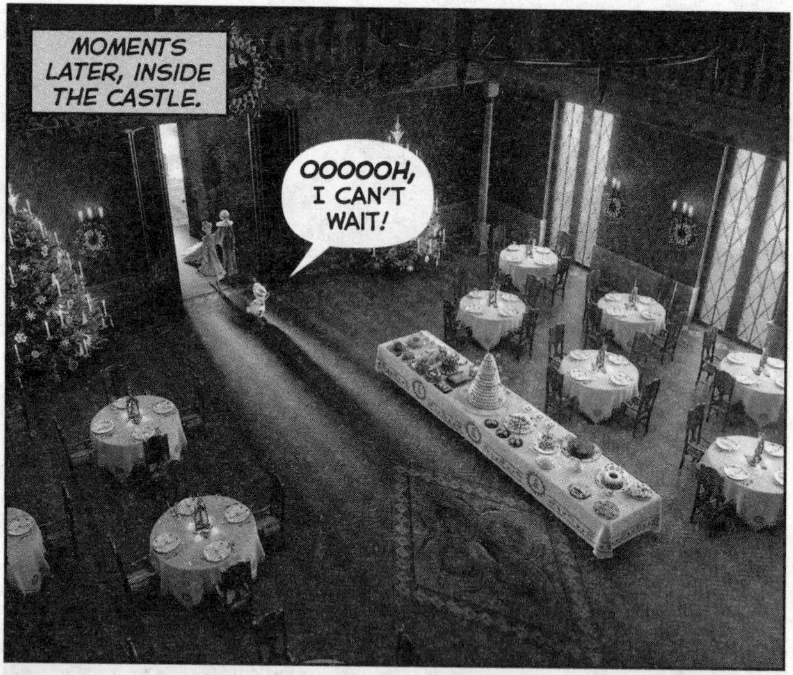
MOMENTS LATER, INSIDE THE CASTLE.
OOOOOH, I CAN'T WAIT!

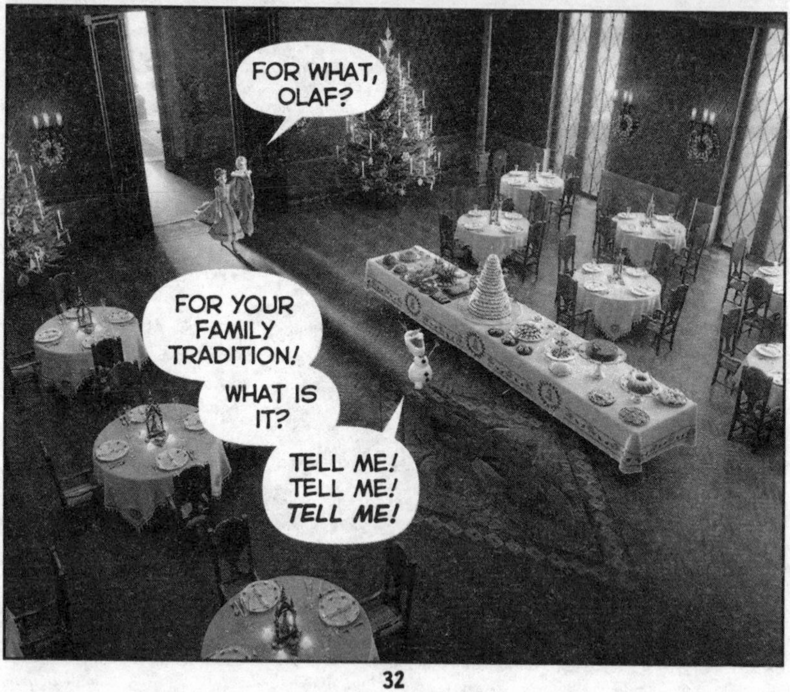
FOR WHAT, OLAF?
FOR YOUR FAMILY TRADITION!
WHAT IS IT?
TELL ME! TELL ME! TELL ME!

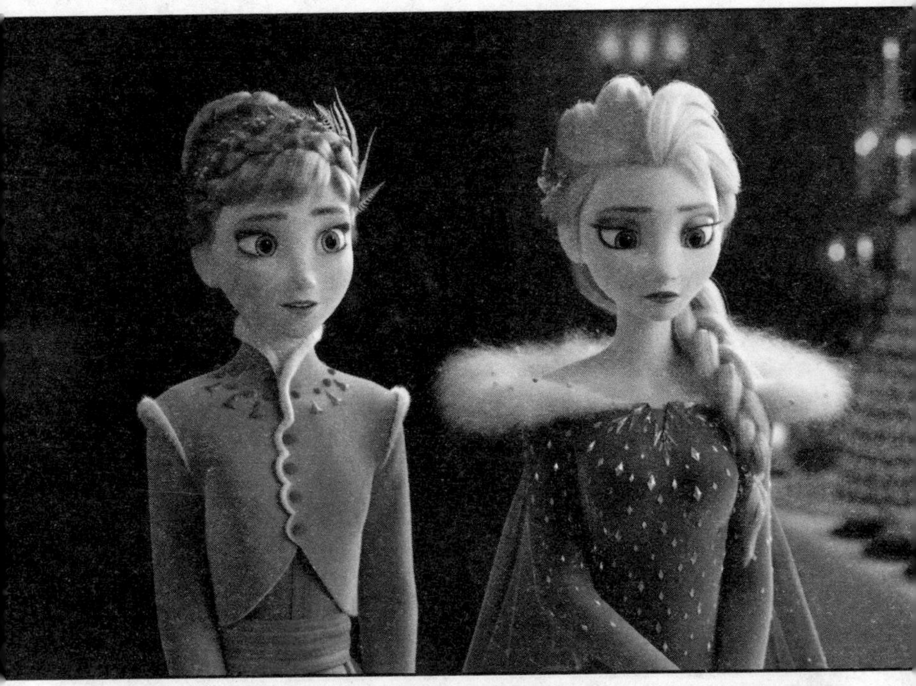

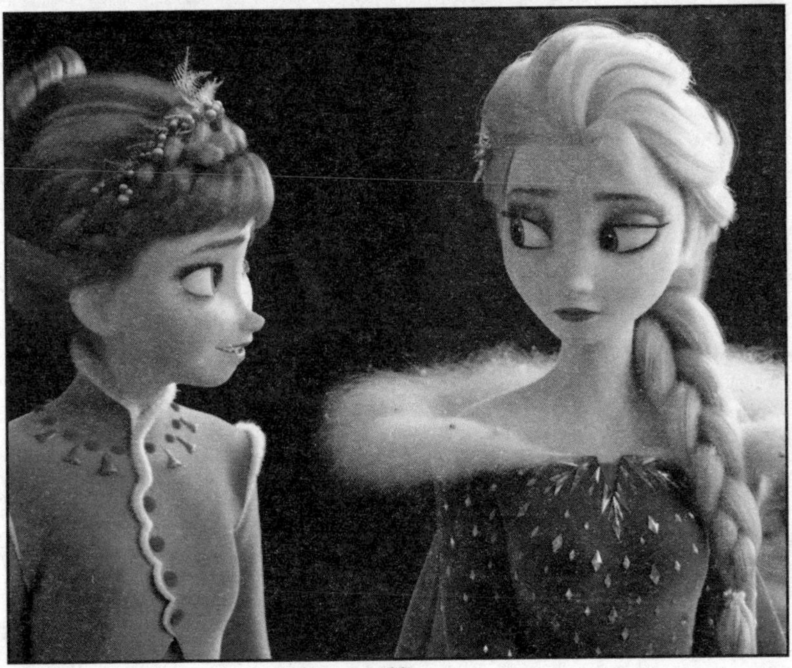

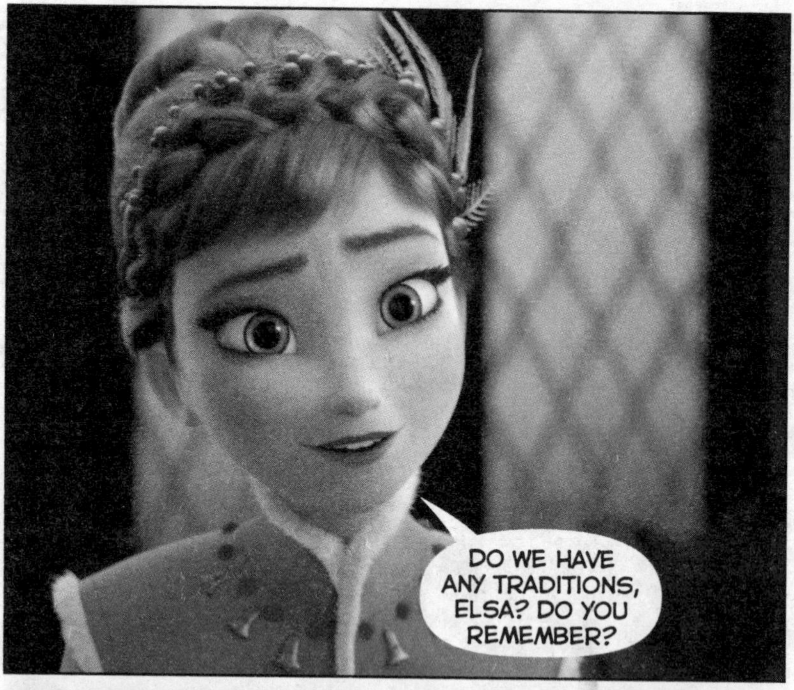
DO WE HAVE ANY TRADITIONS, ELSA? DO YOU REMEMBER?

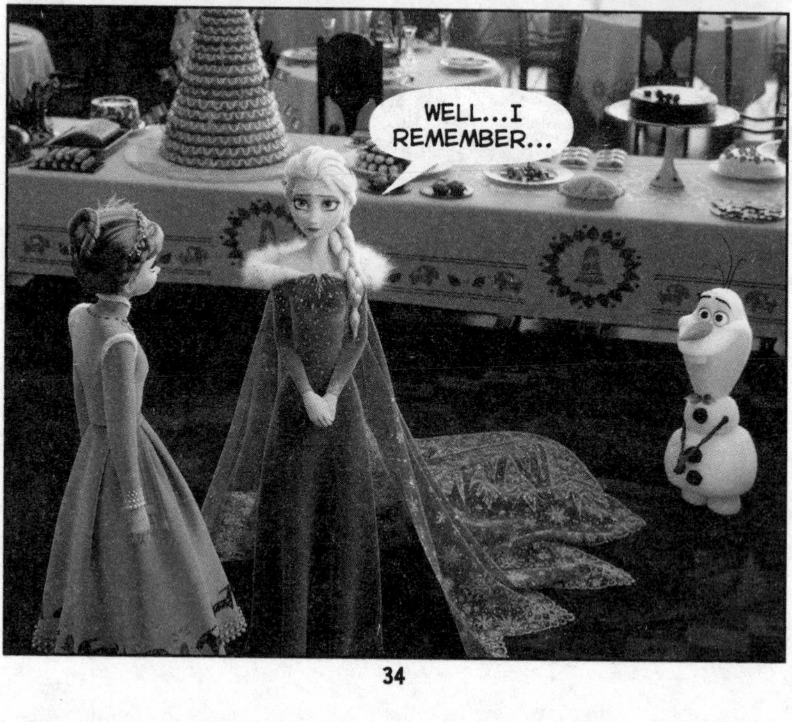
WELL...I REMEMBER...

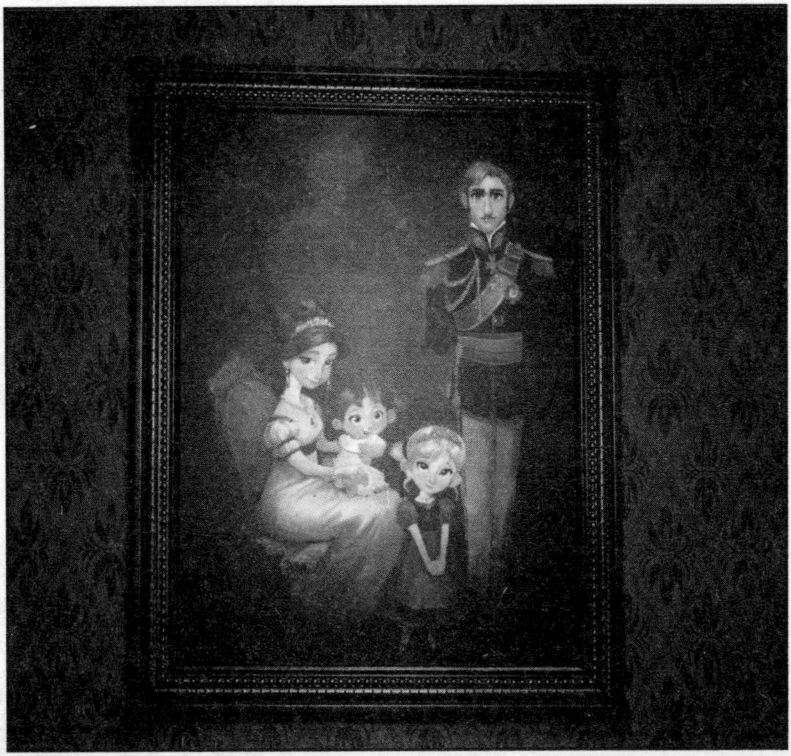

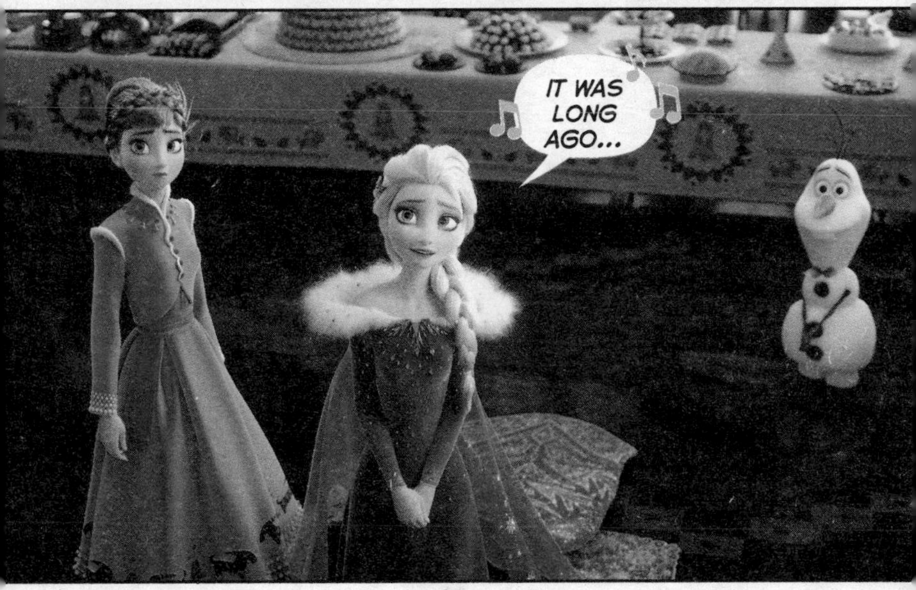
IT WAS LONG AGO...

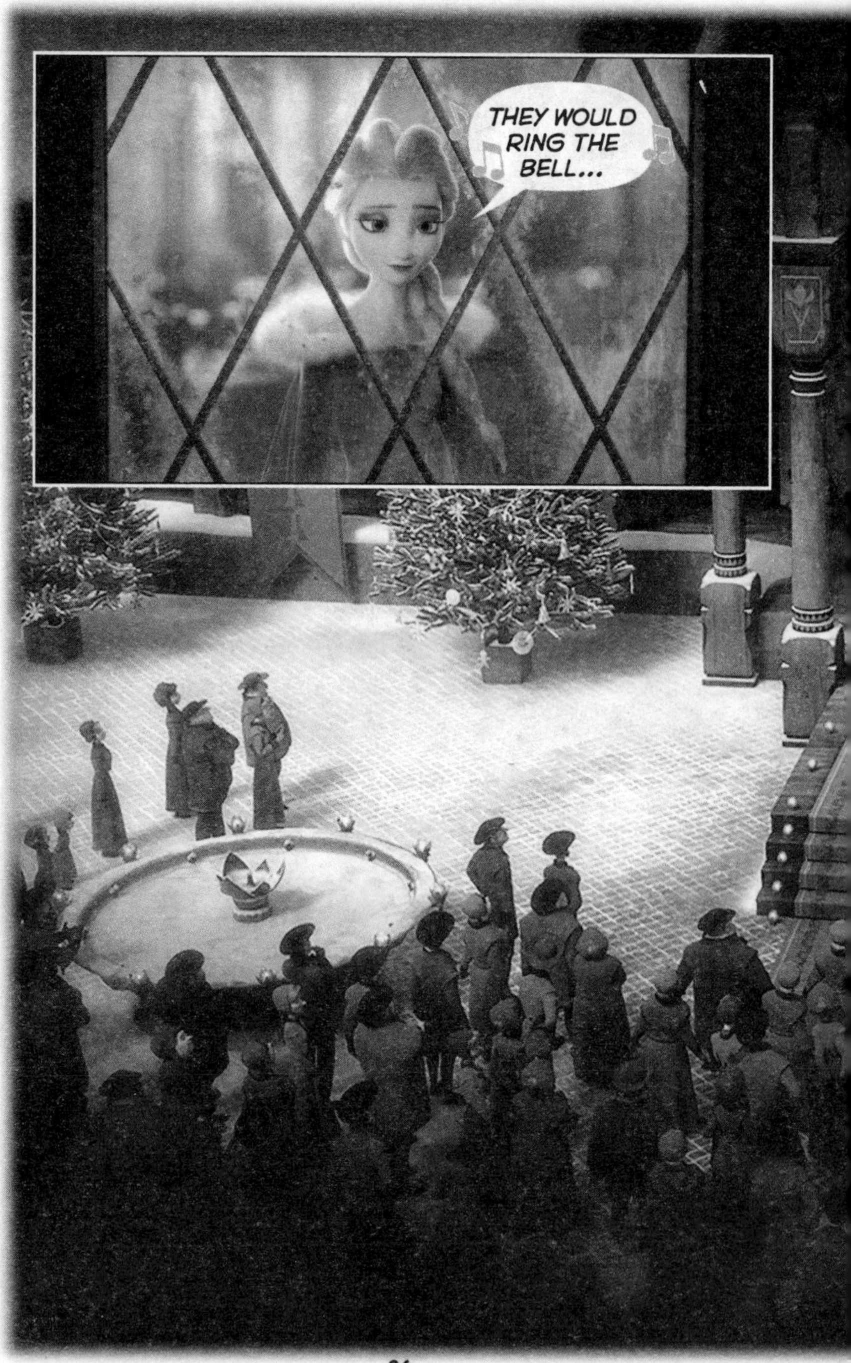
THEY WOULD RING THE BELL...

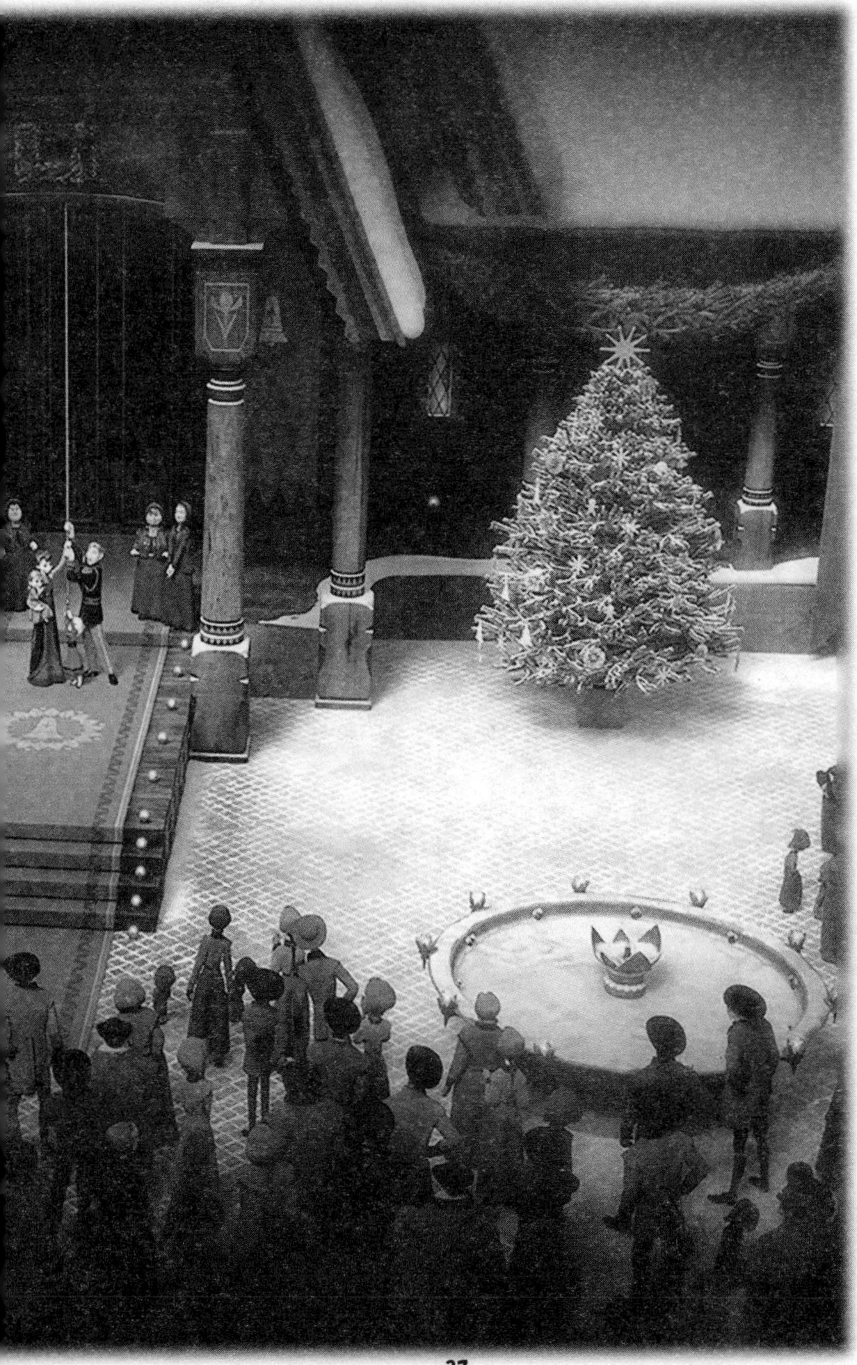

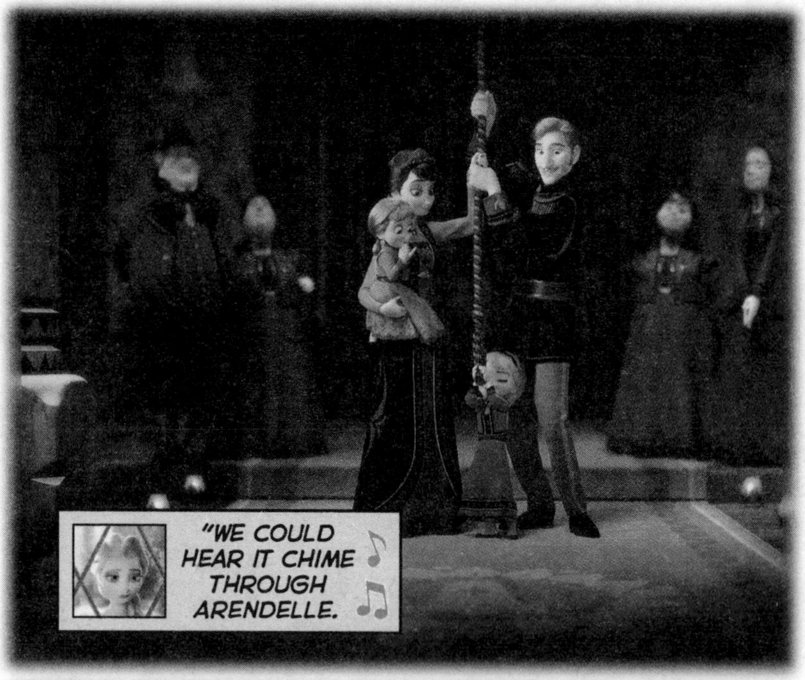
"WE COULD
HEAR IT CHIME
THROUGH
ARENDELLE.

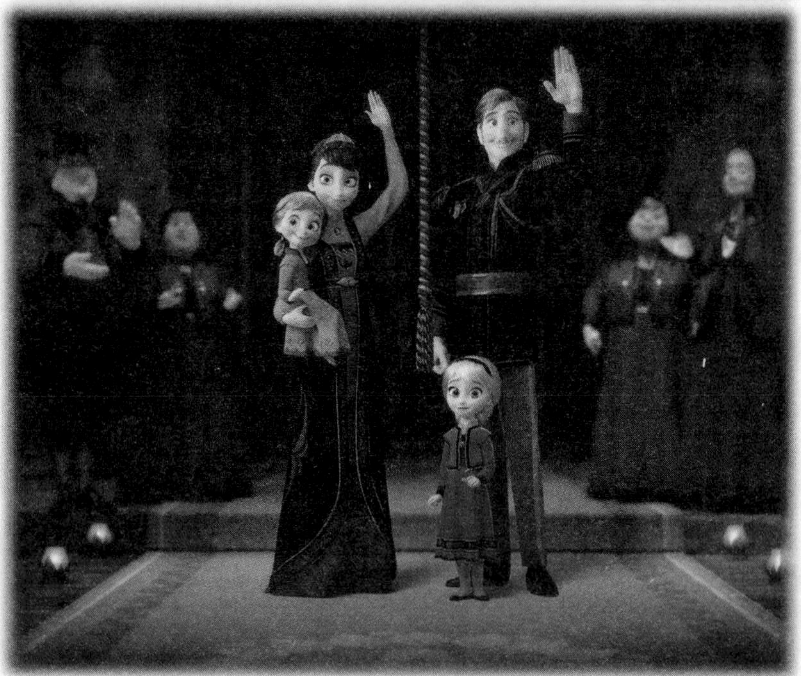

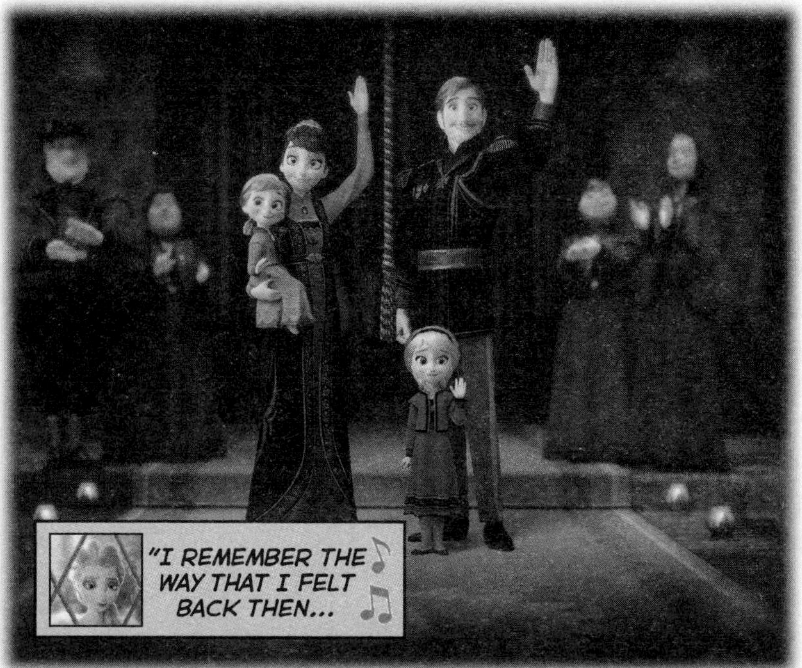
"I REMEMBER THE WAY THAT I FELT BACK THEN...

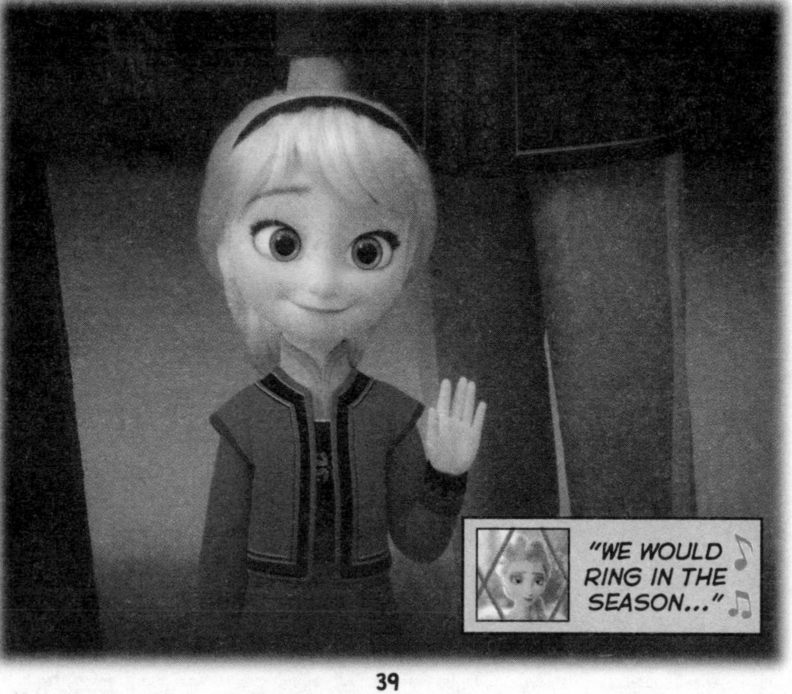
"WE WOULD RING IN THE SEASON..."

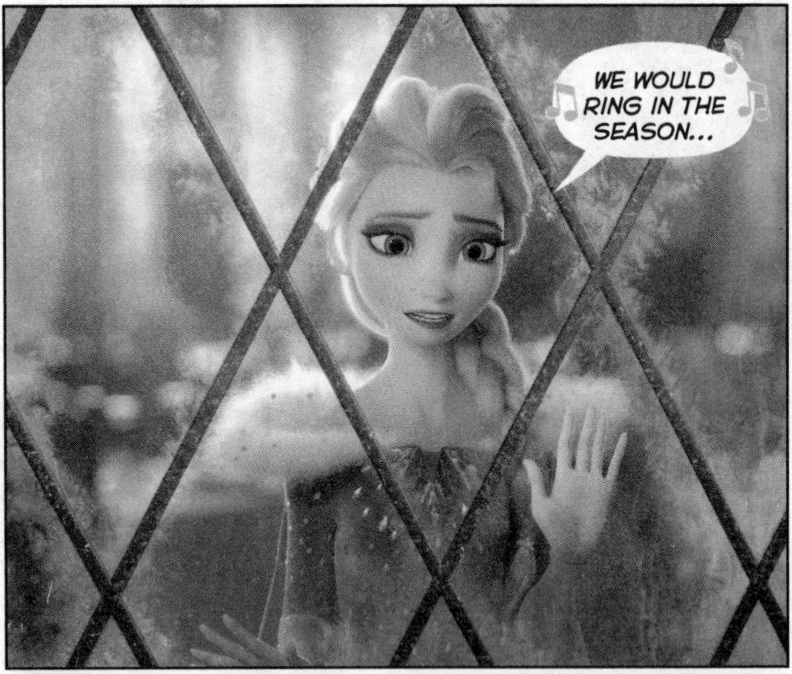
WE WOULD RING IN THE SEASON...

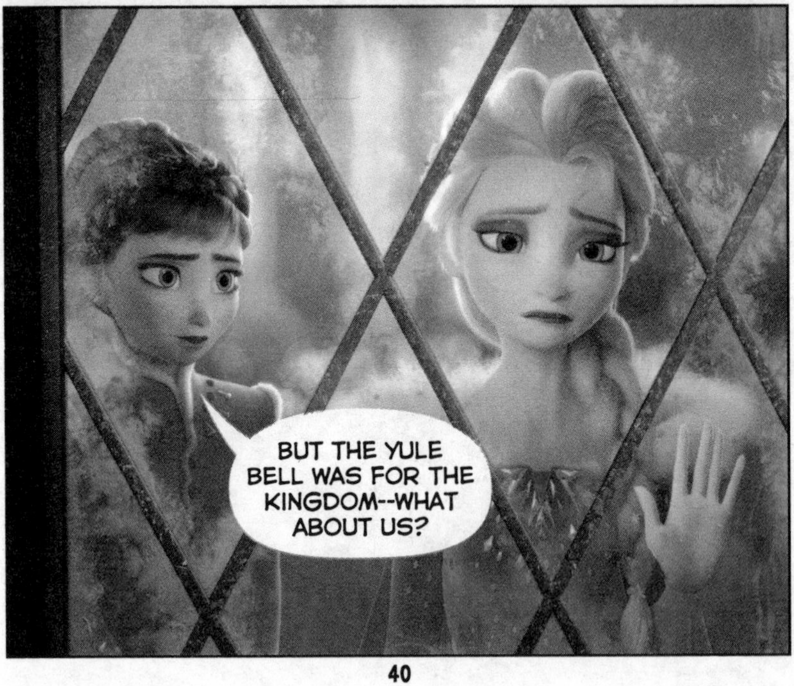
BUT THE YULE BELL WAS FOR THE KINGDOM--WHAT ABOUT US?

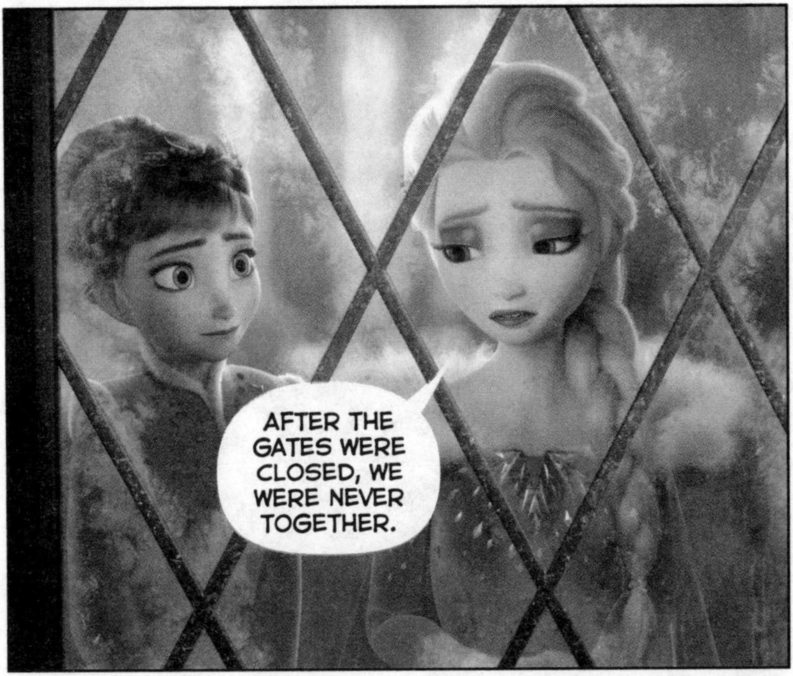
AFTER THE GATES WERE CLOSED, WE WERE NEVER TOGETHER.

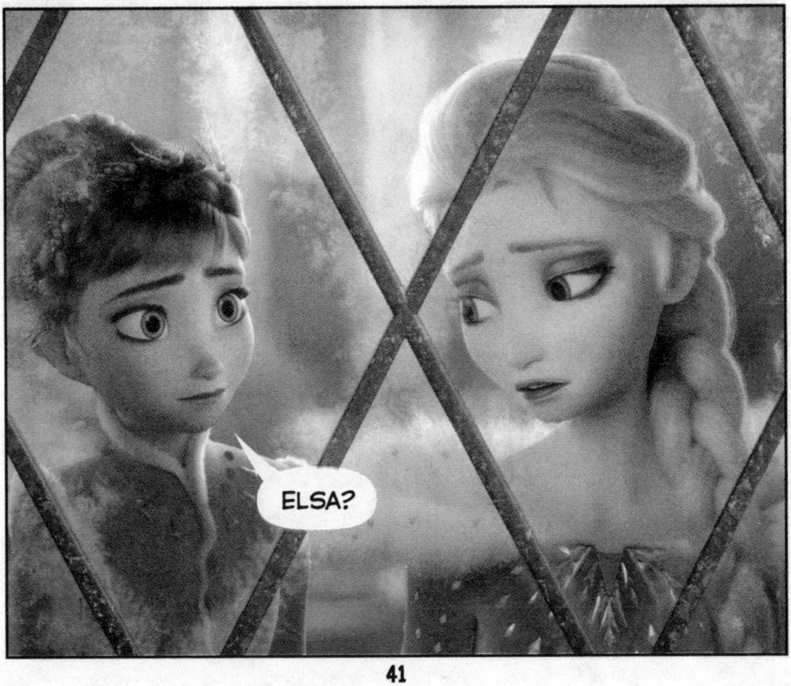
ELSA?

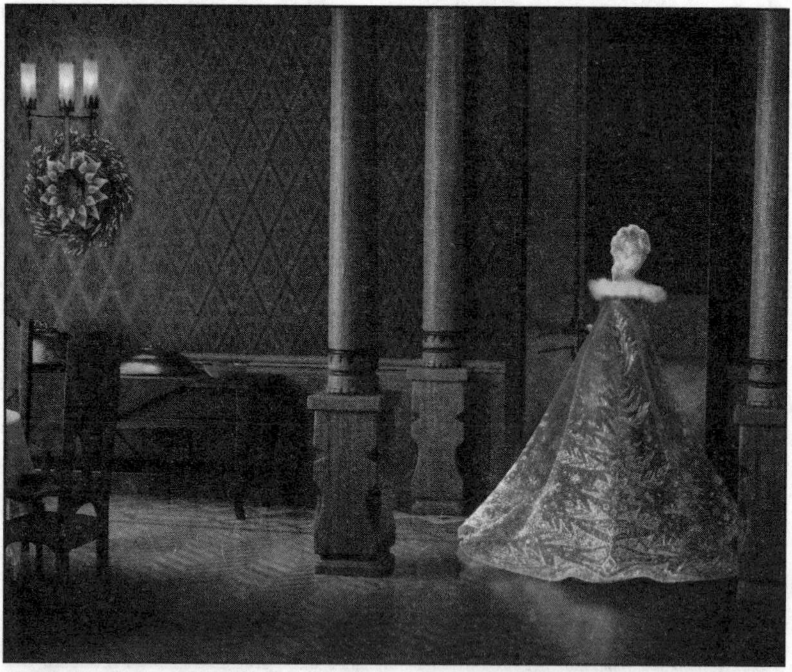

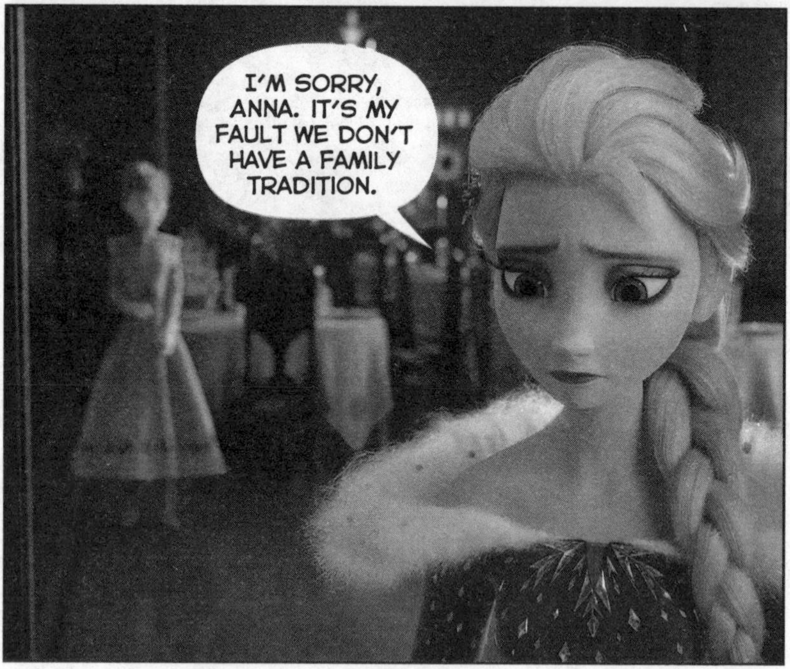
I'M SORRY, ANNA. IT'S MY FAULT WE DON'T HAVE A FAMILY TRADITION.

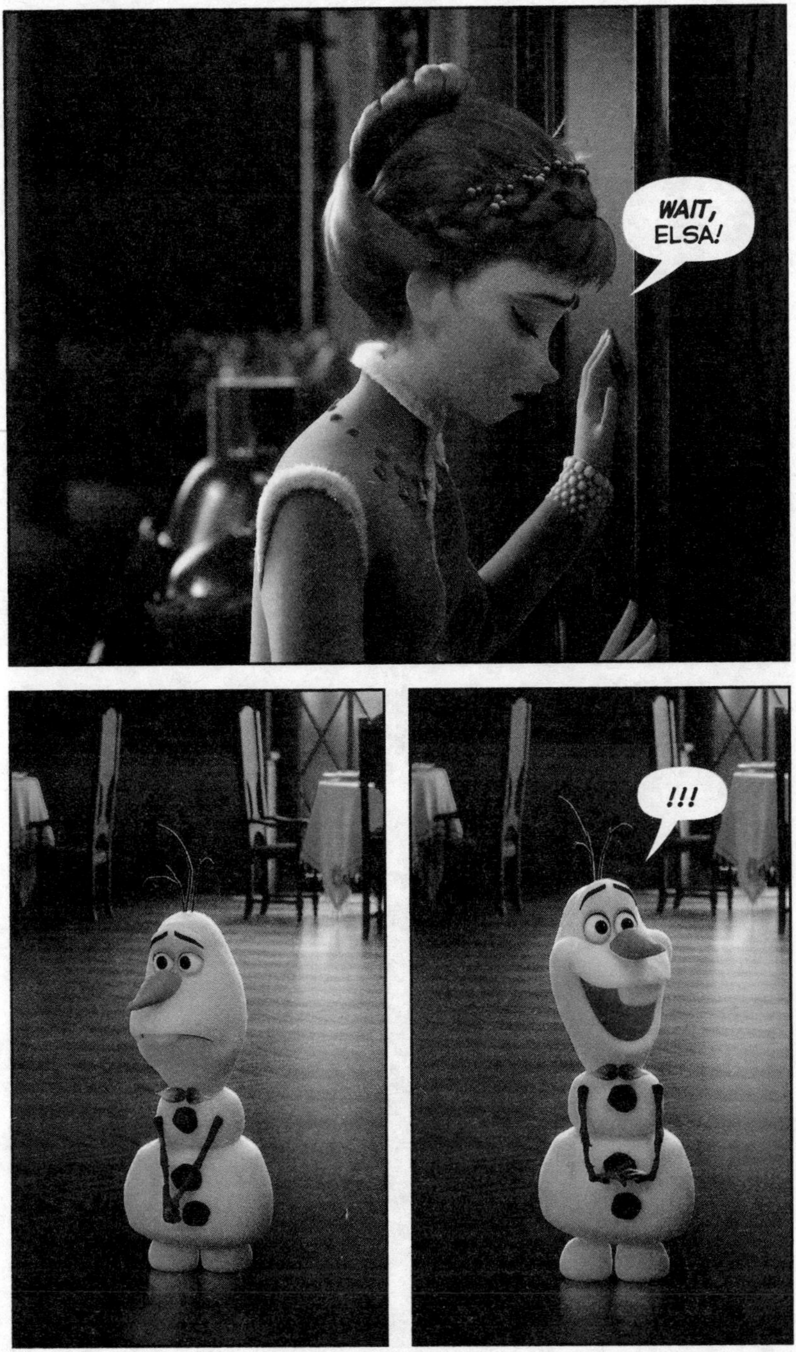
WAIT, ELSA!
!!!

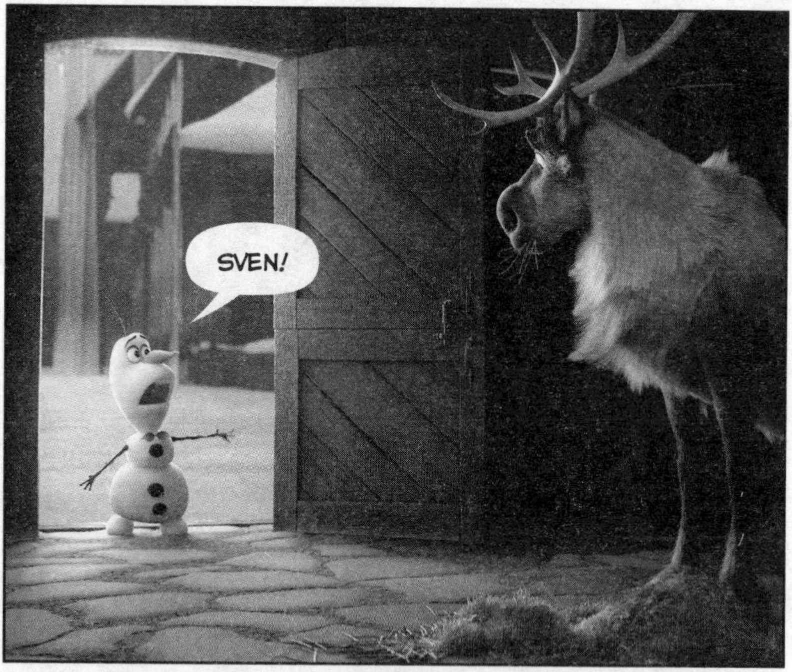
SVEN!

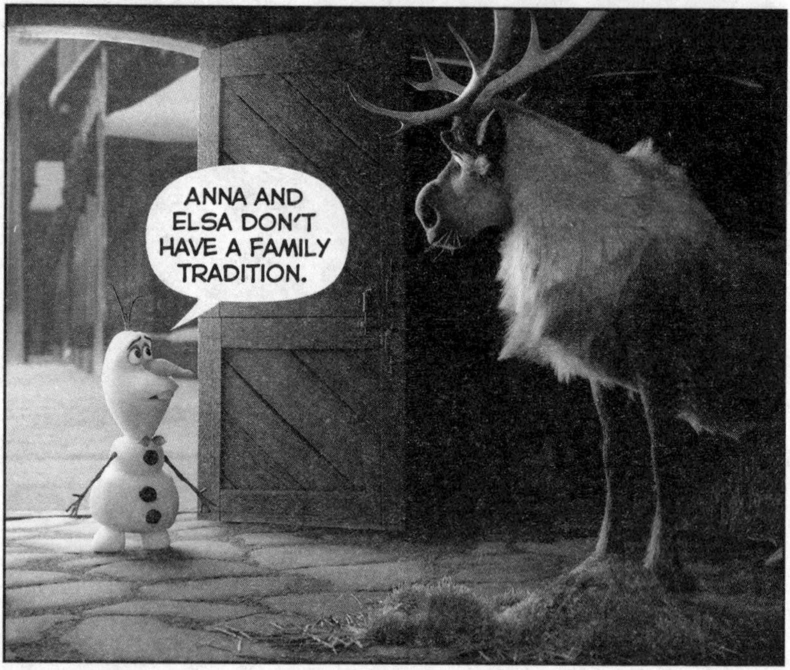
ANNA AND ELSA DON'T HAVE A FAMILY TRADITION.

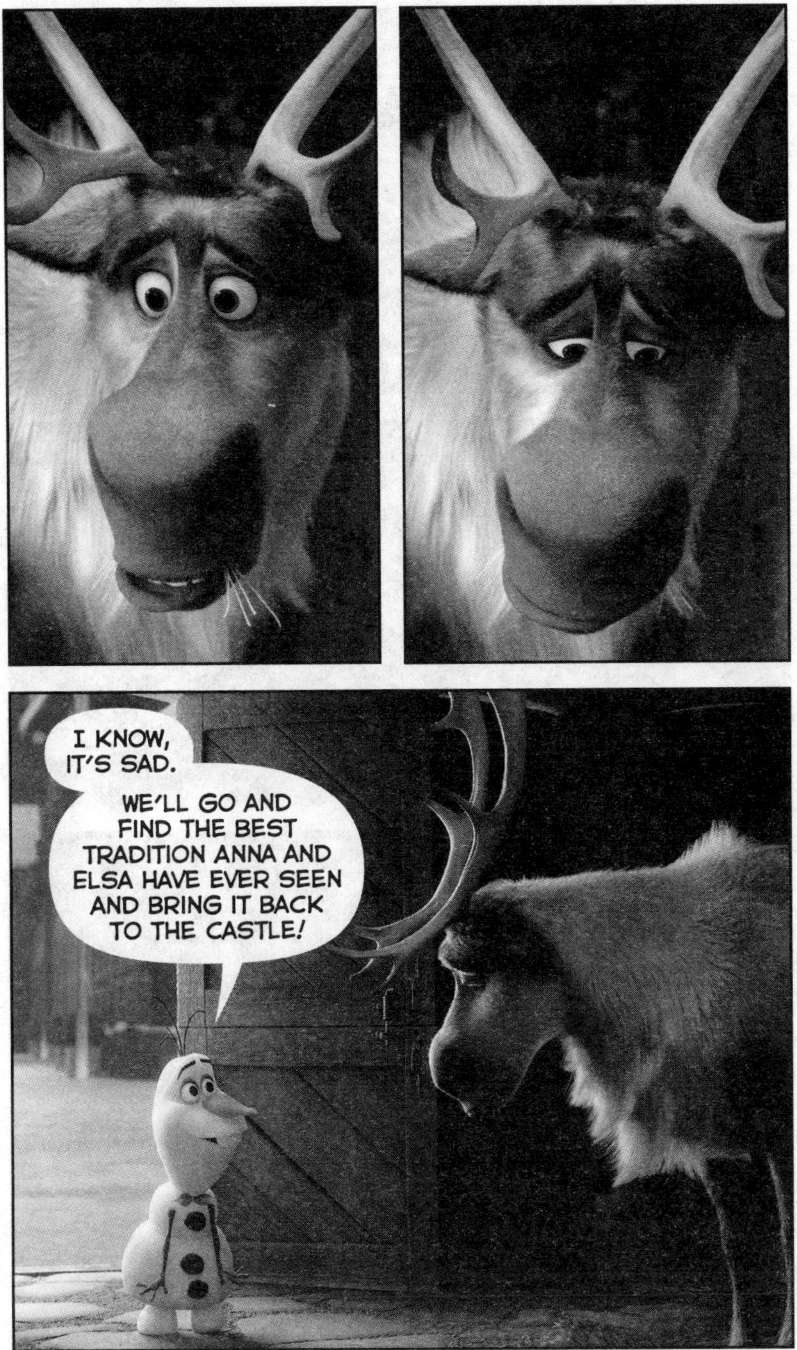
I KNOW, IT'S SAD.
WE'LL GO AND FIND THE BEST TRADITION ANNA AND ELSA HAVE EVER SEEN AND BRING IT BACK TO THE CASTLE!

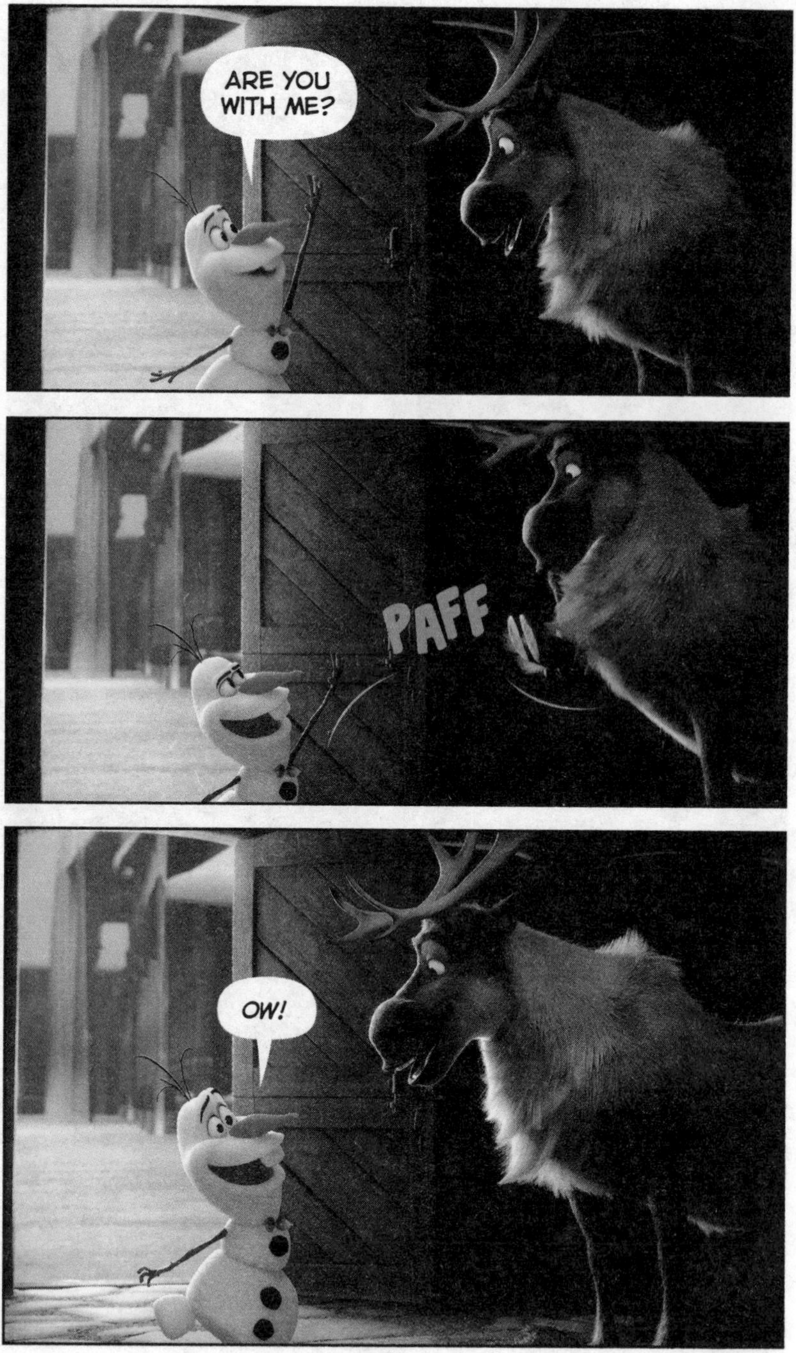
ARE YOU WITH ME?
PAFF
OW!

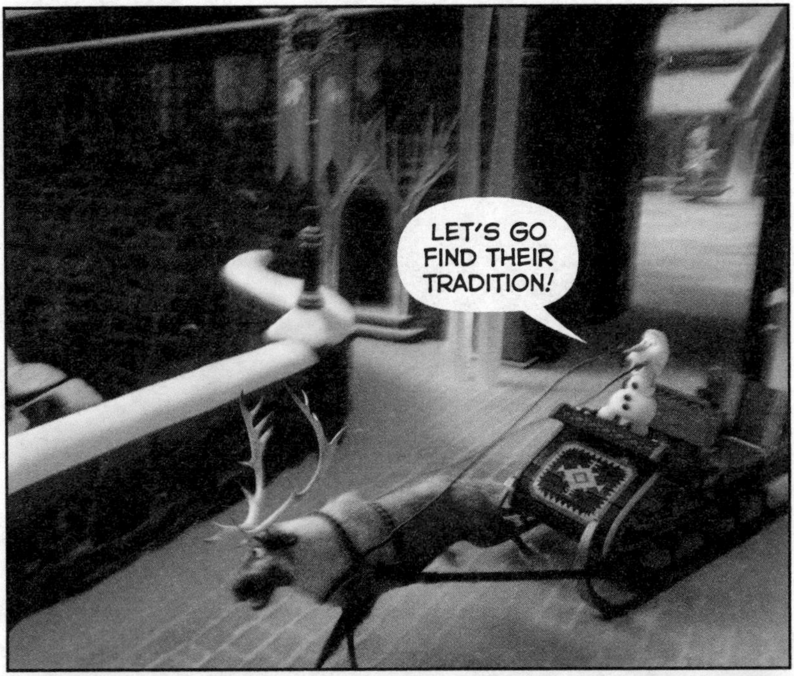
LET'S GO FIND THEIR TRADITION!

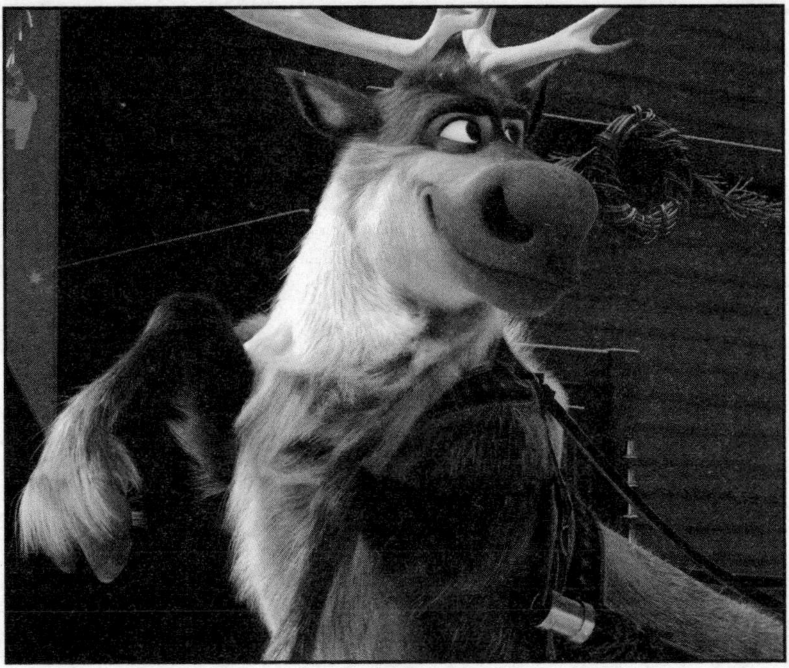

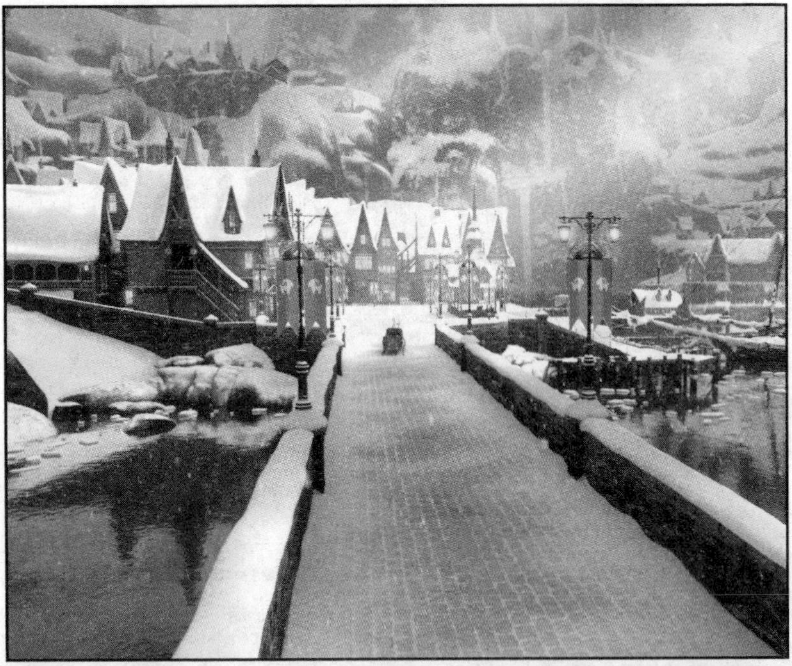

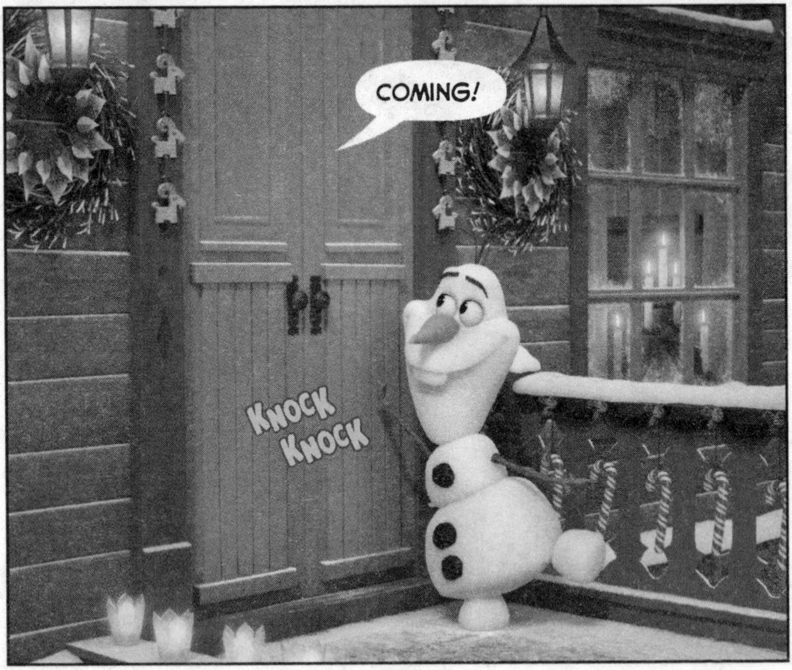
COMING!
KNOCK KNOCK

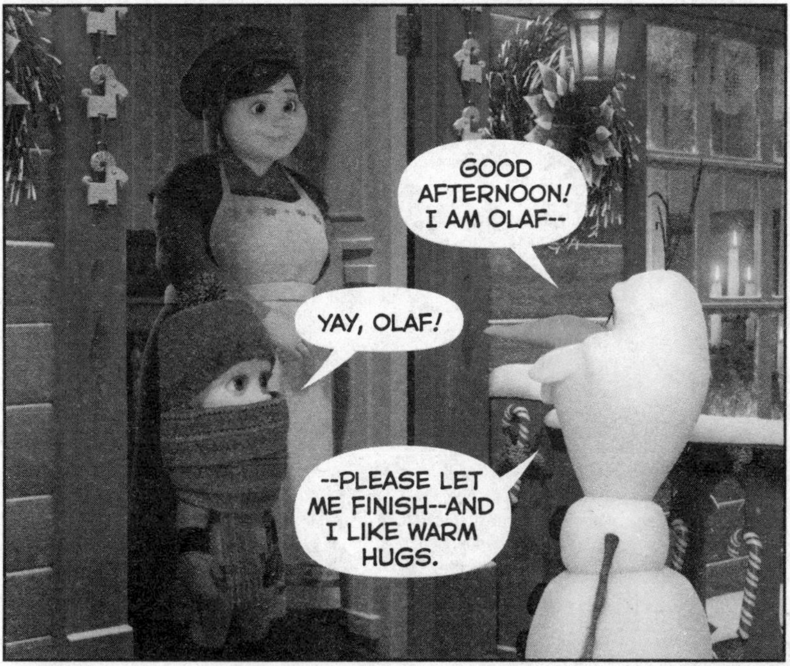
GOOD AFTERNOON! I AM OLAF--
YAY, OLAF!
--PLEASE LET ME FINISH--AND I LIKE WARM HUGS.

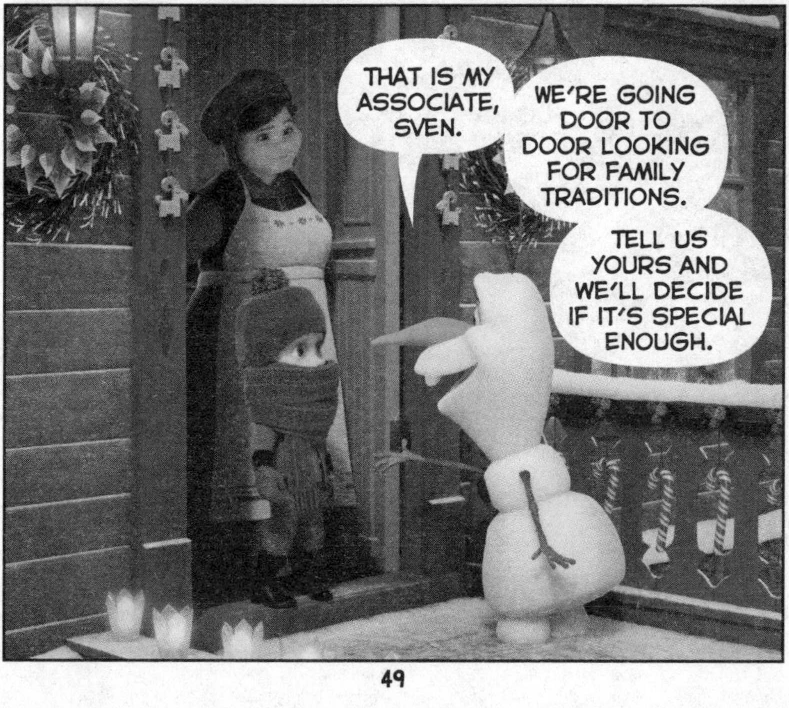
THAT IS MY ASSOCIATE, SVEN.
WE'RE GOING DOOR TO DOOR LOOKING FOR FAMILY TRADITIONS.
TELL US YOURS AND WE'LL DECIDE IF IT'S SPECIAL ENOUGH.

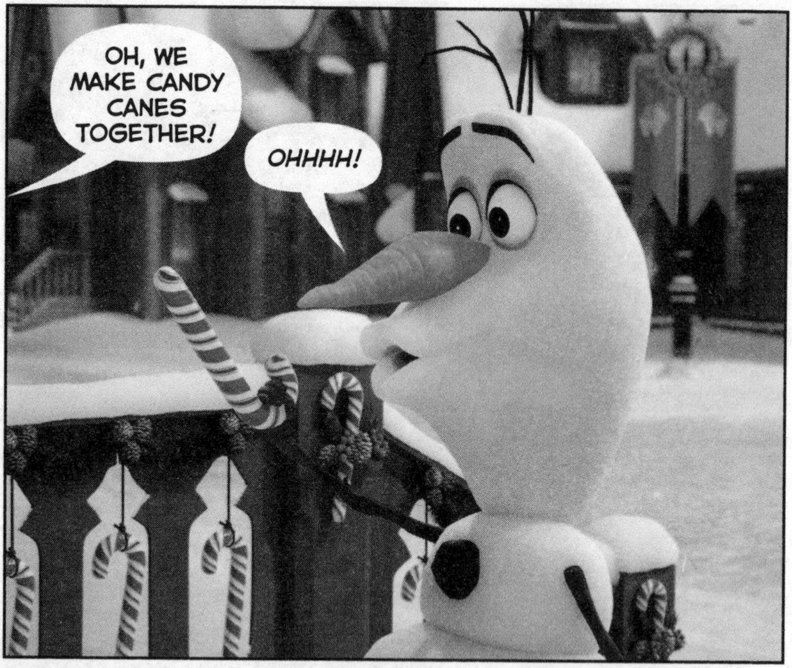
OH, WE MAKE CANDY CANES TOGETHER!
OHHHH!

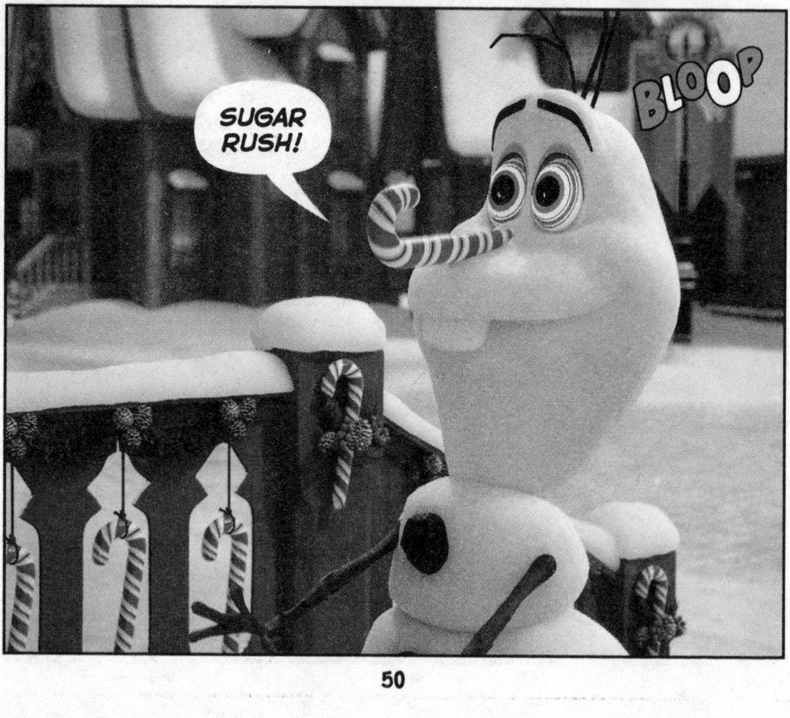
SUGAR RUSH!
BLOOP

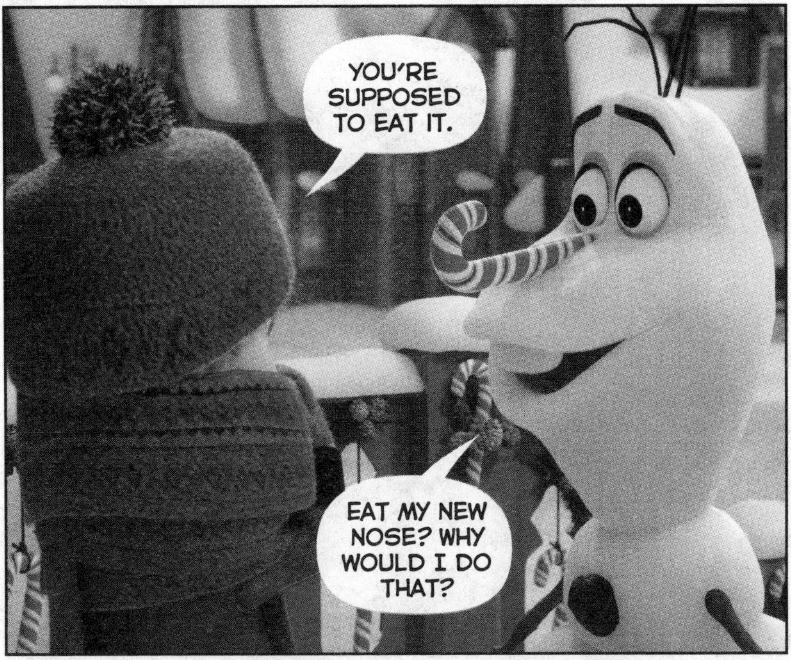
YOU'RE SUPPOSED TO EAT IT.
EAT MY NEW NOSE? WHY WOULD I DO THAT?

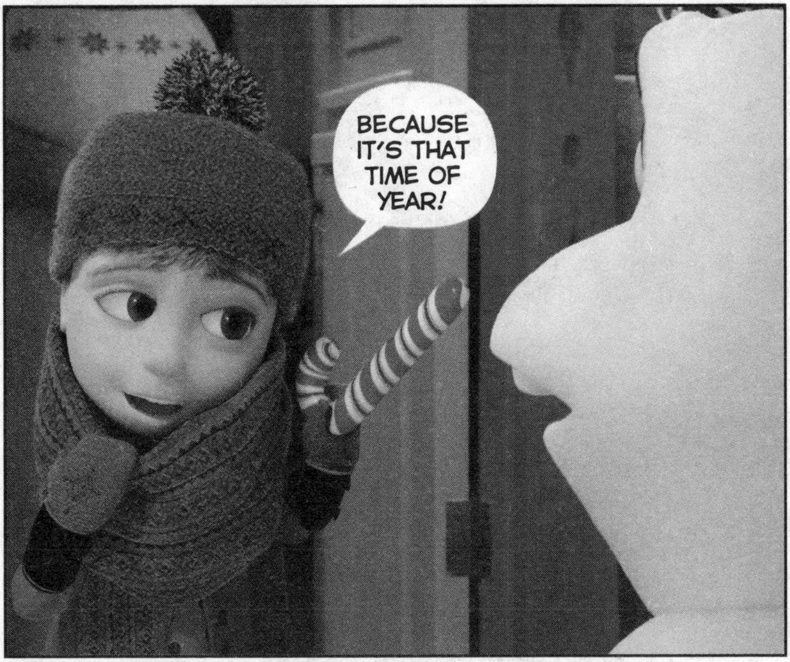
BECAUSE IT'S THAT TIME OF YEAR!

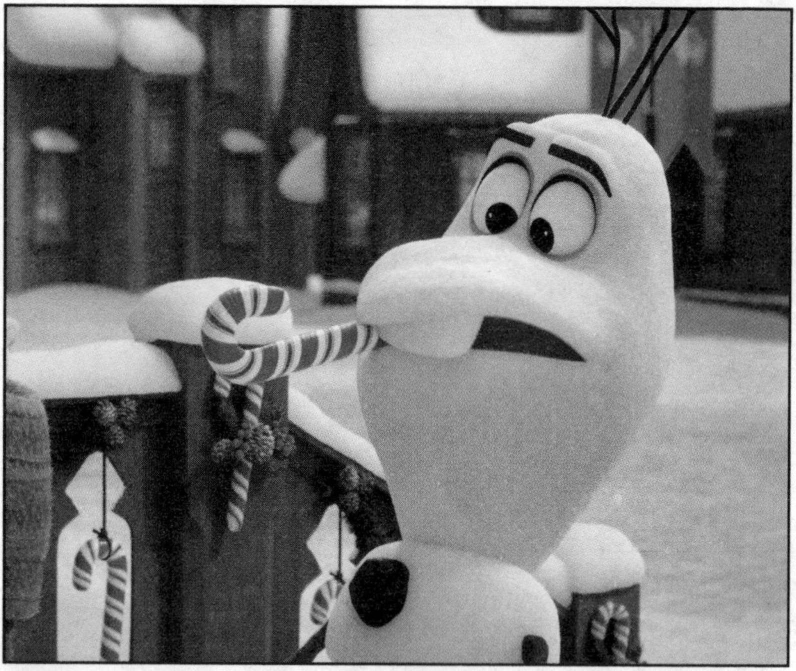

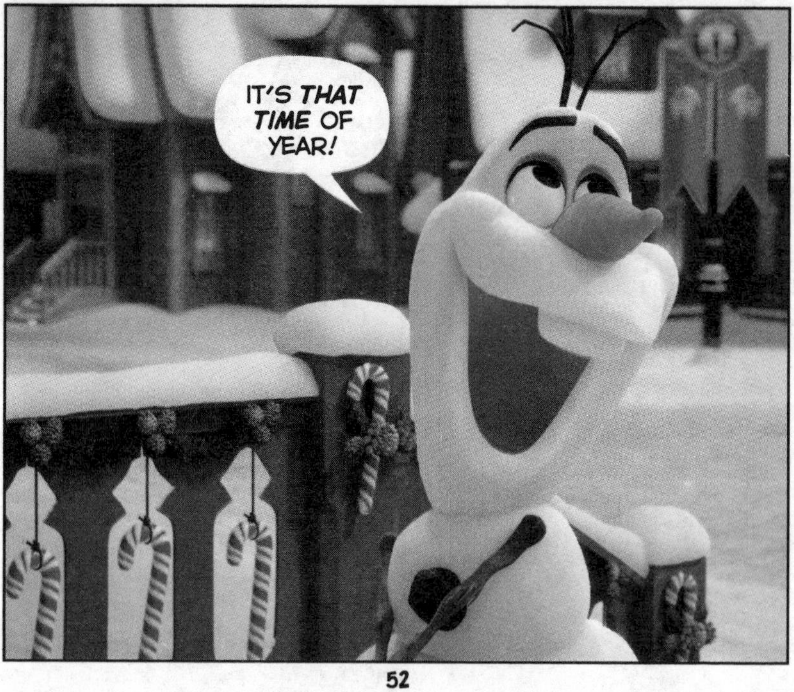
IT'S *THAT* *TIME* OF YEAR!

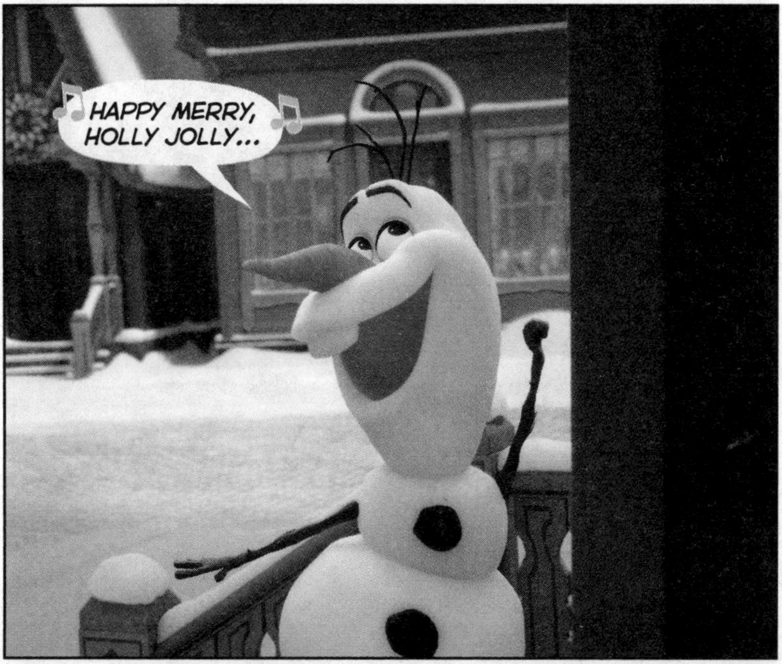
HAPPY MERRY, HOLLY JOLLY...

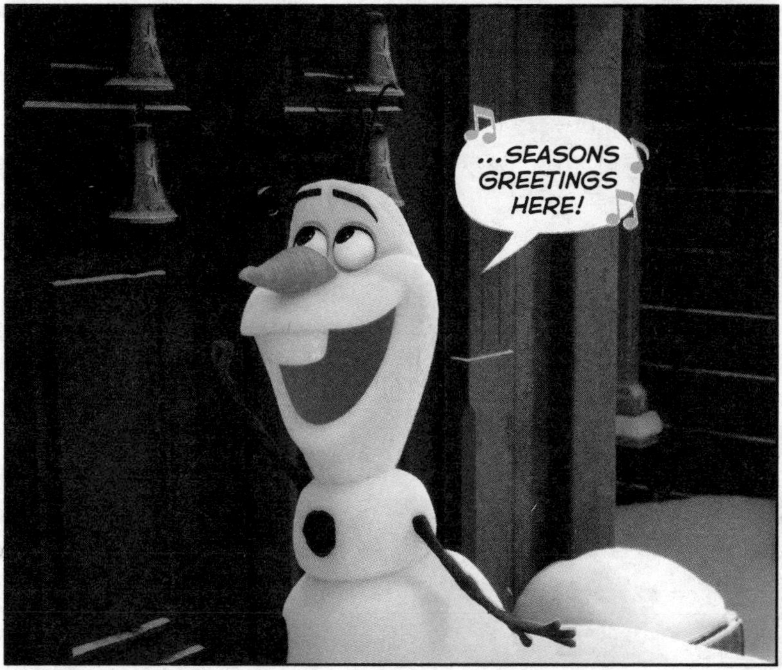
...SEASONS GREETINGS HERE!

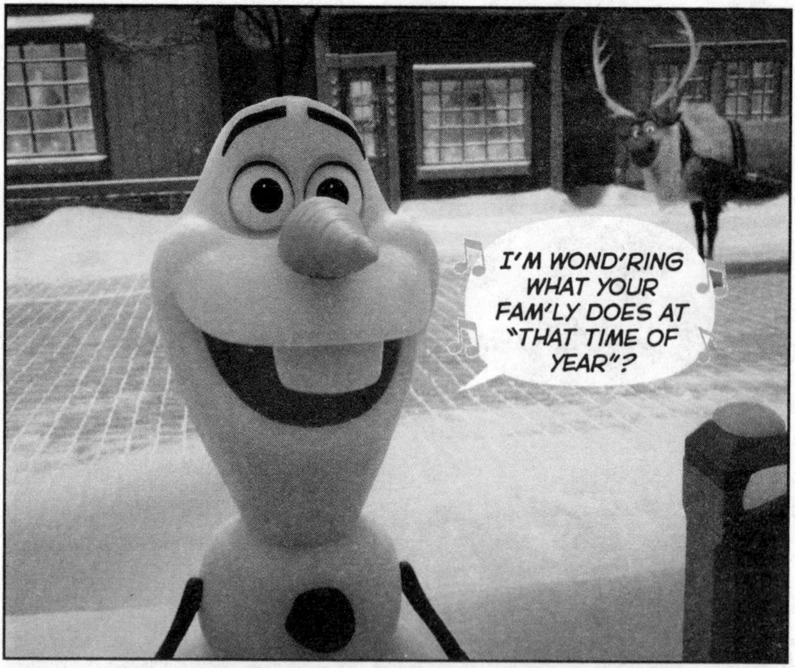
I'M WOND'RING WHAT YOUR FAM'LY DOES AT "THAT TIME OF YEAR"?

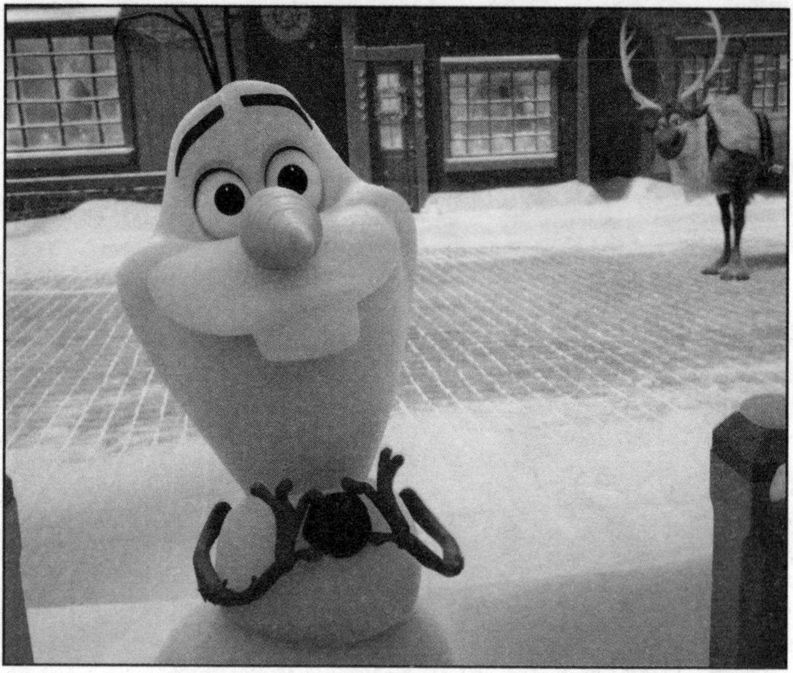

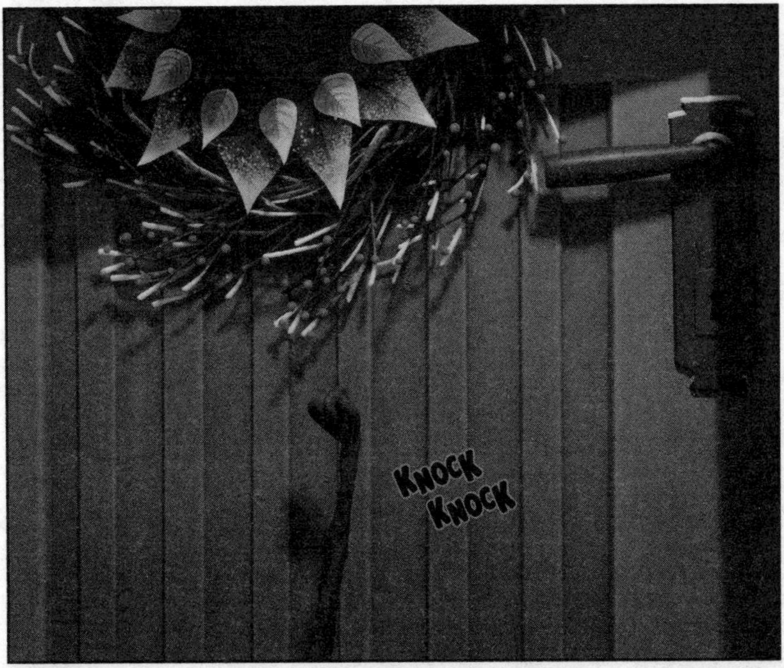
KNOCK
KNOCK

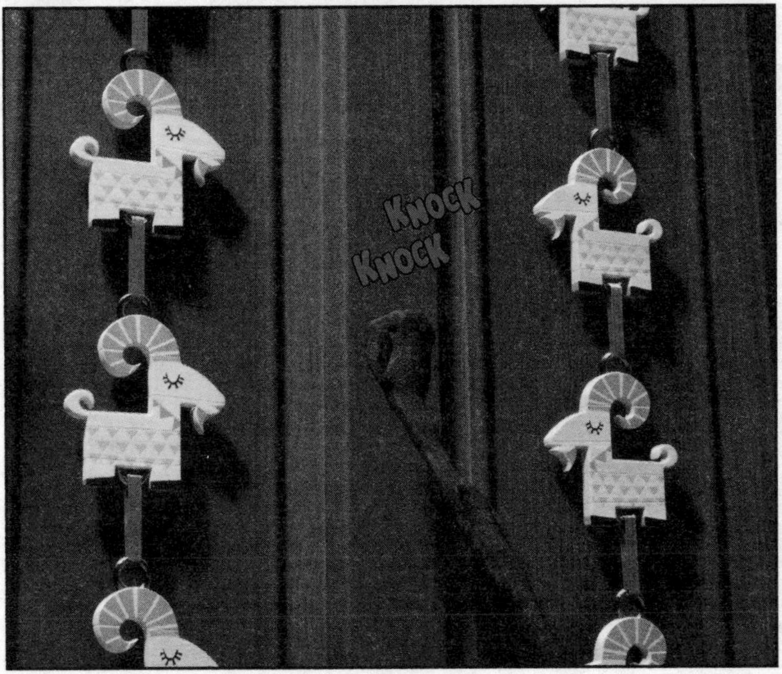
KNOCK
KNOCK

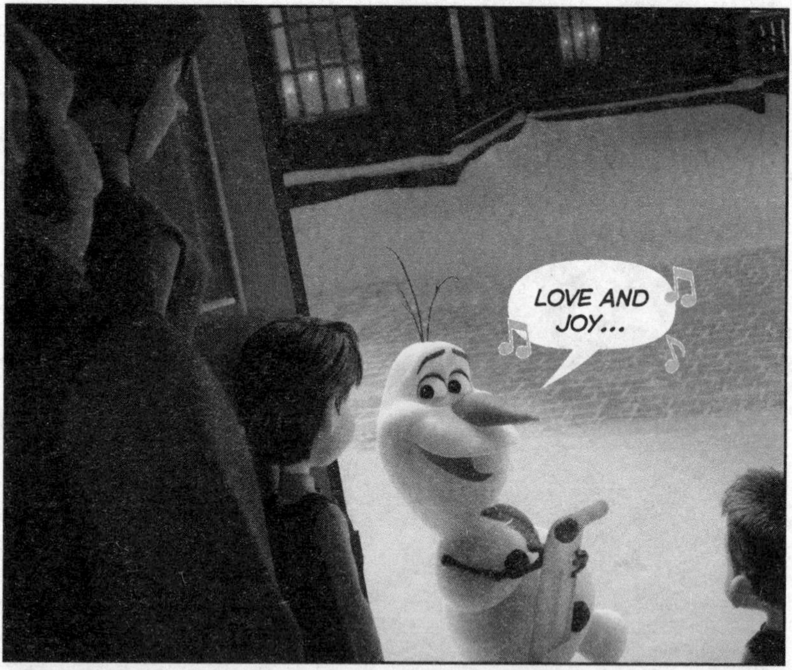
LOVE AND
JOY...

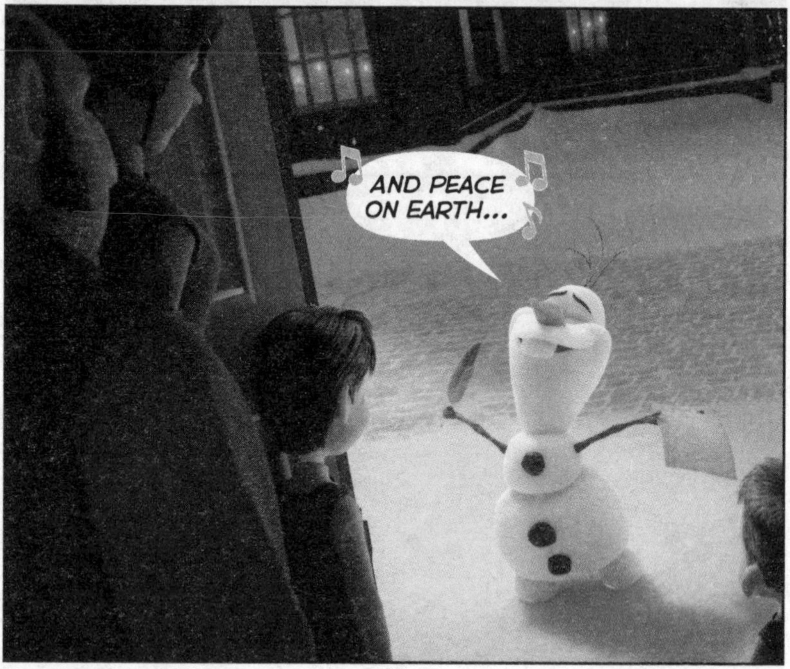
AND PEACE
ON EARTH...

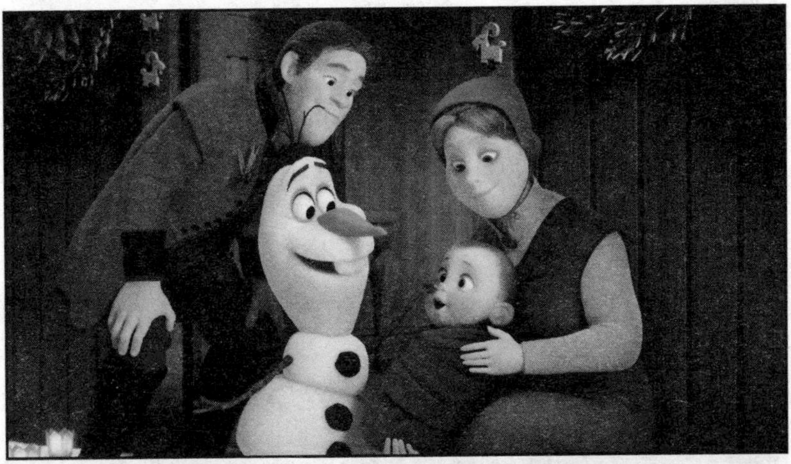

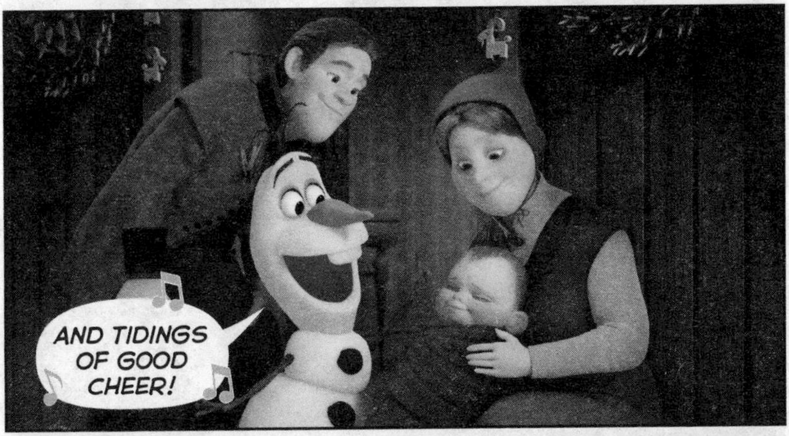
AND TIDINGS OF GOOD CHEER!

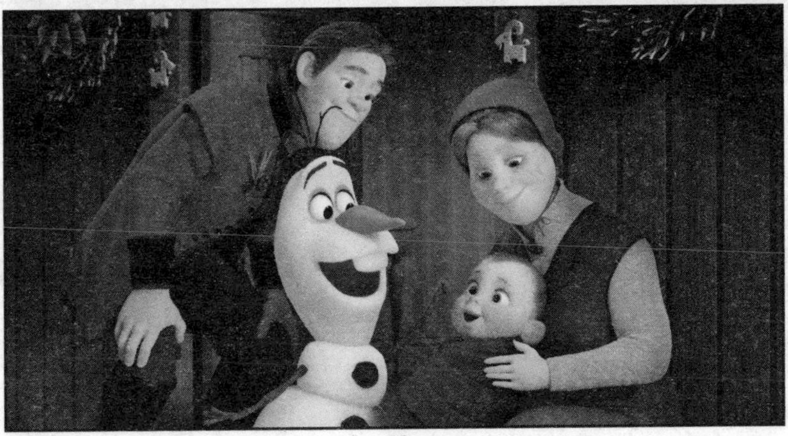

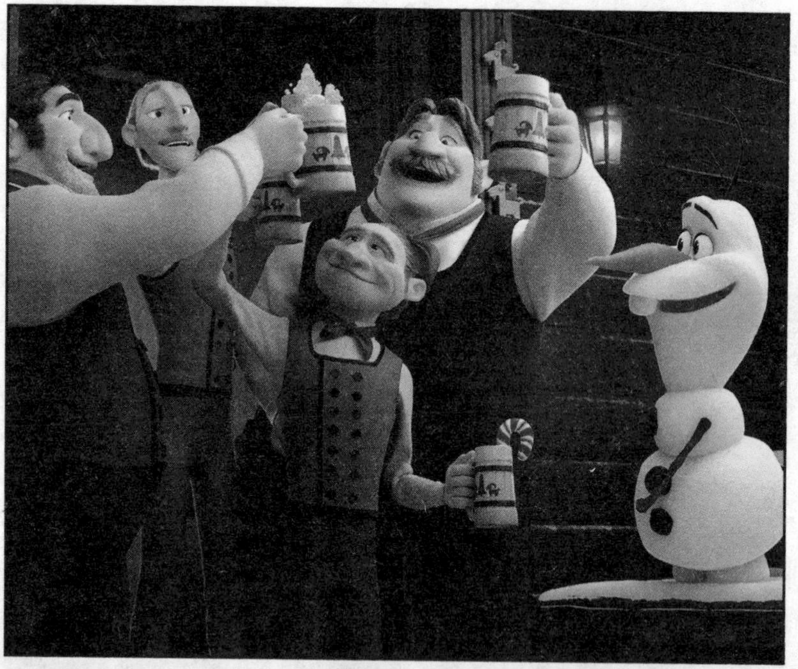

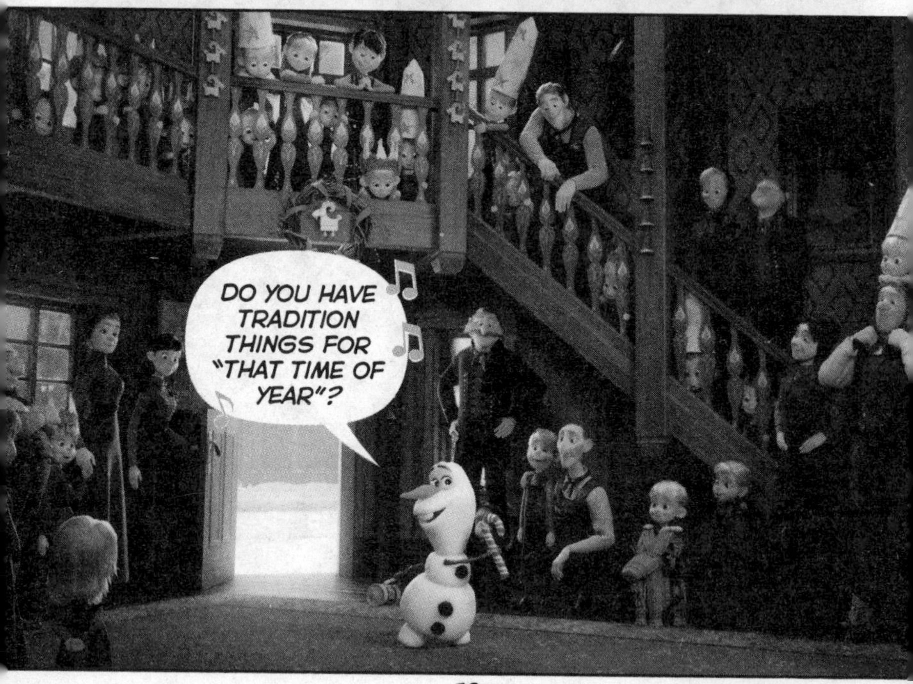
DO YOU HAVE TRADITION THINGS FOR "THAT TIME OF YEAR"?

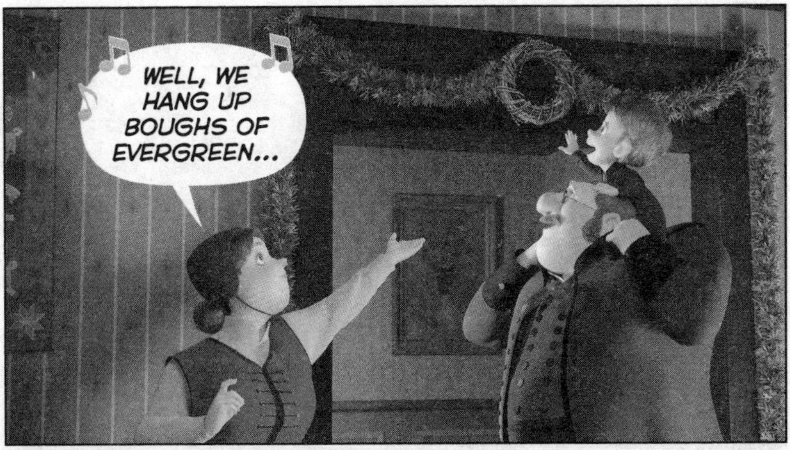
WELL, WE HANG UP BOUGHS OF EVERGREEN...

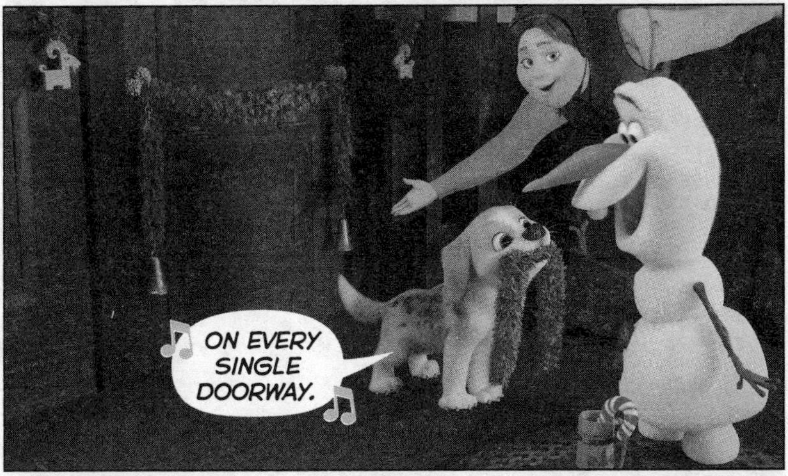
ON EVERY SINGLE DOORWAY.

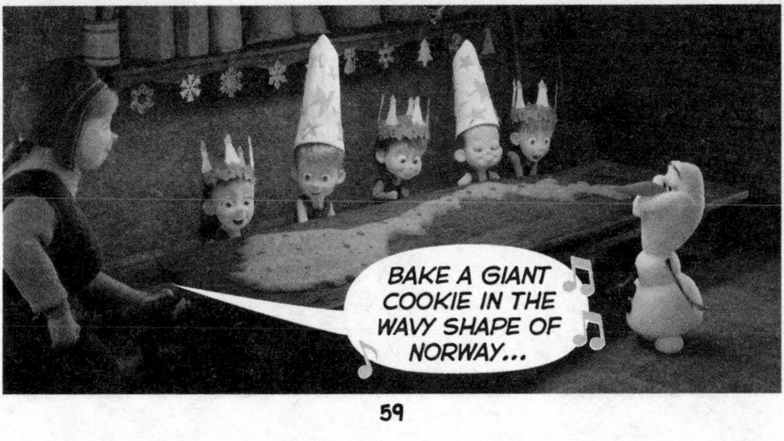
BAKE A GIANT COOKIE IN THE WAVY SHAPE OF NORWAY...

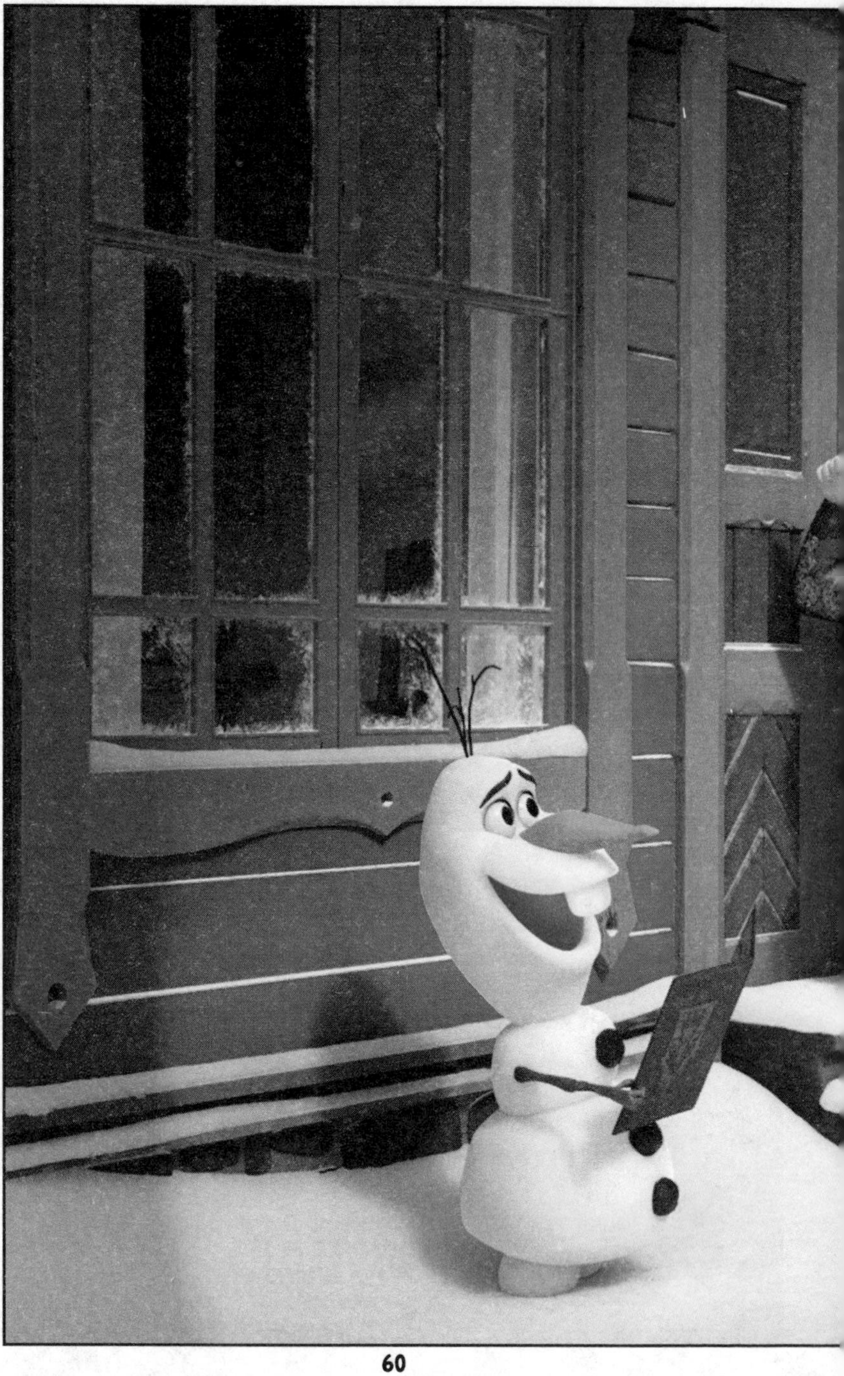

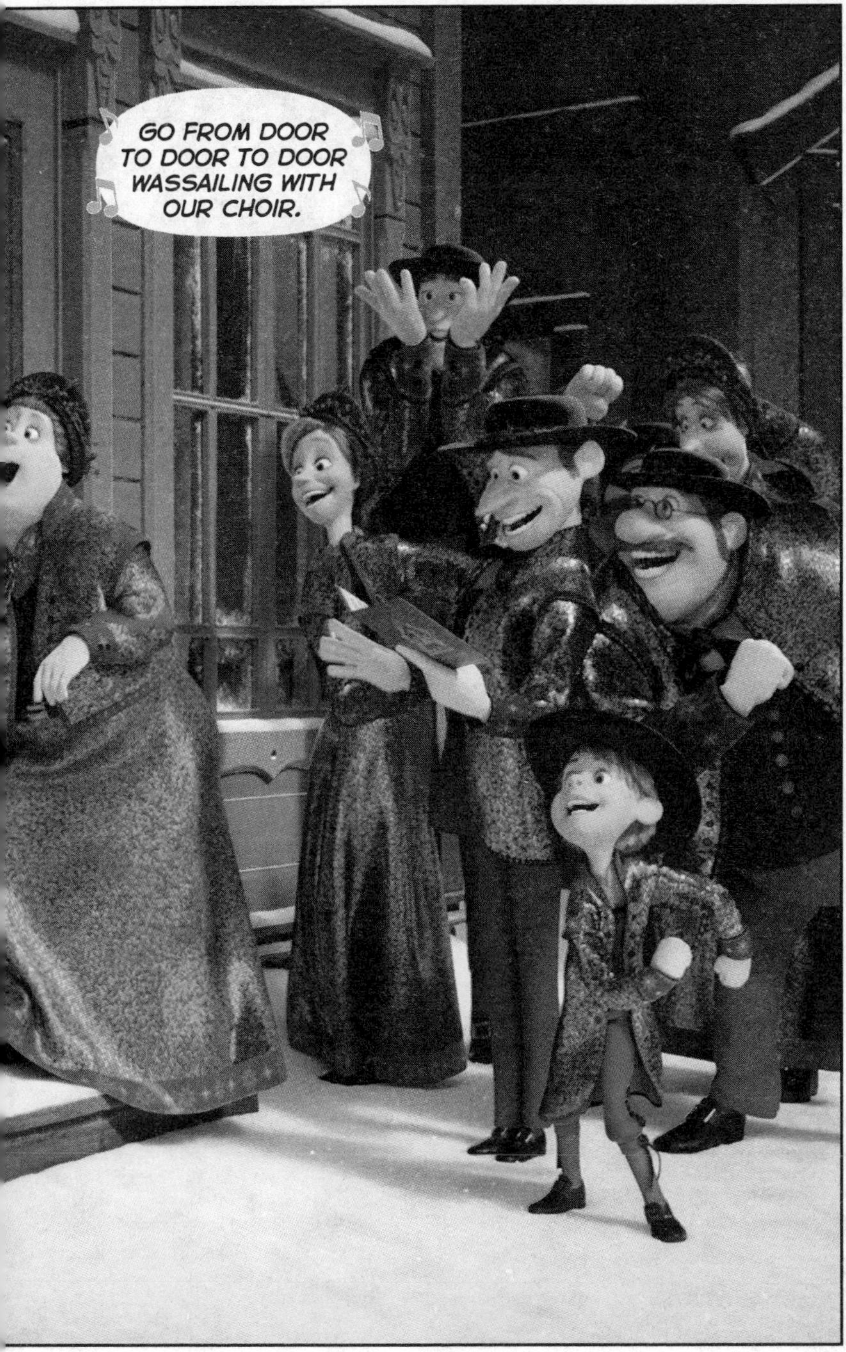
GO FROM DOOR TO DOOR TO DOOR WASSAILING WITH OUR CHOIR.

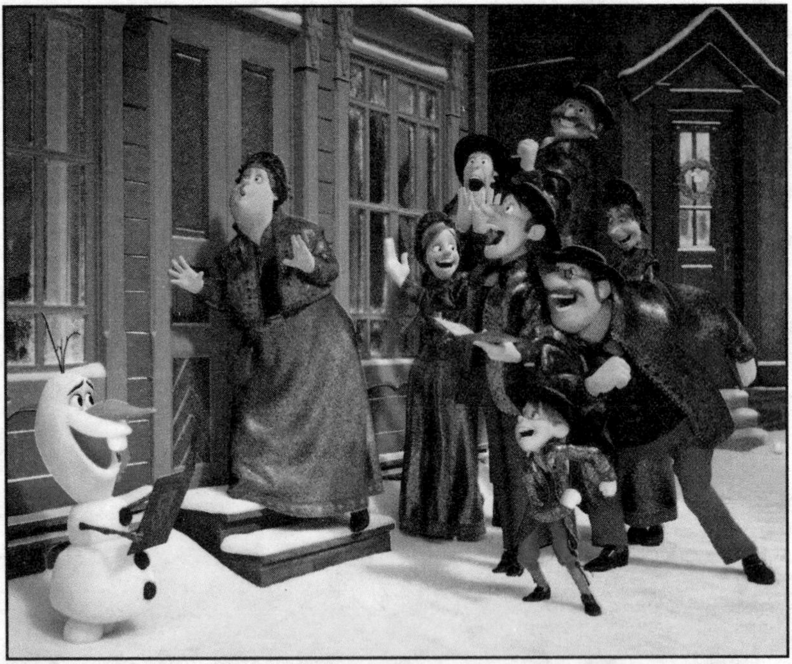

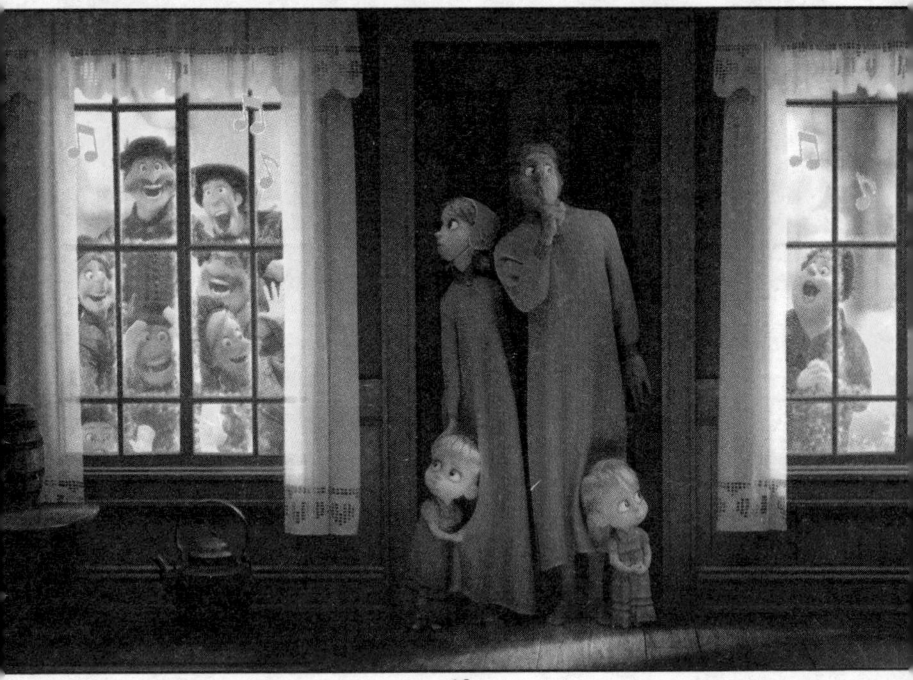

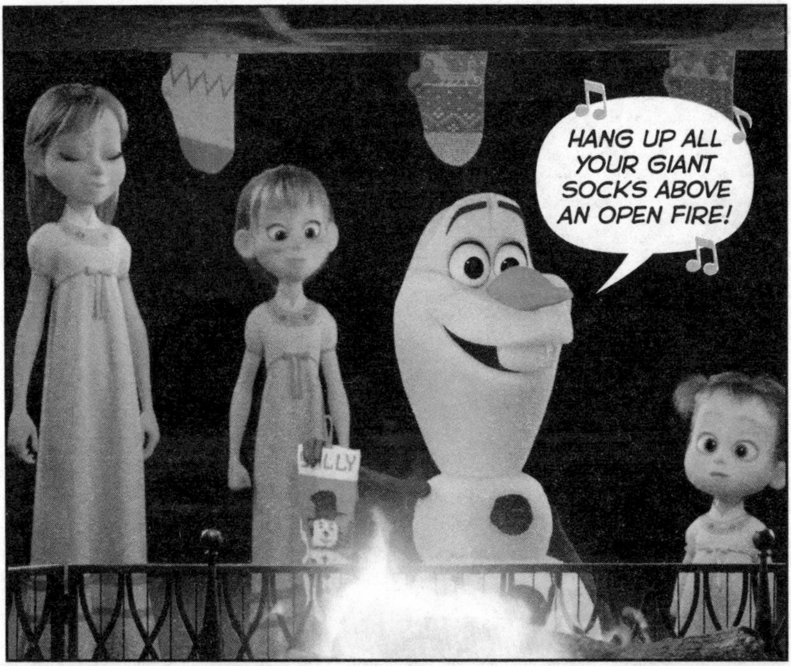
HANG UP ALL YOUR GIANT SOCKS ABOVE AN OPEN FIRE!

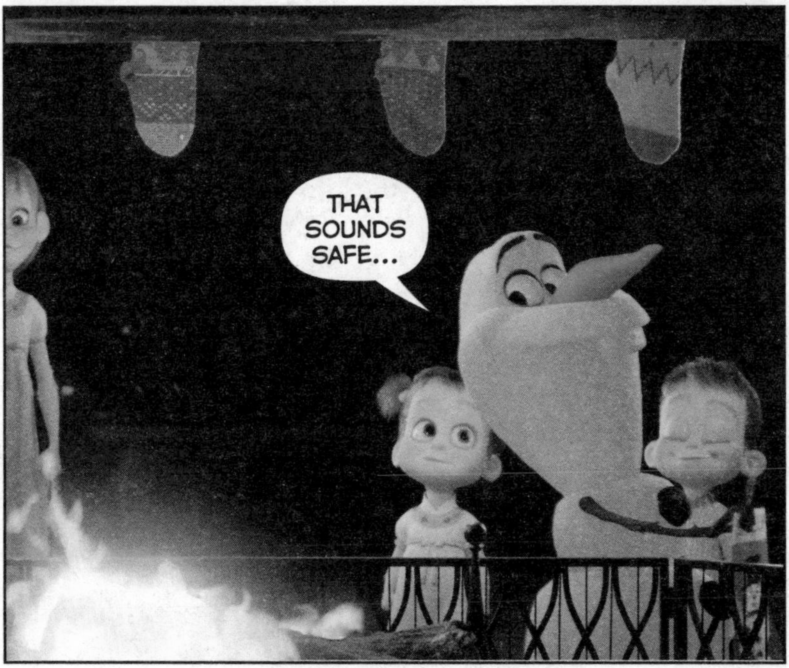
THAT SOUNDS SAFE...

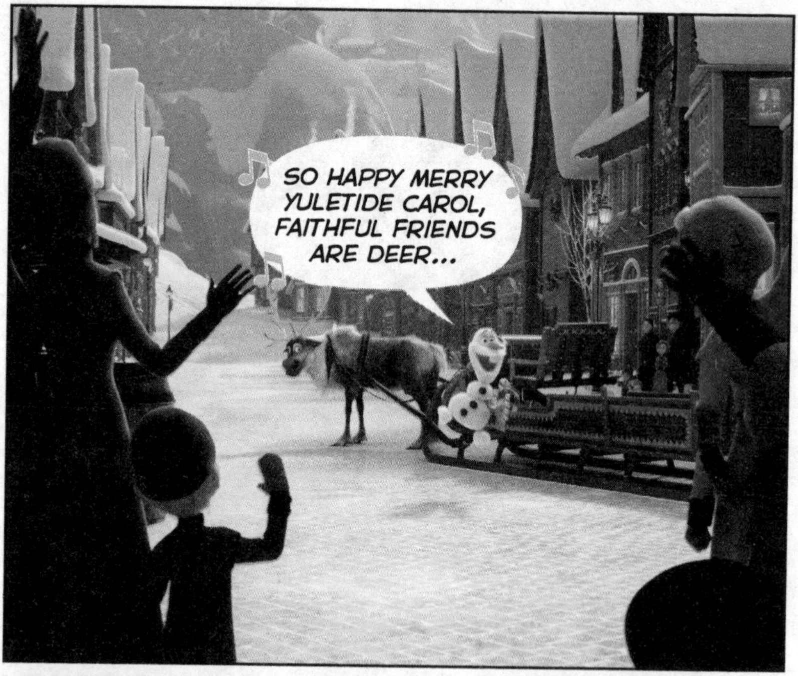
SO HAPPY MERRY YULETIDE CAROL, FAITHFUL FRIENDS ARE DEER...

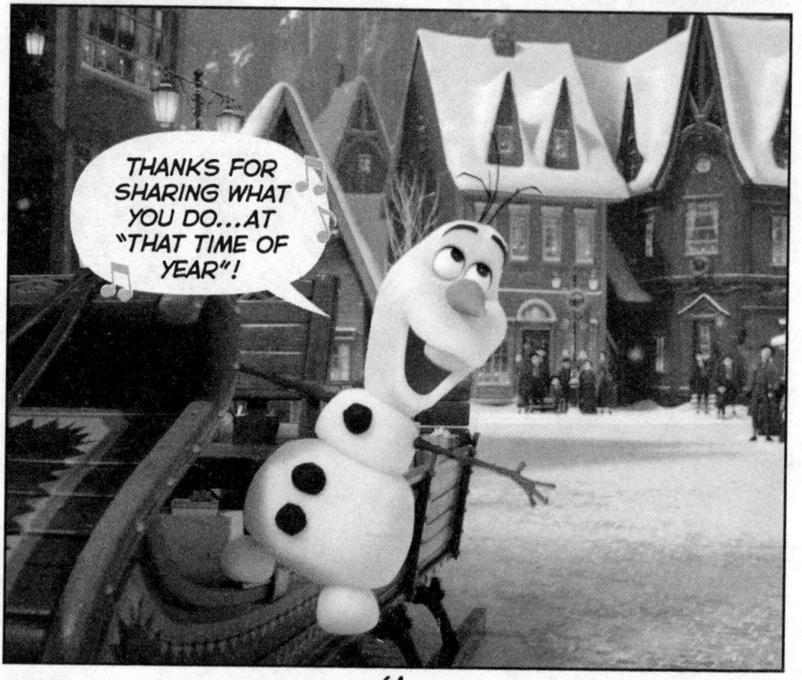
THANKS FOR SHARING WHAT YOU DO...AT "THAT TIME OF YEAR"!

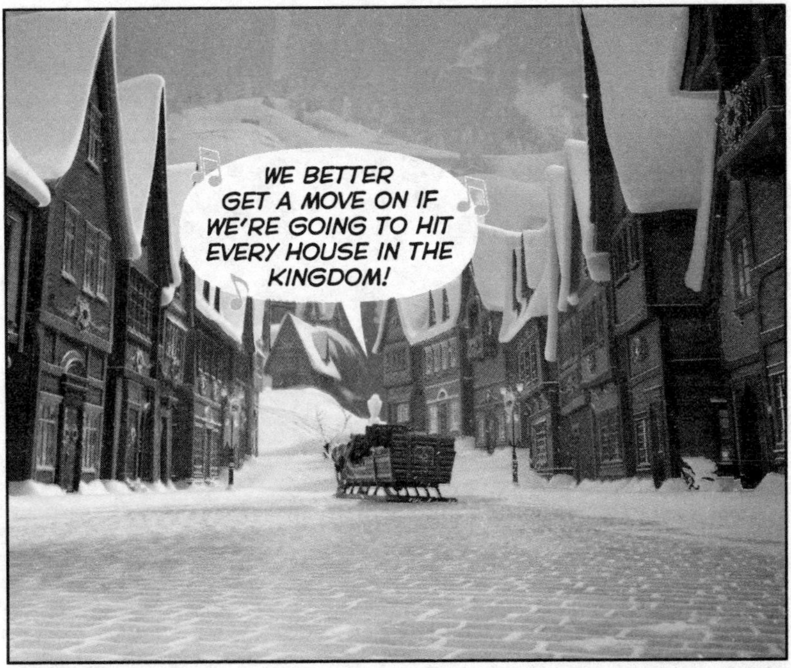
WE BETTER GET A MOVE ON IF WE'RE GOING TO HIT EVERY HOUSE IN THE KINGDOM!

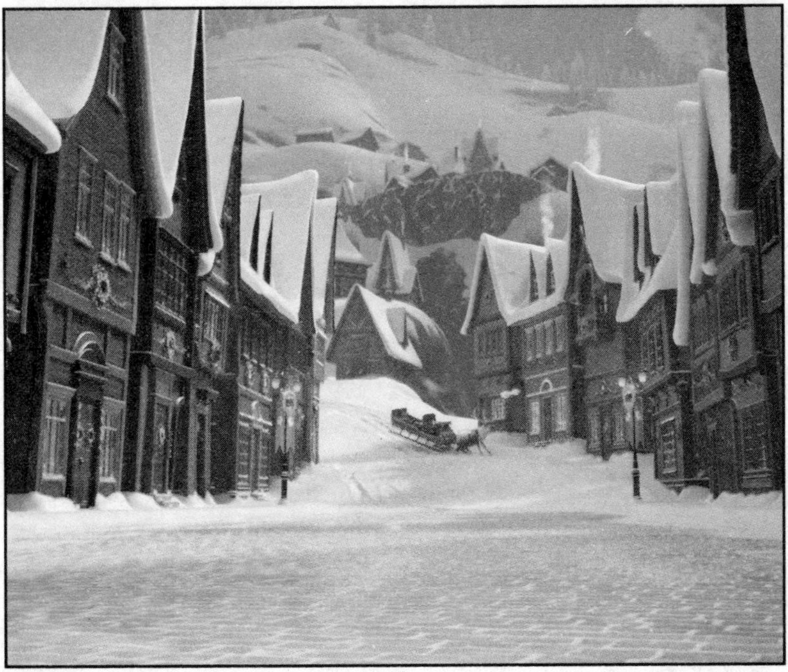

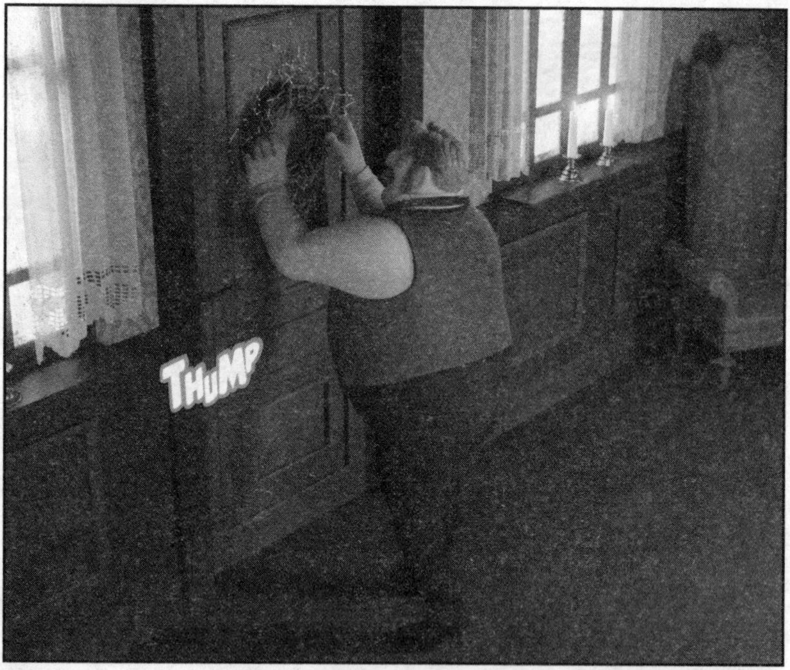
THUMP

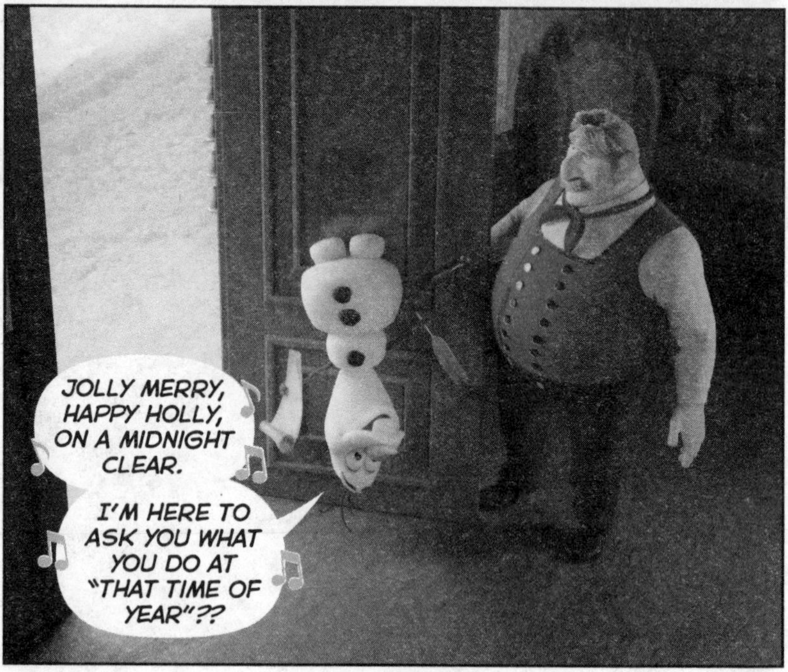
JOLLY MERRY, HAPPY HOLLY, ON A MIDNIGHT CLEAR.
I'M HERE TO ASK YOU WHAT YOU DO AT "THAT TIME OF YEAR"??

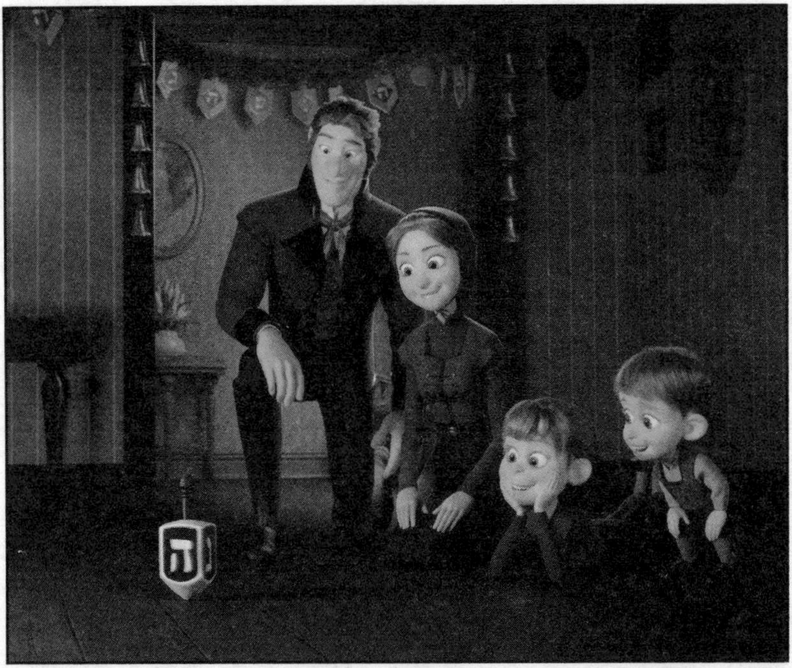

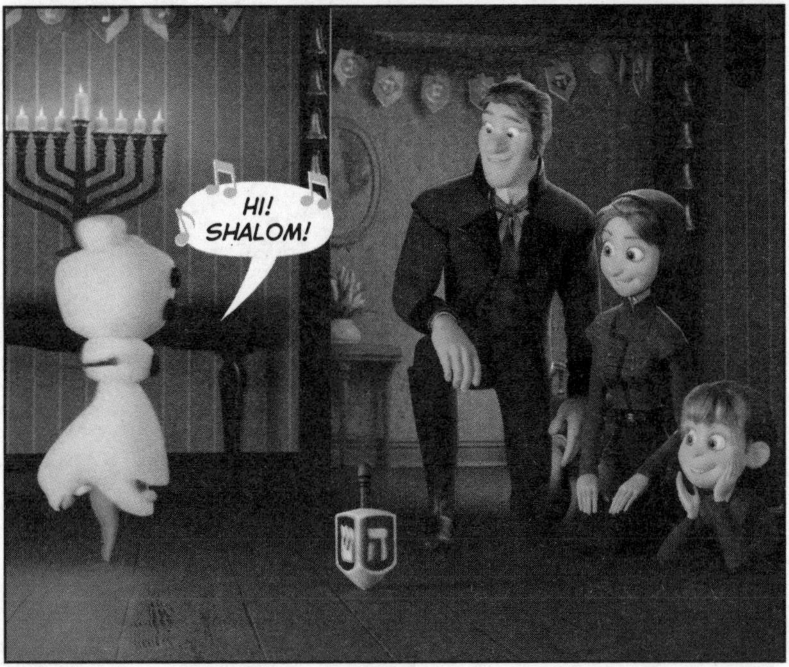
HI! SHALOM!

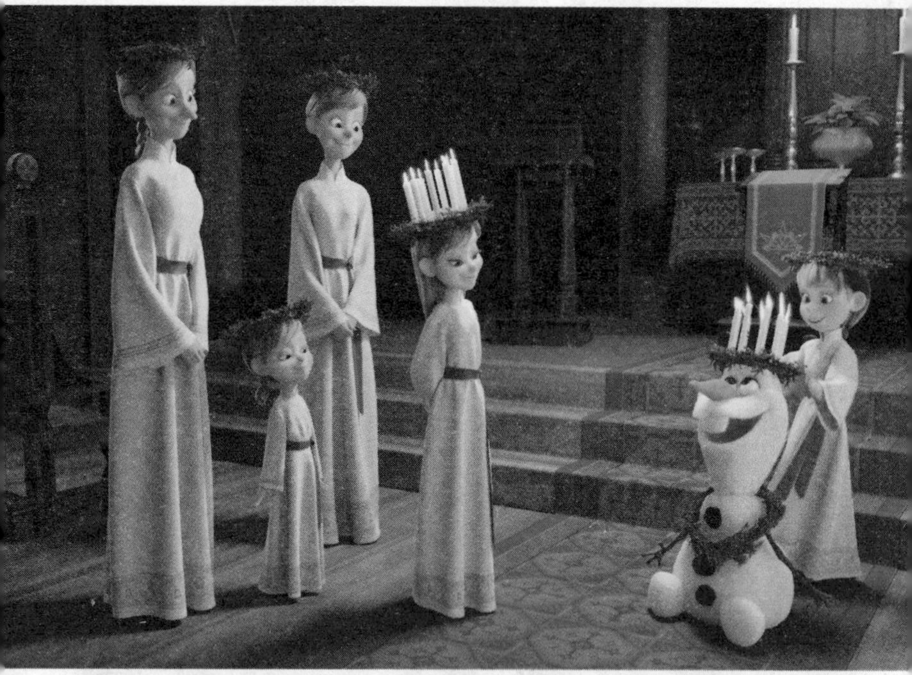

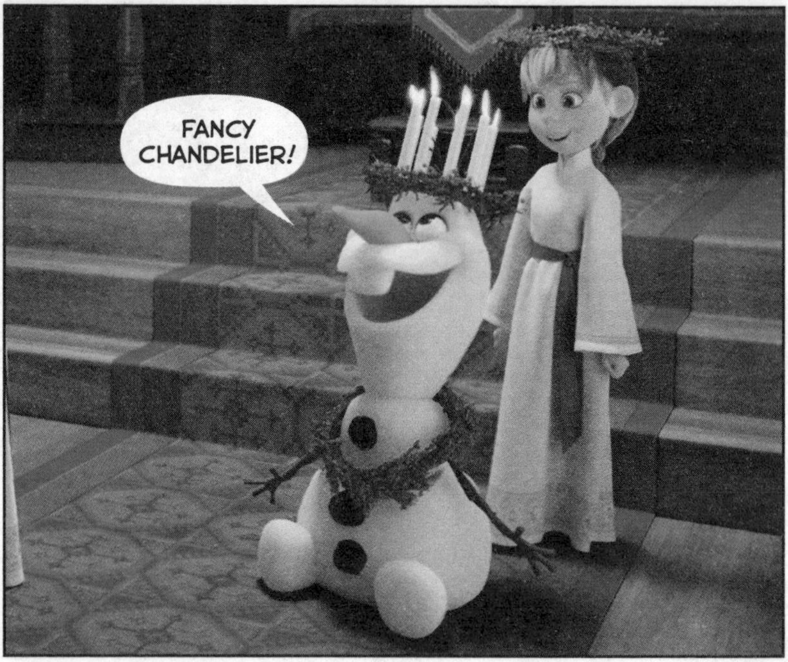
FANCY CHANDELIER!

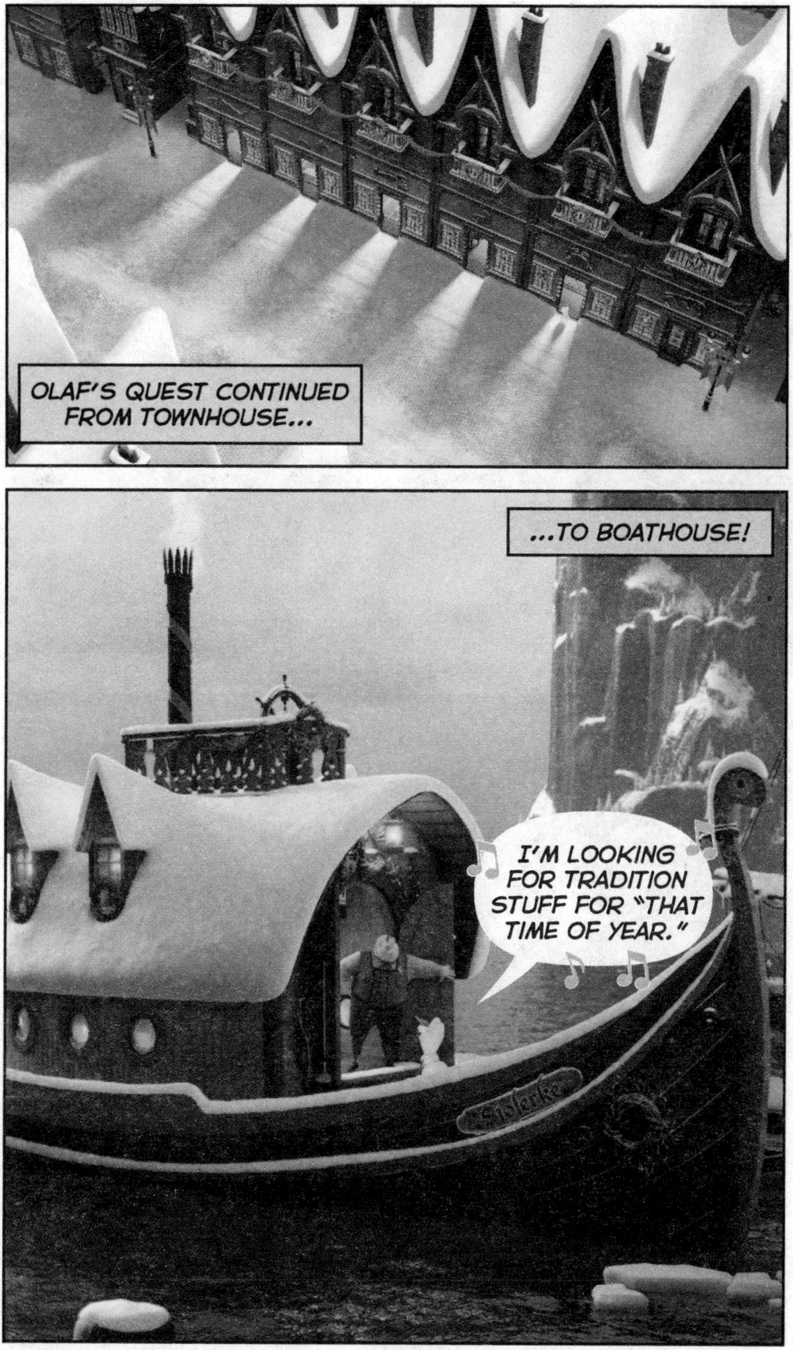
OLAF'S QUEST CONTINUED FROM TOWNHOUSE...
...TO BOATHOUSE!
I'M LOOKING FOR TRADITION STUFF FOR "THAT TIME OF YEAR."

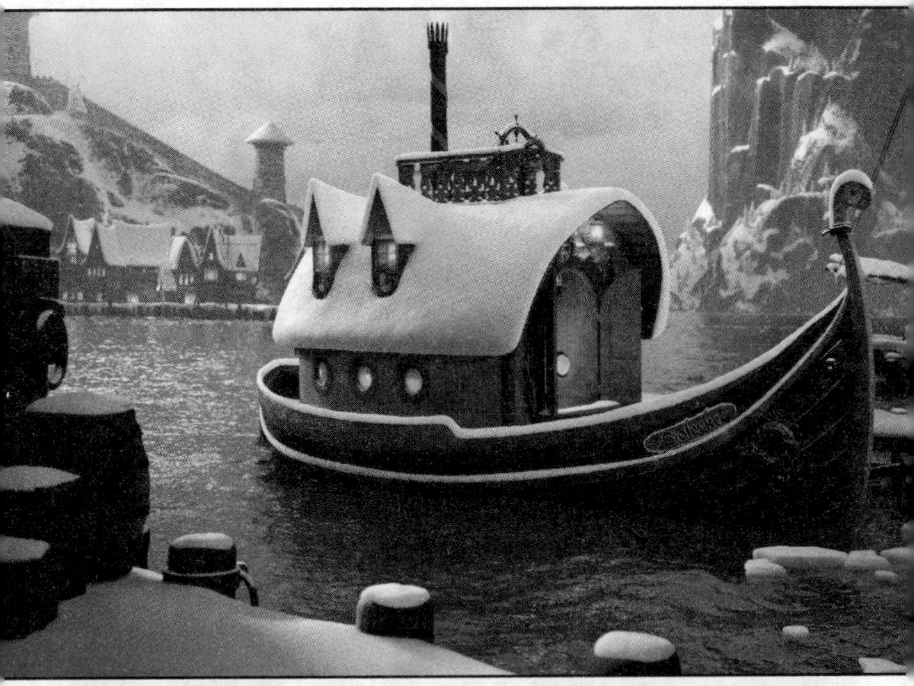

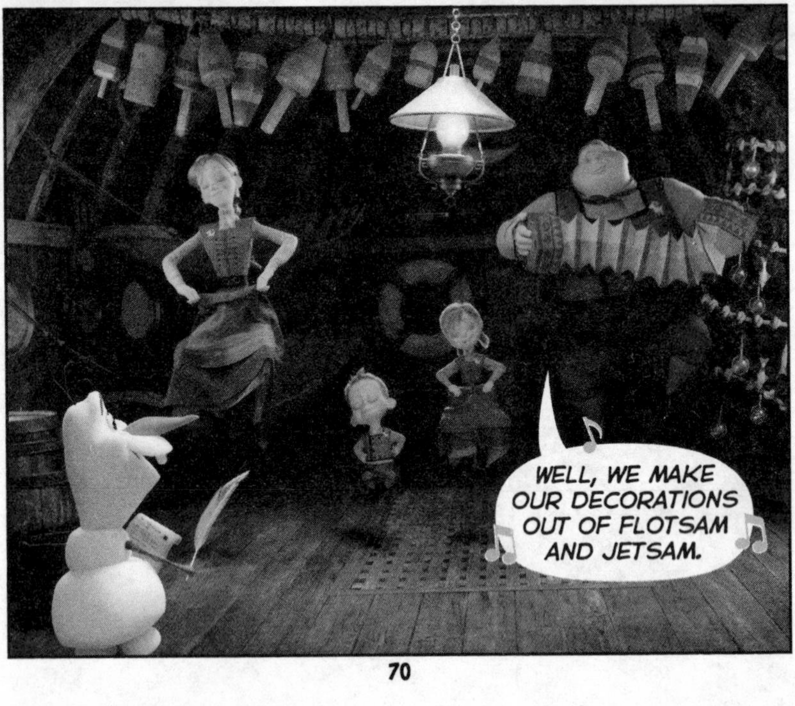
WELL, WE MAKE OUR DECORATIONS OUT OF FLOTSAM AND JETSAM.

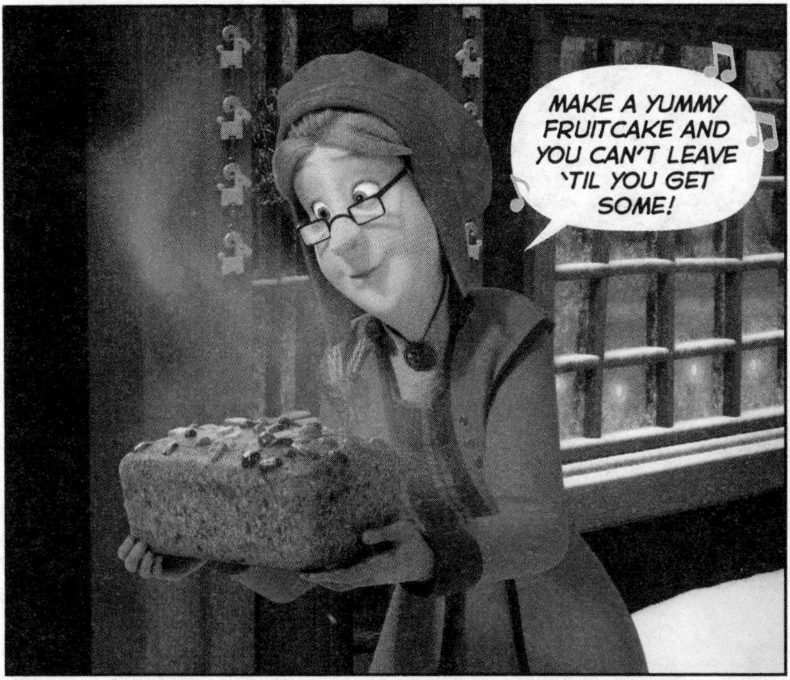
MAKE A YUMMY FRUITCAKE AND YOU CAN'T LEAVE 'TIL YOU GET SOME!

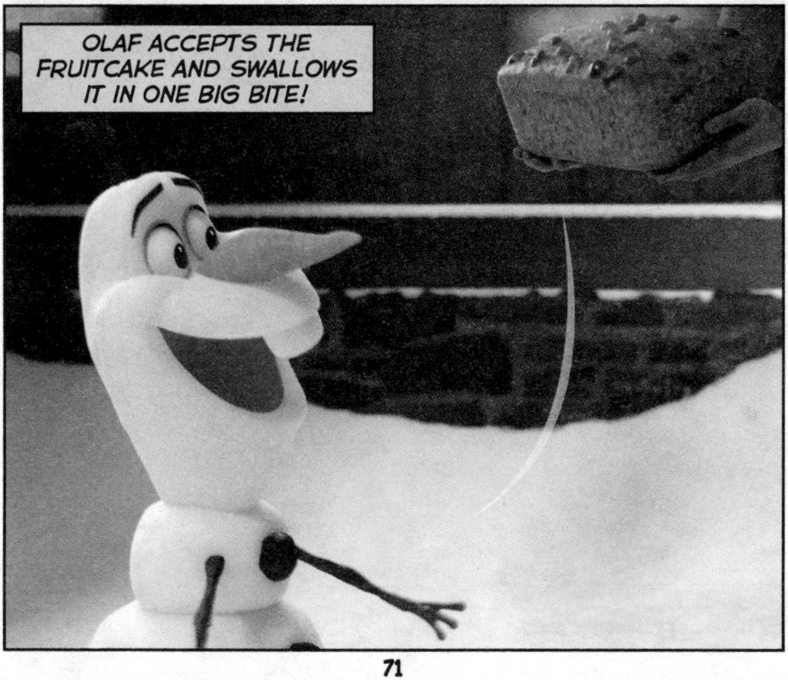
OLAF ACCEPTS THE FRUITCAKE AND SWALLOWS IT IN ONE BIG BITE!

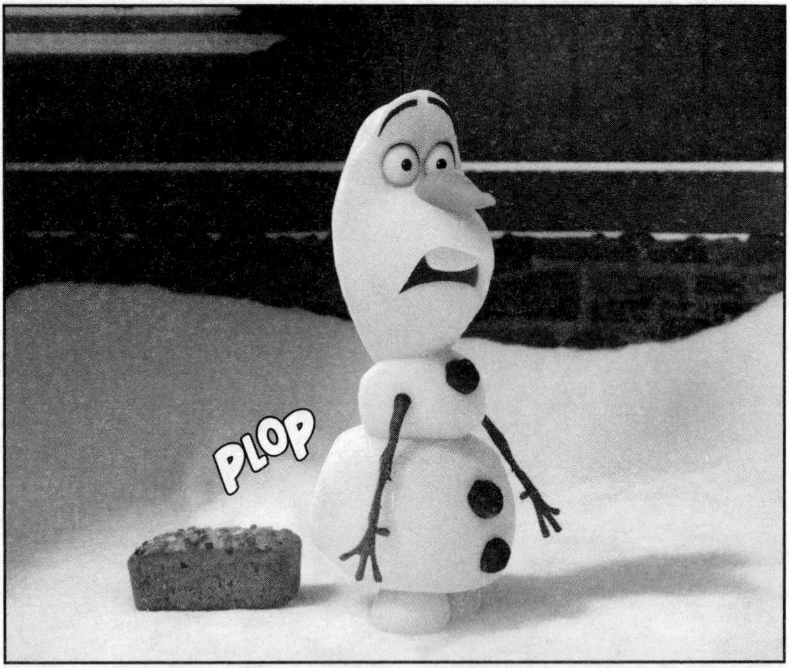
PLOP

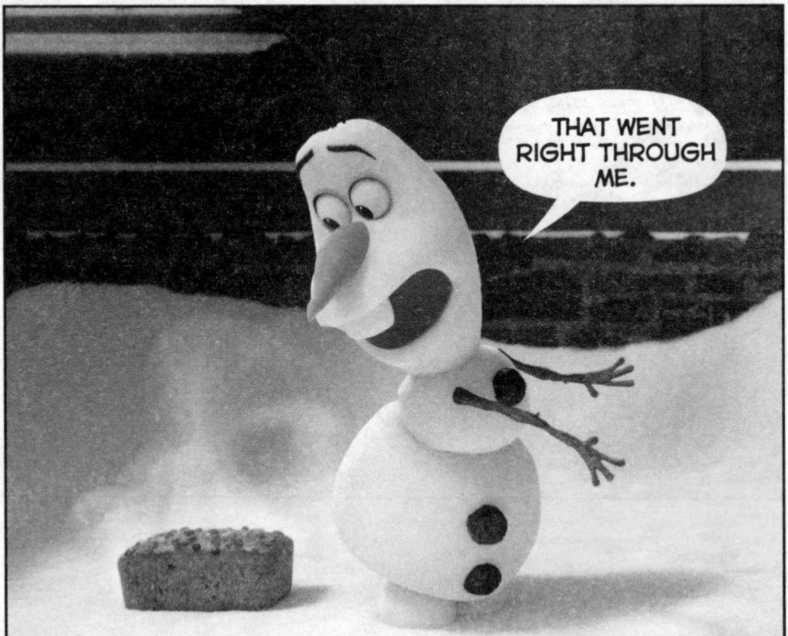
THAT WENT RIGHT THROUGH ME.

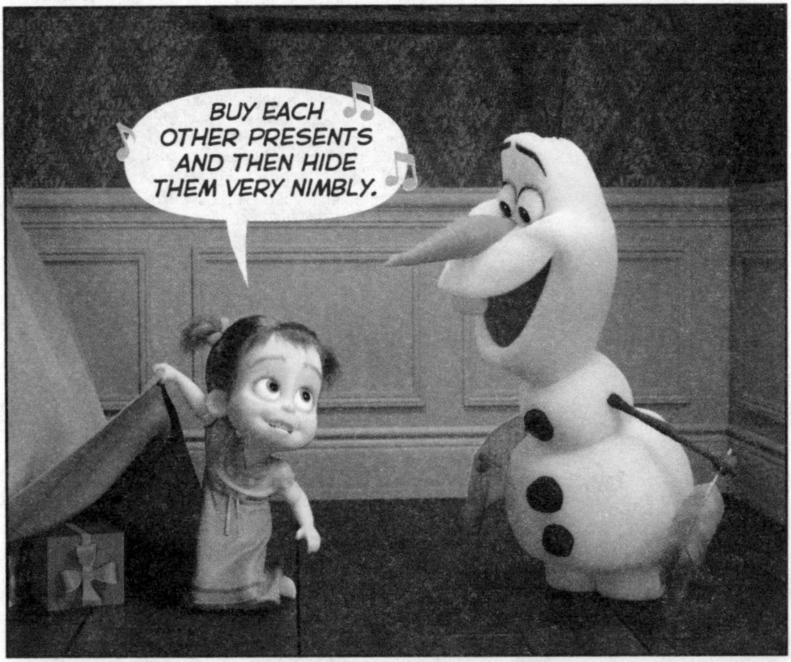
BUY EACH OTHER PRESENTS AND THEN HIDE THEM VERY NIMBLY.

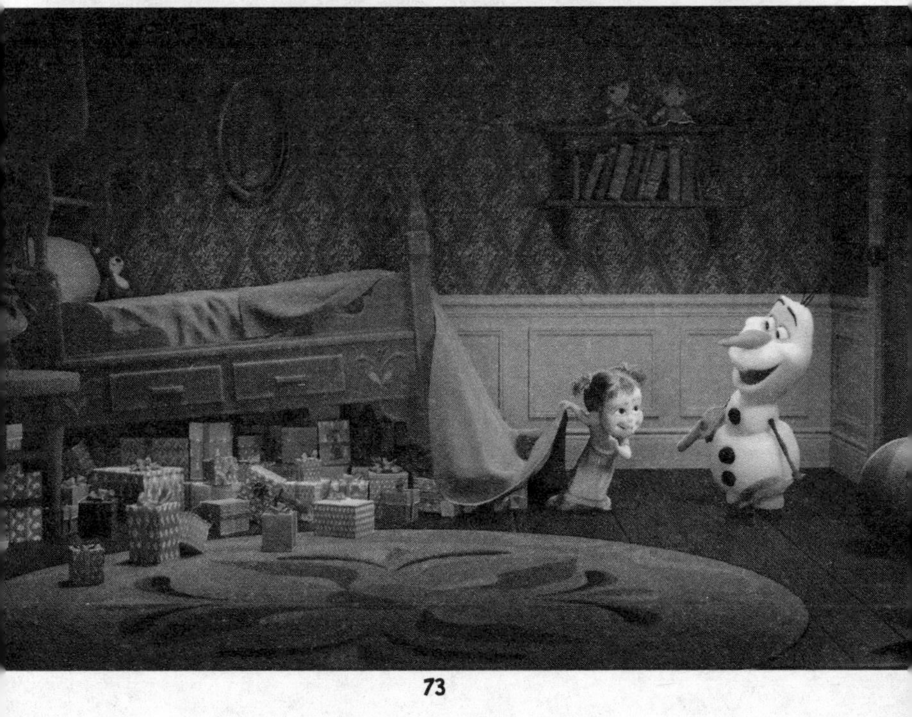

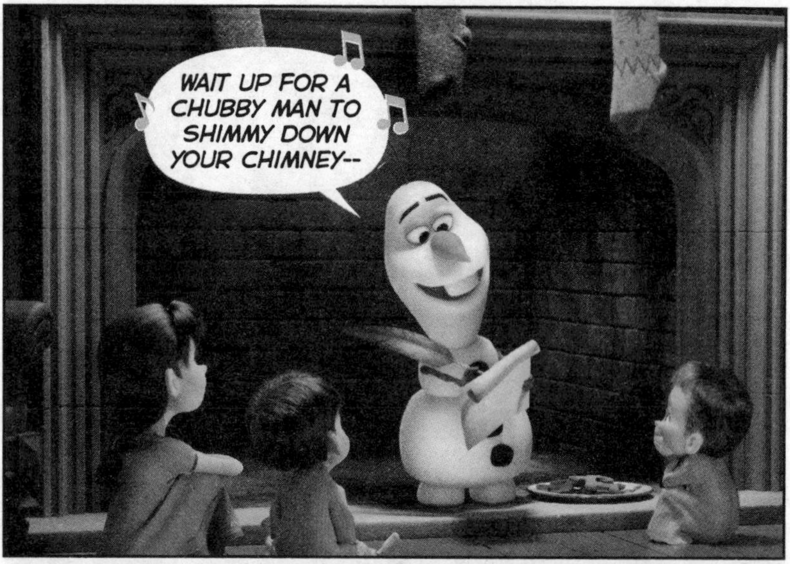
WAIT UP FOR A CHUBBY MAN TO SHIMMY DOWN YOUR CHIMNEY--

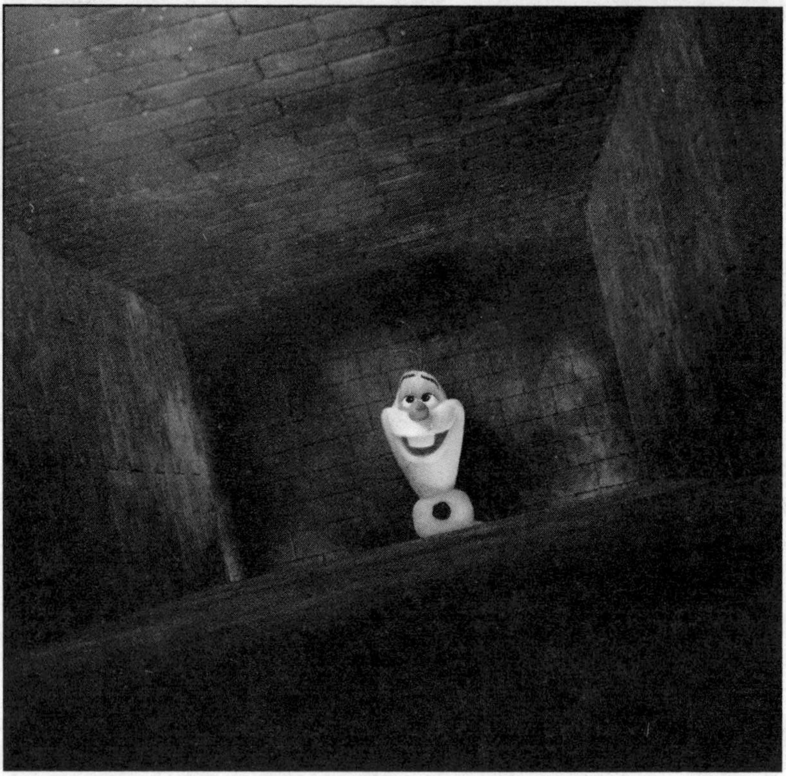

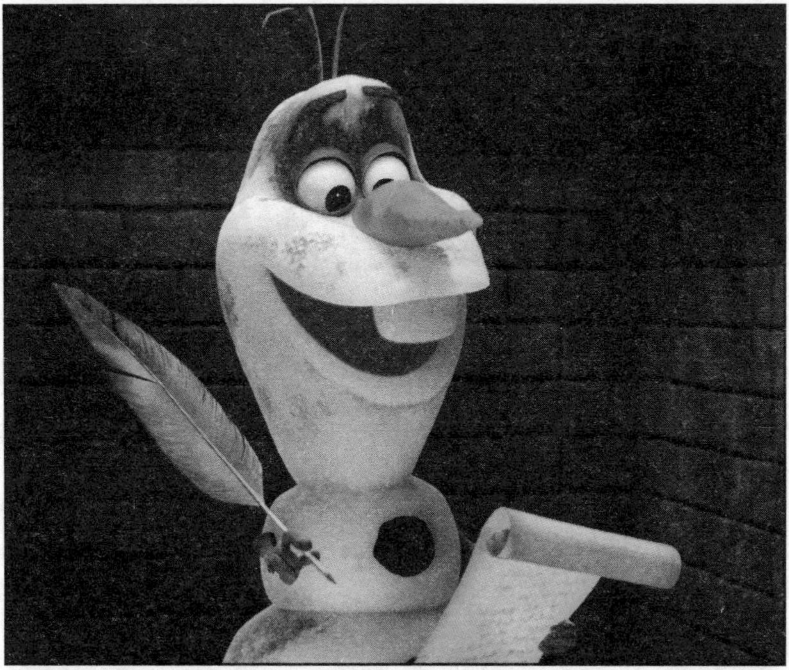

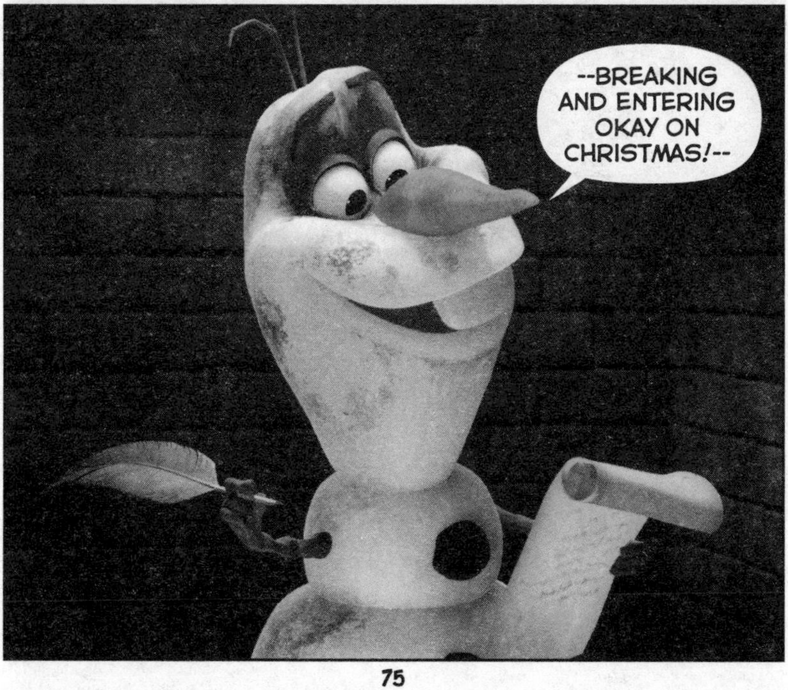
--BREAKING AND ENTERING OKAY ON CHRISTMAS!--

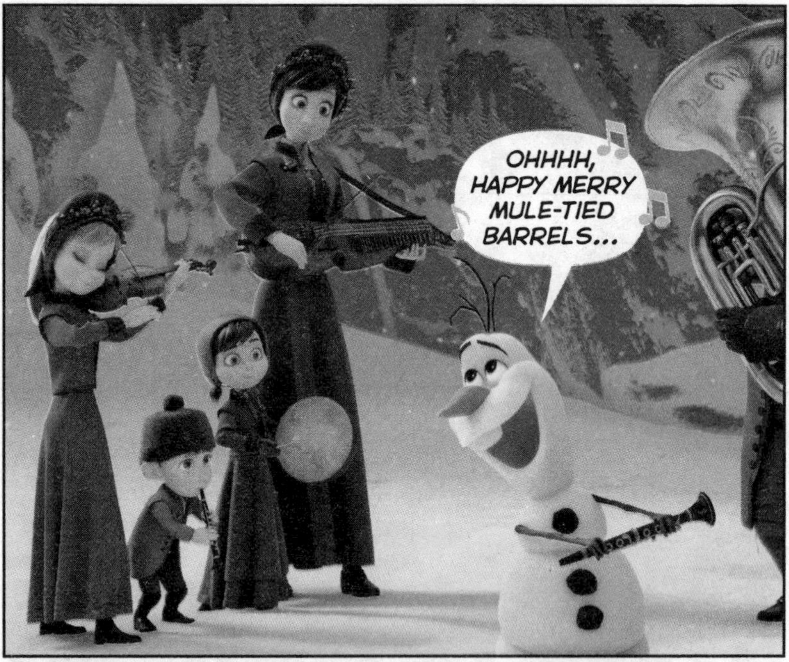
OHHHH, HAPPY MERRY MULE-TIED BARRELS...

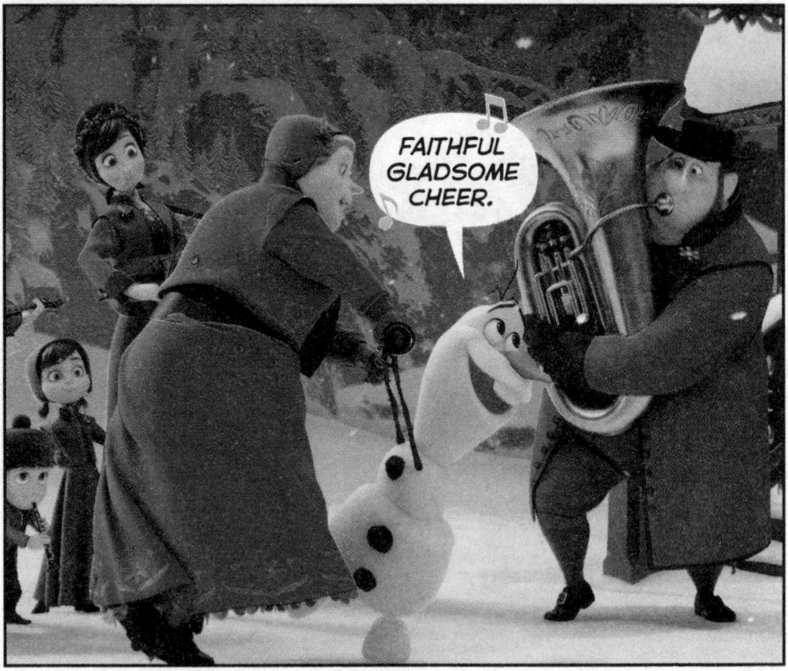
FAITHFUL GLADSOME CHEER.

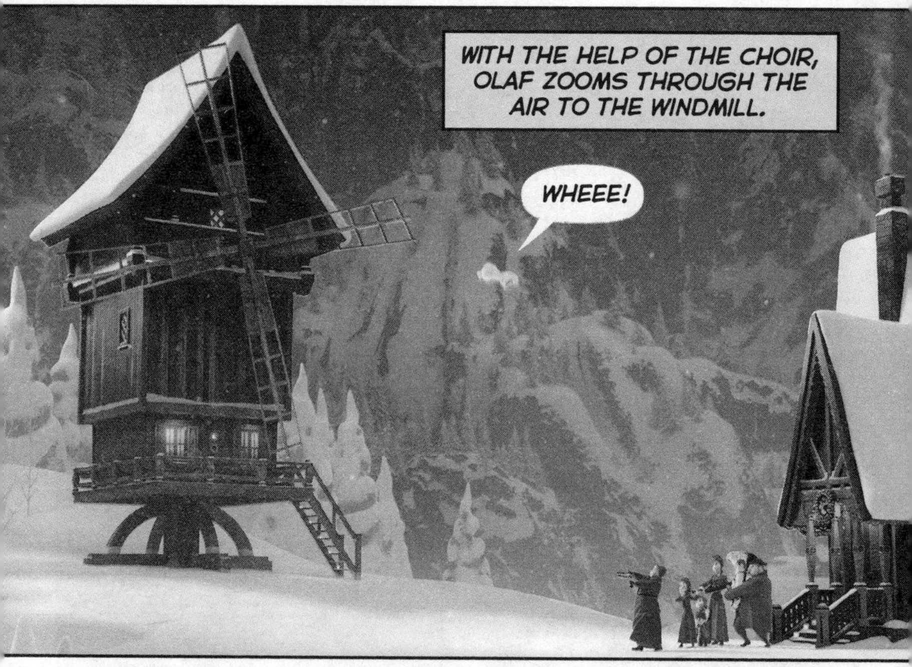
WITH THE HELP OF THE CHOIR, OLAF ZOOMS THROUGH THE AIR TO THE WINDMILL.
WHEEE!

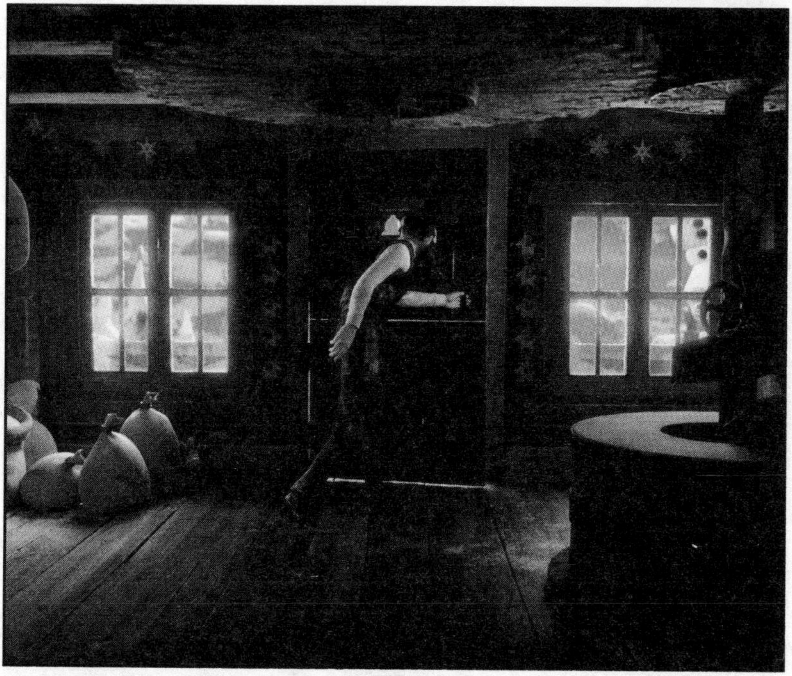

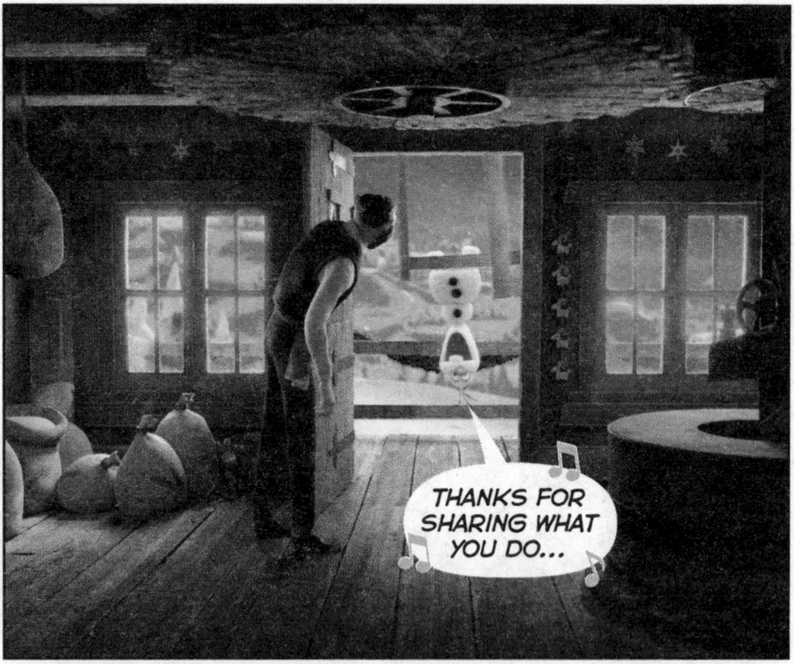
THANKS FOR SHARING WHAT YOU DO...

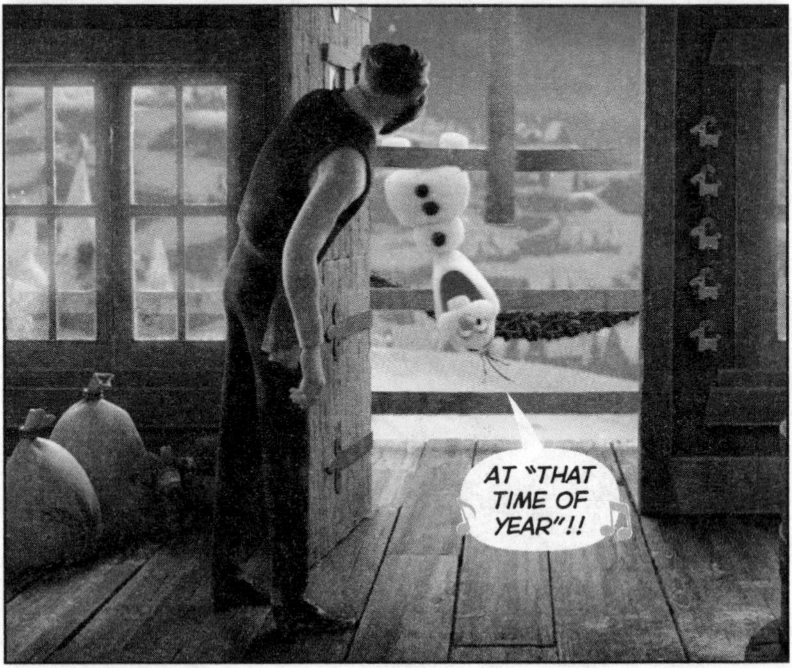
AT "THAT TIME OF YEAR"!!

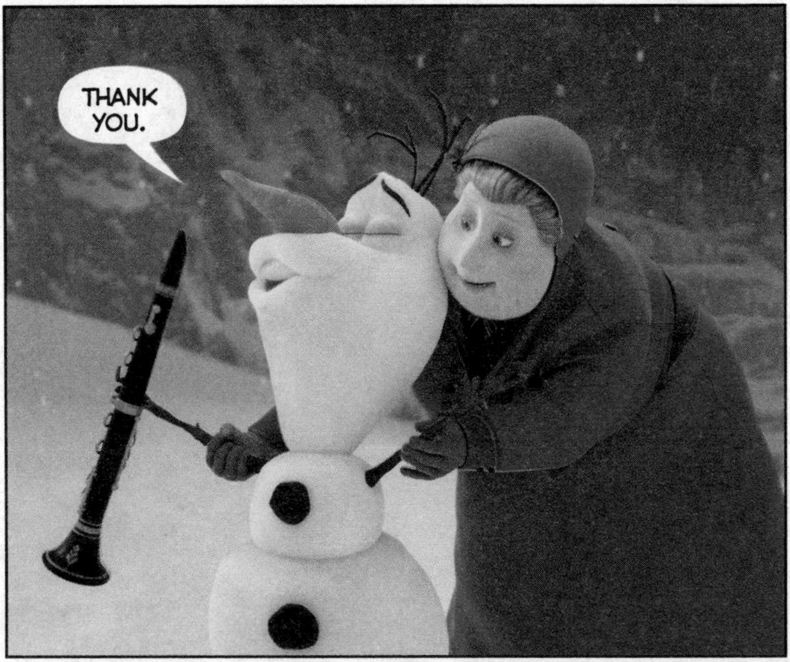
THANK YOU.

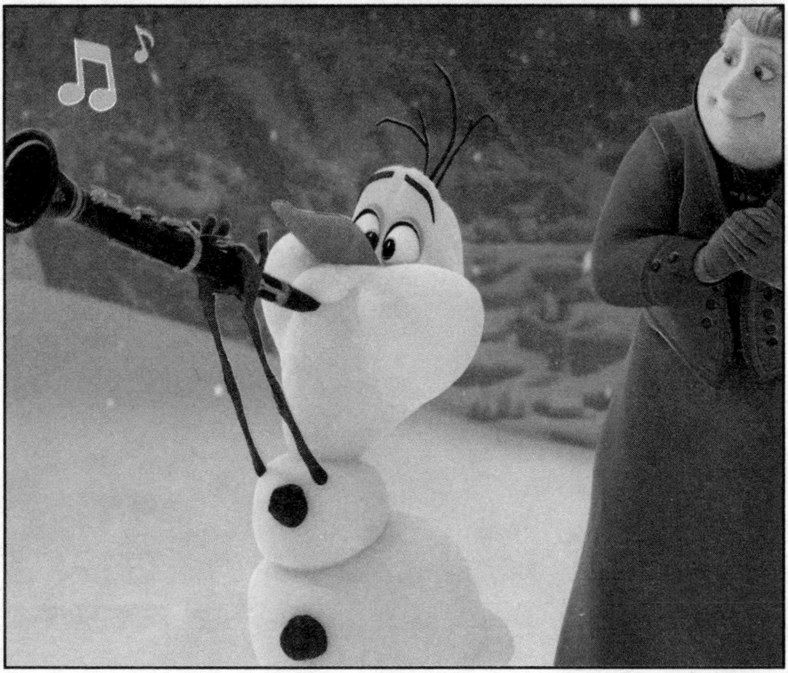

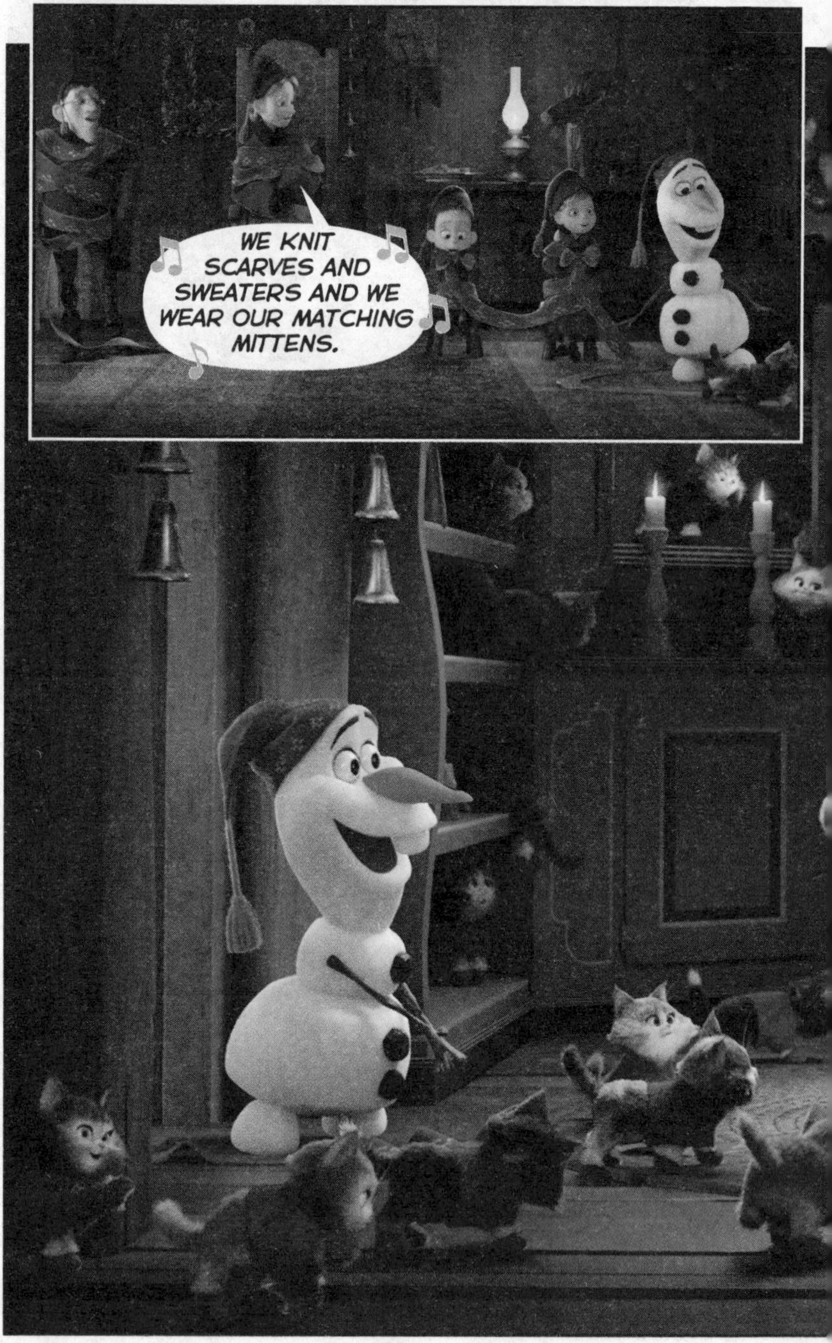
WE KNIT SCARVES AND SWEATERS AND WE WEAR OUR MATCHING MITTENS.

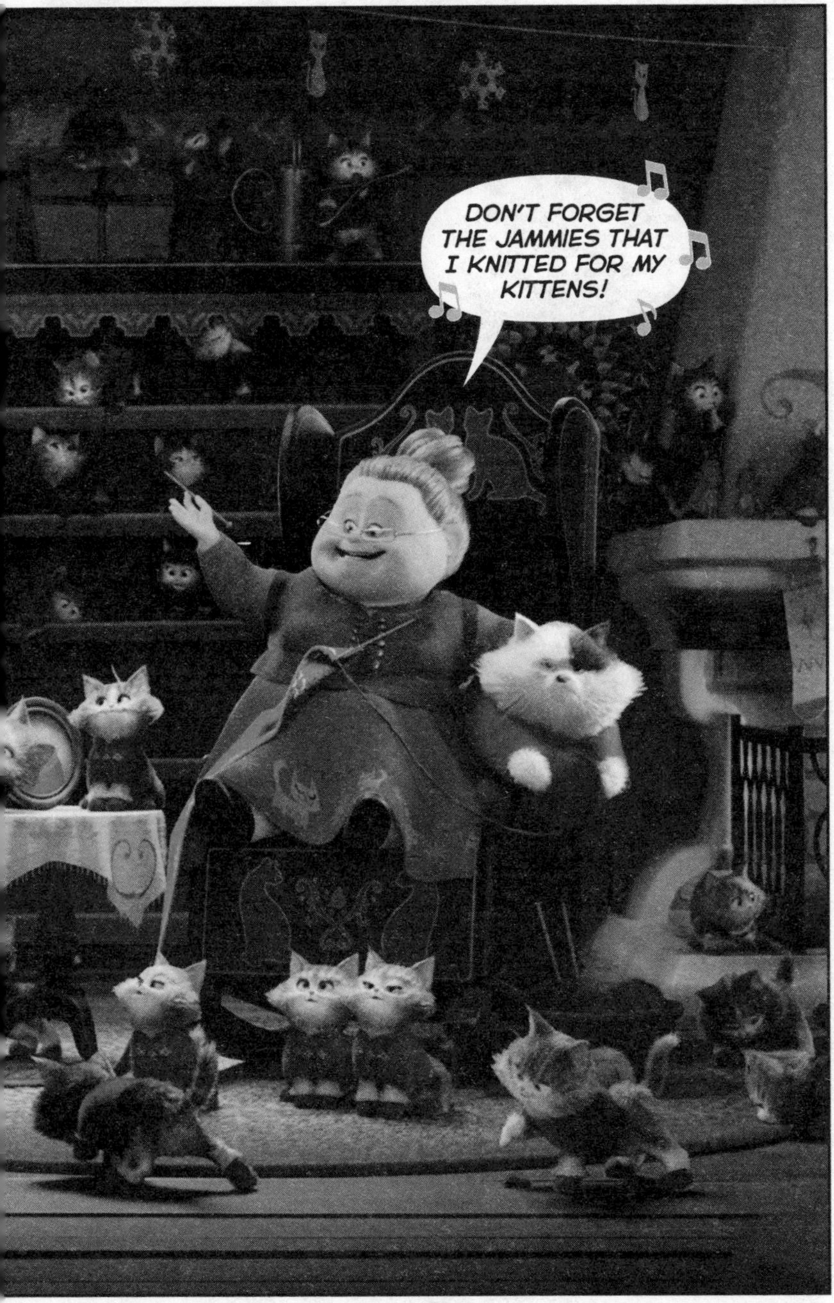
DON'T FORGET THE JAMMIES THAT I KNITTED FOR MY KITTENS!

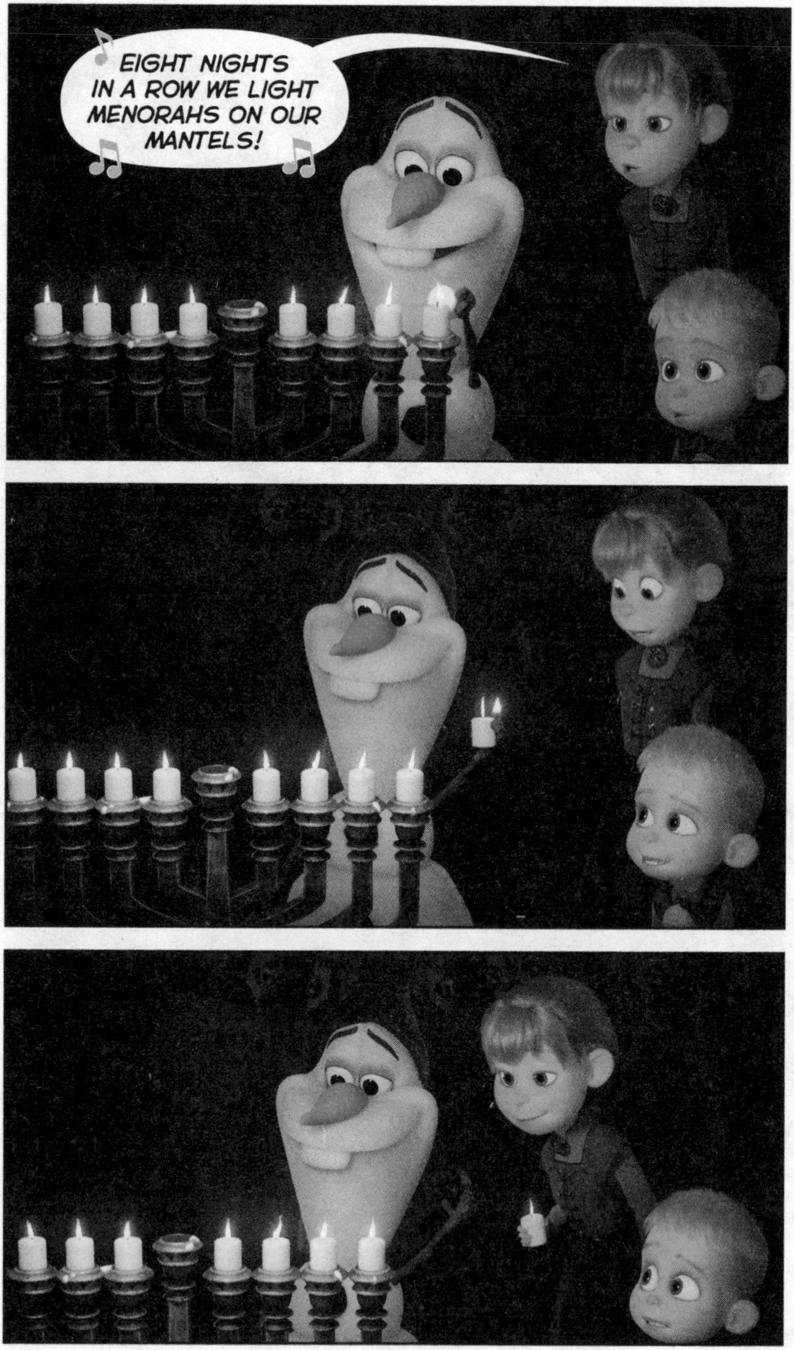
EIGHT NIGHTS IN A ROW WE LIGHT MENORAHS ON OUR MANTELS!

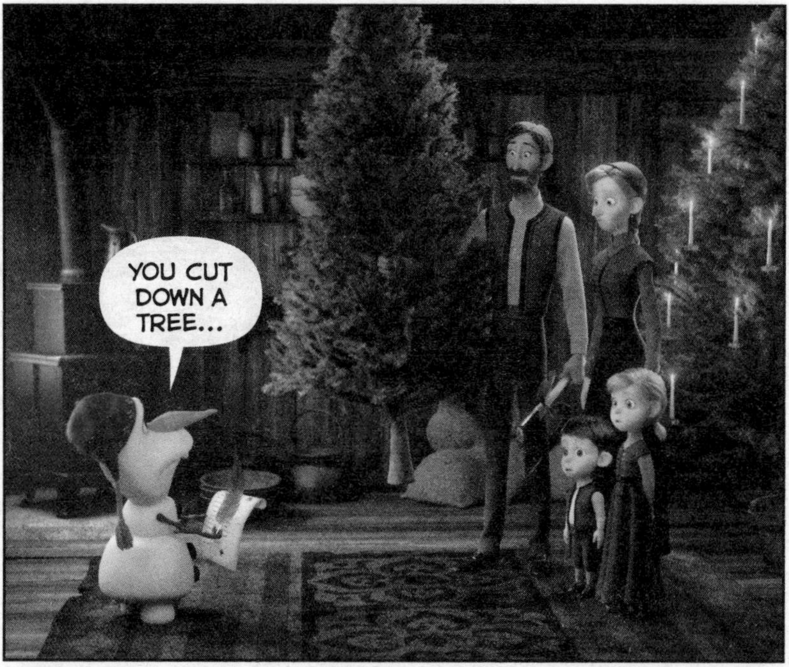
YOU CUT DOWN A TREE...

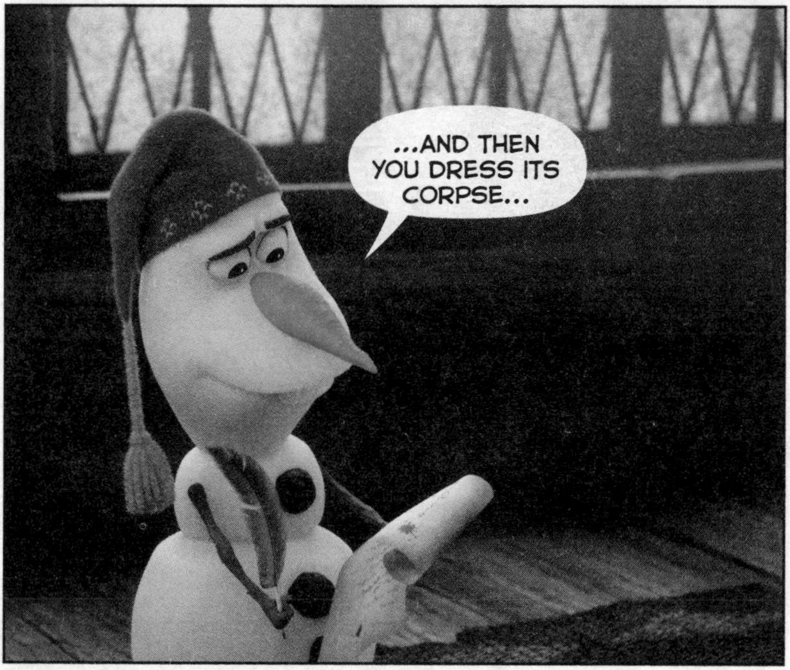
...AND THEN YOU DRESS ITS CORPSE...

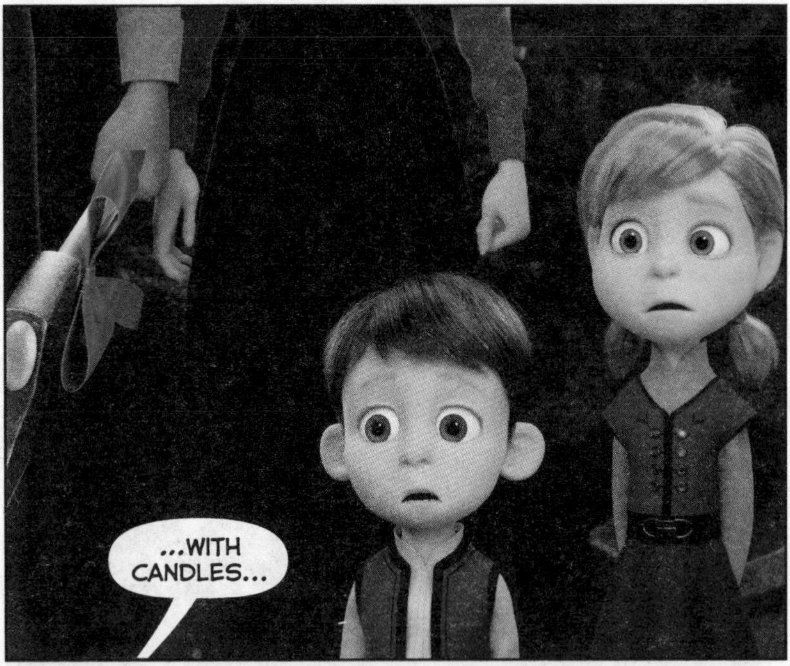
...WITH CANDLES...

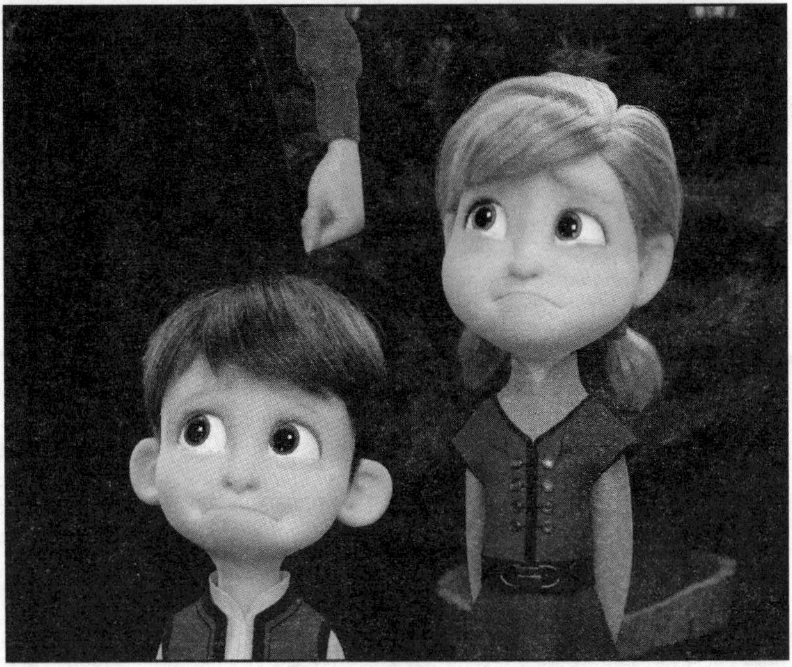

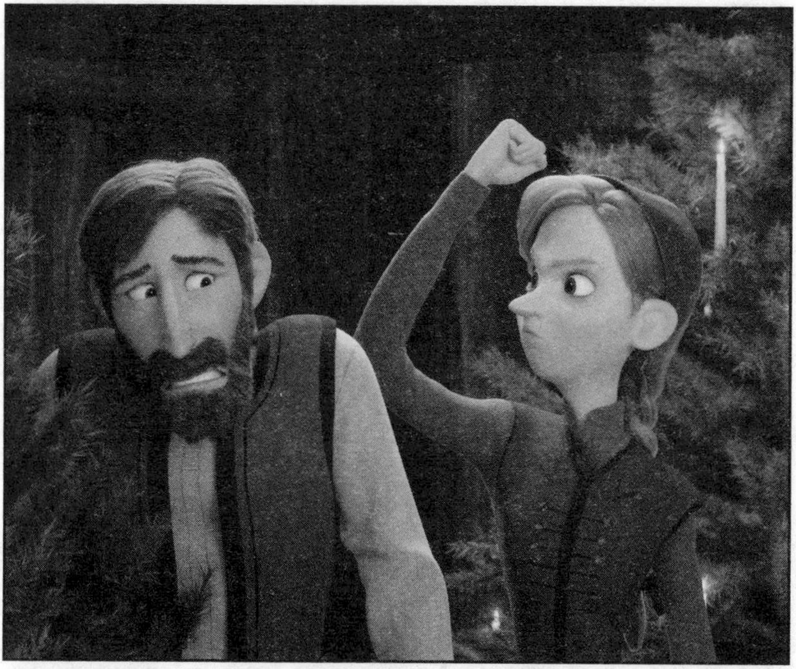

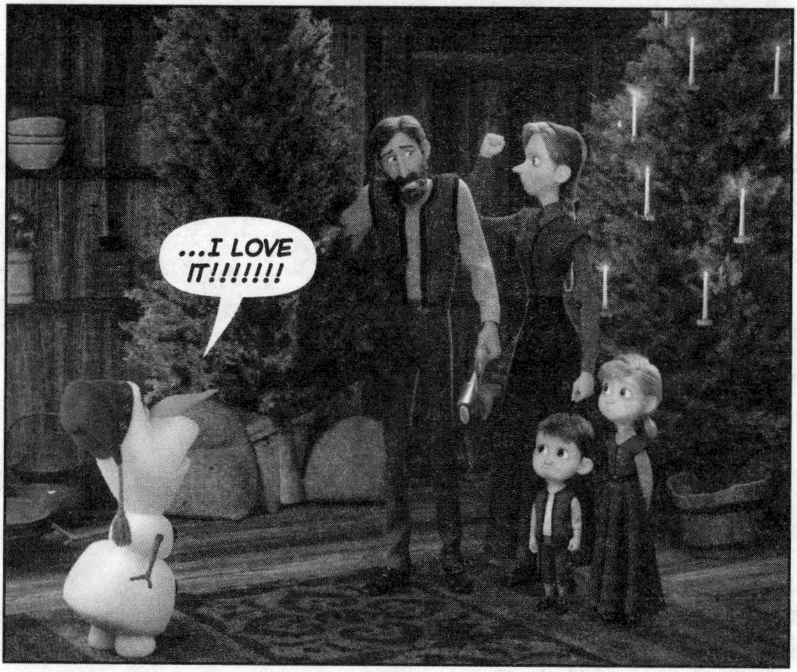
...I LOVE IT!!!!!!!!

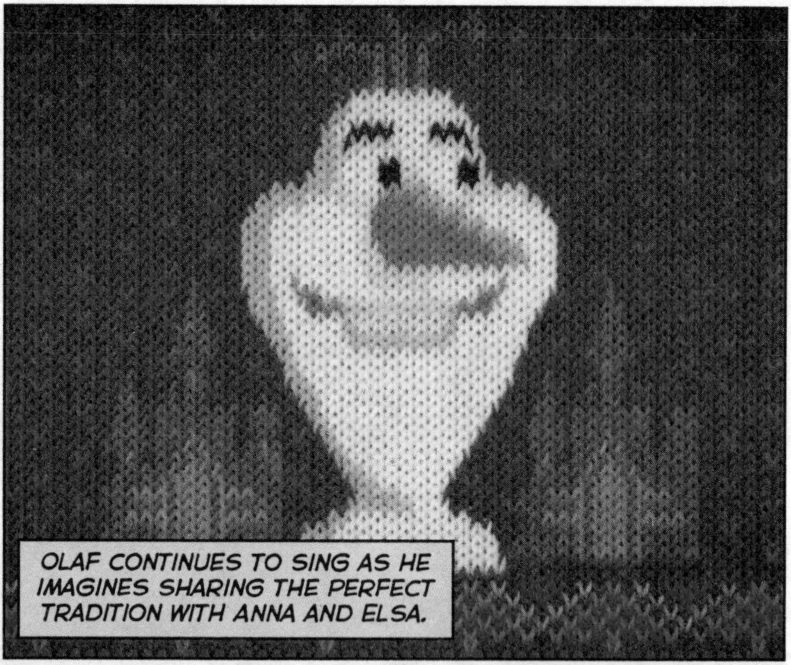
OLAF CONTINUES TO SING AS HE IMAGINES SHARING THE PERFECT TRADITION WITH ANNA AND ELSA.

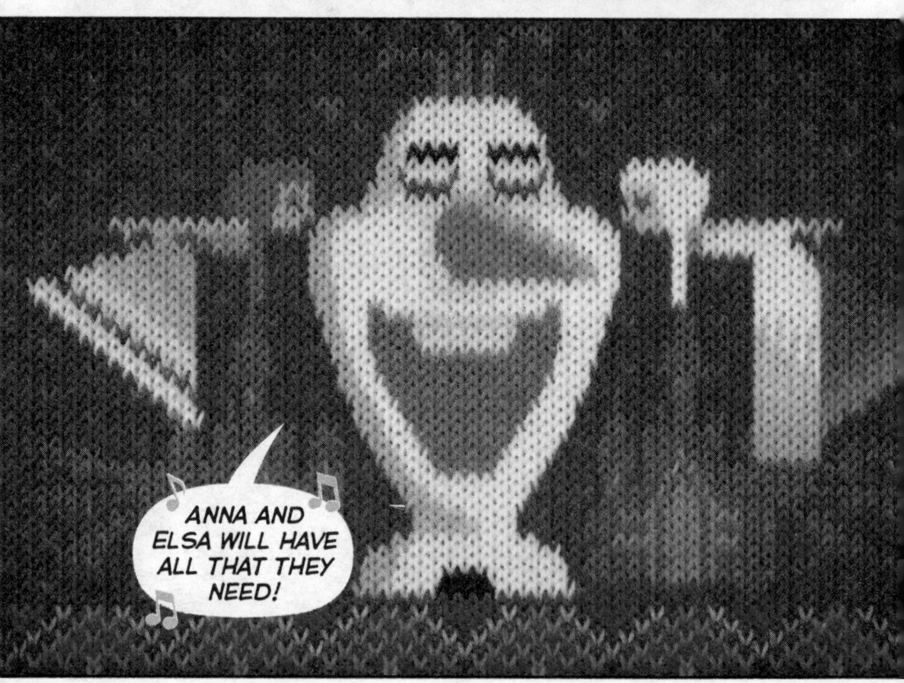
ANNA AND ELSA WILL HAVE ALL THAT THEY NEED!

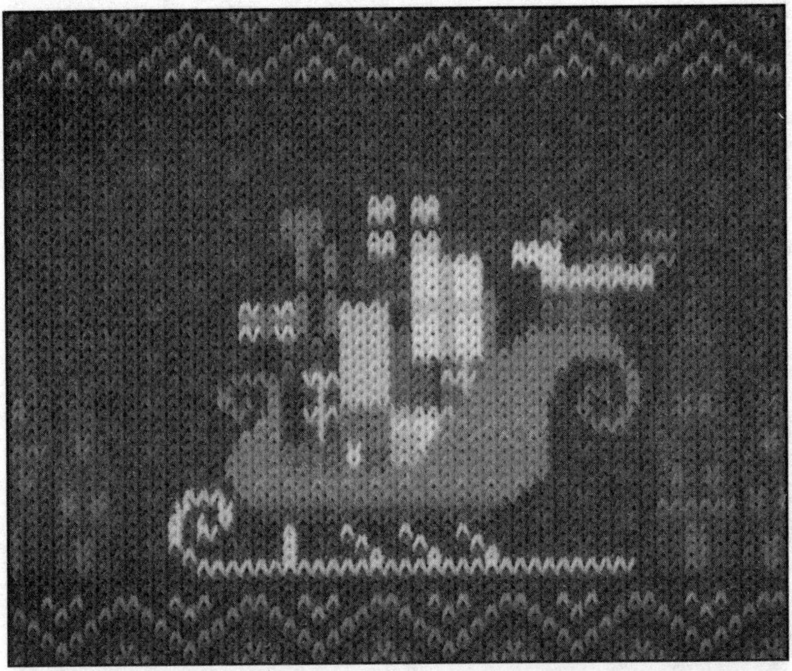

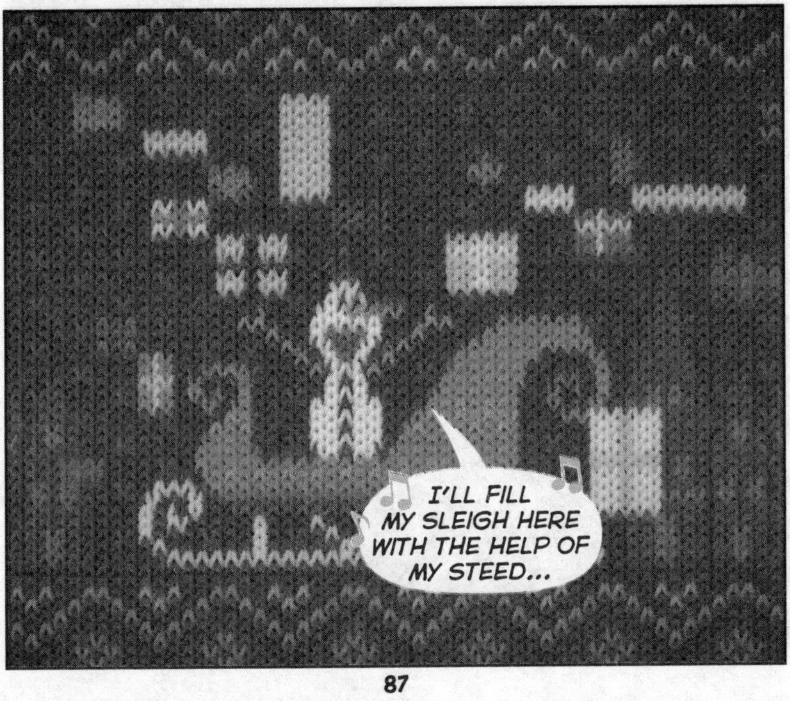
I'LL FILL MY SLEIGH HERE WITH THE HELP OF MY STEED...

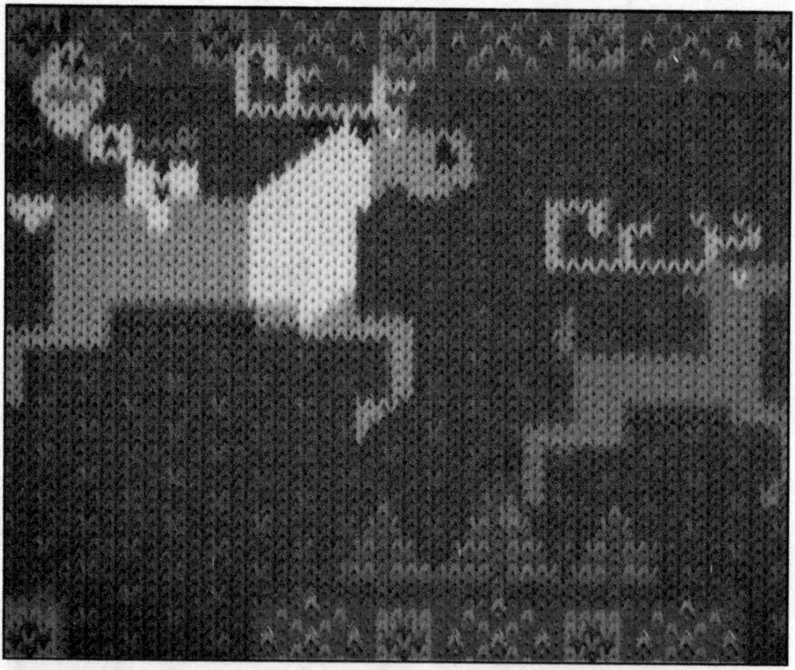

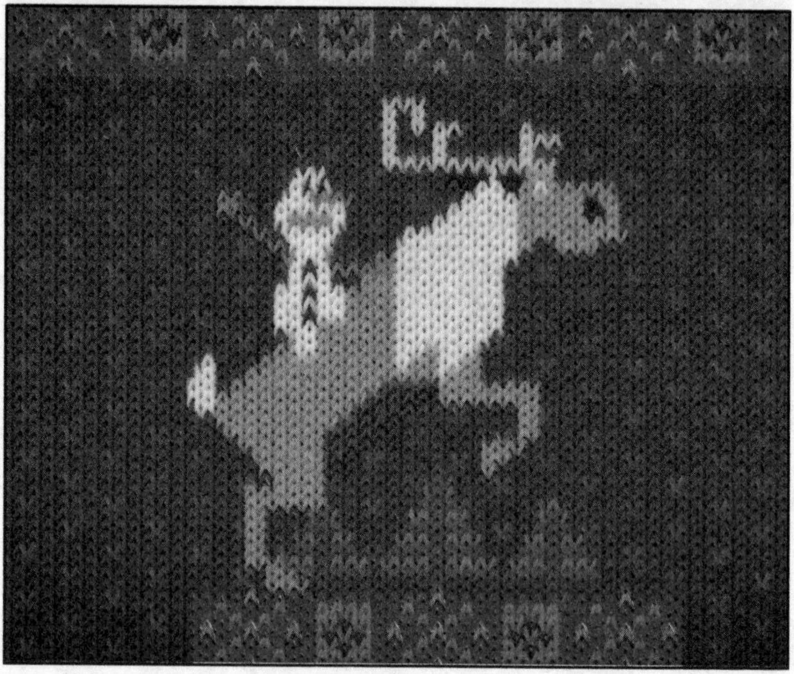

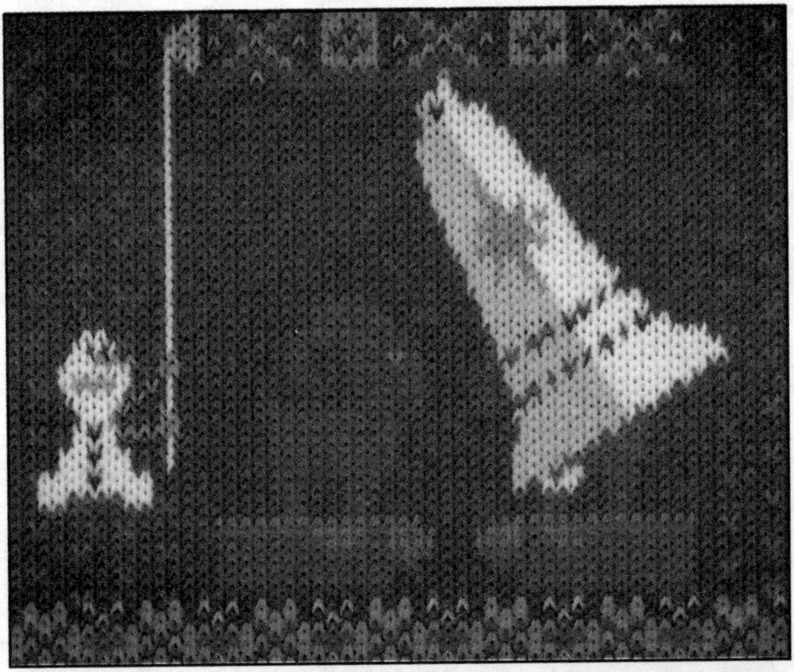

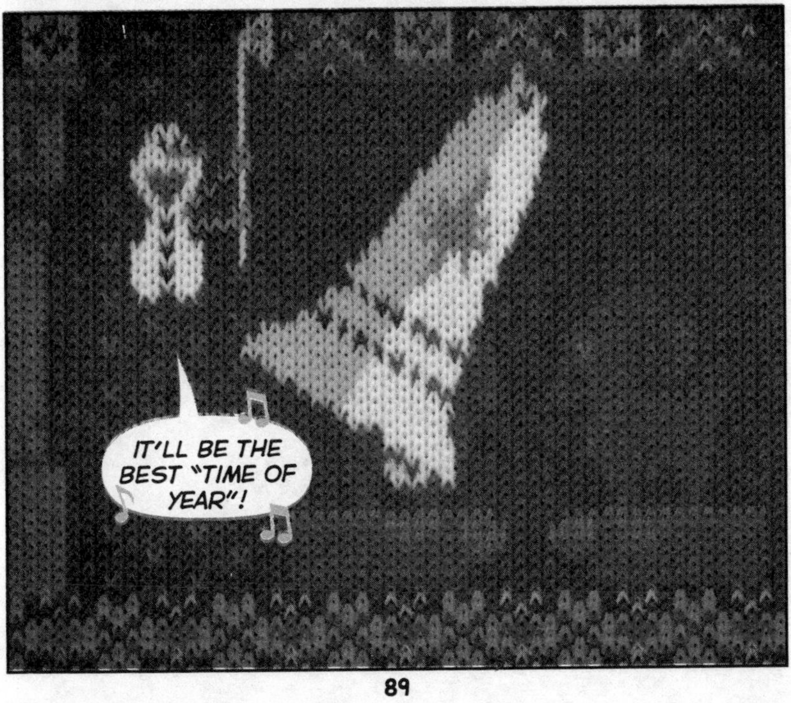
IT'LL BE THE BEST "TIME OF YEAR"!

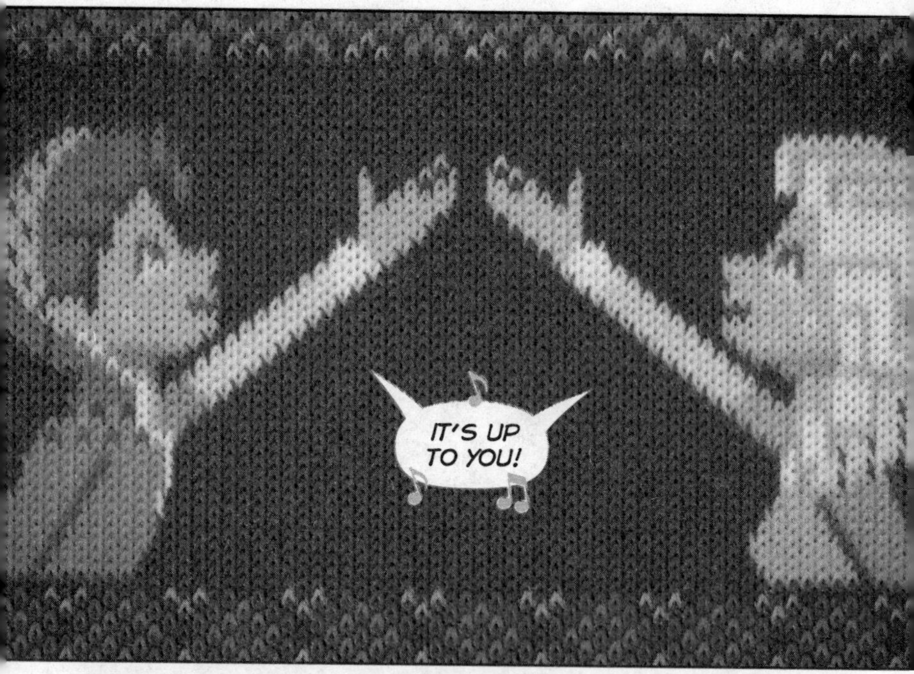
IT'S UP TO YOU!

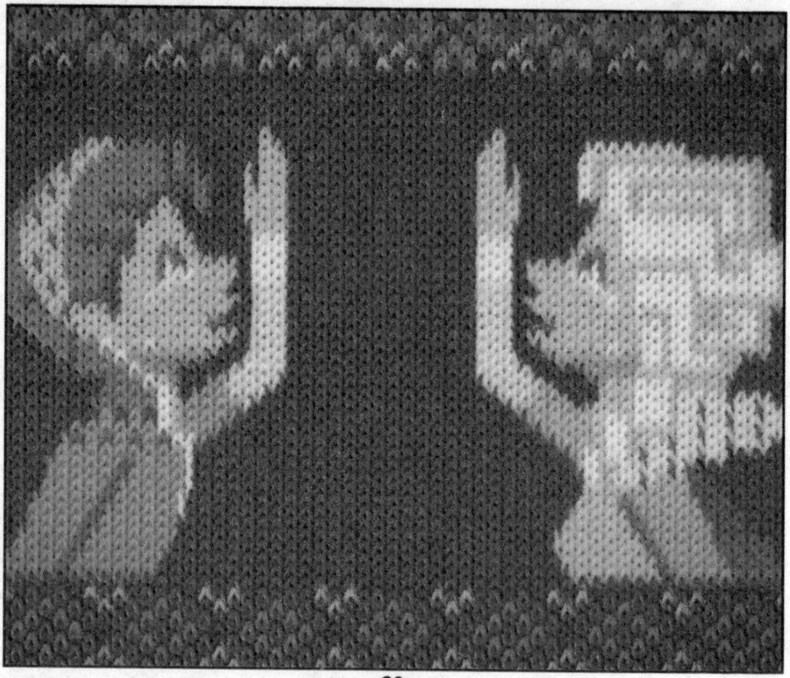

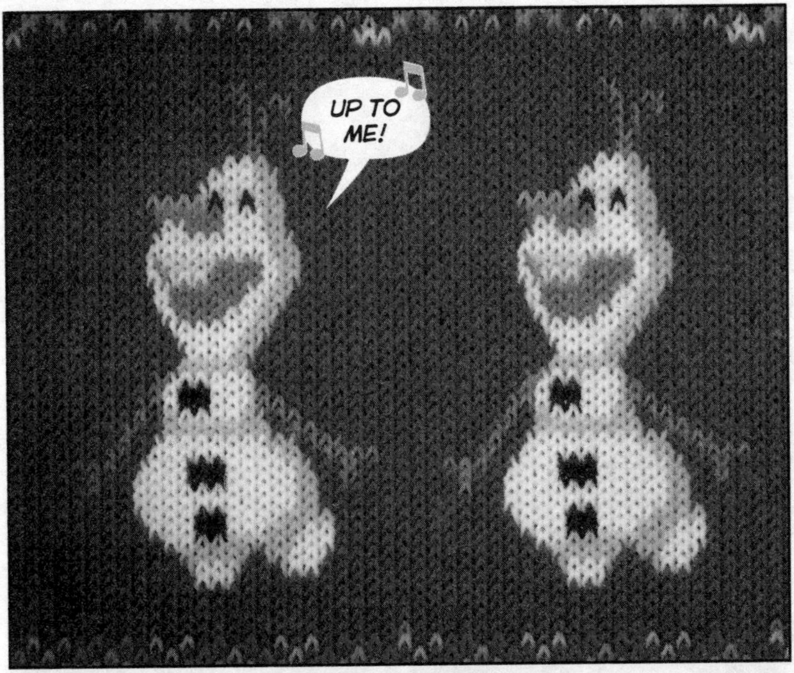
UP TO
ME!

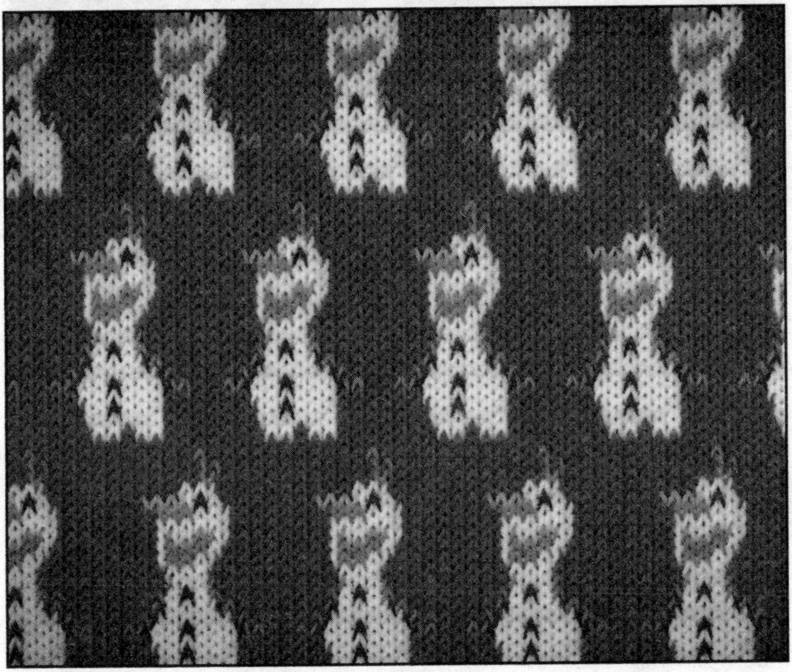

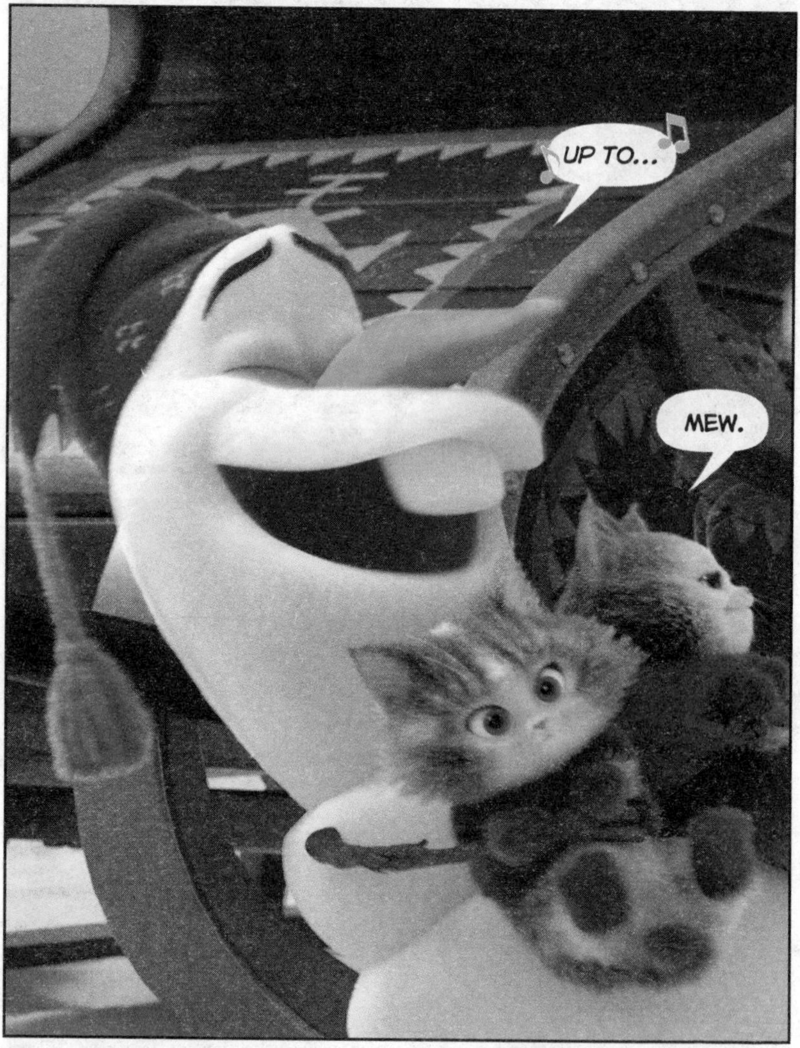
UP TO...
MEW.

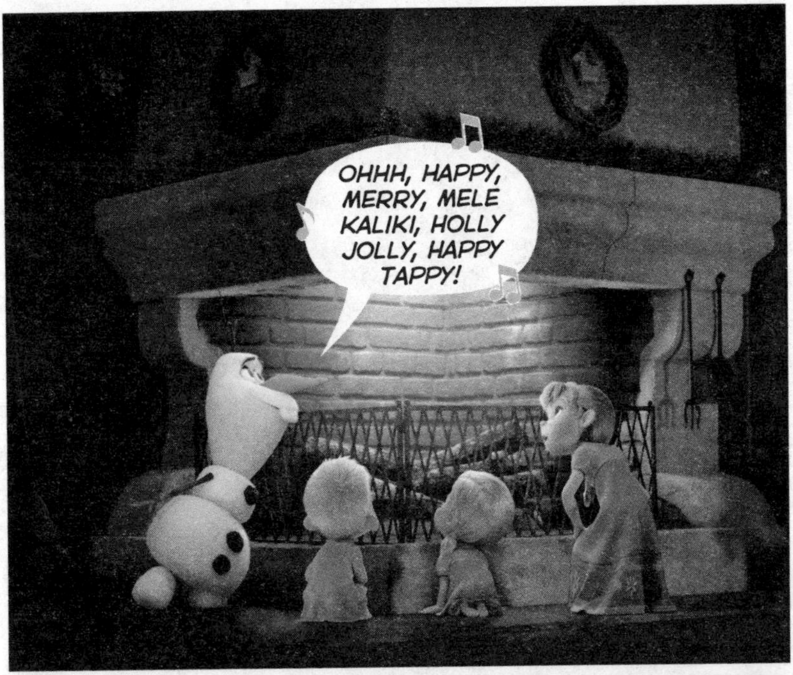
OHHH, HAPPY, MERRY, MELE KALIKI, HOLLY JOLLY, HAPPY TAPPY!

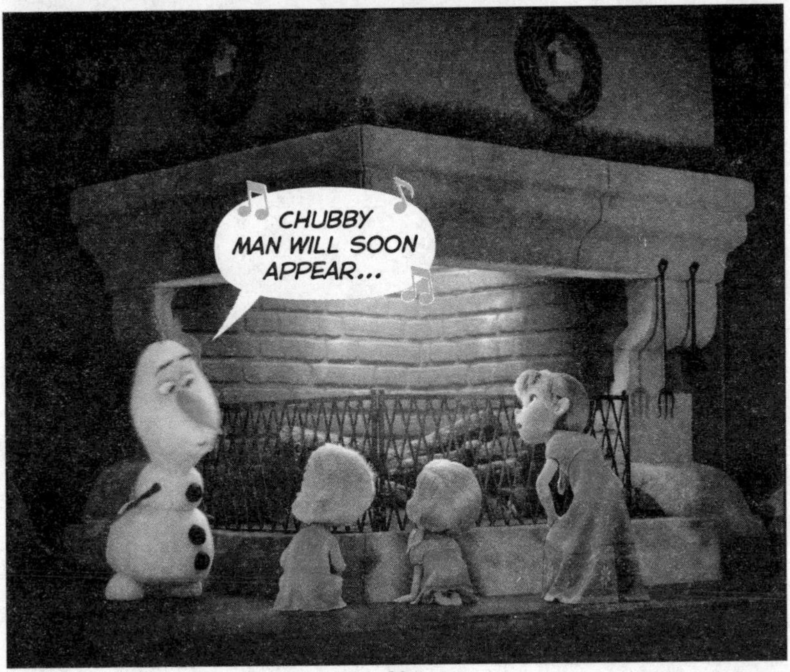
CHUBBY MAN WILL SOON APPEAR...

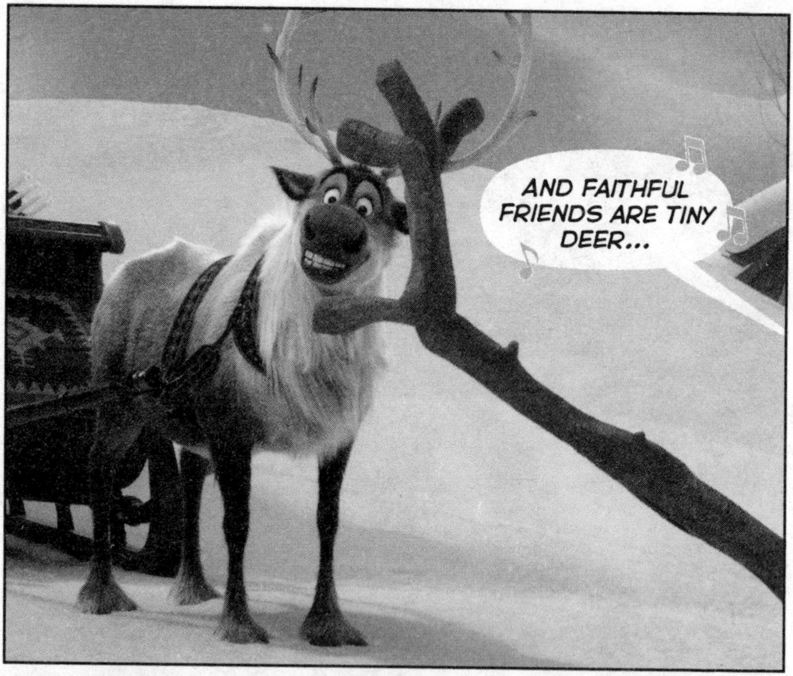
AND FAITHFUL FRIENDS ARE TINY DEER...

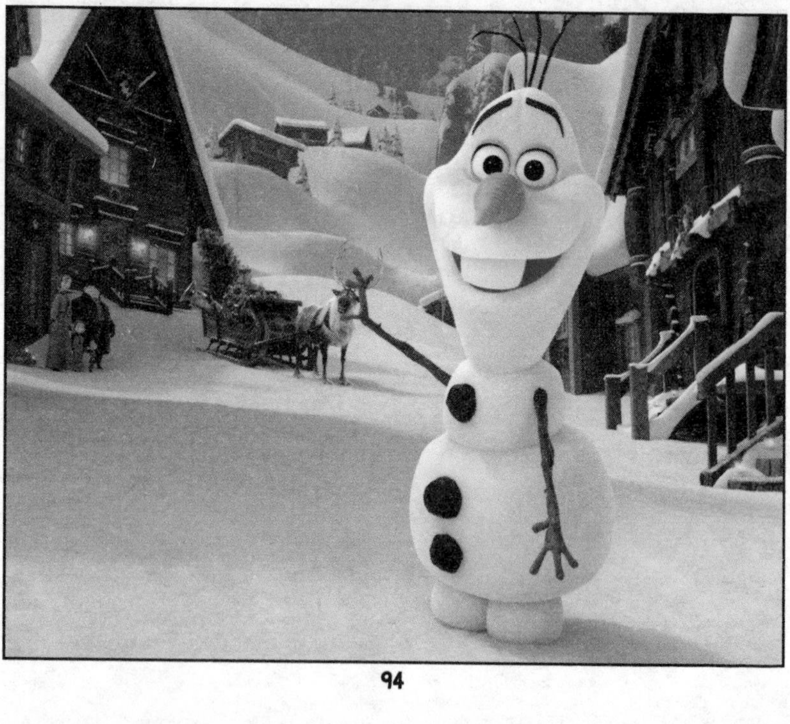

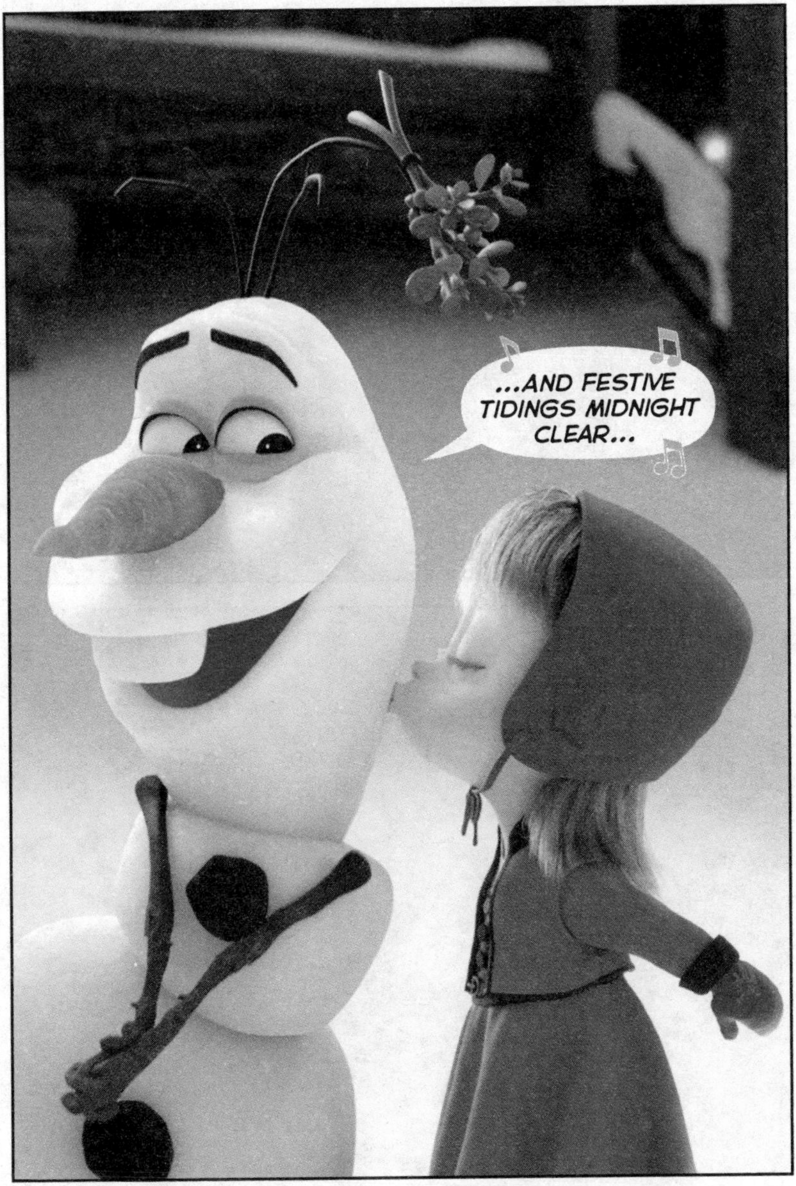
...AND FESTIVE TIDINGS MIDNIGHT CLEAR...

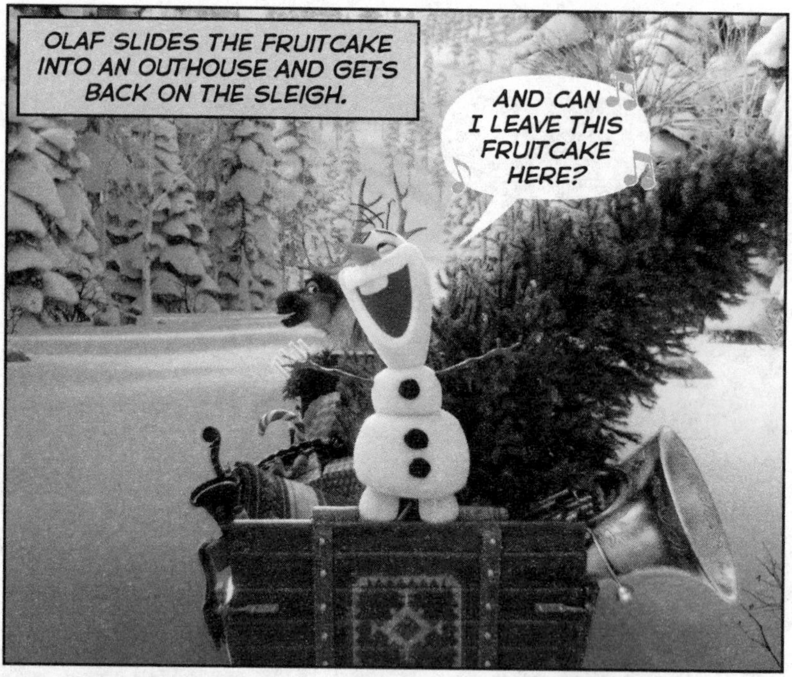
OLAF SLIDES THE FRUITCAKE INTO AN OUTHOUSE AND GETS BACK ON THE SLEIGH.
AND CAN I LEAVE THIS FRUITCAKE HERE?

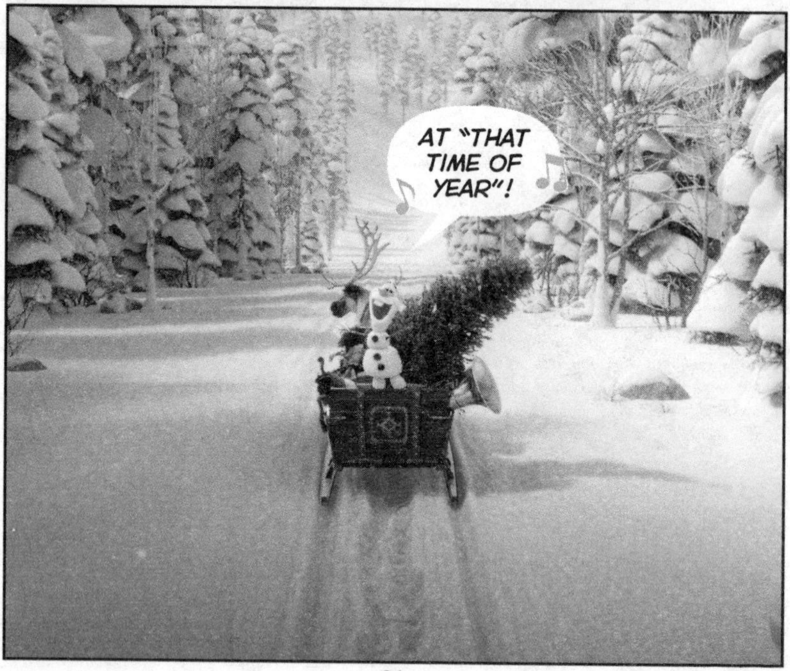
AT "THAT TIME OF YEAR"!

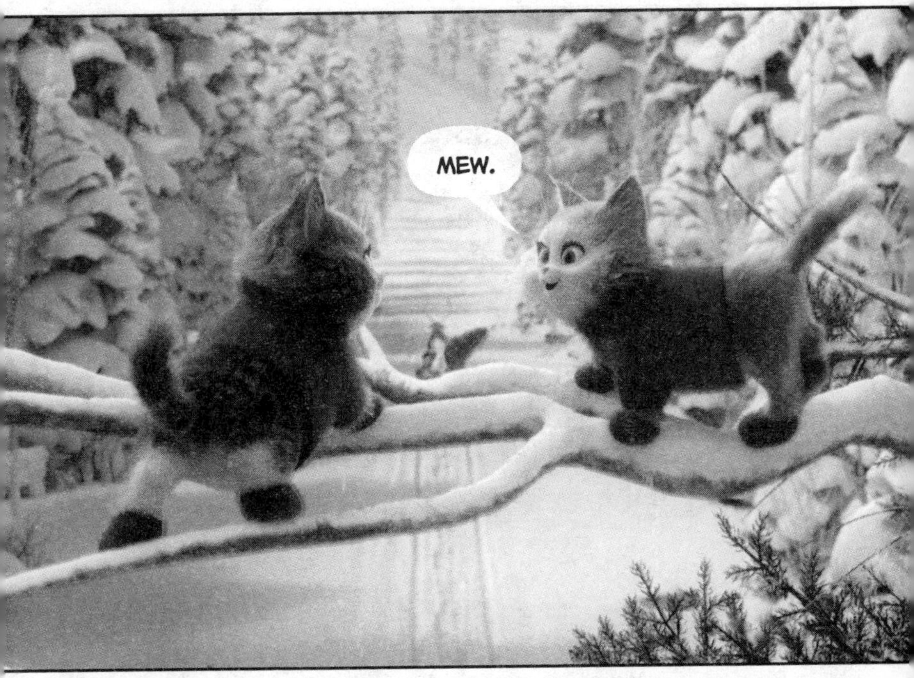
MEW.

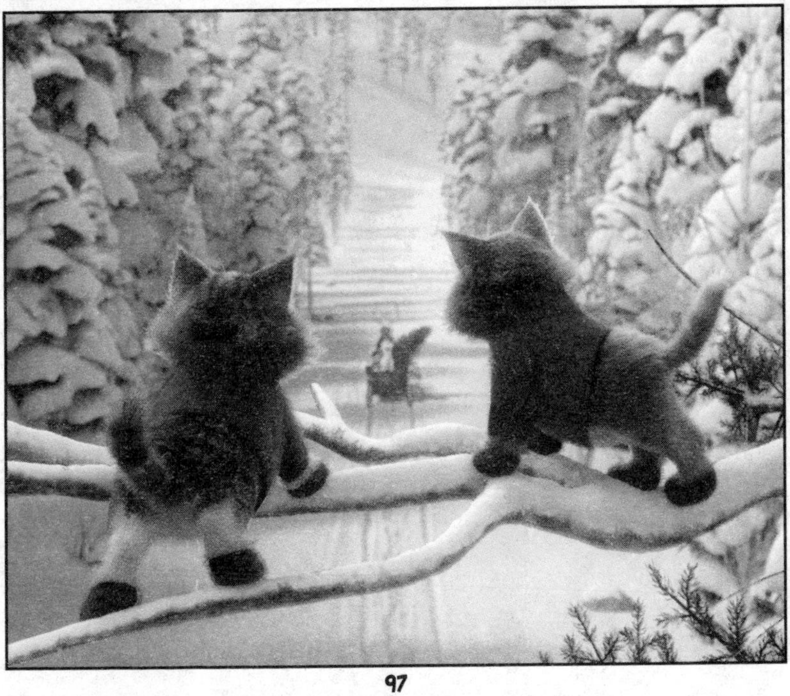

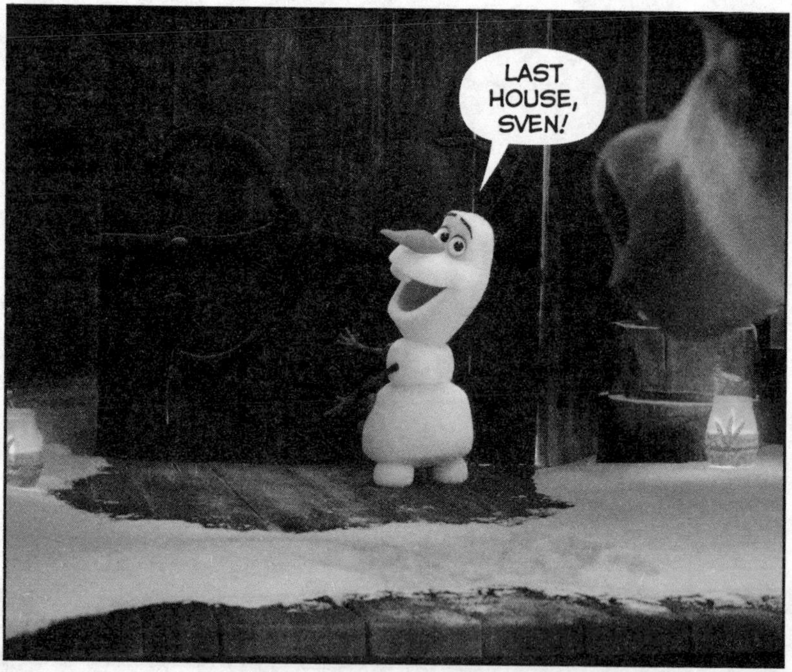
LAST HOUSE, SVEN!

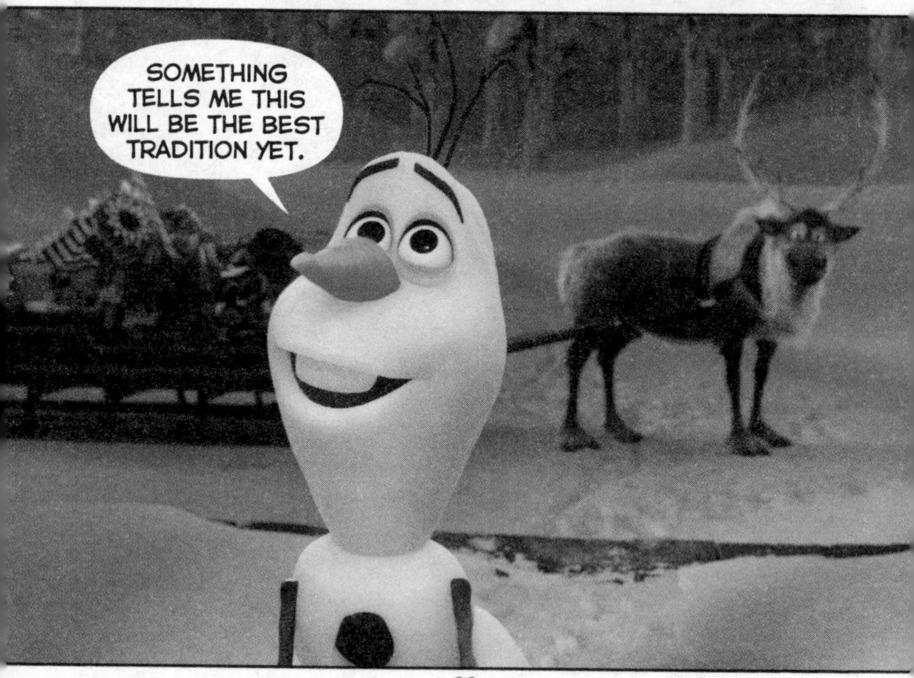
SOMETHING TELLS ME THIS WILL BE THE BEST TRADITION YET.

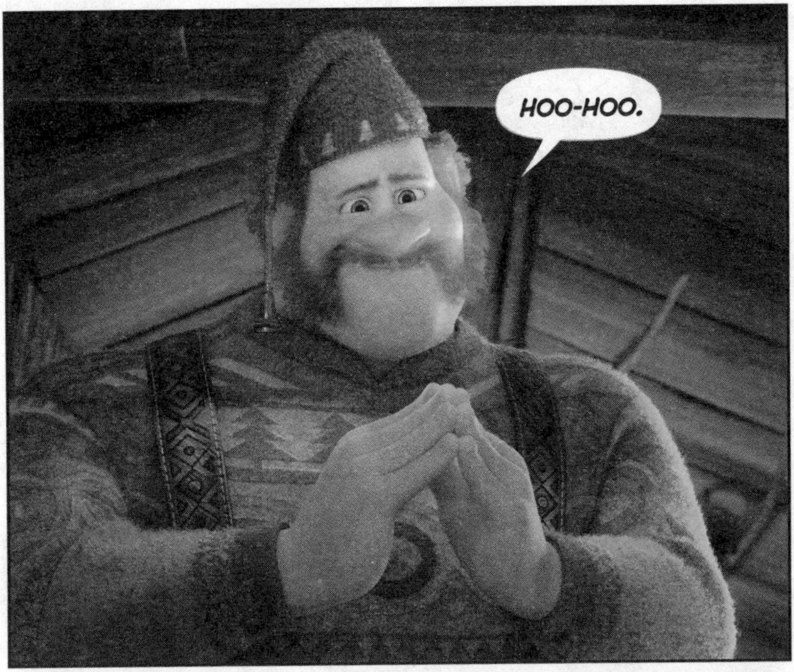
HOO-HOO.

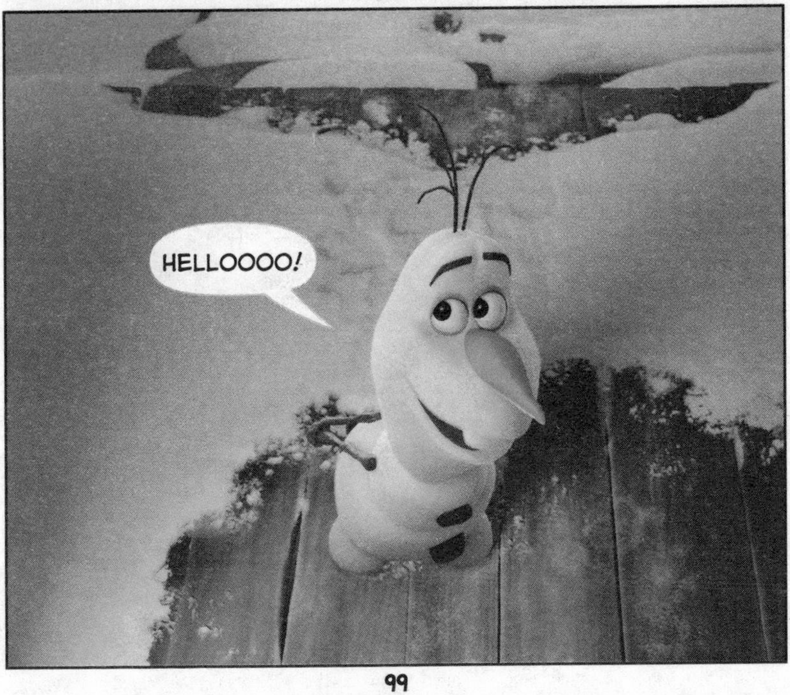
HELLOOOO!

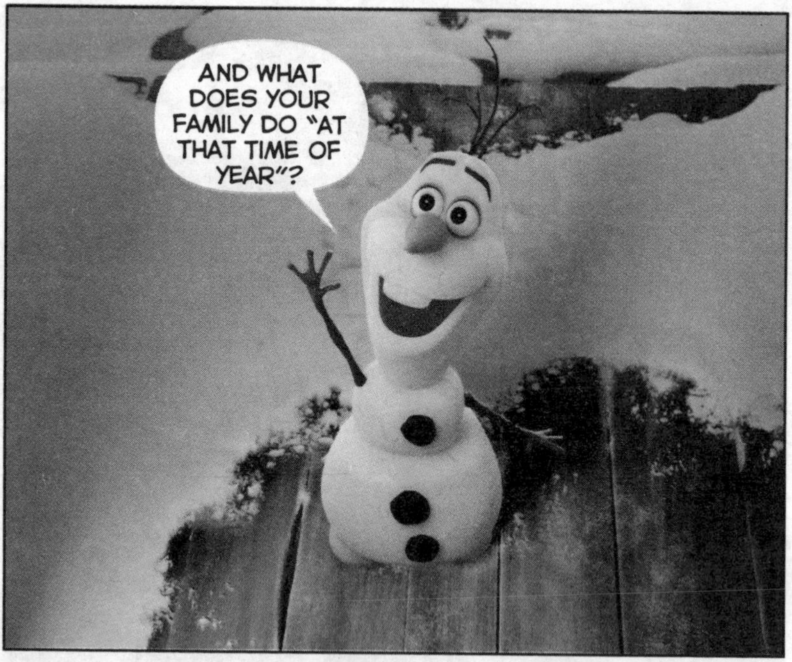
AND WHAT DOES YOUR FAMILY DO "AT THAT TIME OF YEAR"?

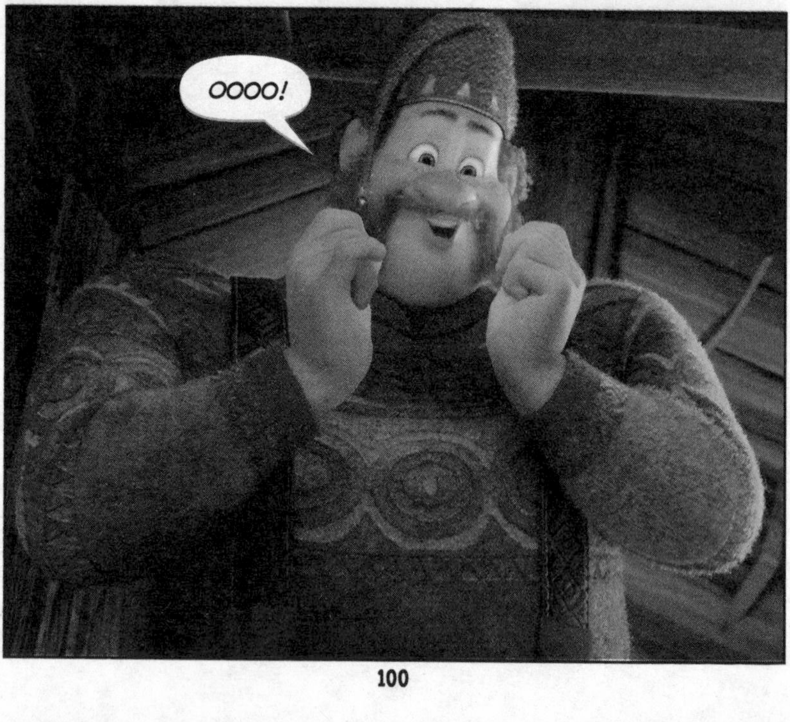
OOOO!

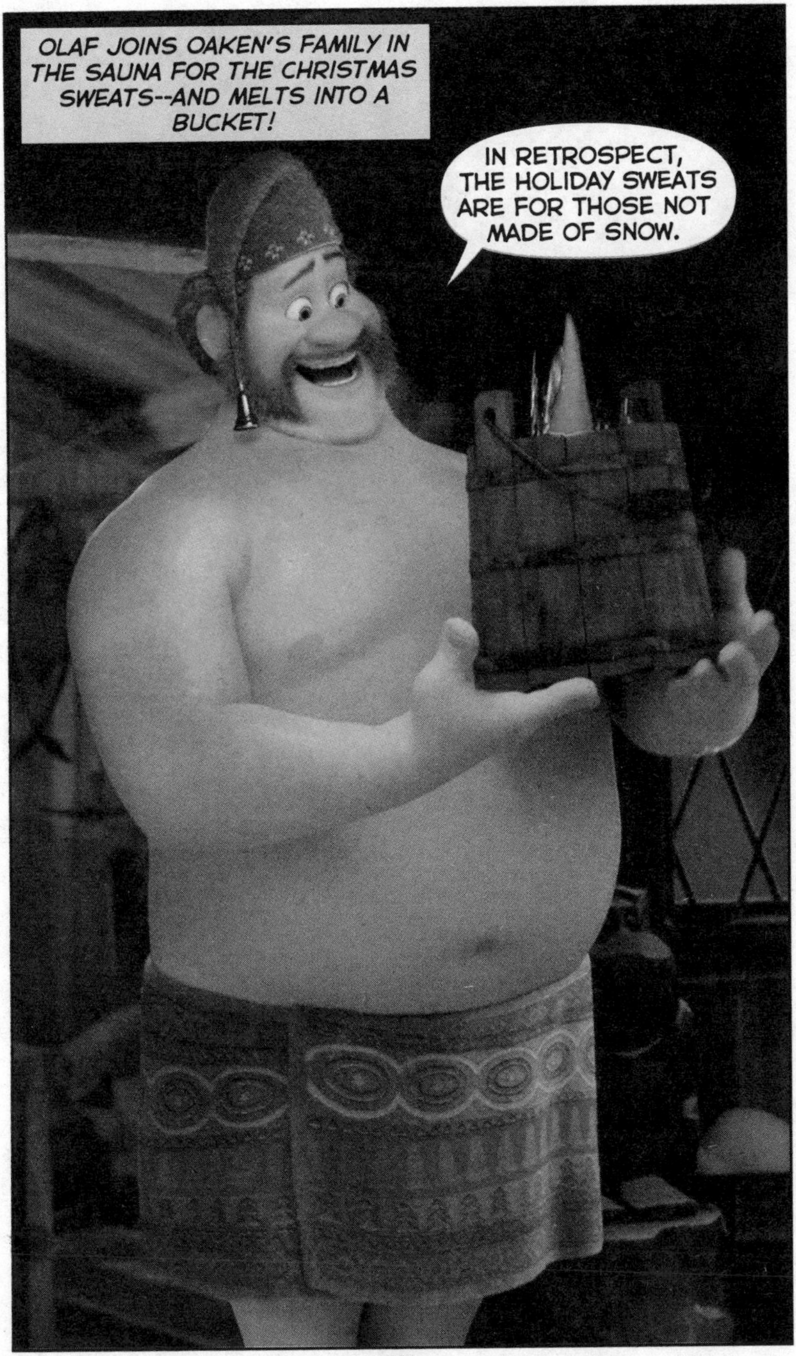

OLAF JOINS OAKEN'S FAMILY IN THE SAUNA FOR THE CHRISTMAS SWEATS--AND MELTS INTO A BUCKET!
IN RETROSPECT, THE HOLIDAY SWEATS ARE FOR THOSE NOT MADE OF SNOW.

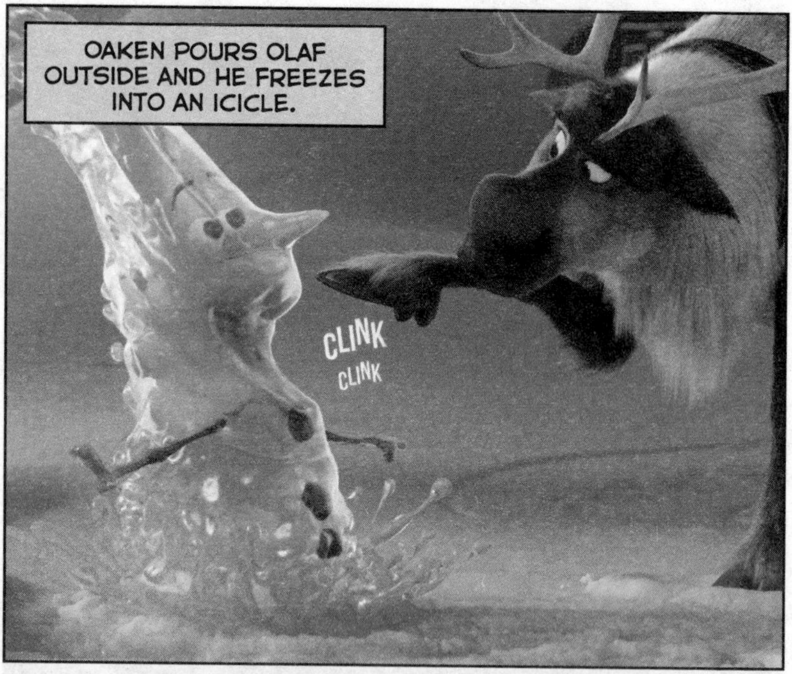
OAKEN POURS OLAF OUTSIDE AND HE FREEZES INTO AN ICICLE.
CLINK
CLINK

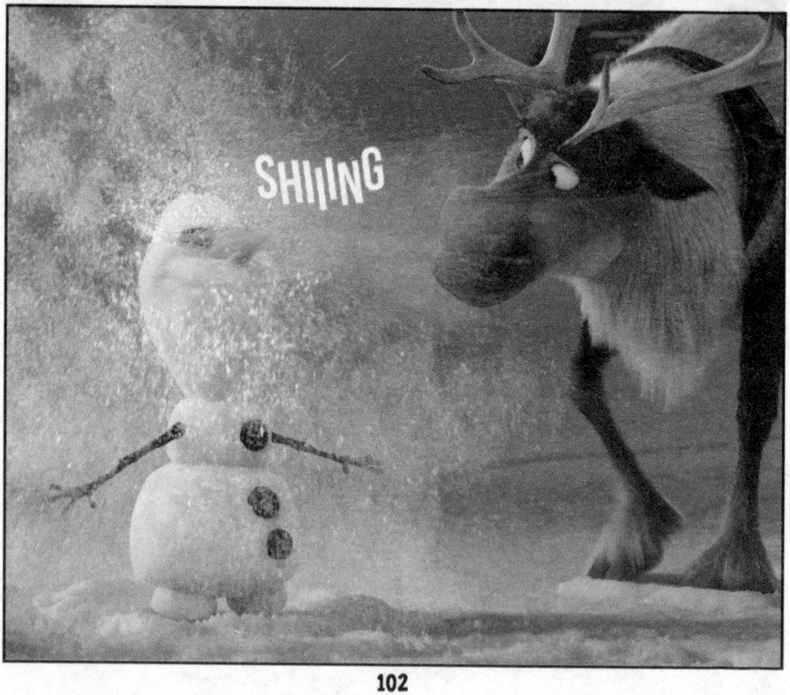
SHIIING

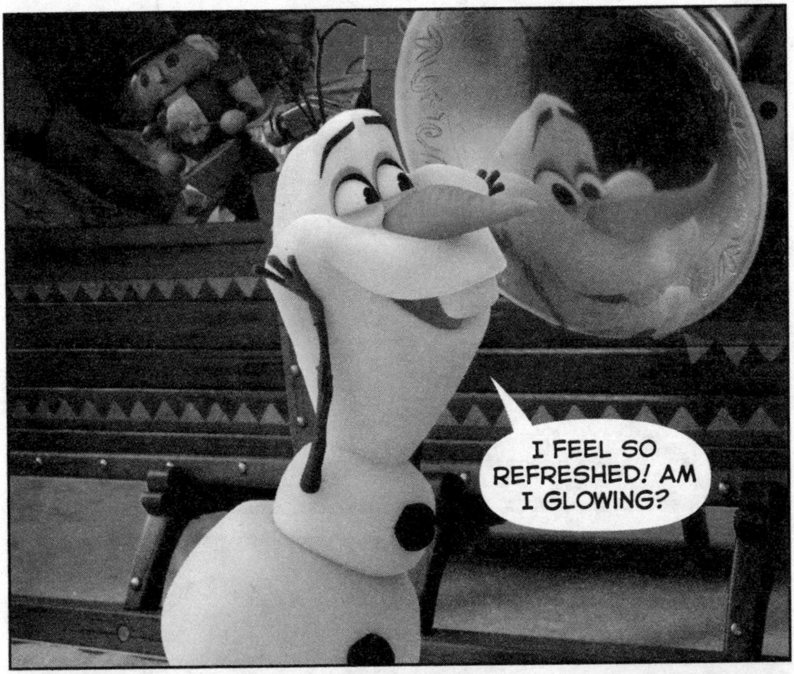
I FEEL SO REFRESHED! AM I GLOWING?

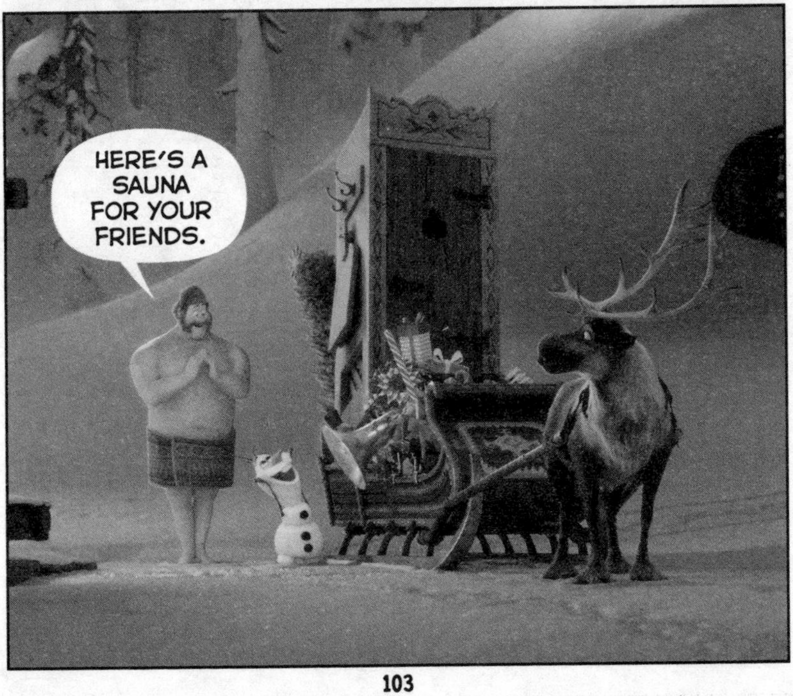
HERE'S A SAUNA FOR YOUR FRIENDS.

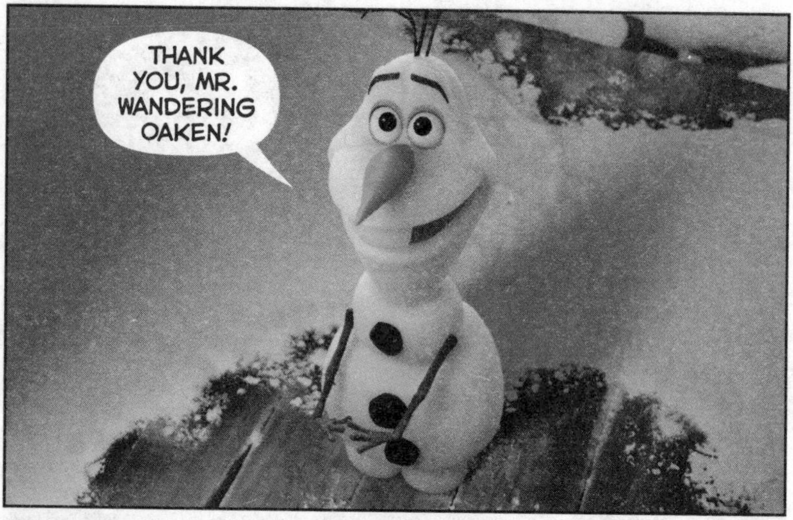
THANK YOU, MR. WANDERING OAKEN!

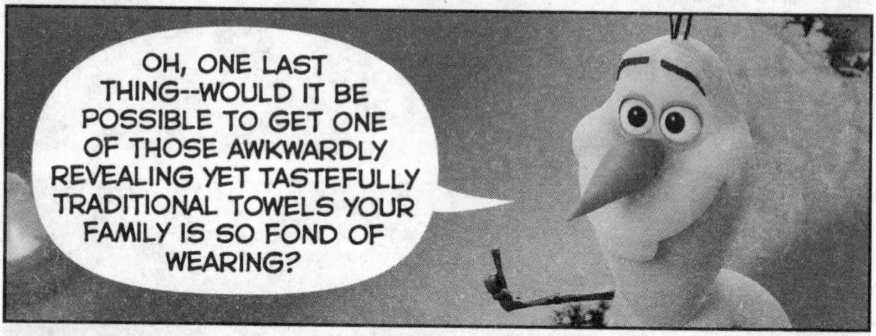
OH, ONE LAST THING--WOULD IT BE POSSIBLE TO GET ONE OF THOSE AWKWARDLY REVEALING YET TASTEFULLY TRADITIONAL TOWELS YOUR FAMILY IS SO FOND OF WEARING?

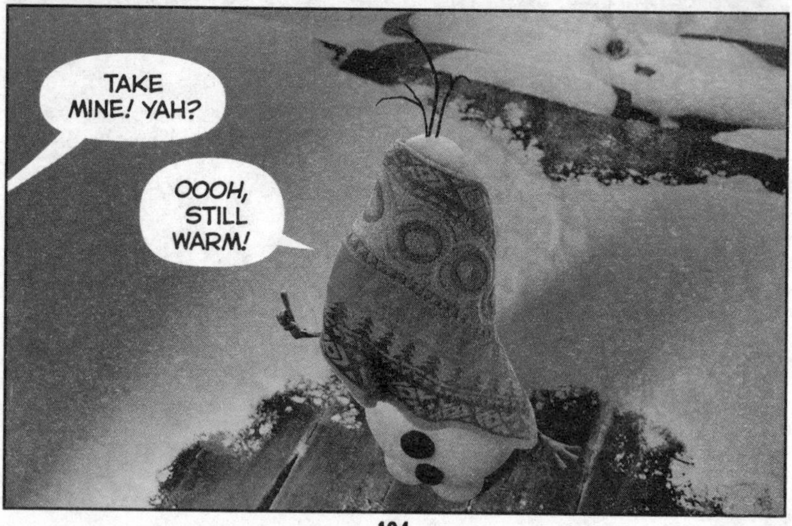
TAKE MINE! YAH?
OOOH, STILL WARM!

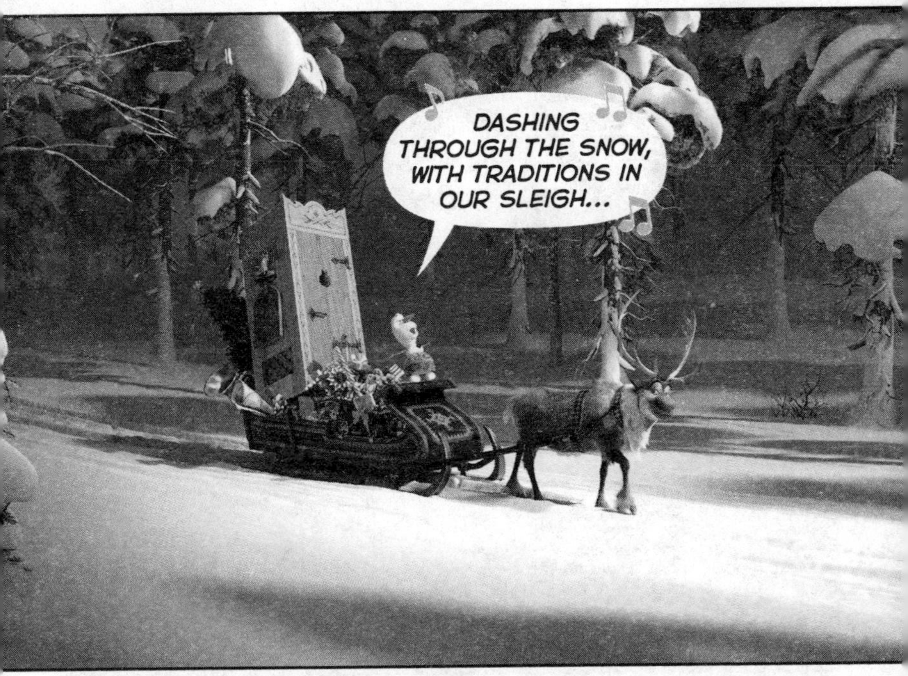
DASHING THROUGH THE SNOW, WITH TRADITIONS IN OUR SLEIGH...

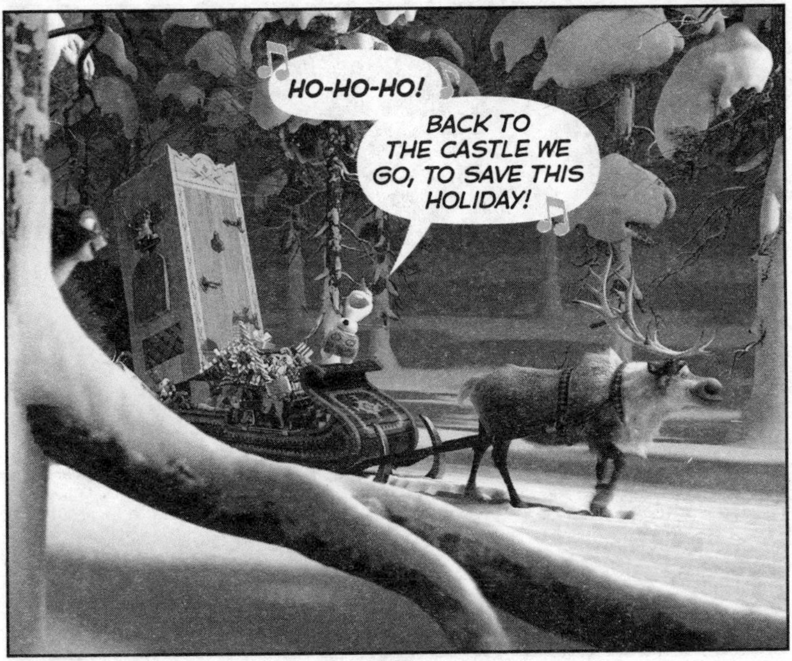
HO-HO-HO!
BACK TO THE CASTLE WE GO, TO SAVE THIS HOLIDAY!

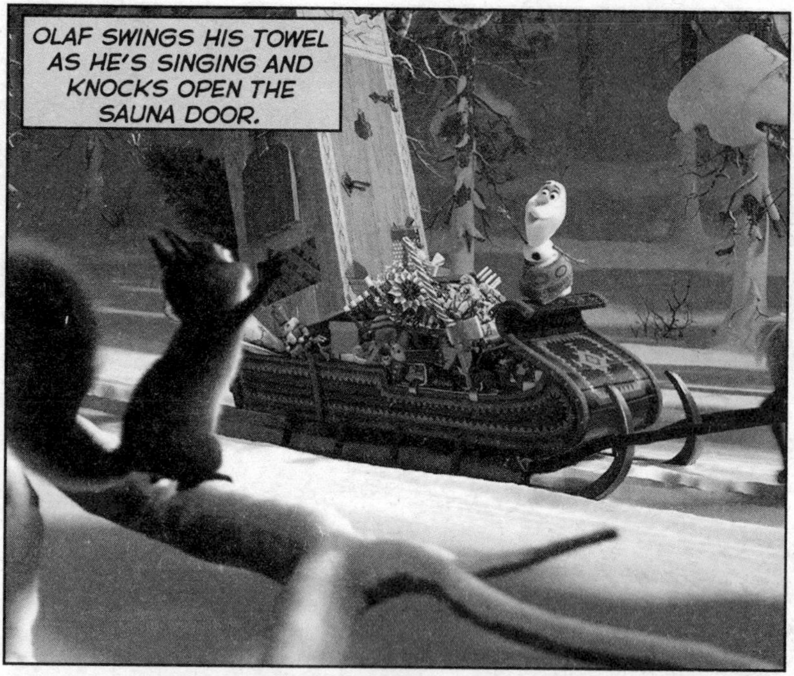
OLAF SWINGS HIS TOWEL AS HE'S SINGING AND KNOCKS OPEN THE SAUNA DOOR.

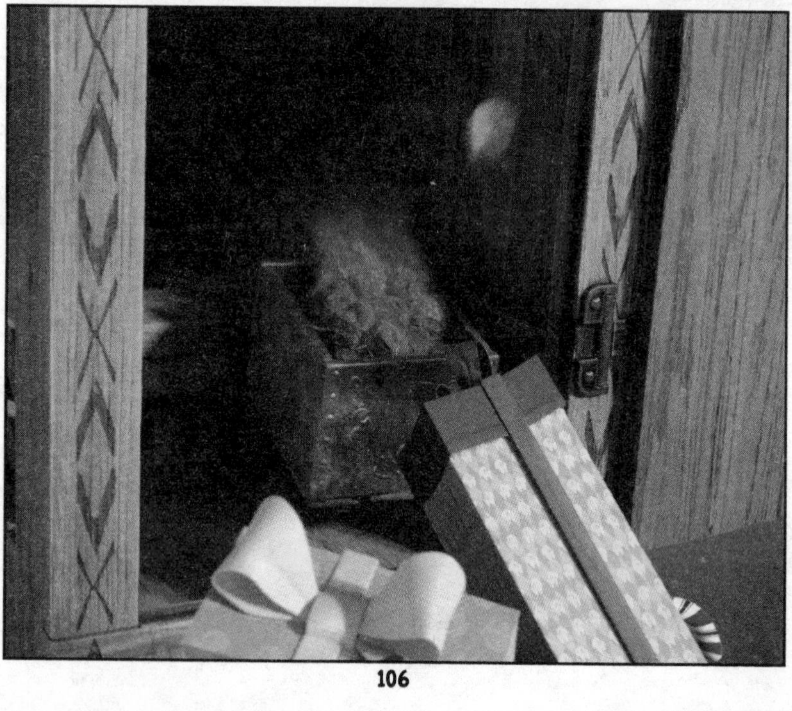

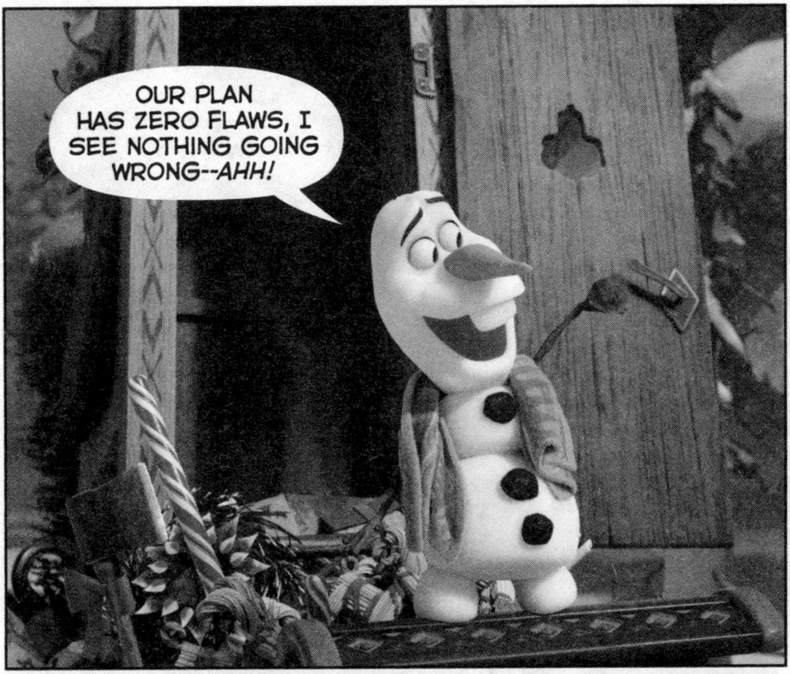
OUR PLAN HAS ZERO FLAWS, I SEE NOTHING GOING WRONG--AHH!

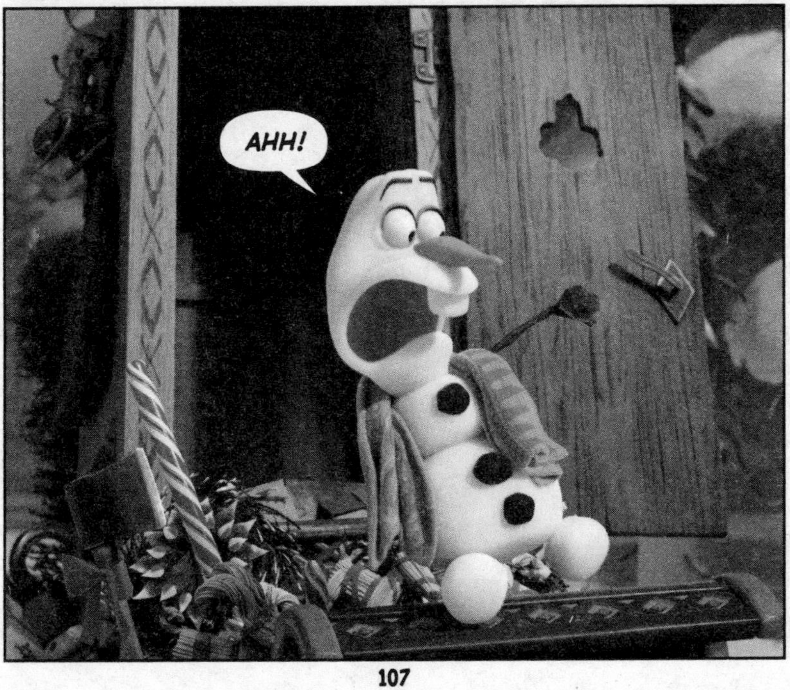
AHH!

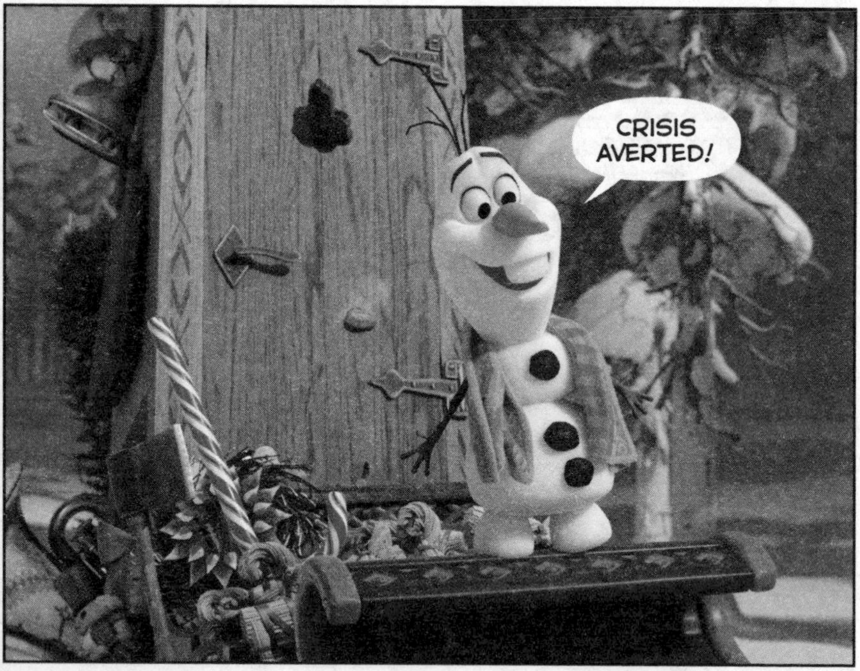
CRISIS AVERTED!

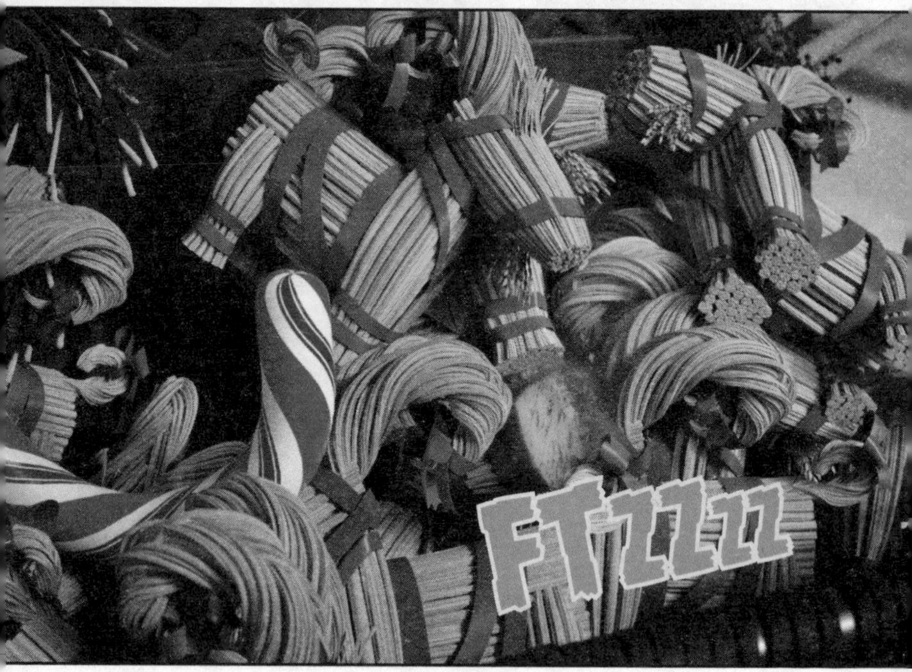
FTZZZZ

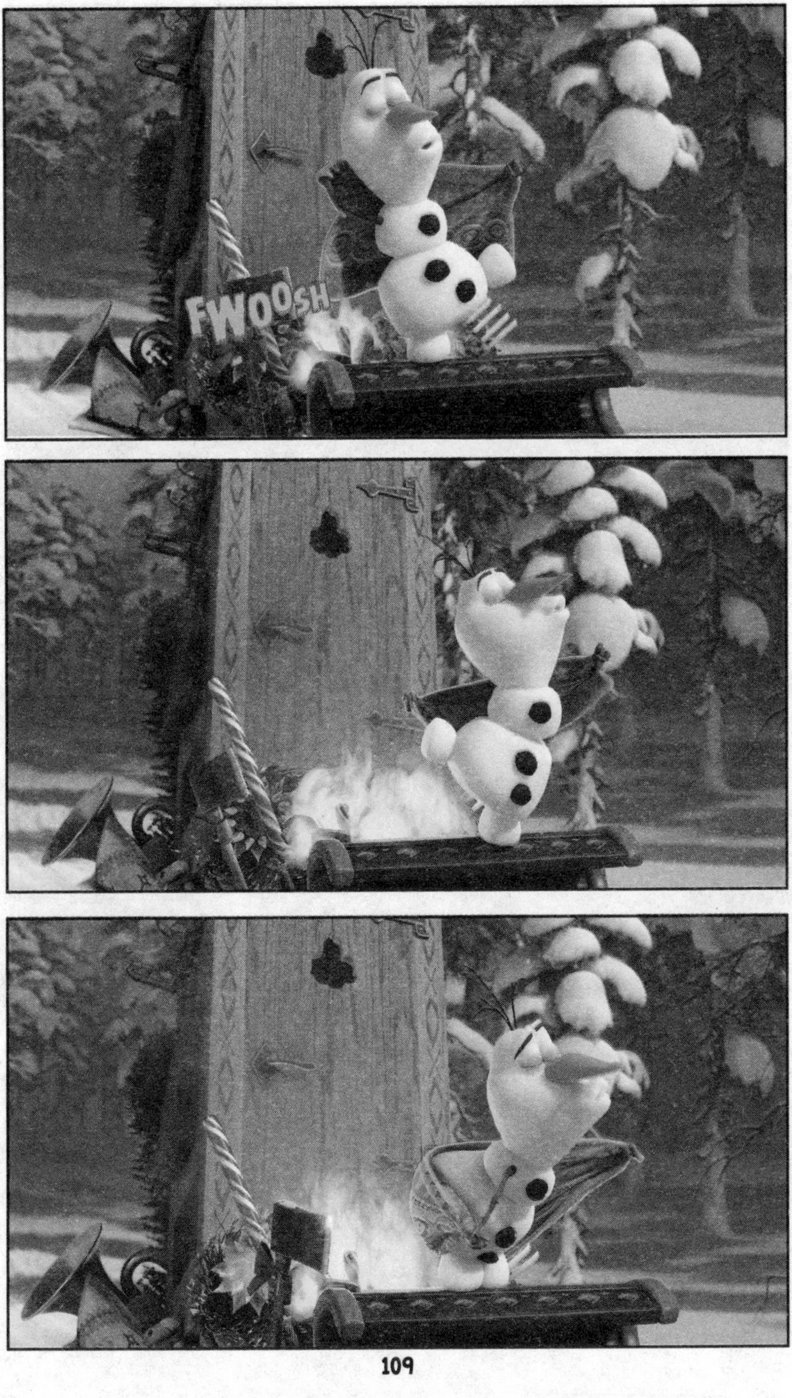
FWOOSH

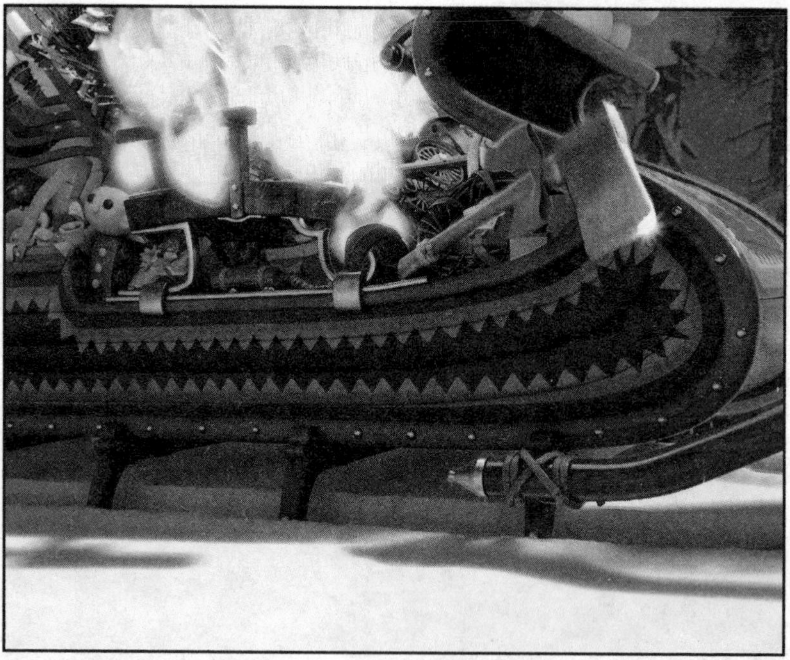

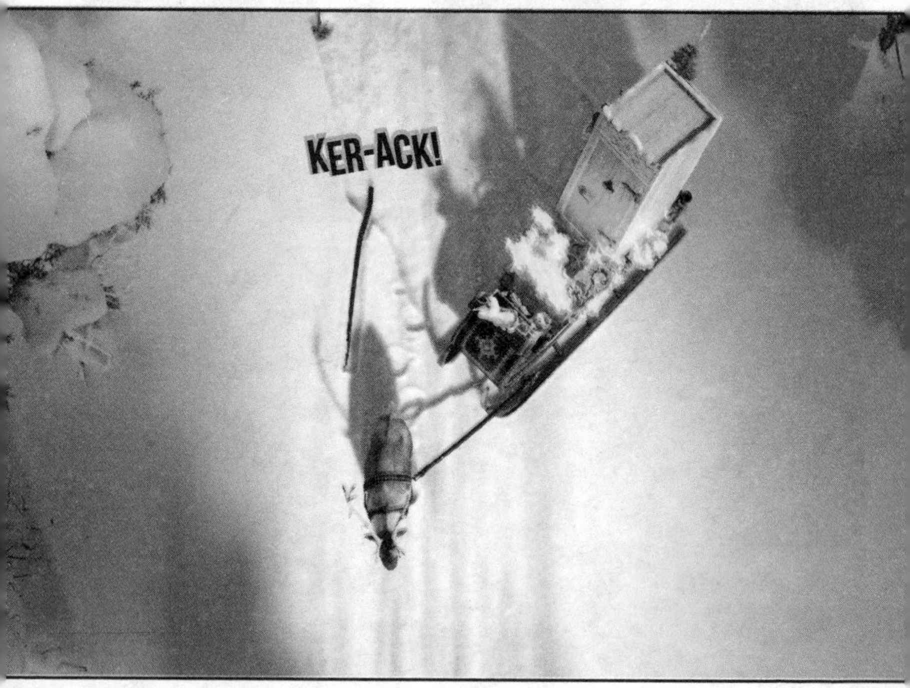
KER-ACK!

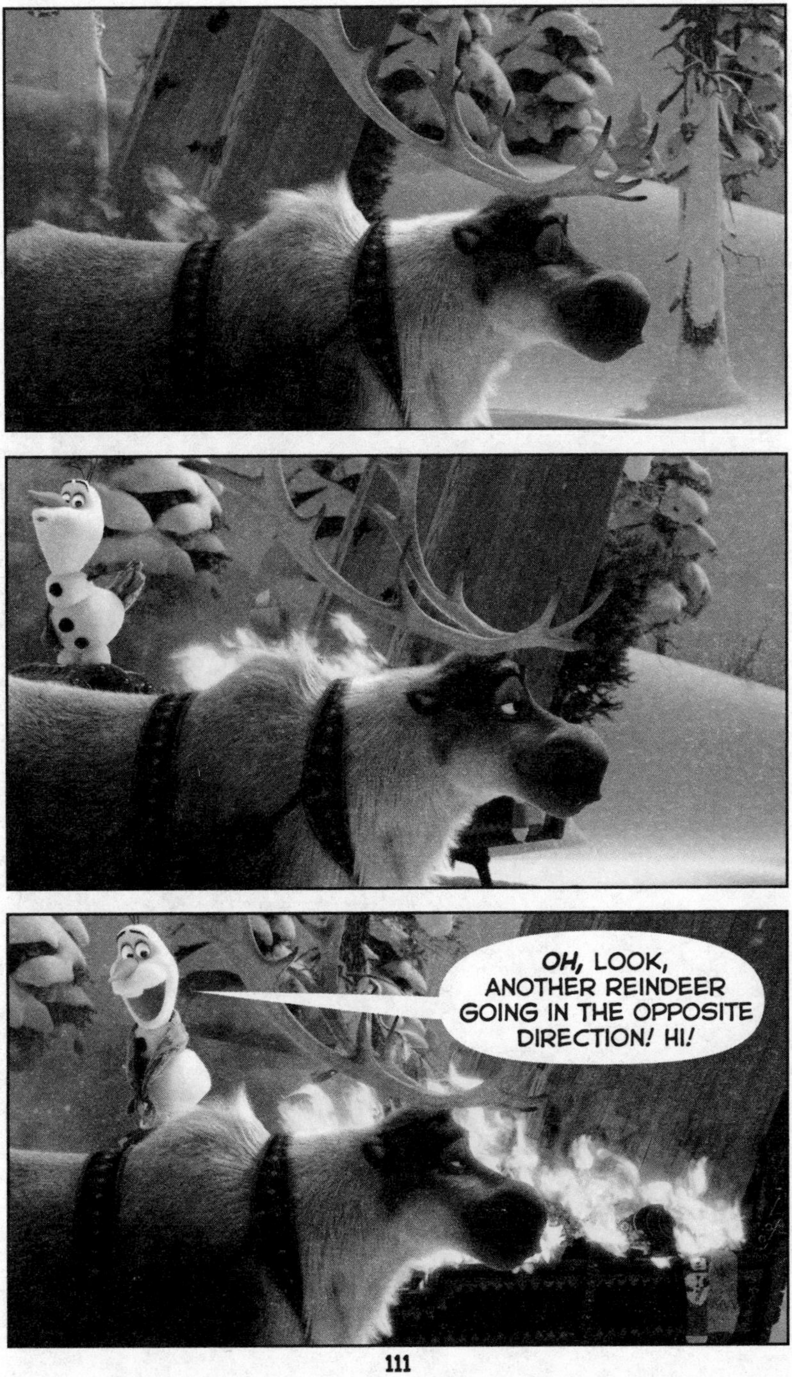
OH, LOOK, ANOTHER REINDEER GOING IN THE OPPOSITE DIRECTION! HI!

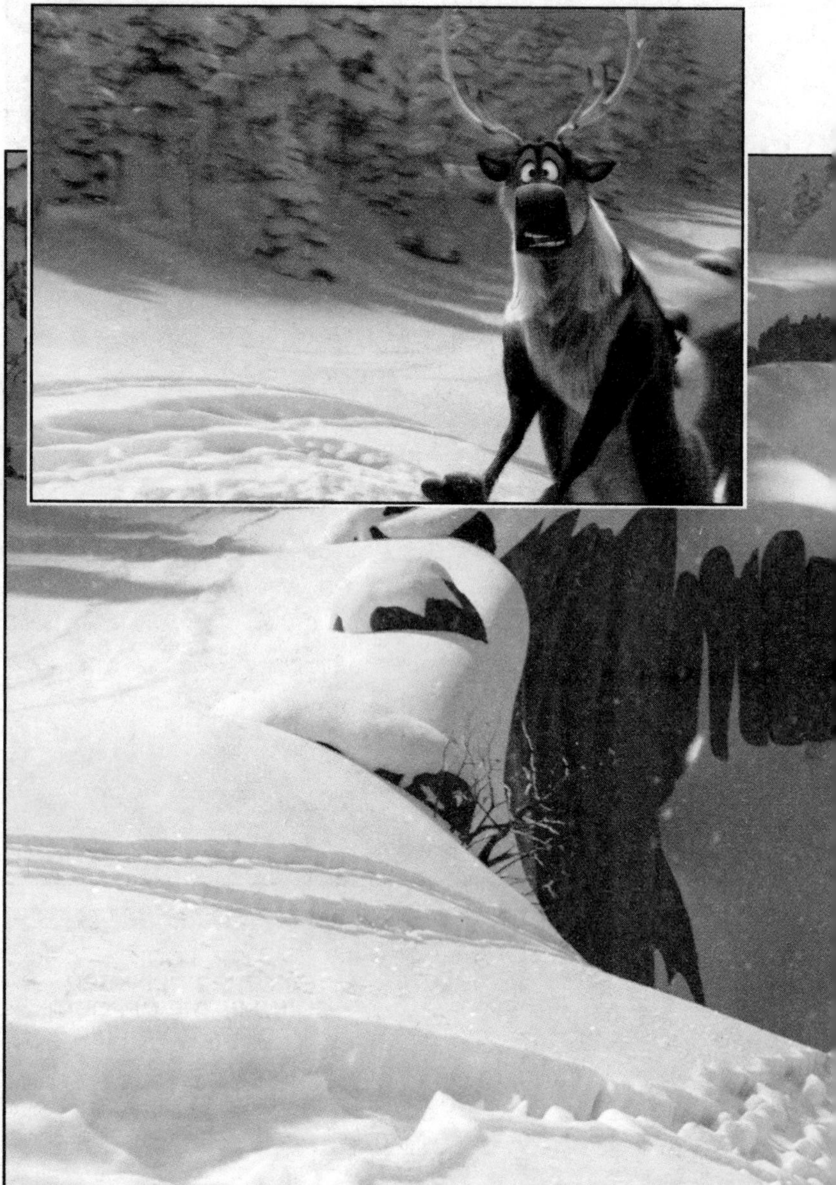

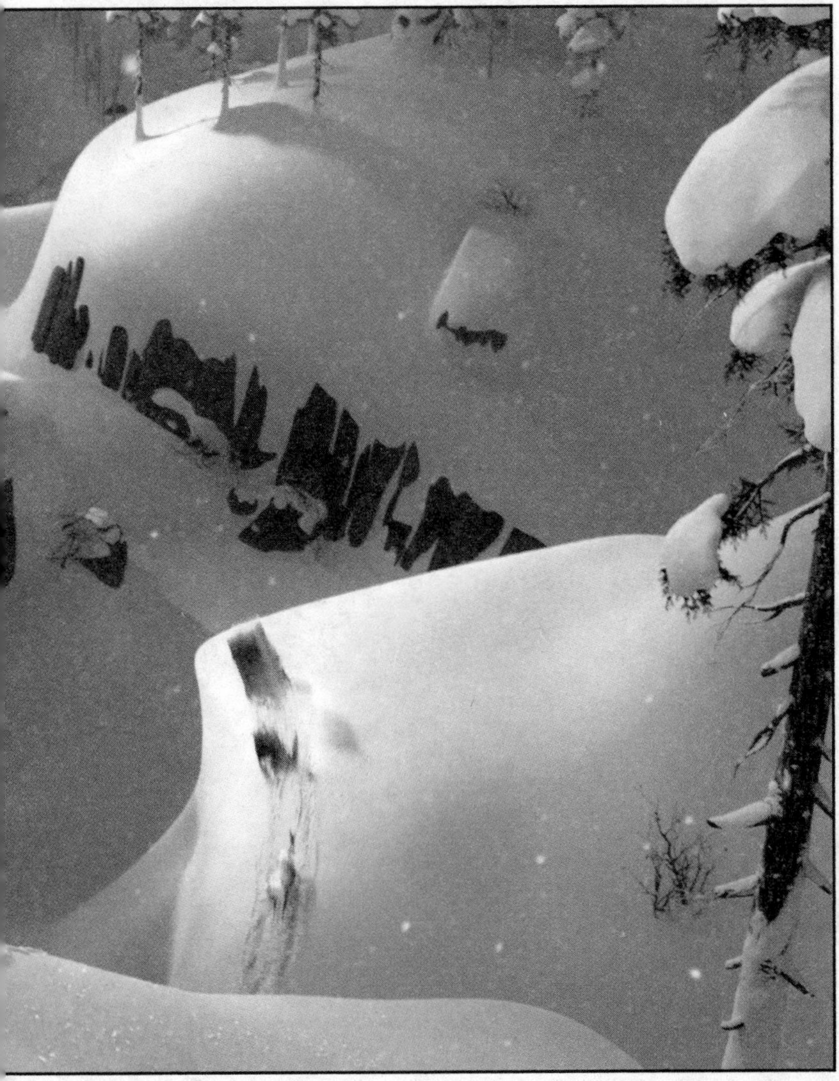

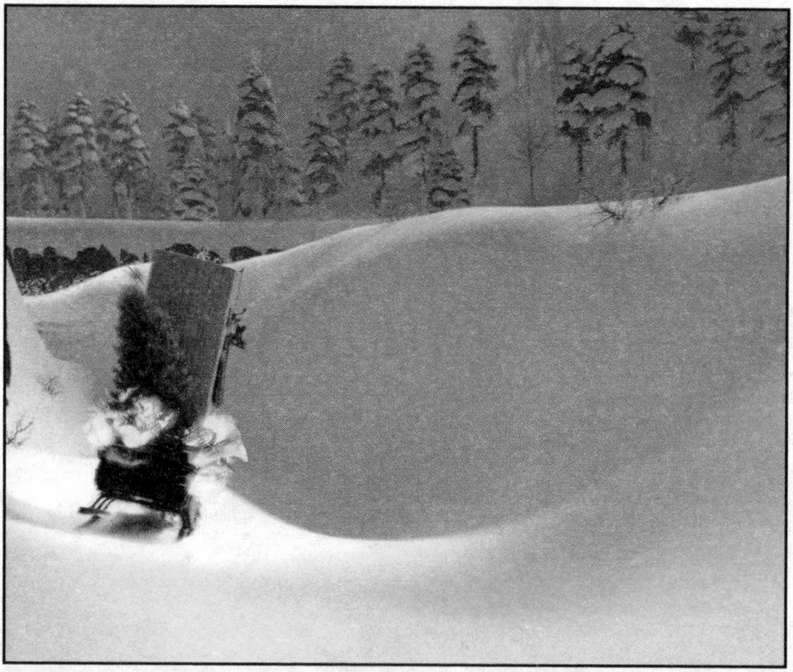

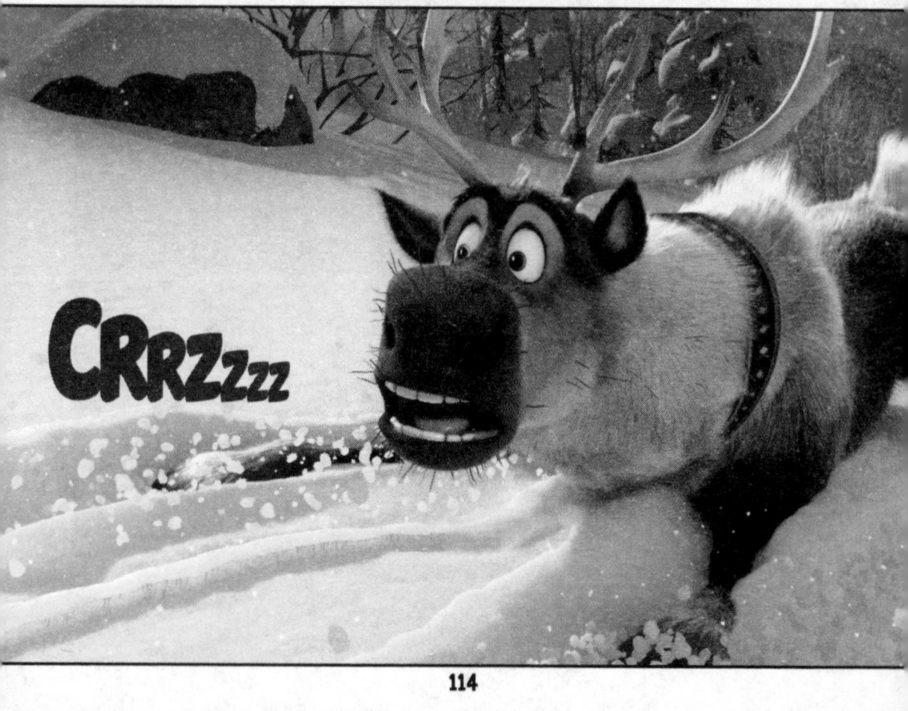
CRRZzzz

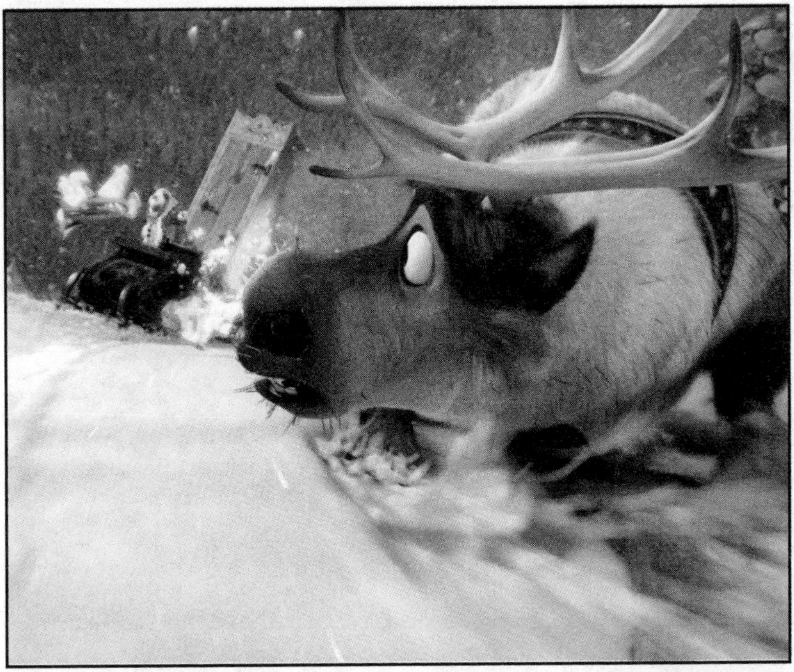

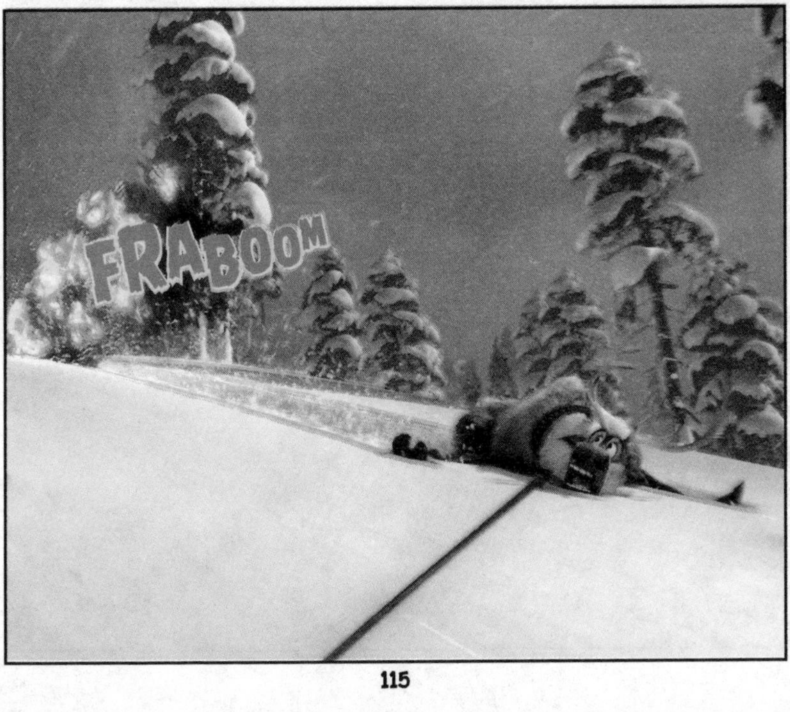
FRABOOM

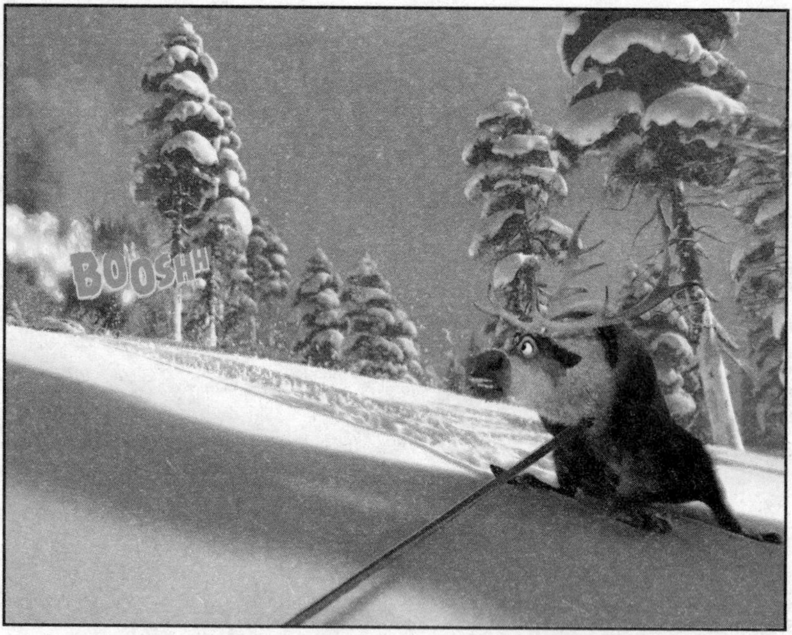
BOOSHH

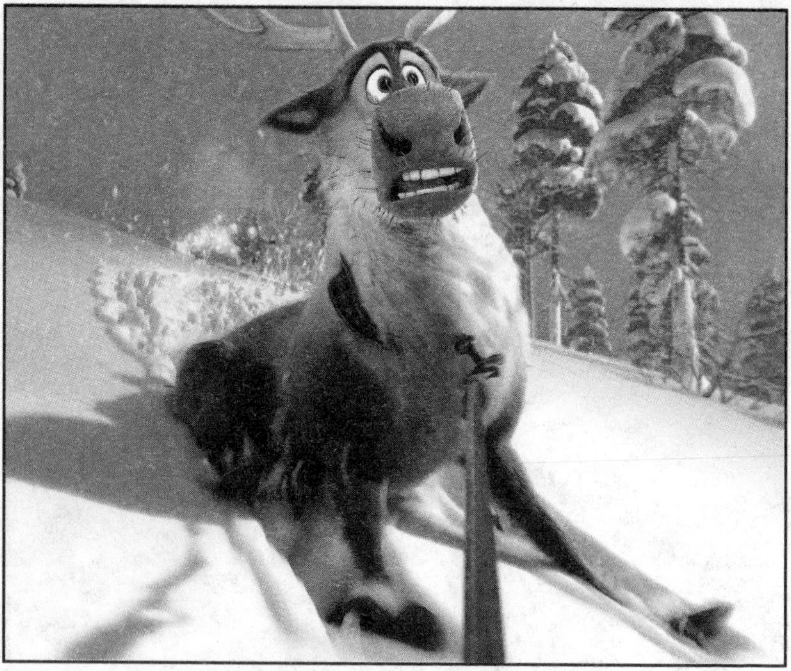

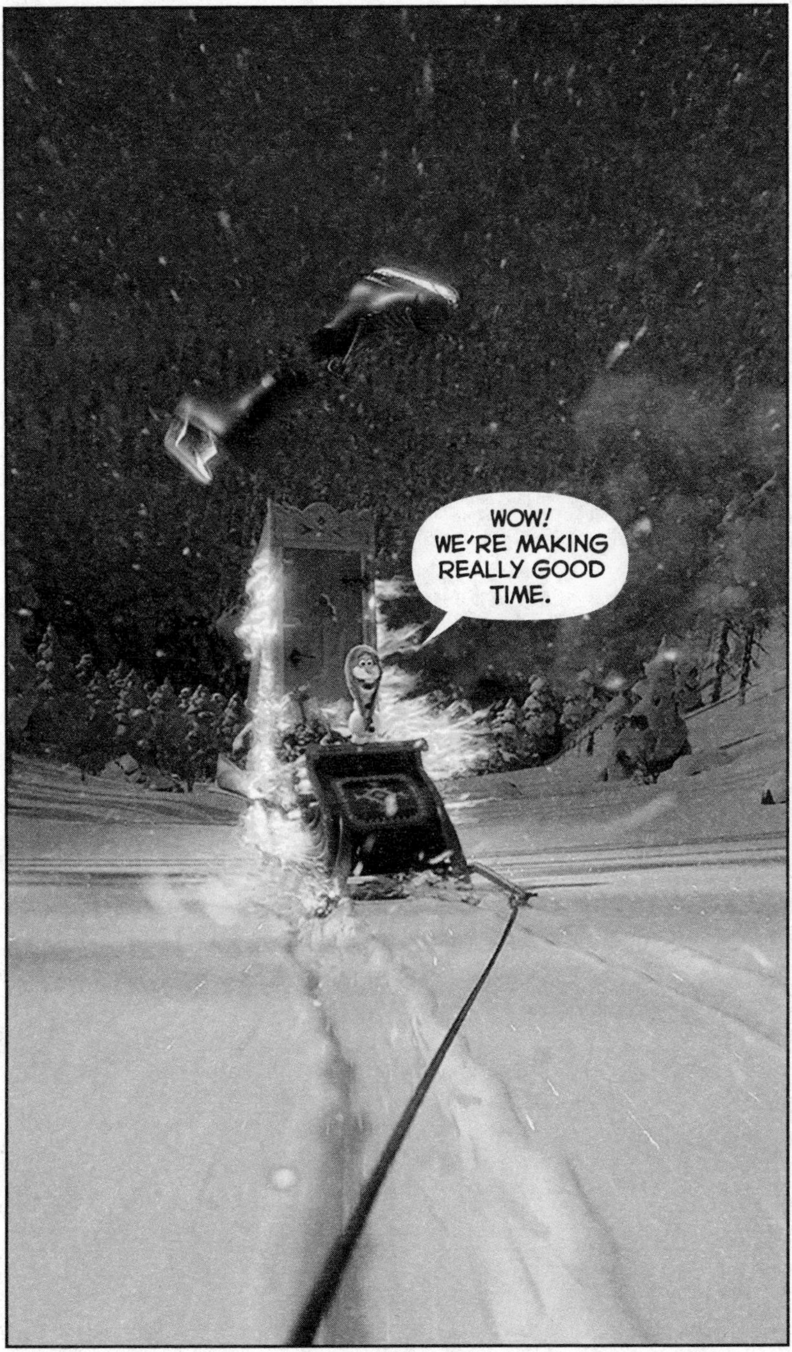
WOW!
WE'RE MAKING
REALLY GOOD
TIME.

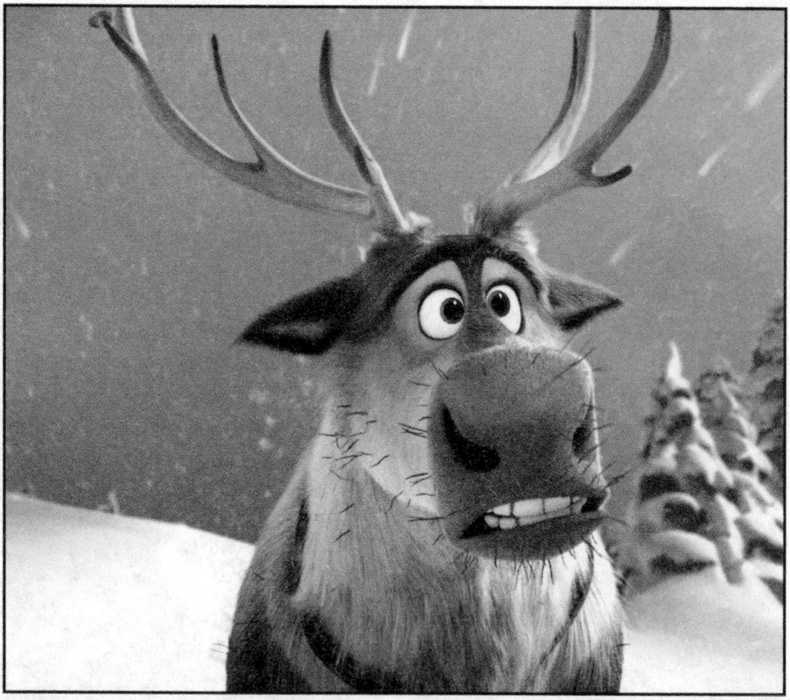

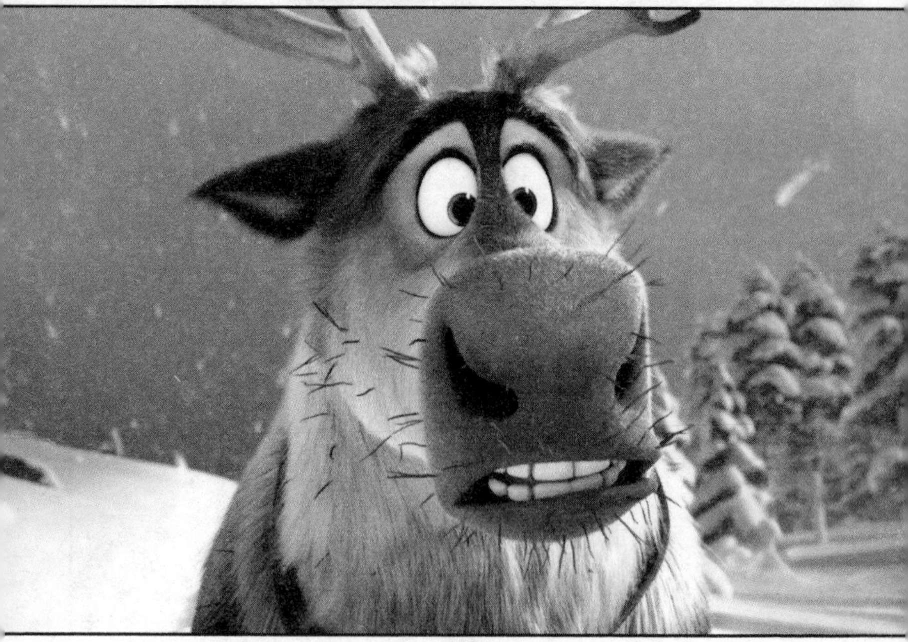

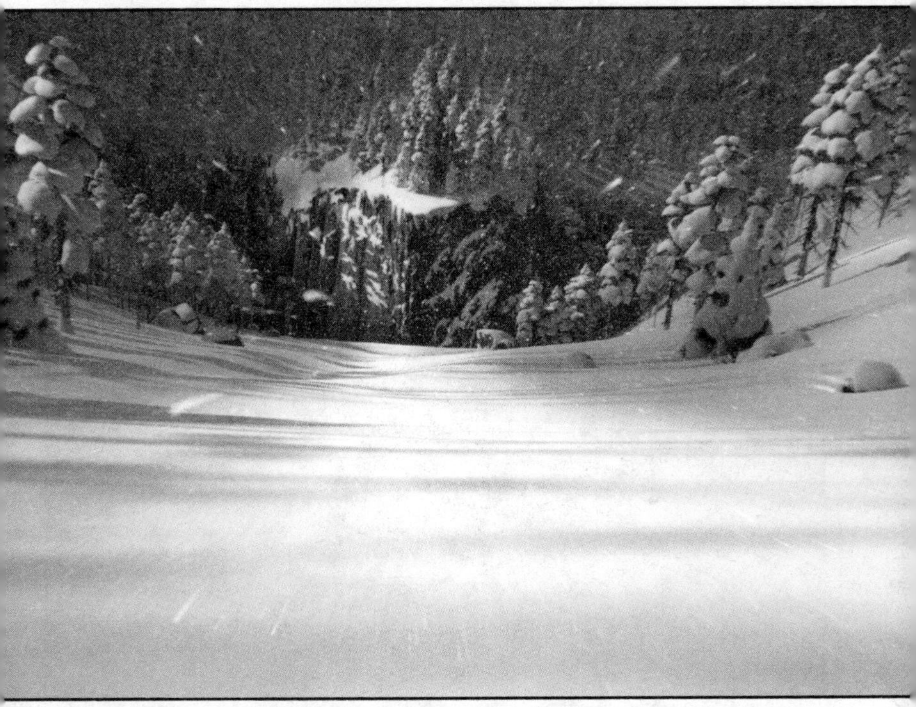

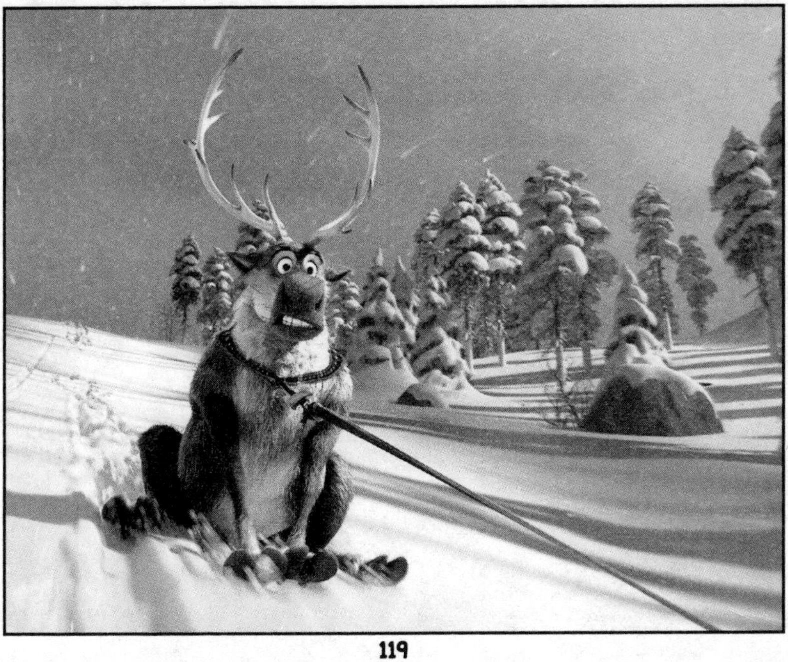

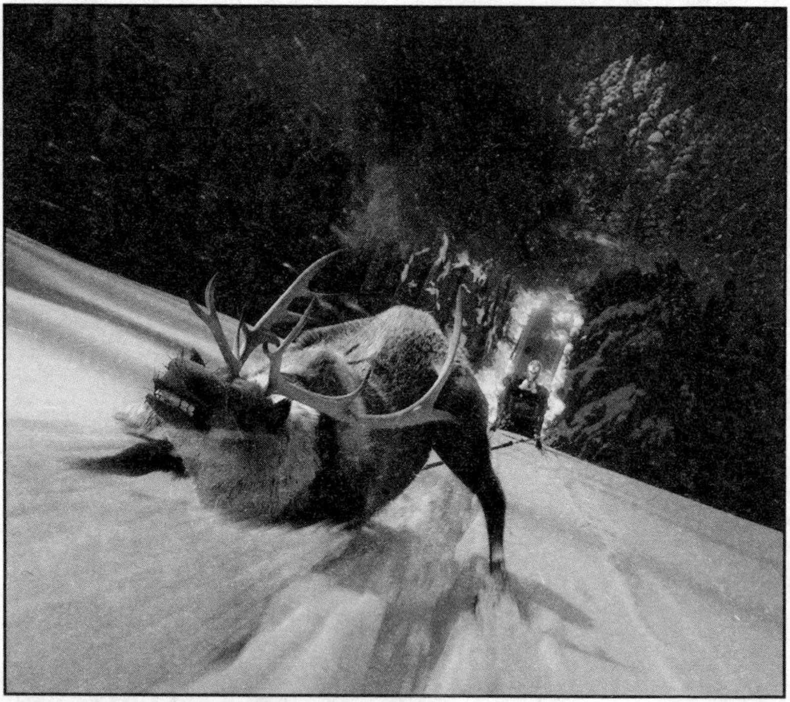

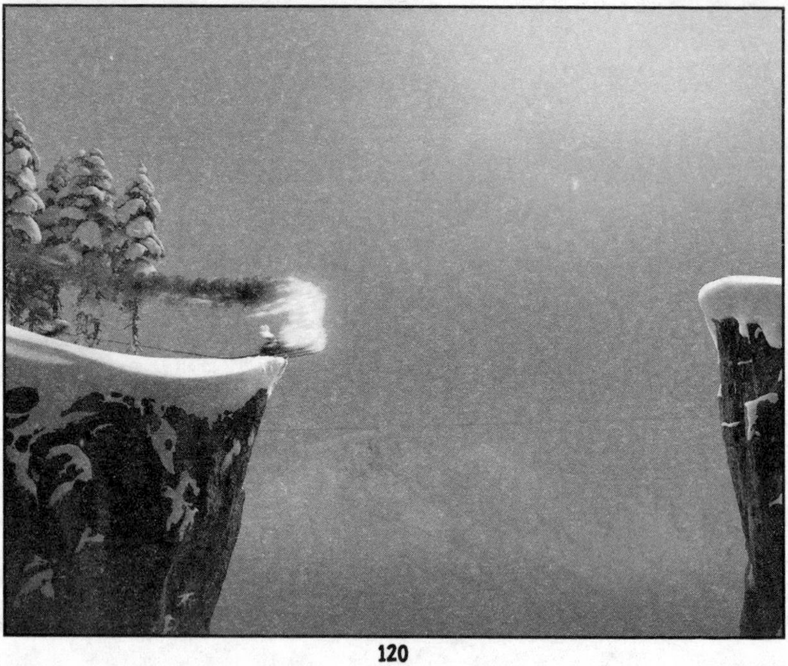

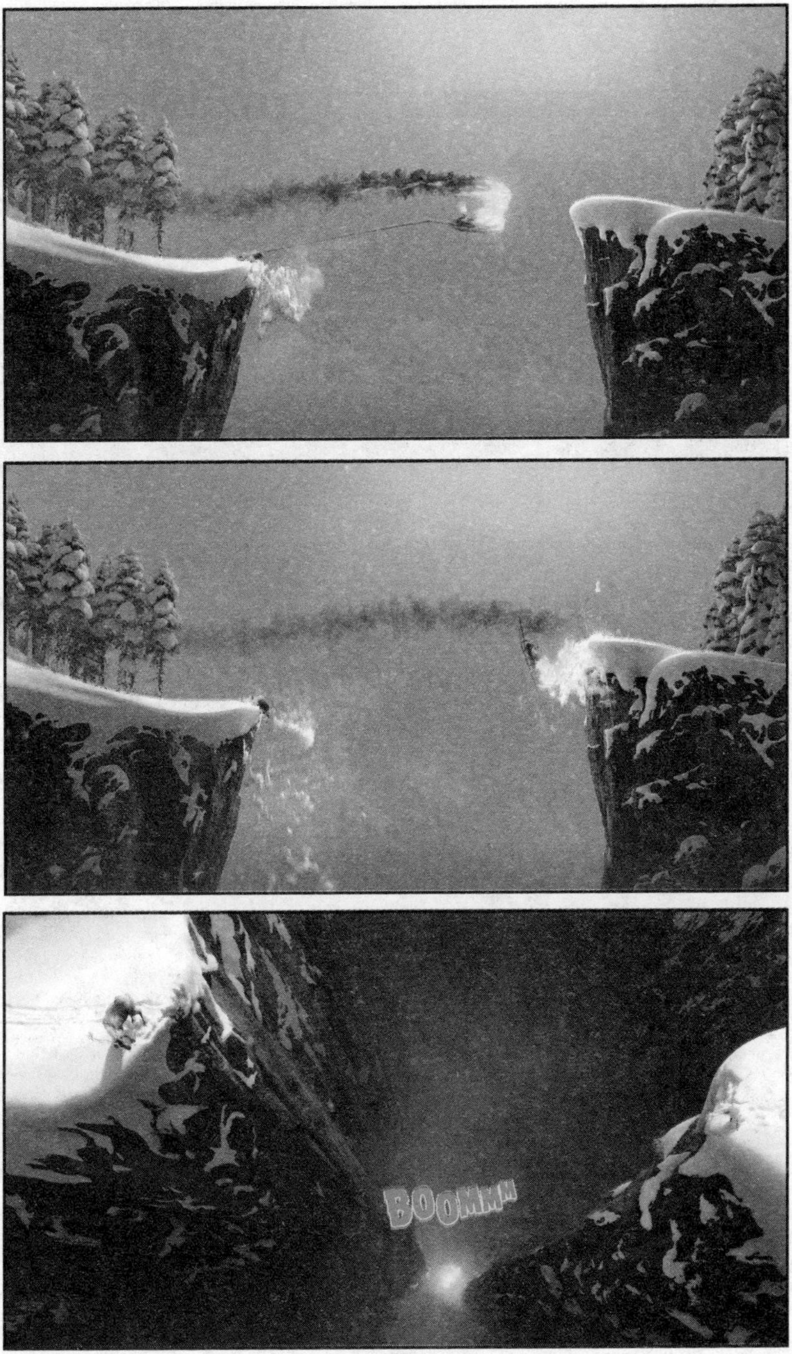
BOOMMM

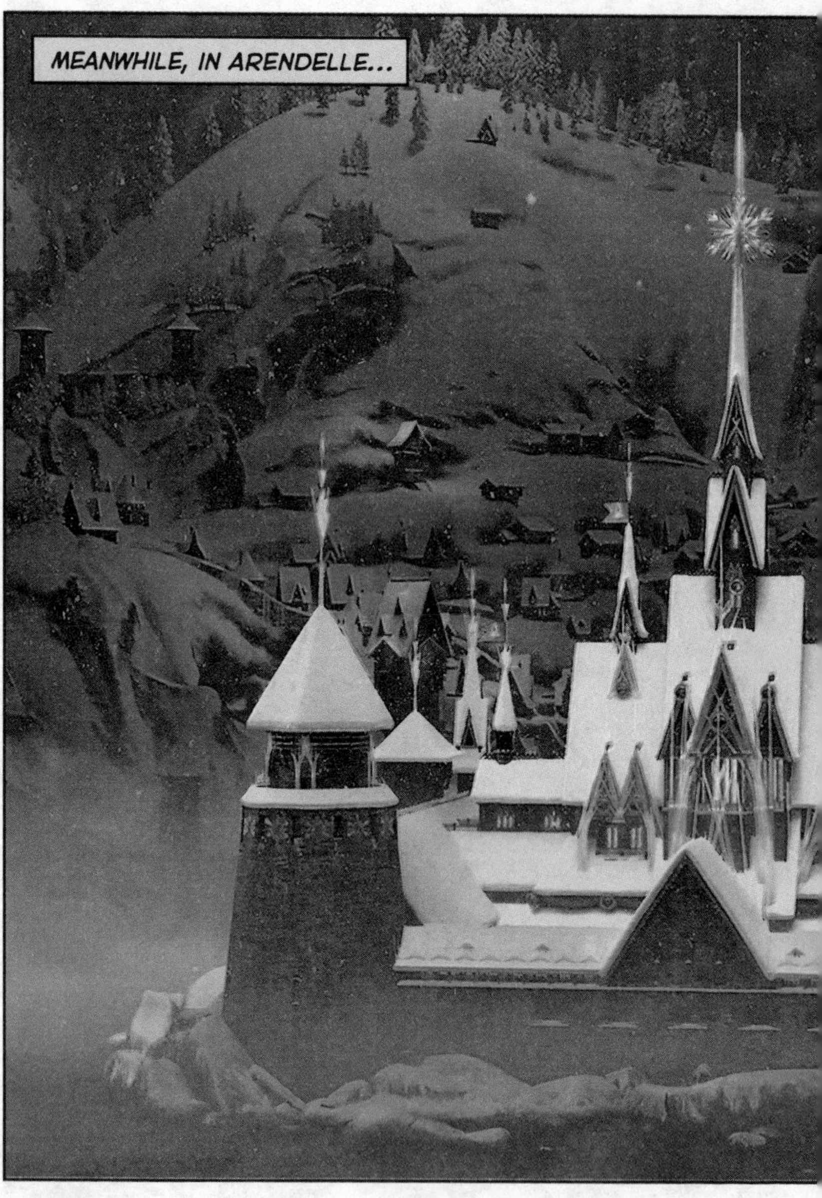
MEANWHILE, IN ARENDELLE...

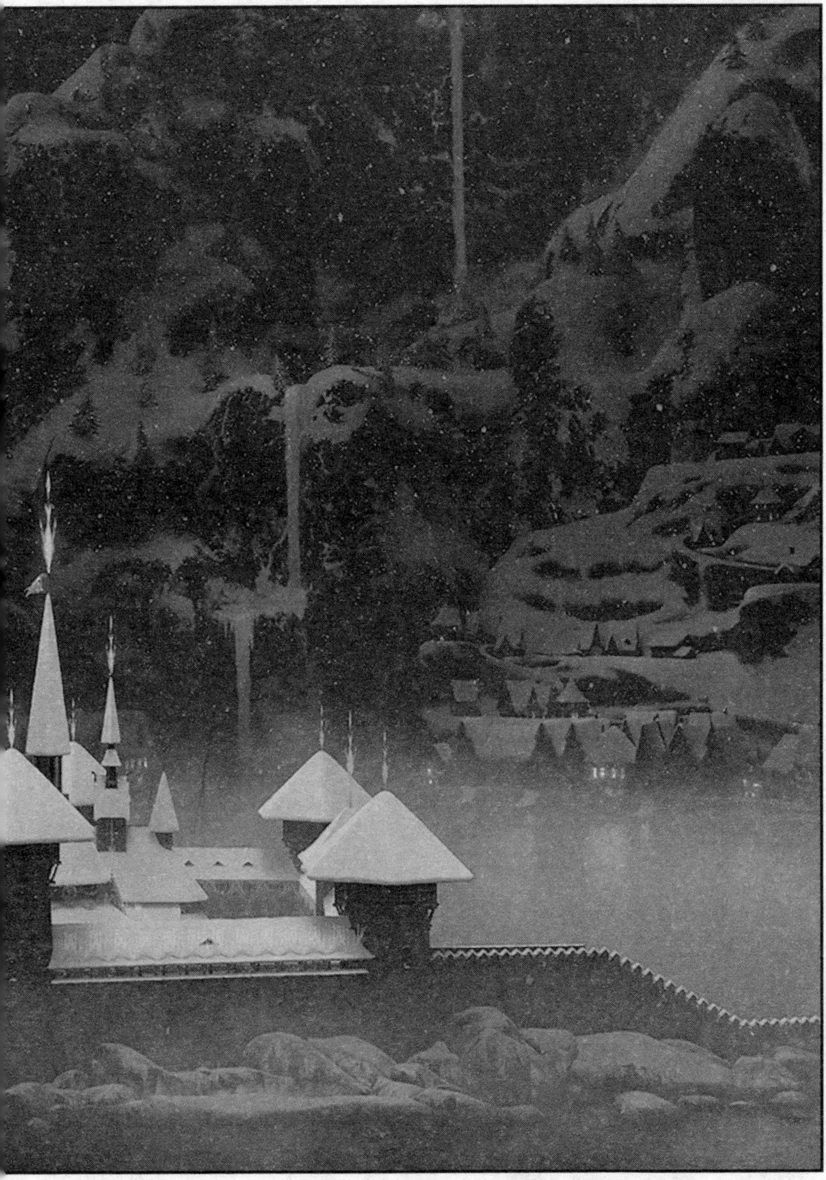

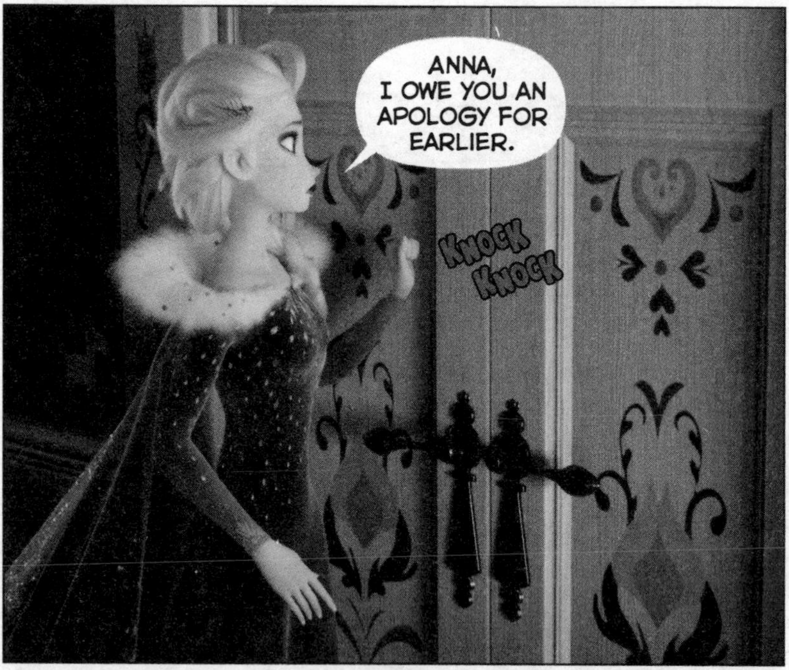
ANNA, I OWE YOU AN APOLOGY FOR EARLIER.
KNOCK KNOCK

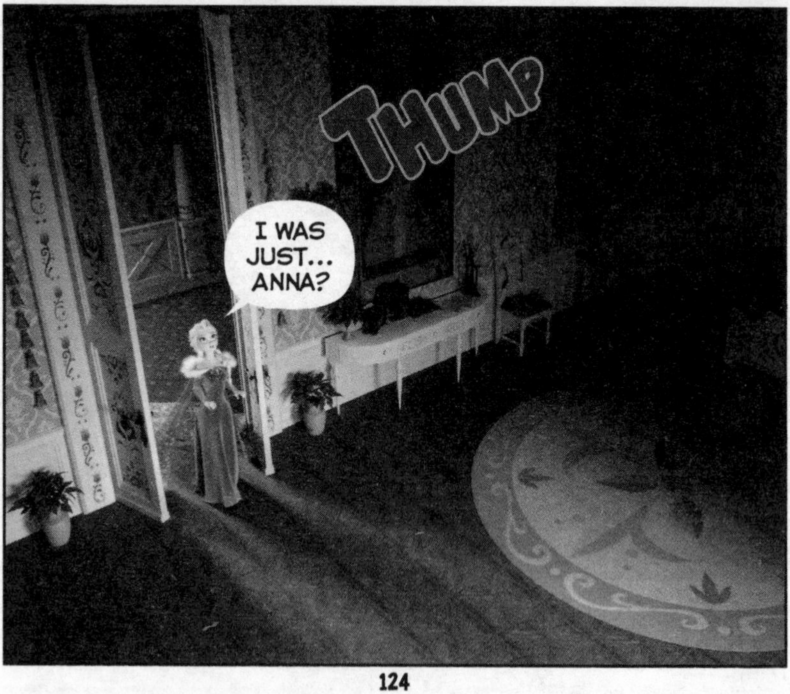
THUMP
I WAS JUST... ANNA?

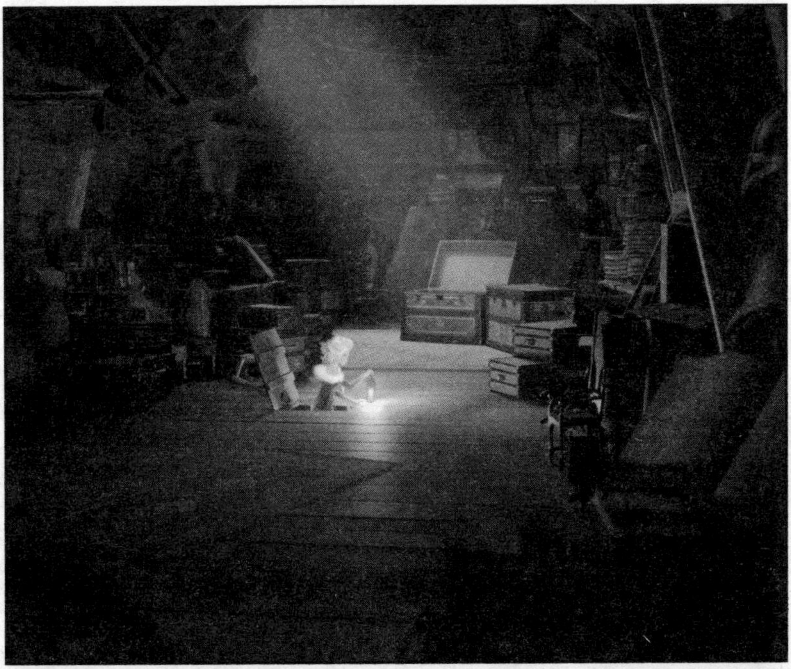

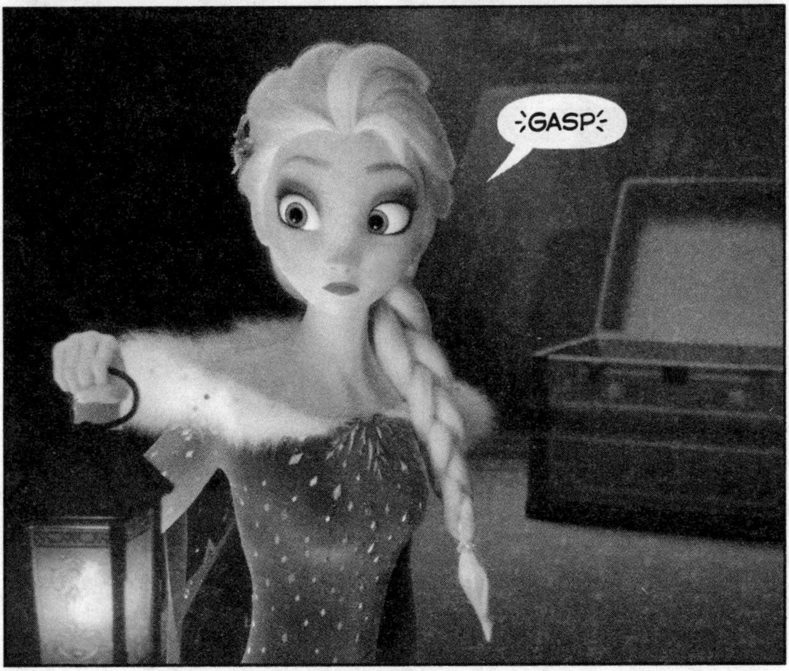
GASP

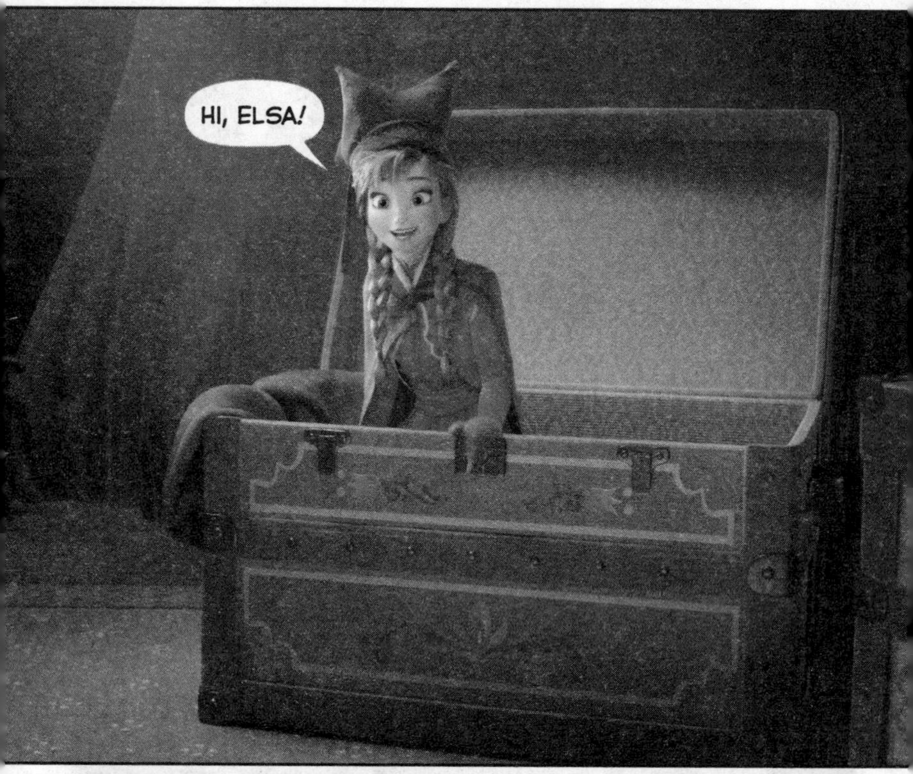
HI, ELSA!

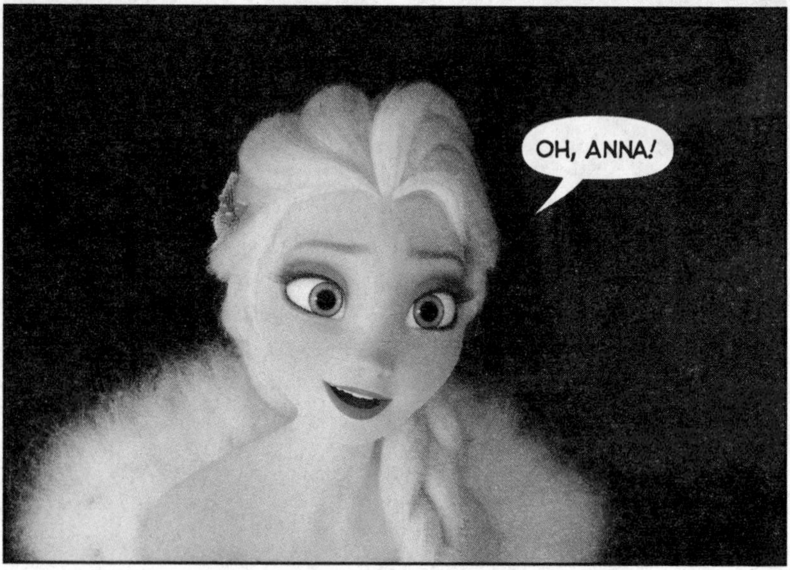
OH, ANNA!

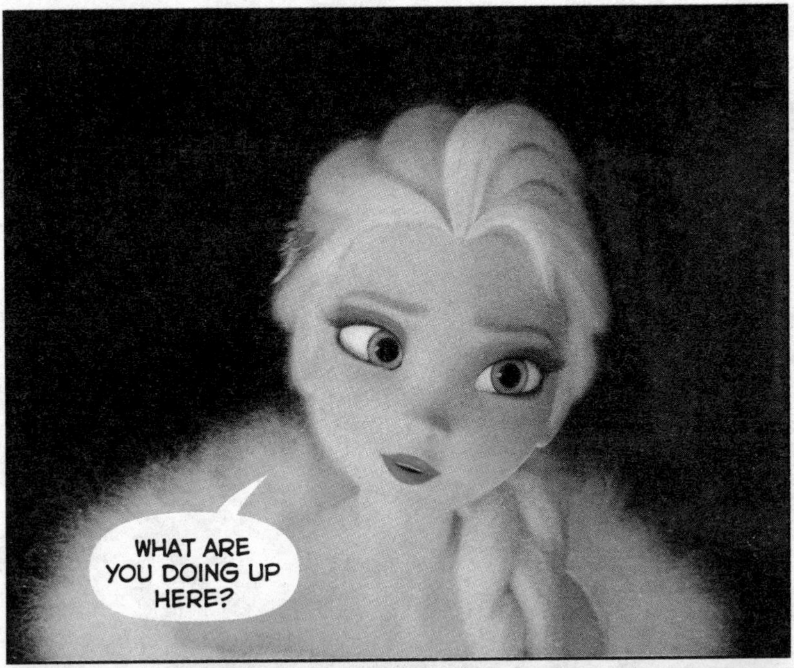
WHAT ARE YOU DOING UP HERE?

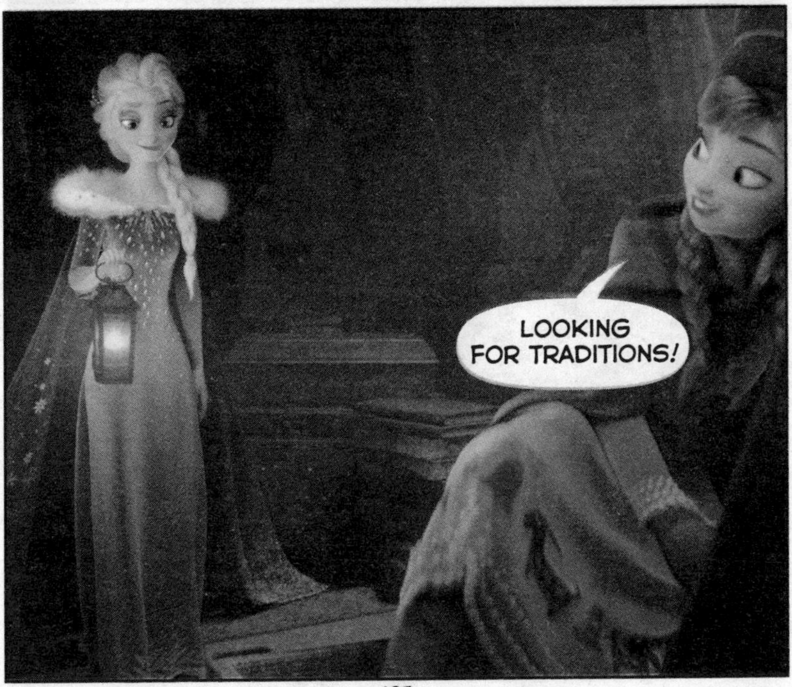
LOOKING FOR TRADITIONS!

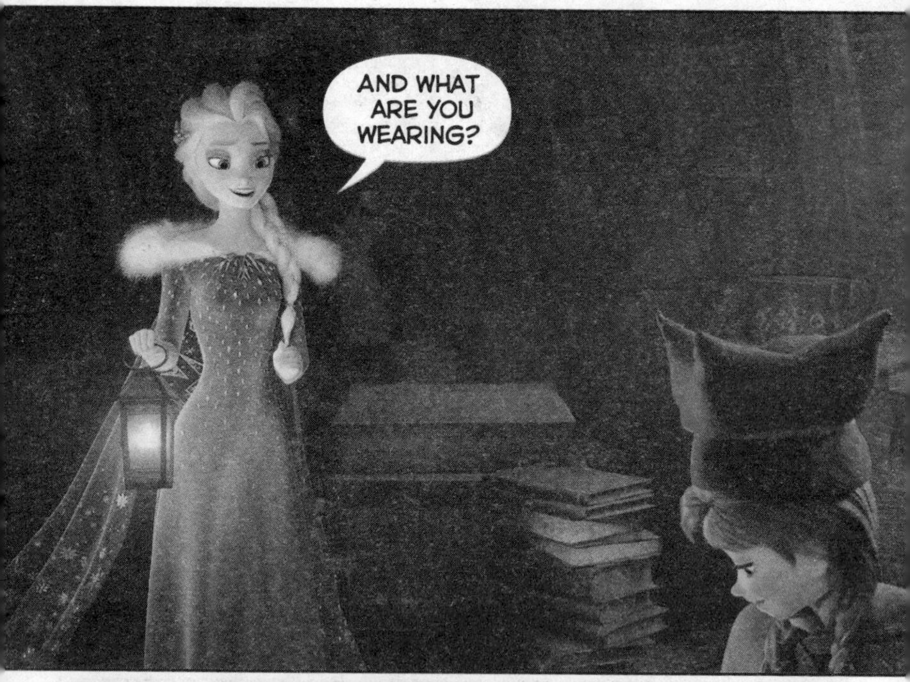
AND WHAT ARE YOU WEARING?

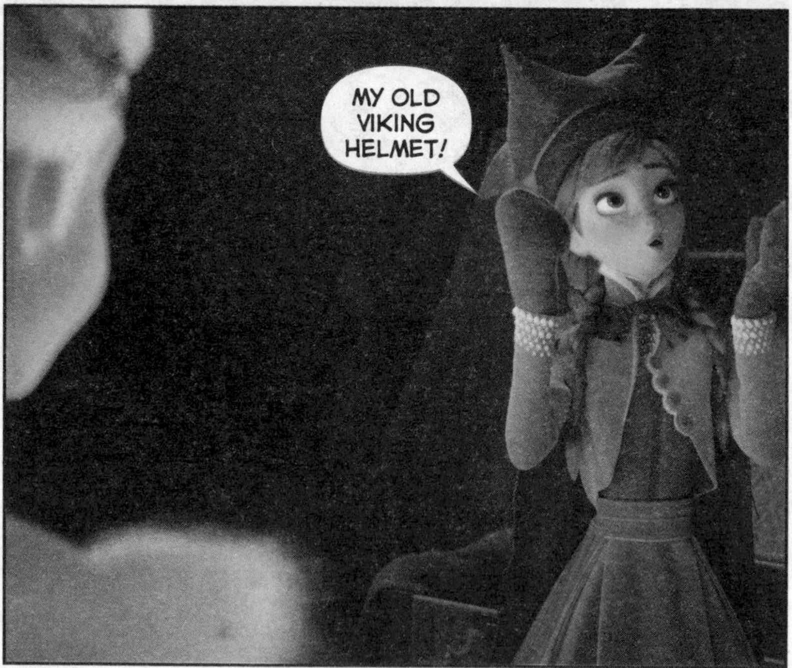
MY OLD VIKING HELMET!

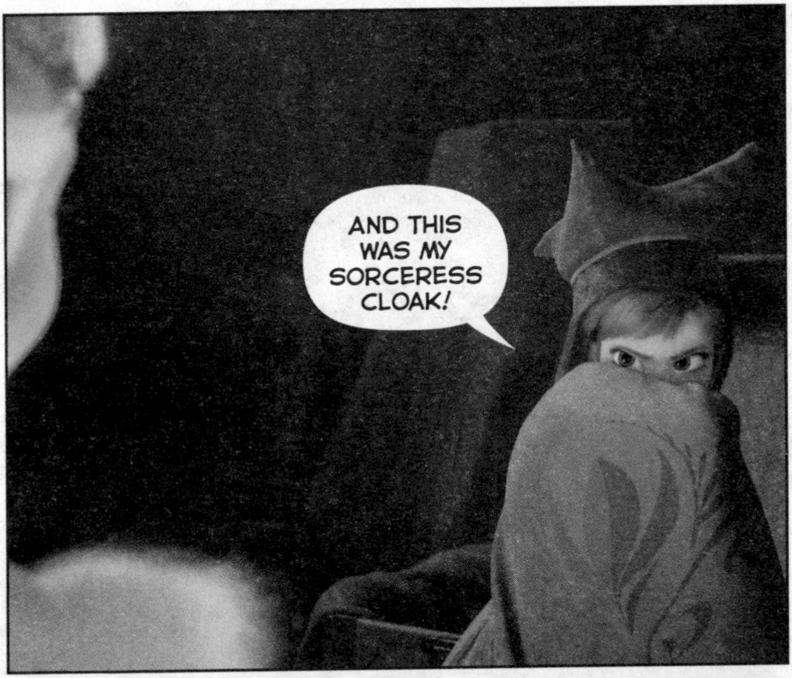
AND THIS WAS MY SORCERESS CLOAK!

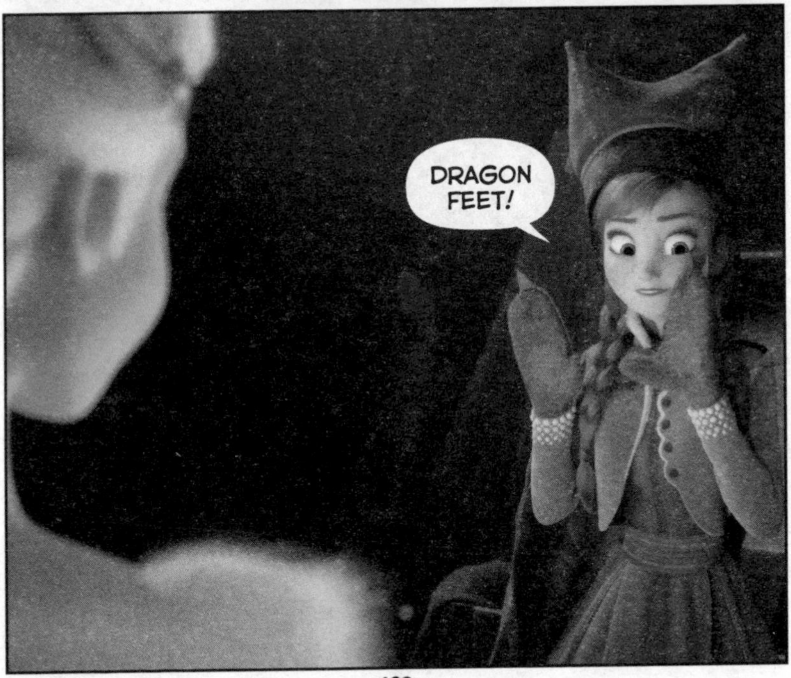
DRAGON FEET!

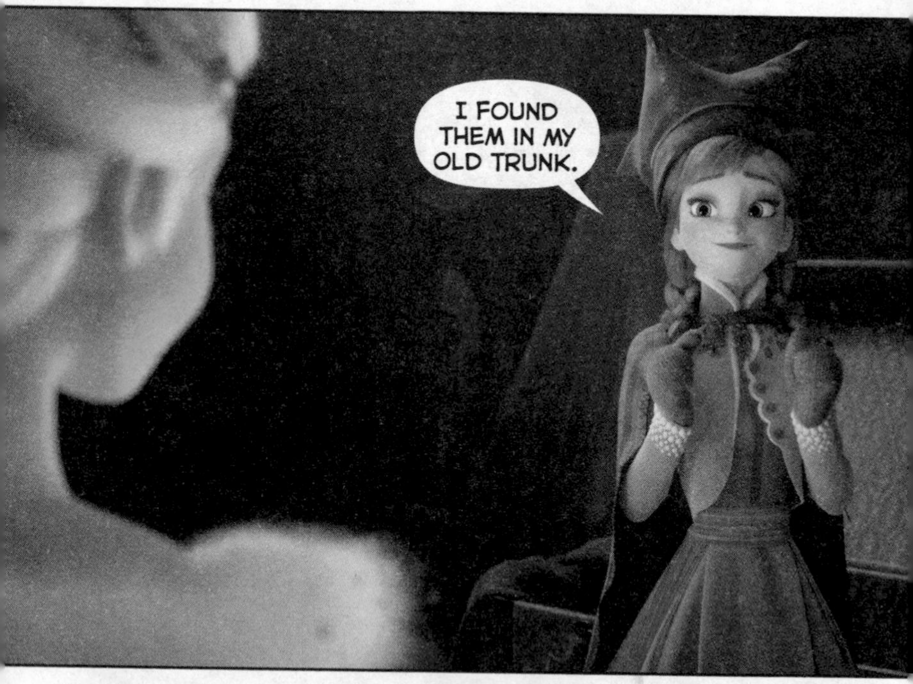
I FOUND THEM IN MY OLD TRUNK.

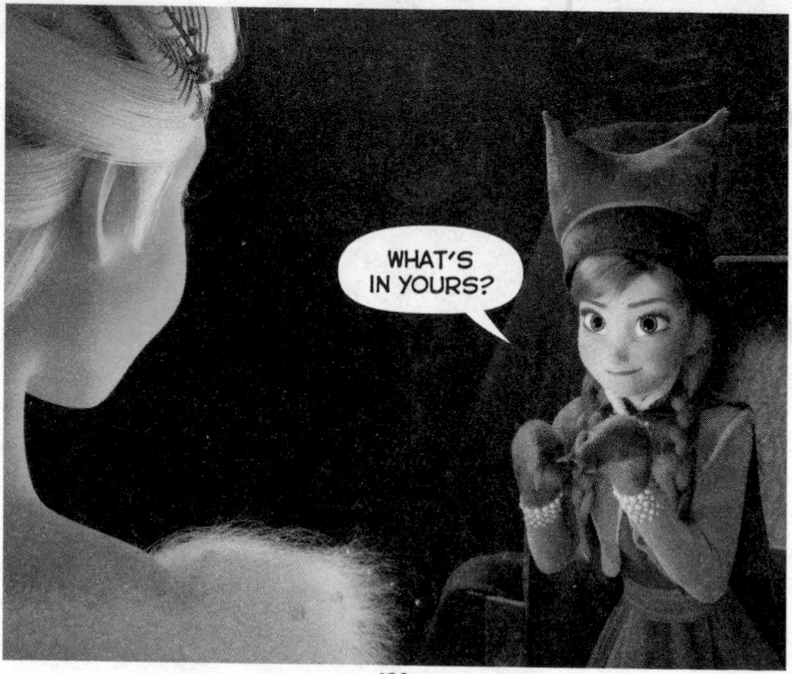
WHAT'S IN YOURS?

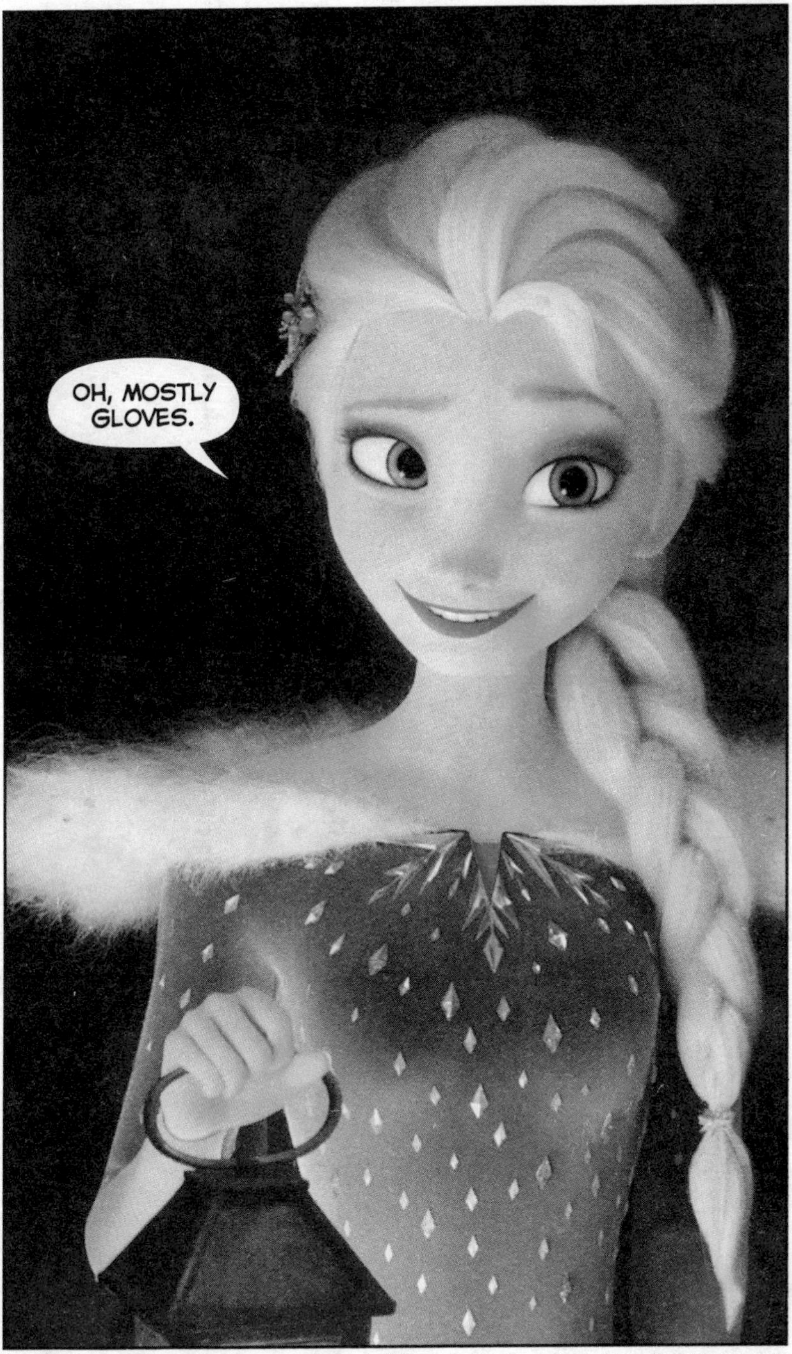
OH, MOSTLY GLOVES.

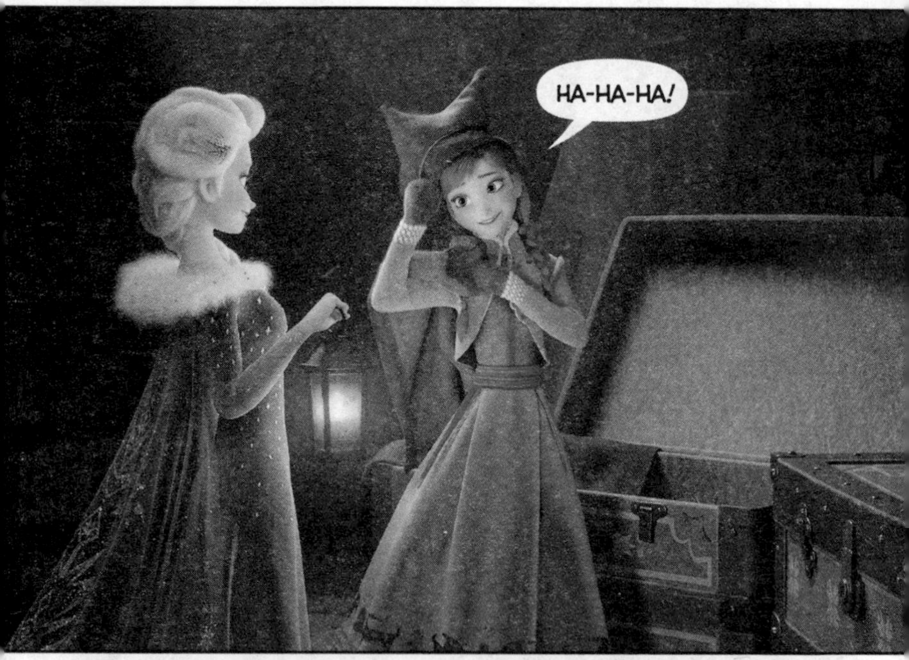
HA-HA-HA!

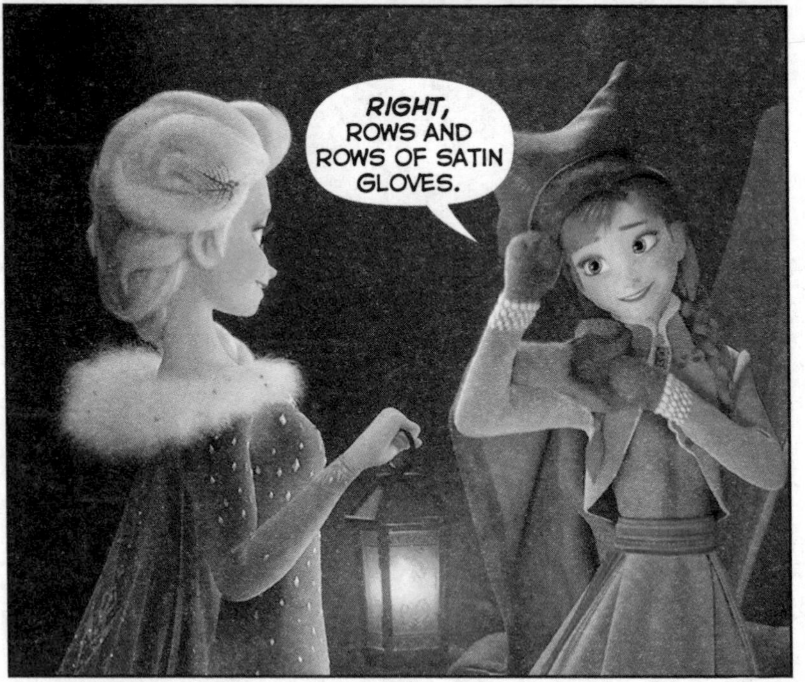
RIGHT, ROWS AND ROWS OF SATIN GLOVES.

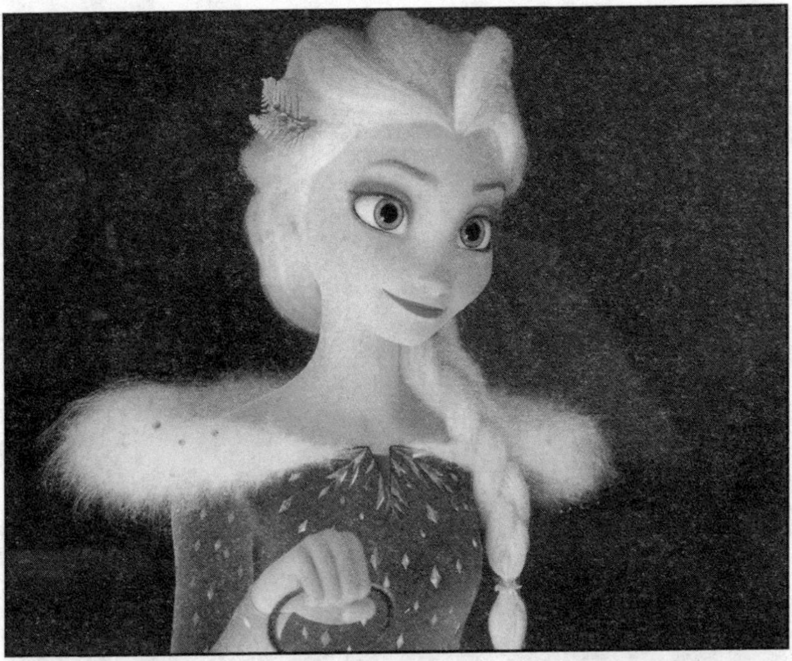

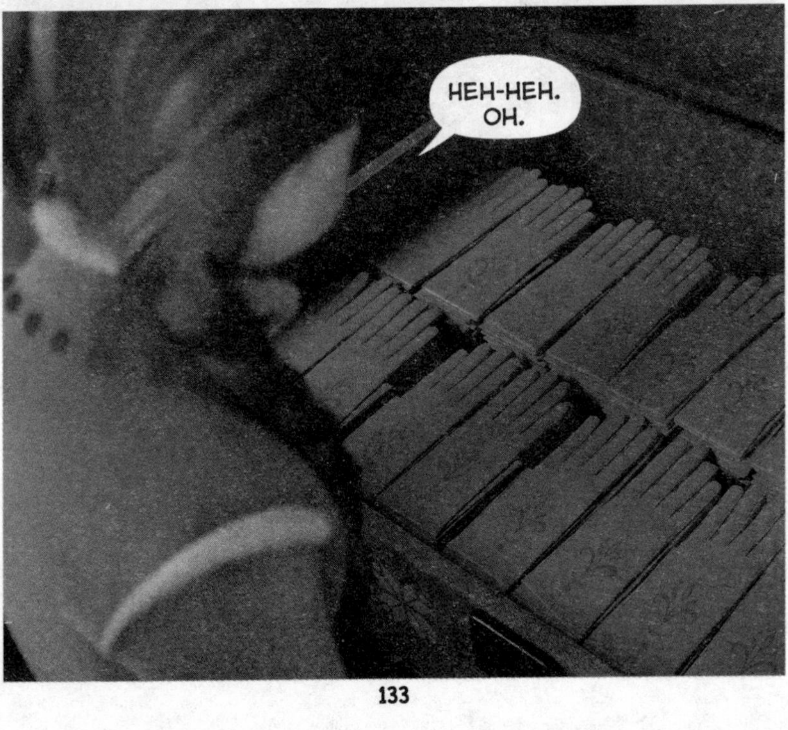
HEH-HEH.
OH.

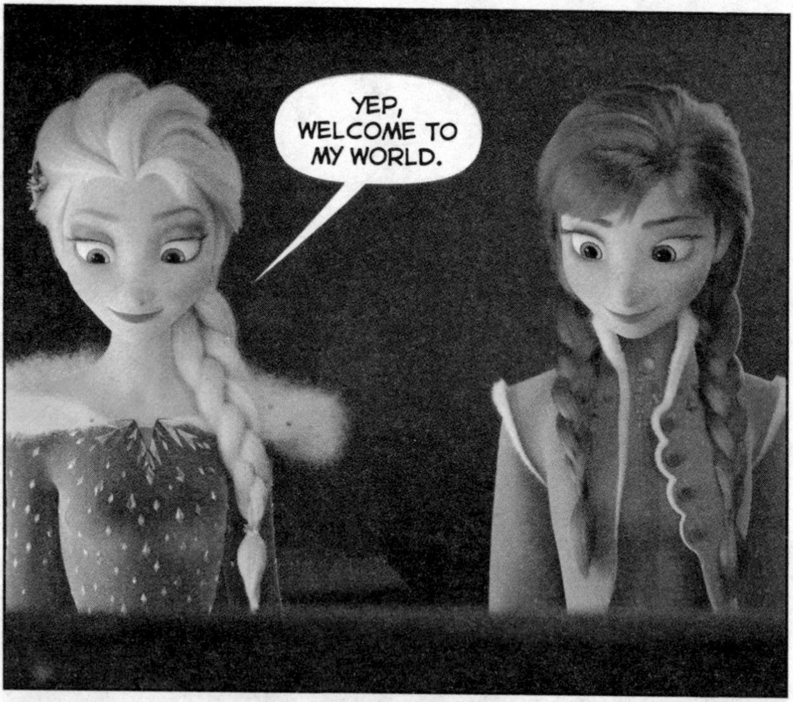
YEP, WELCOME TO MY WORLD.

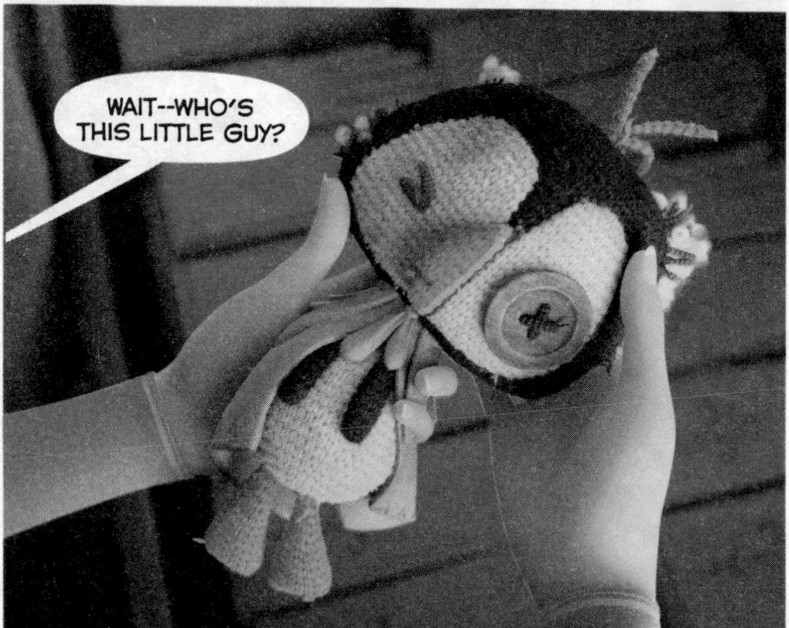
WAIT--WHO'S THIS LITTLE GUY?

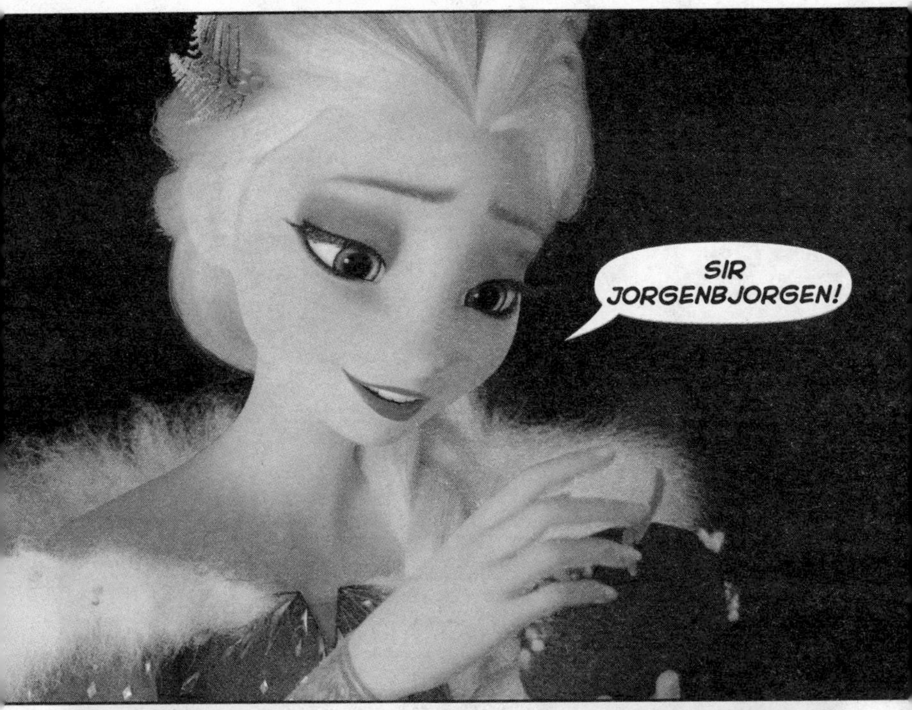
SIR JORGENBJORGEN!

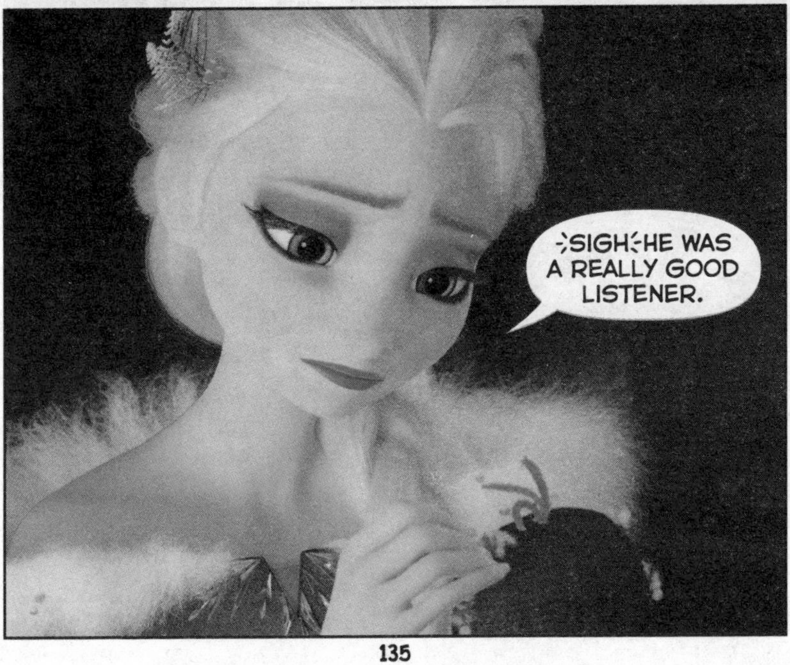
SIGH HE WAS A REALLY GOOD LISTENER.

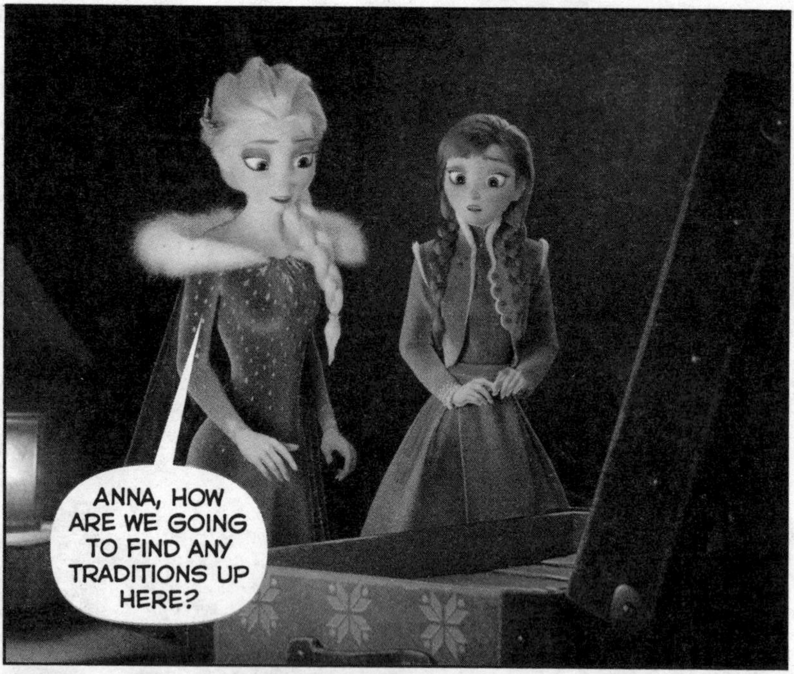
ANNA, HOW ARE WE GOING TO FIND ANY TRADITIONS UP HERE?

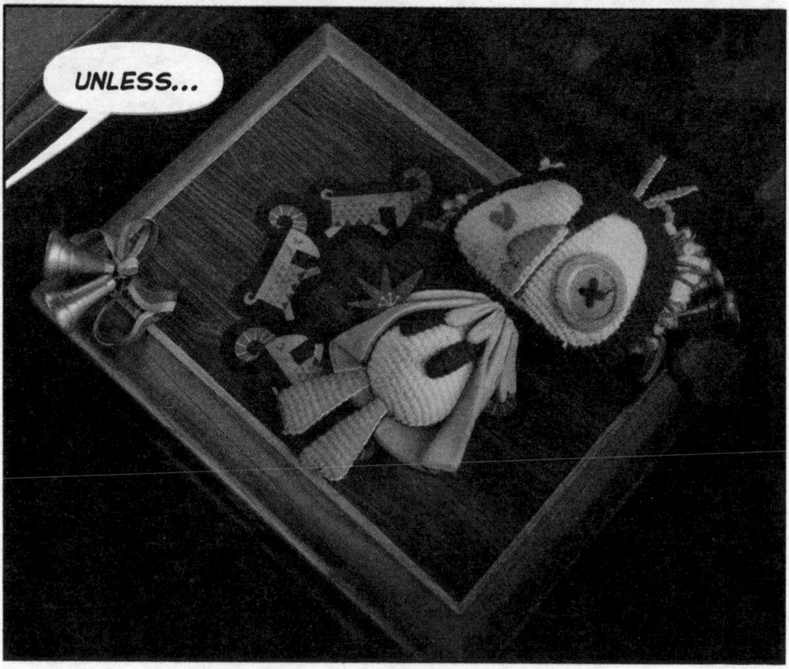
UNLESS...

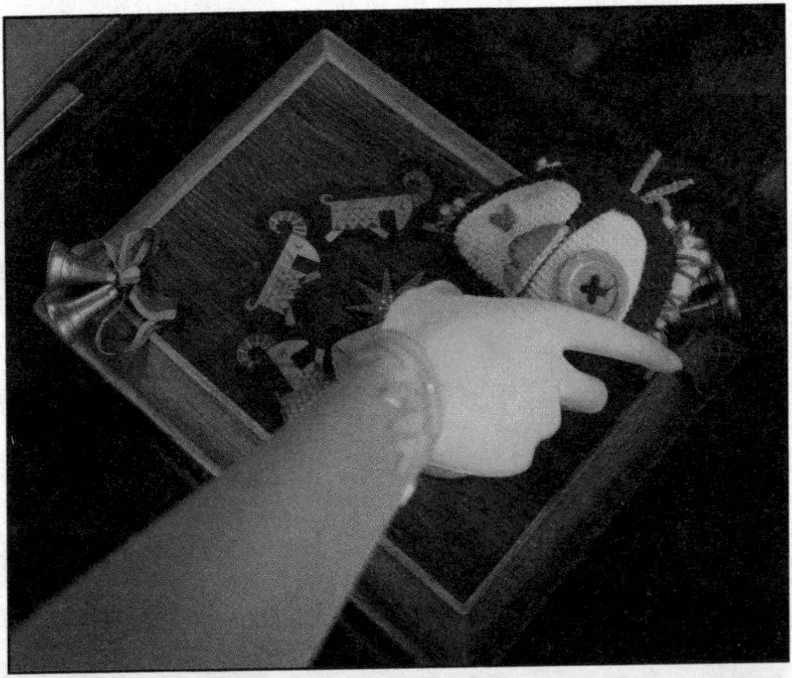

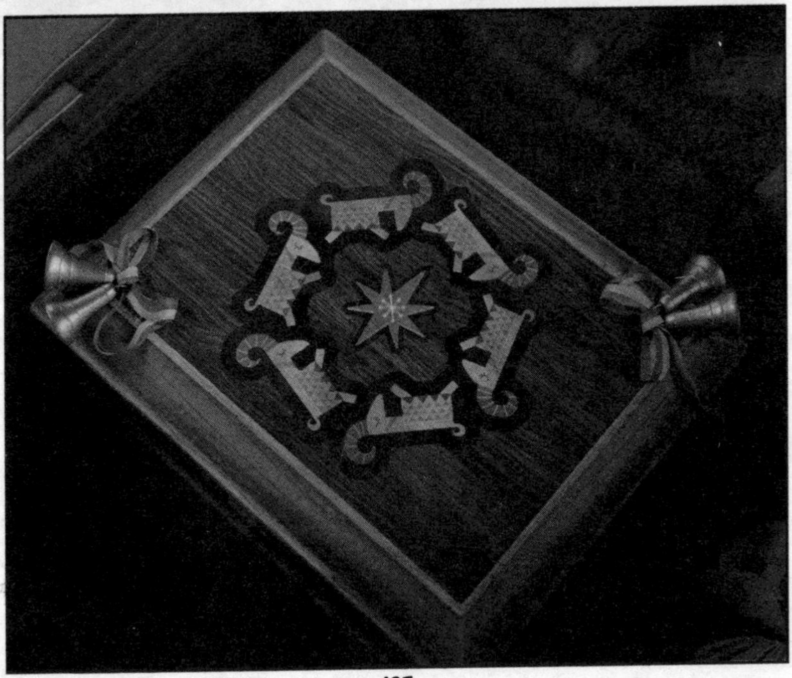

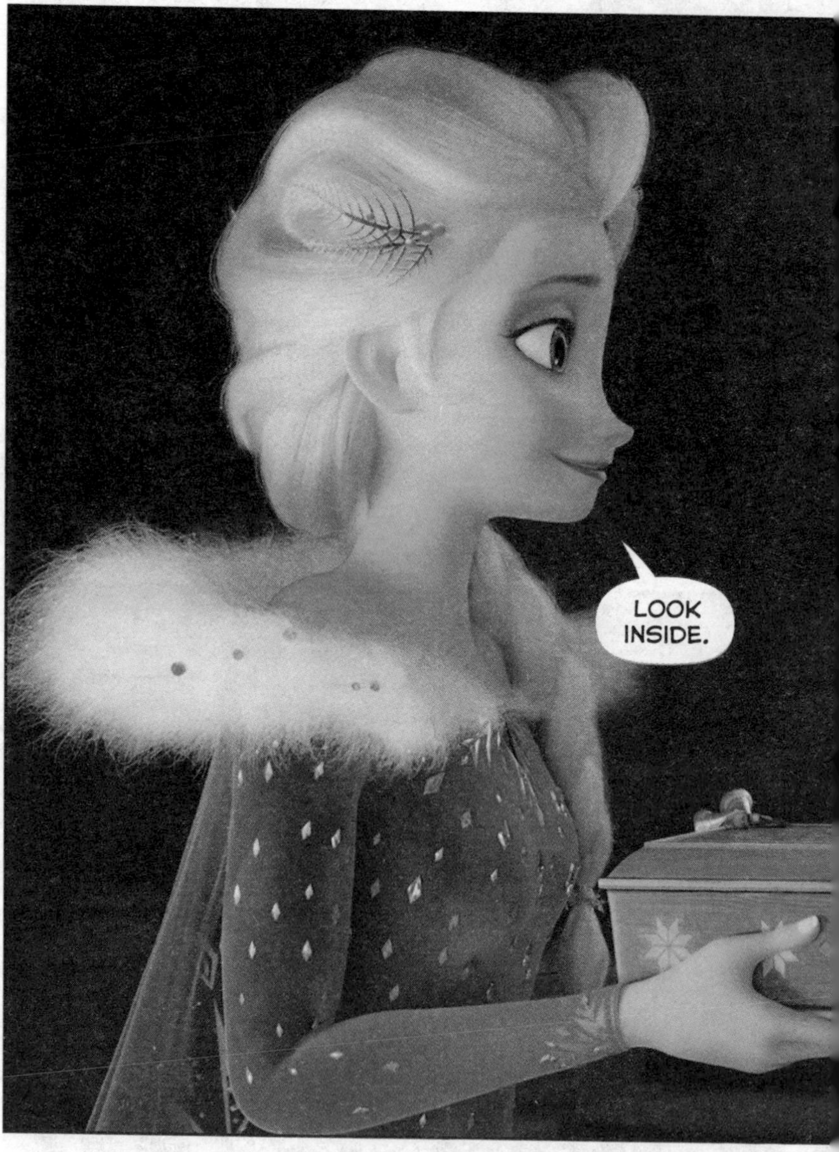
LOOK
INSIDE.

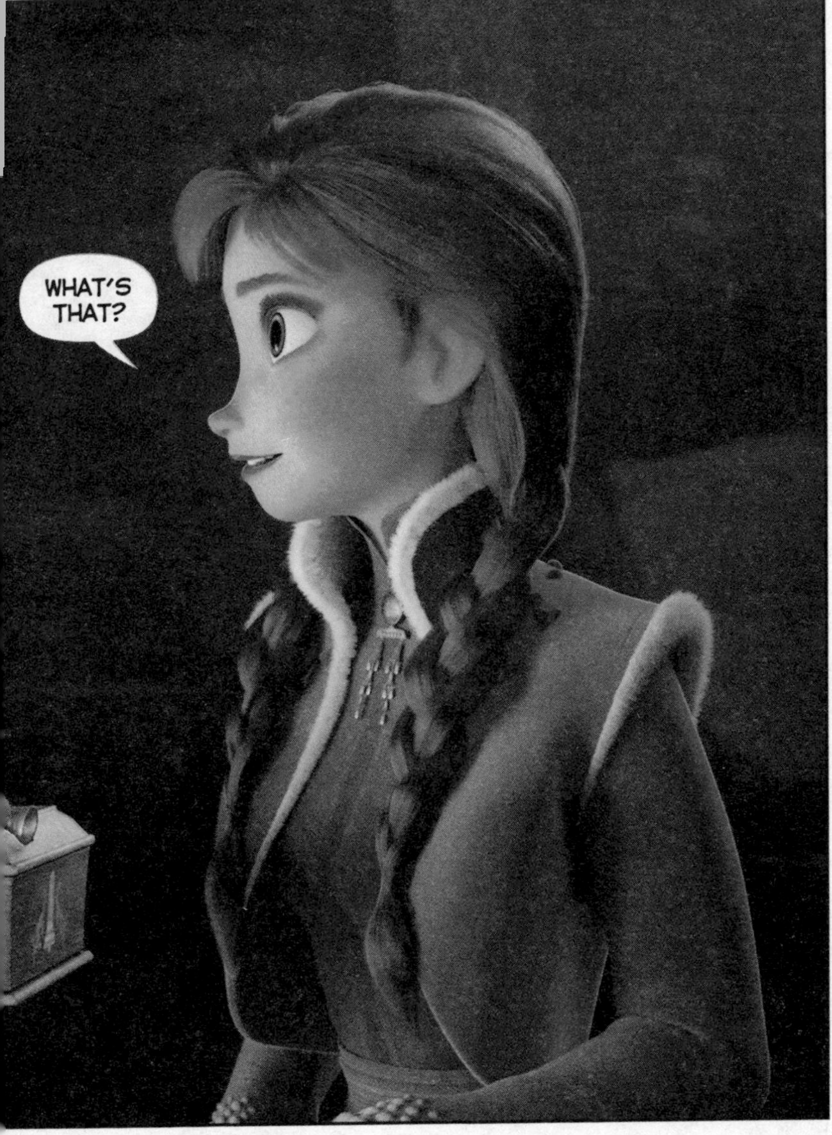
WHAT'S THAT?

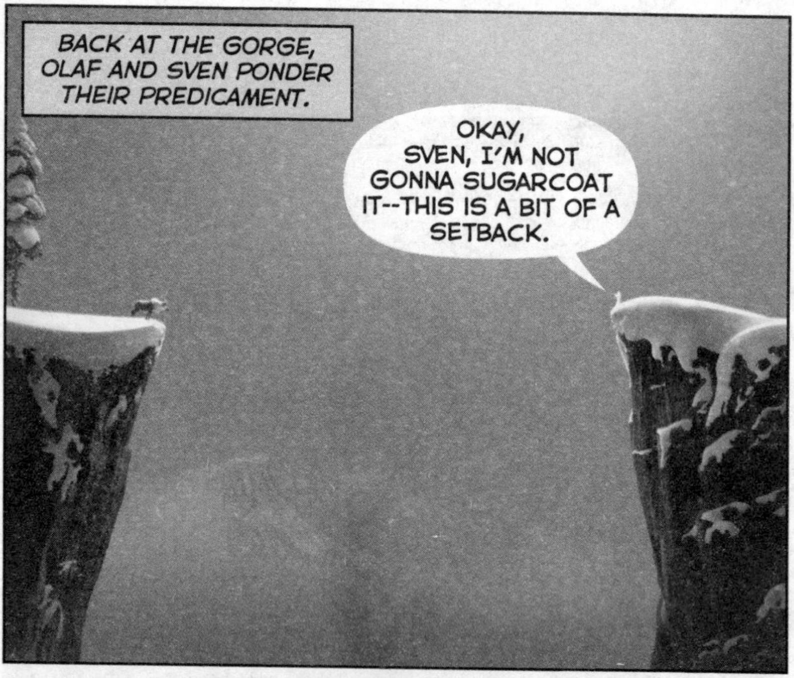
BACK AT THE GORGE, OLAF AND SVEN PONDER THEIR PREDICAMENT.
OKAY, SVEN, I'M NOT GONNA SUGARCOAT IT--THIS IS A BIT OF A SETBACK.

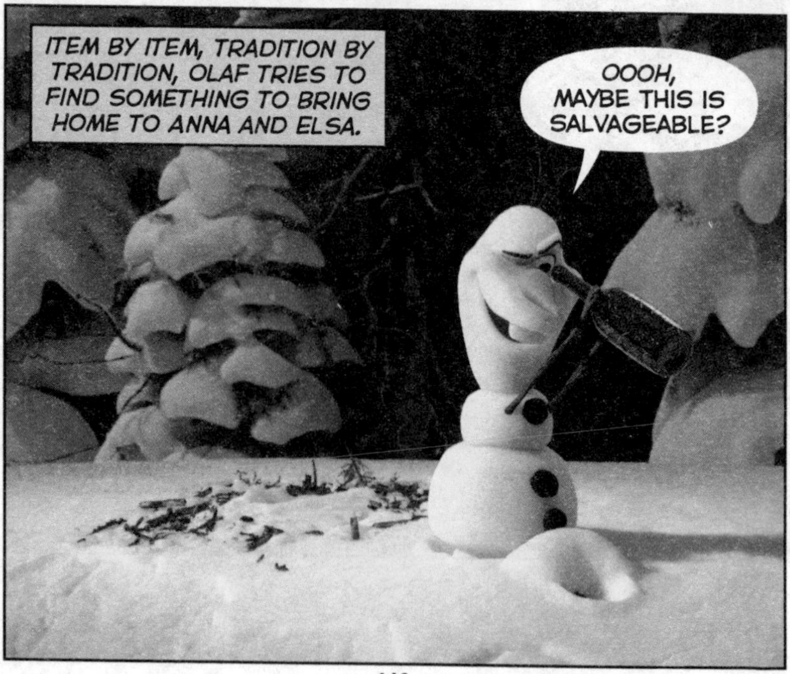
ITEM BY ITEM, TRADITION BY TRADITION, OLAF TRIES TO FIND SOMETHING TO BRING HOME TO ANNA AND ELSA.
OOOH, MAYBE THIS IS SALVAGEABLE?

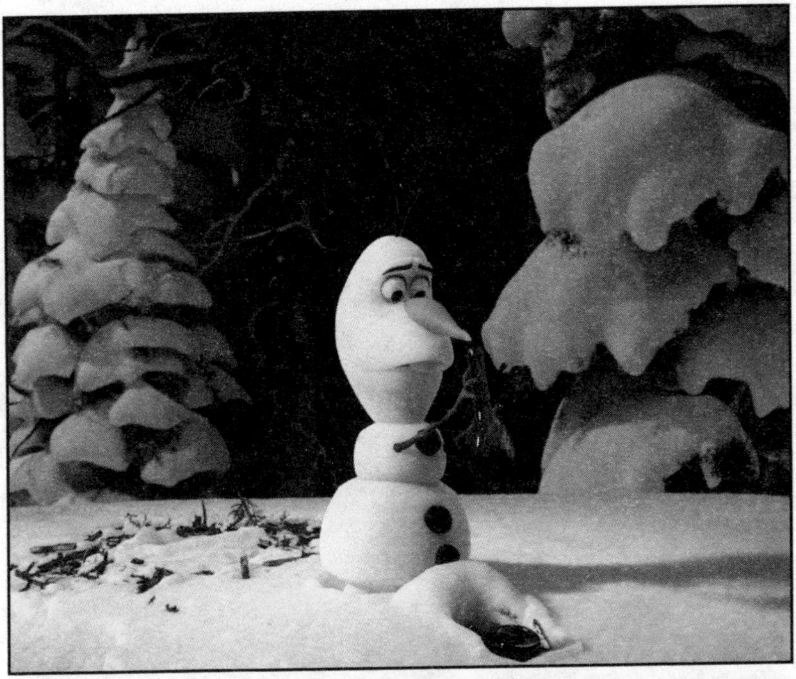

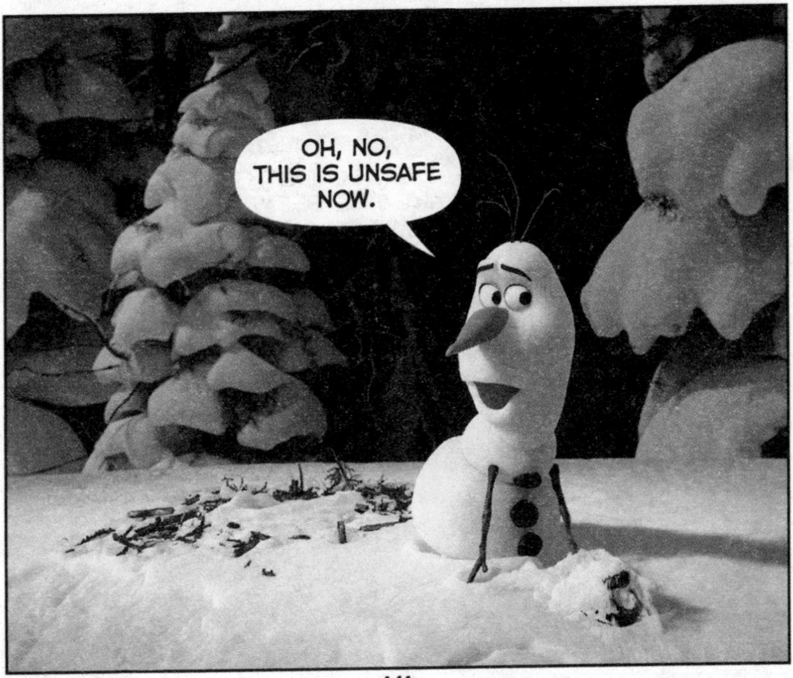
OH, NO, THIS IS UNSAFE NOW.

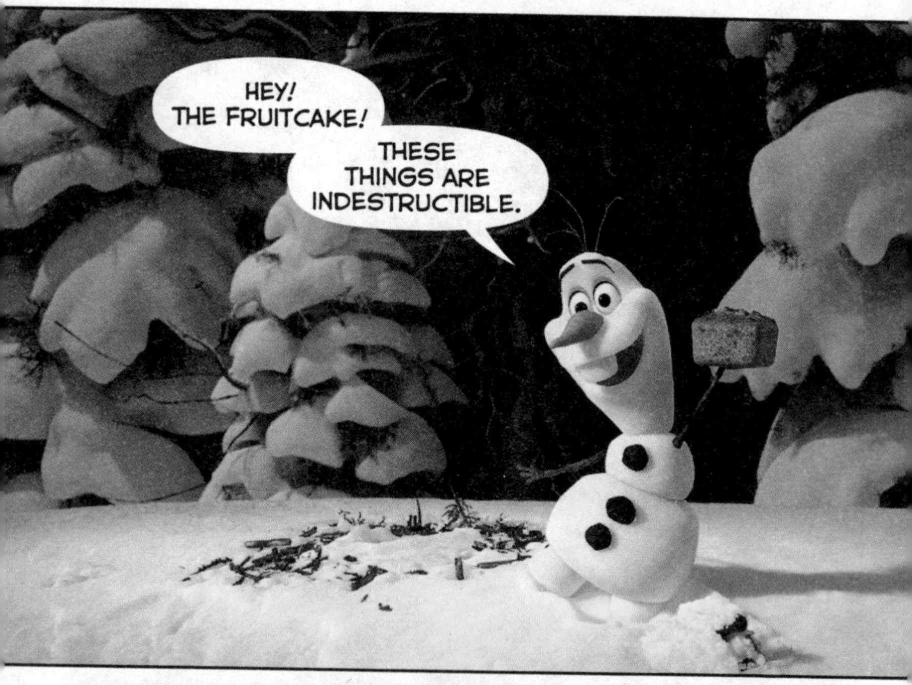
HEY!
THE FRUITCAKE!
THESE THINGS ARE INDESTRUCTIBLE.

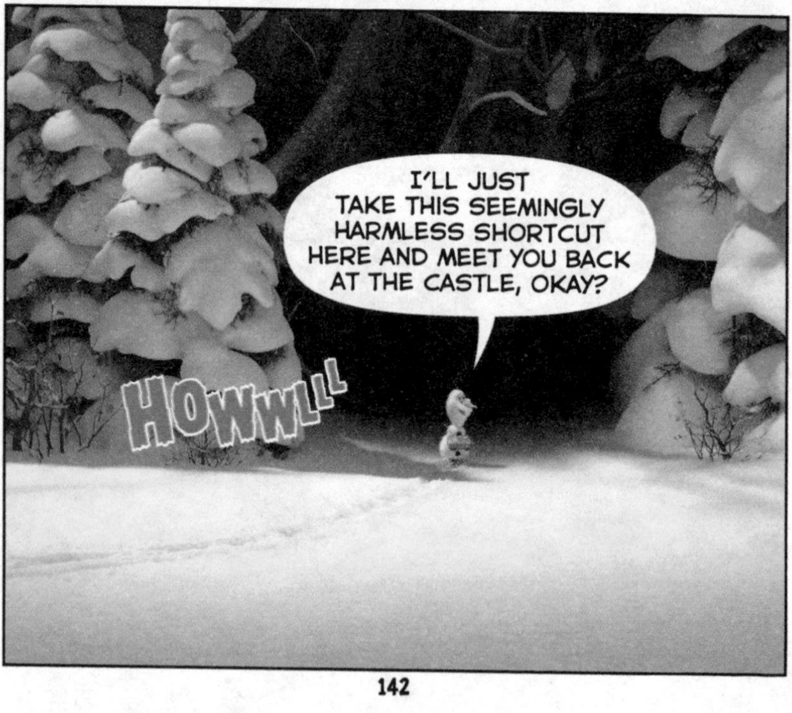
I'LL JUST TAKE THIS SEEMINGLY HARMLESS SHORTCUT HERE AND MEET YOU BACK AT THE CASTLE, OKAY?
HOWWLLL

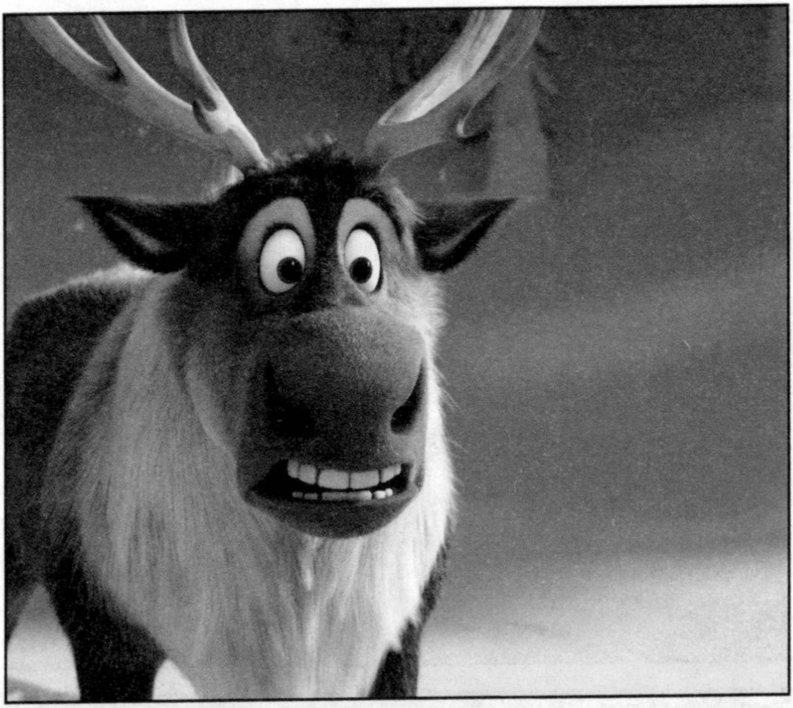

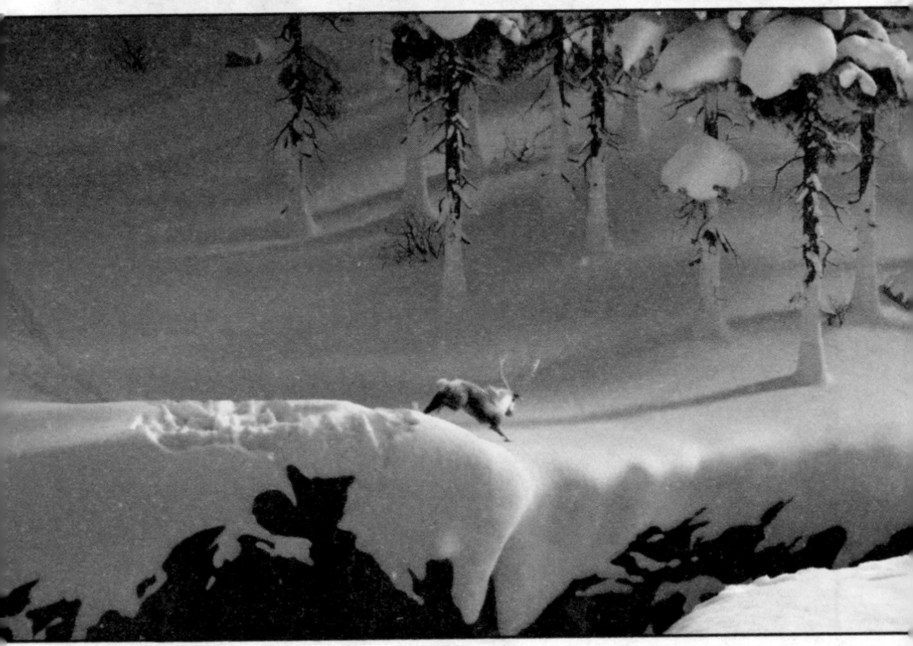

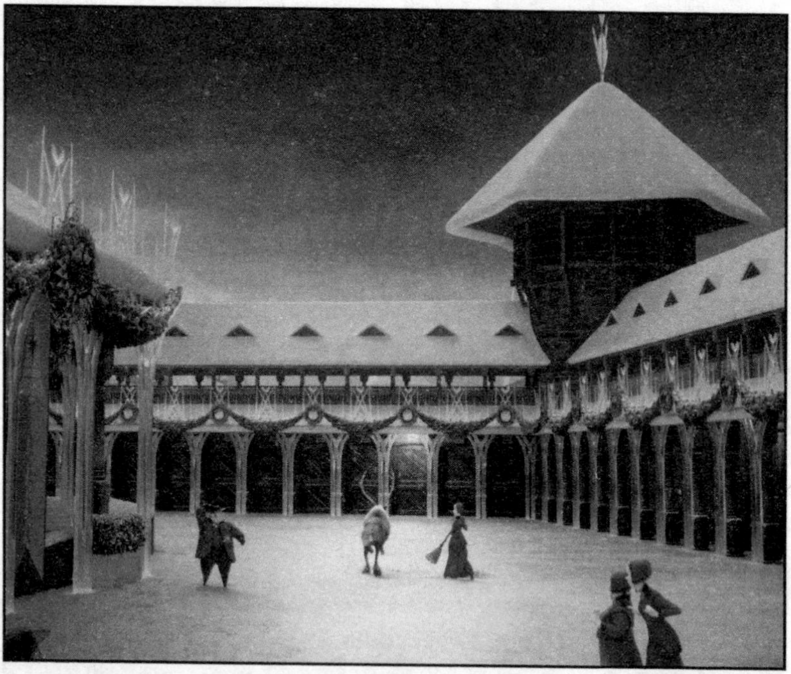

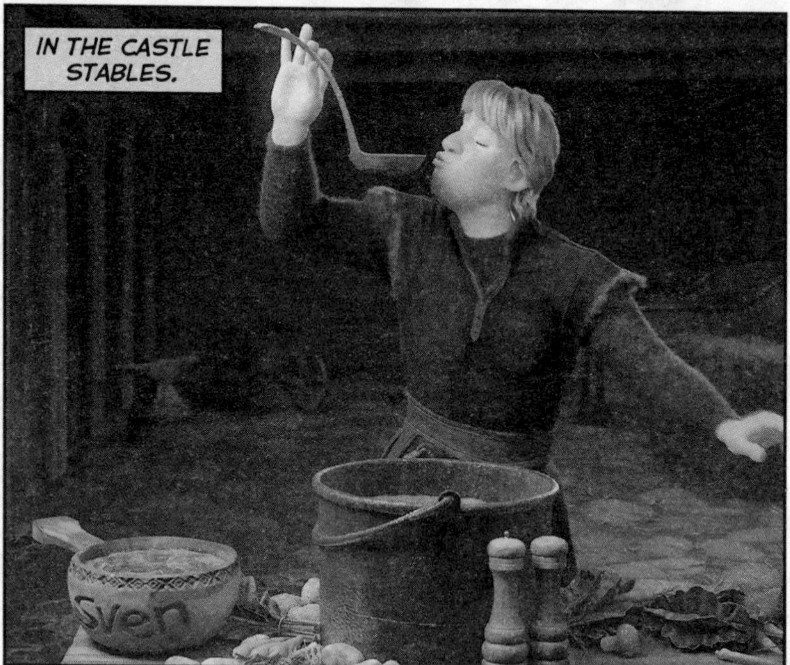
IN THE CASTLE STABLES.
Sven

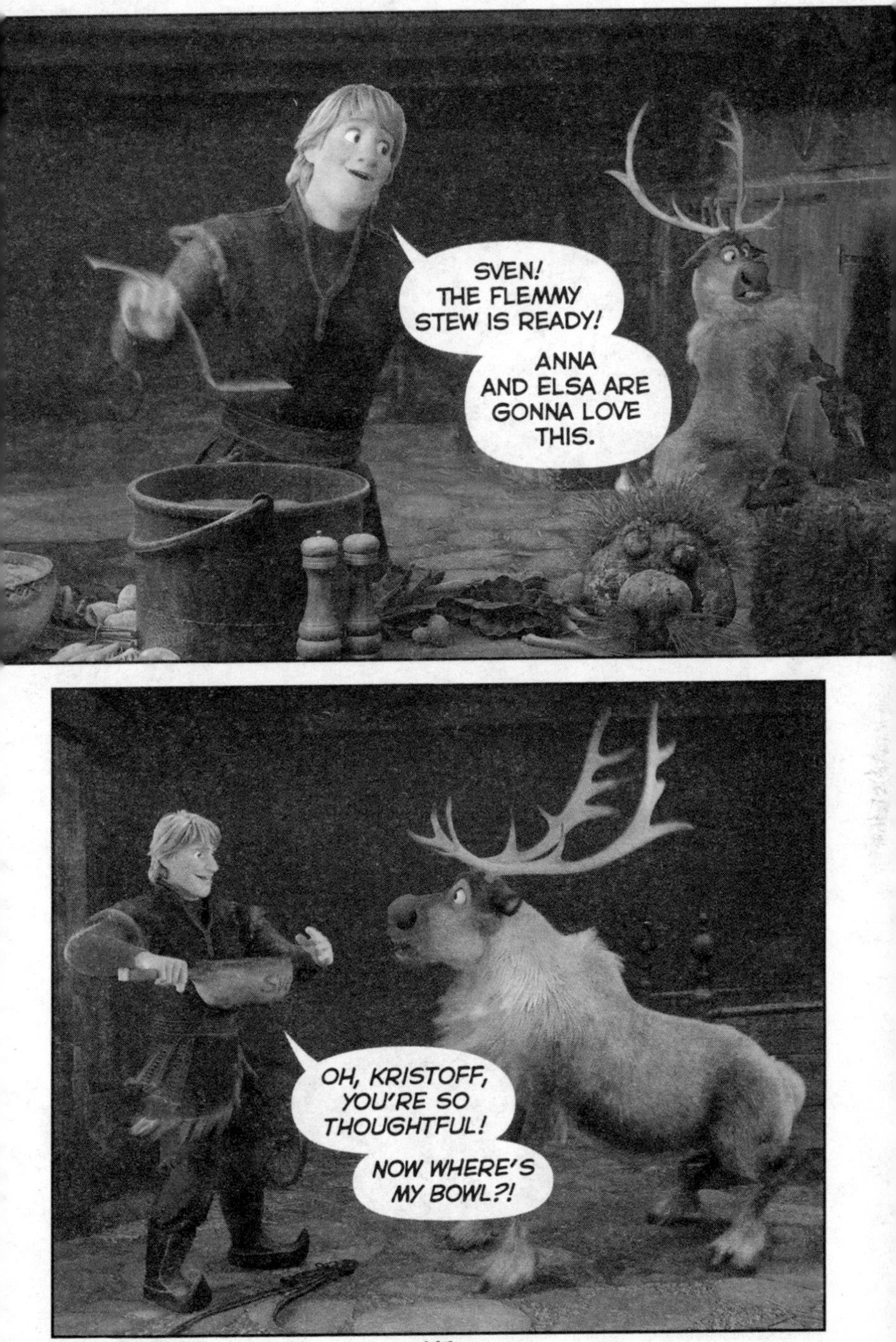
SVEN! THE FLEMMY STEW IS READY!
ANNA AND ELSA ARE GONNA LOVE THIS.
OH, KRISTOFF, YOU'RE SO THOUGHTFUL!
NOW WHERE'S MY BOWL?!

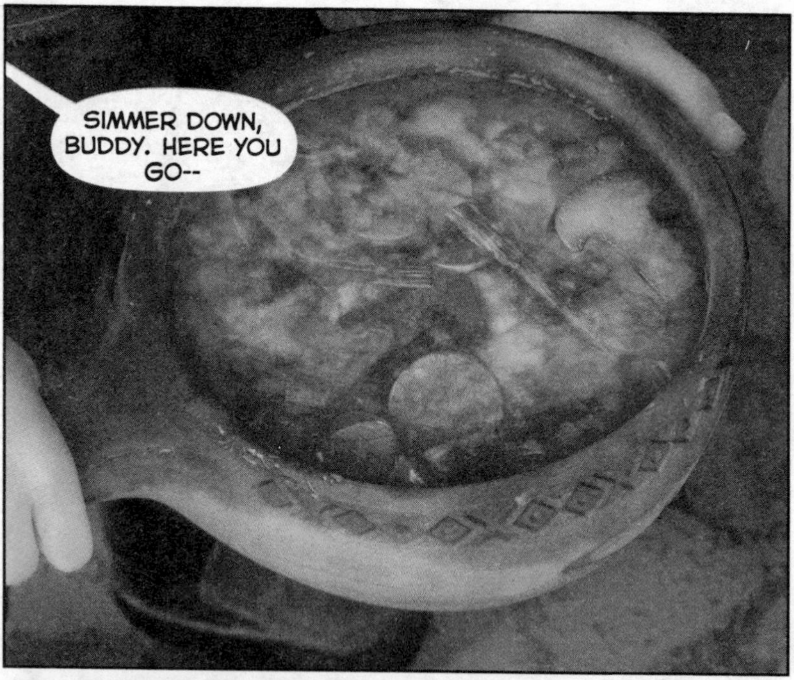
SIMMER DOWN, BUDDY. HERE YOU GO--

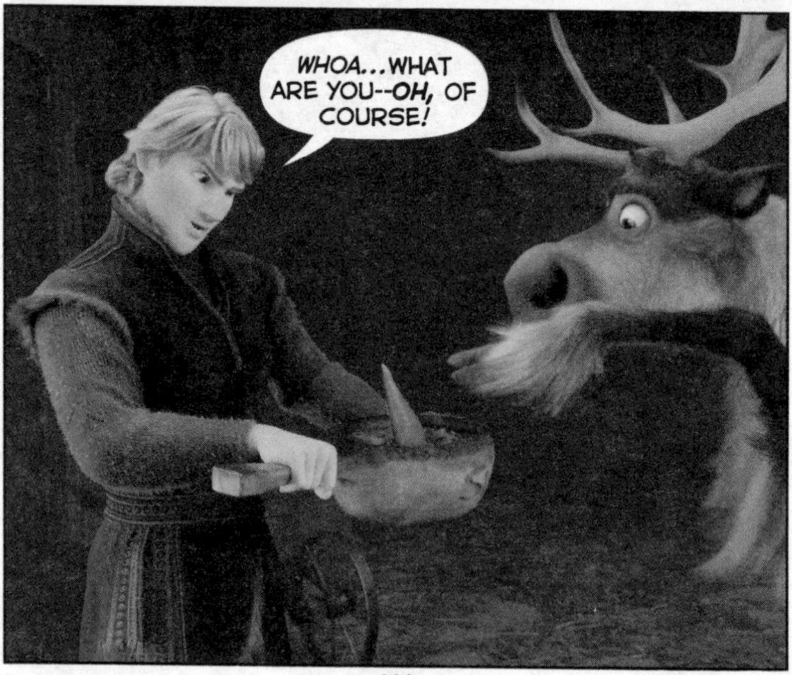
*WHOA...*WHAT ARE YOU--***OH,*** OF COURSE!

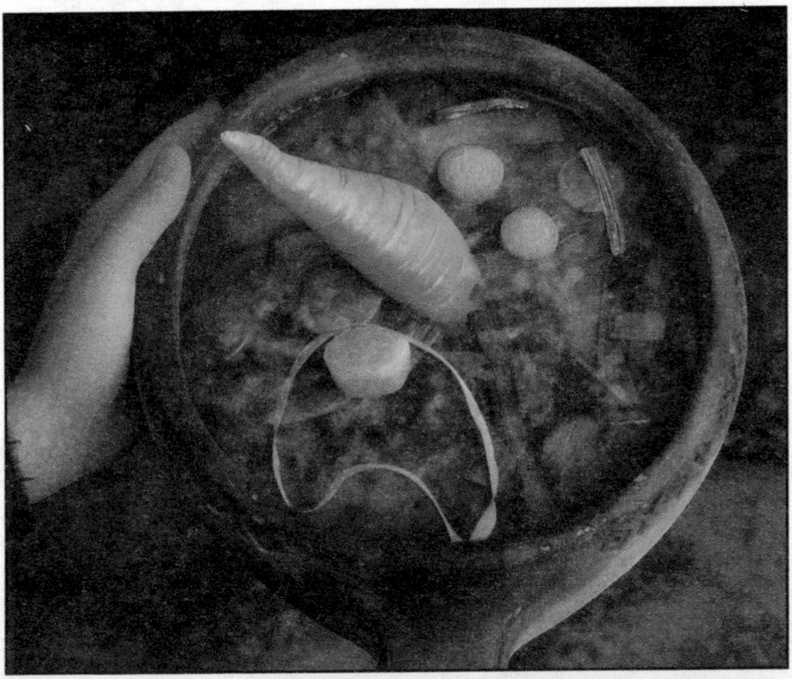

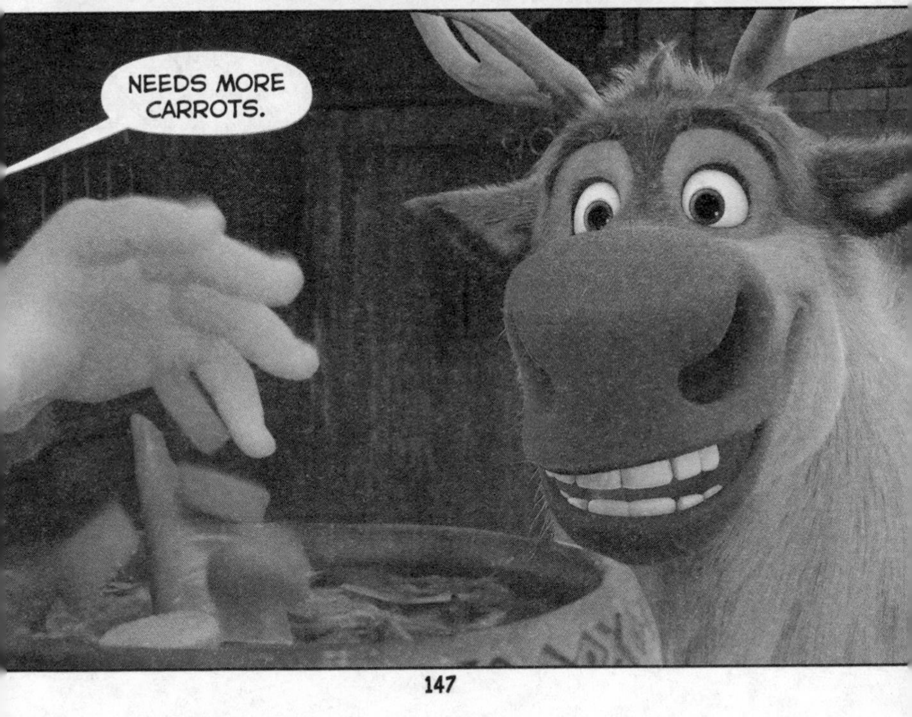
NEEDS MORE CARROTS.

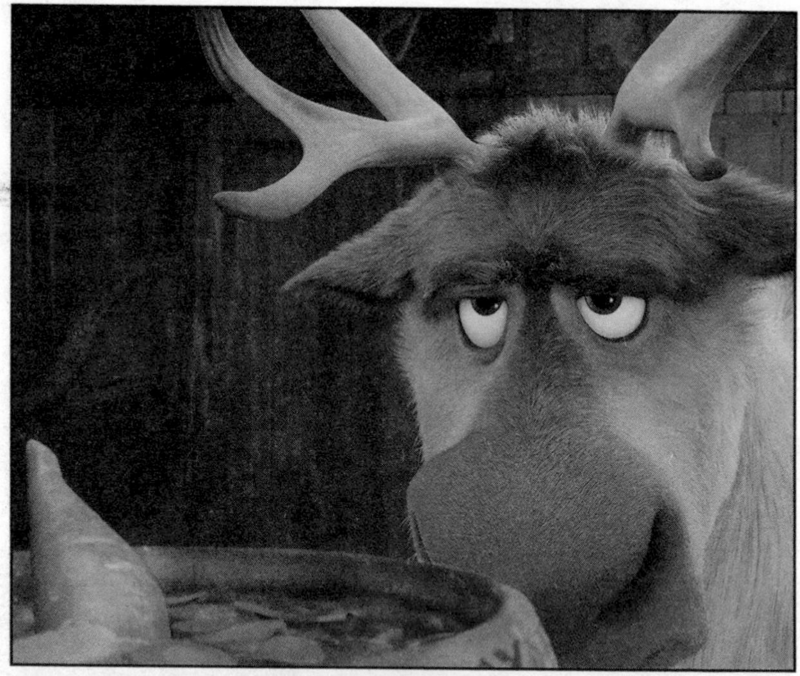

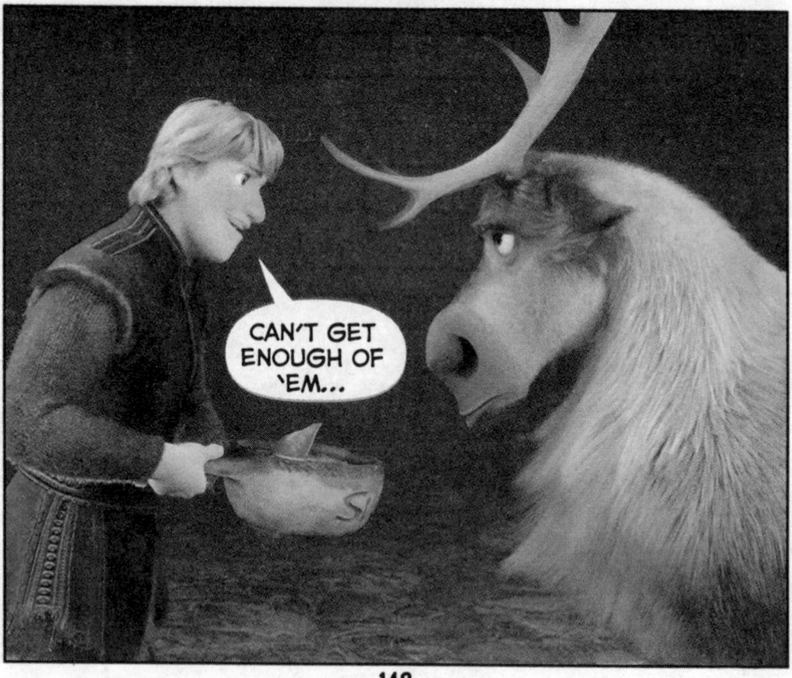
CAN'T GET ENOUGH OF 'EM...

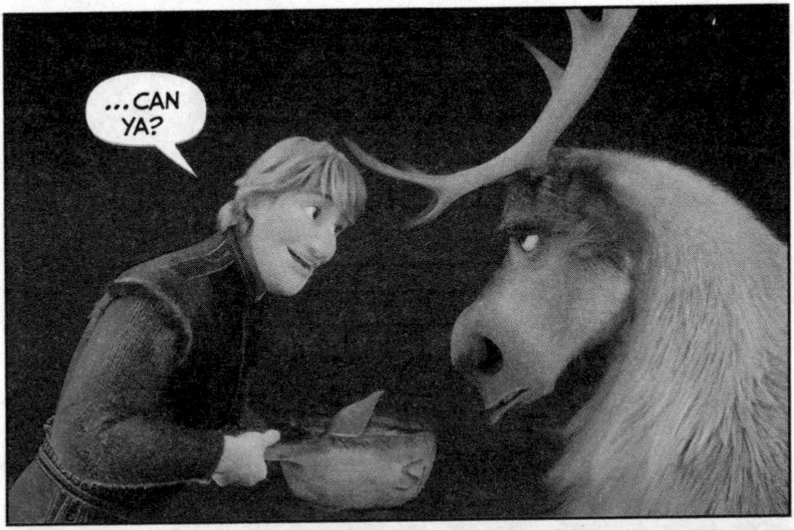
...CAN YA?

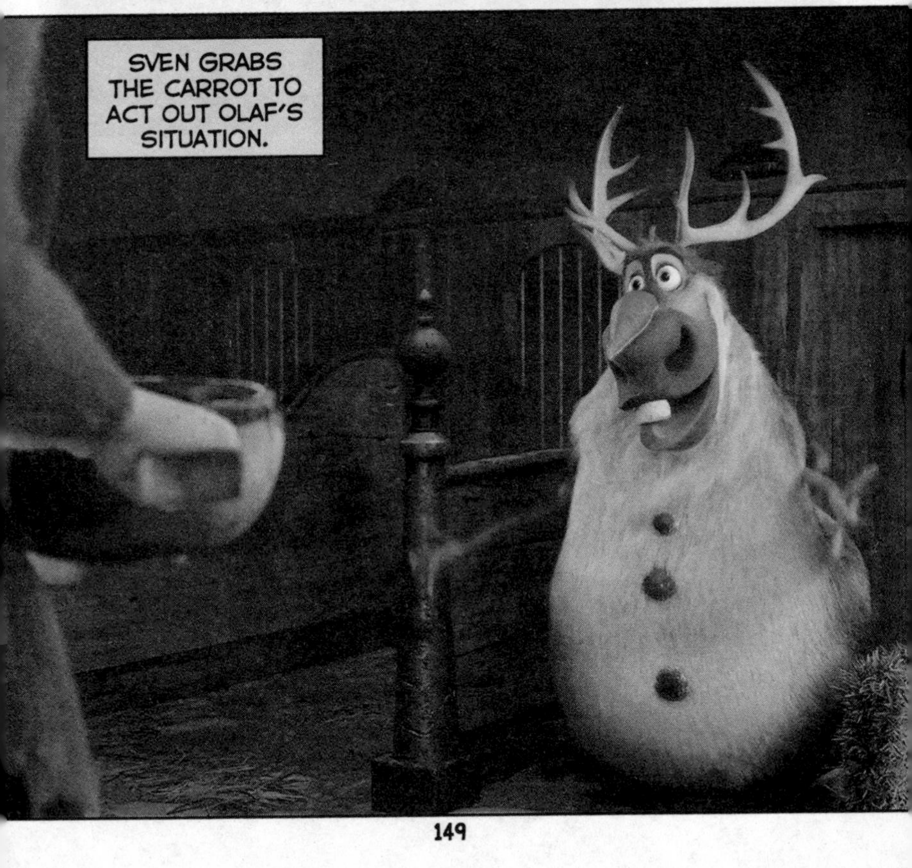
SVEN GRABS THE CARROT TO ACT OUT OLAF'S SITUATION.

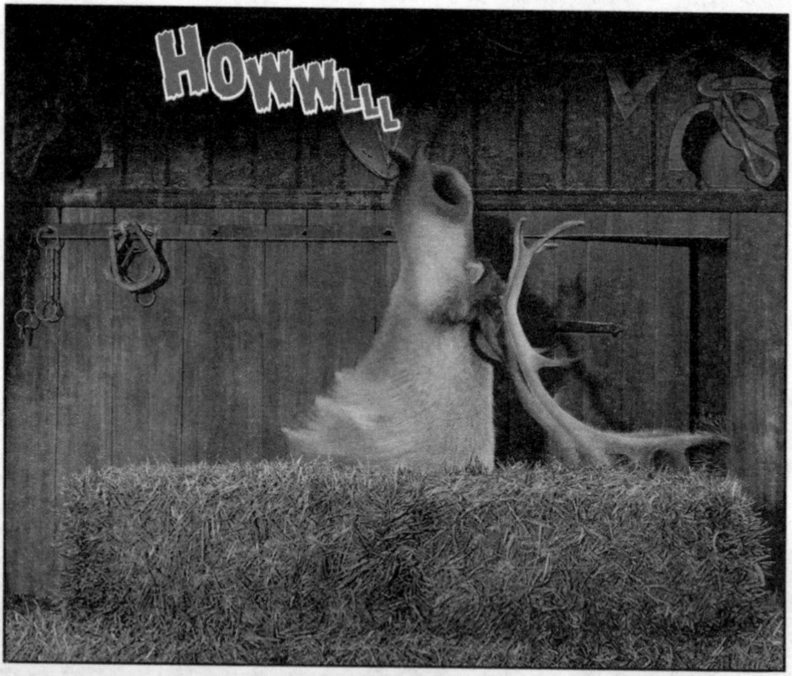
HOWWLLL

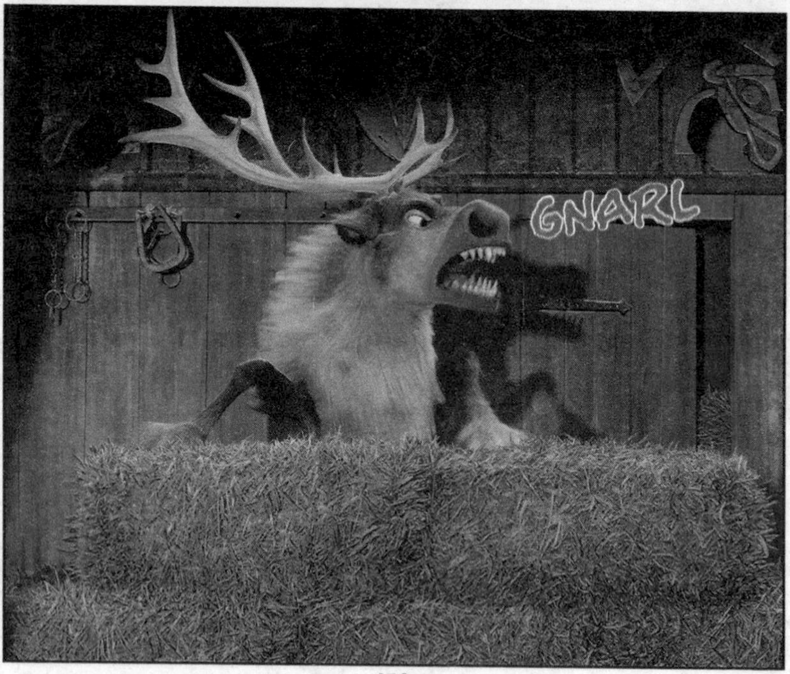
GNARL

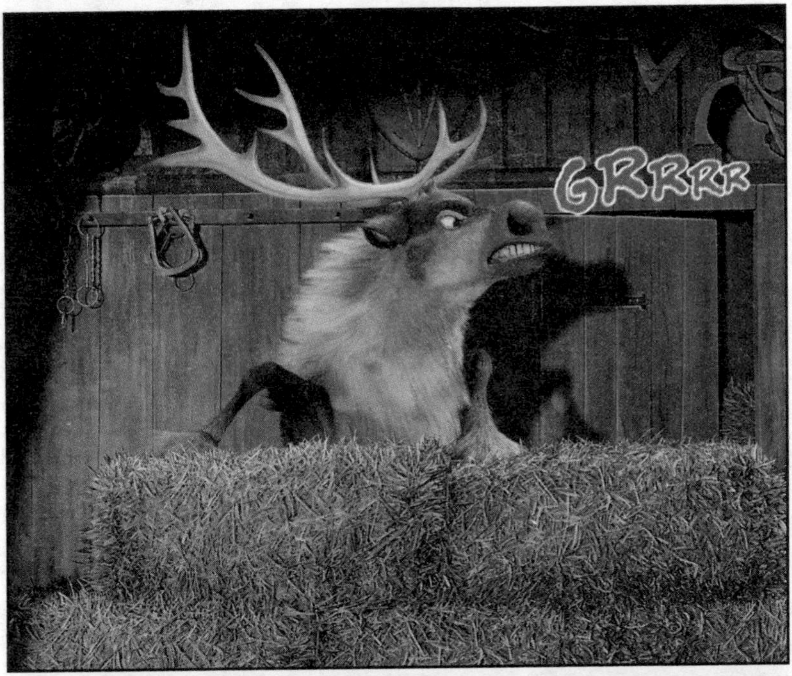
GRRRR

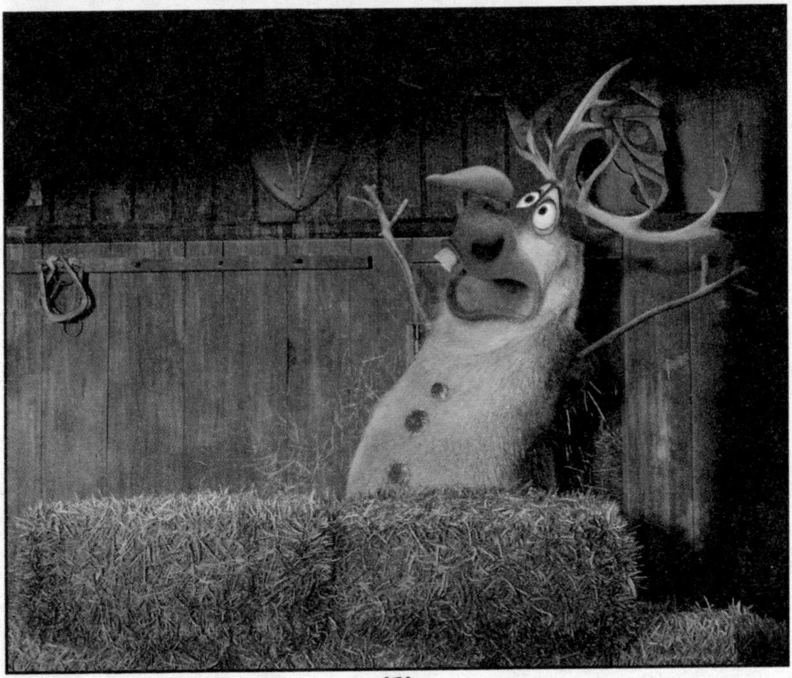

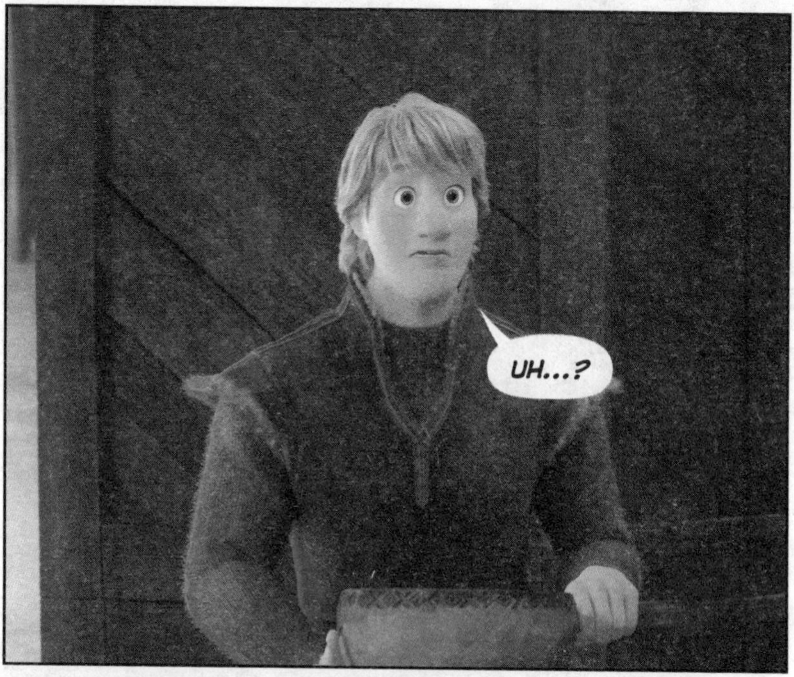
UH...?

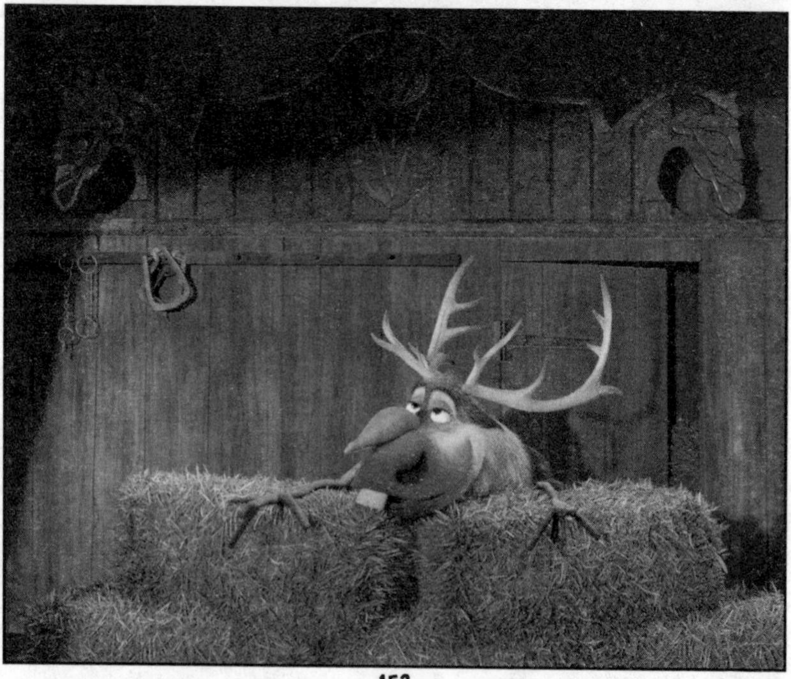

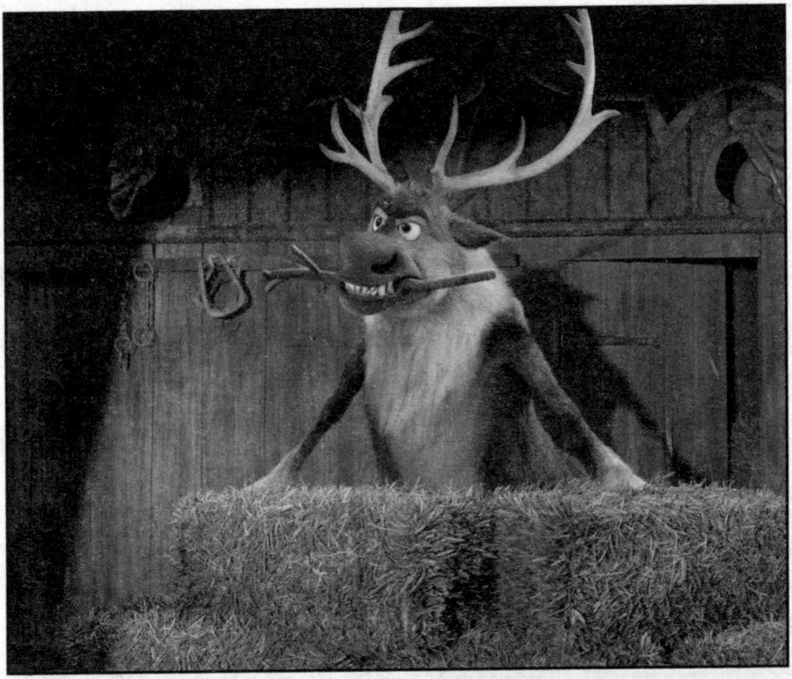

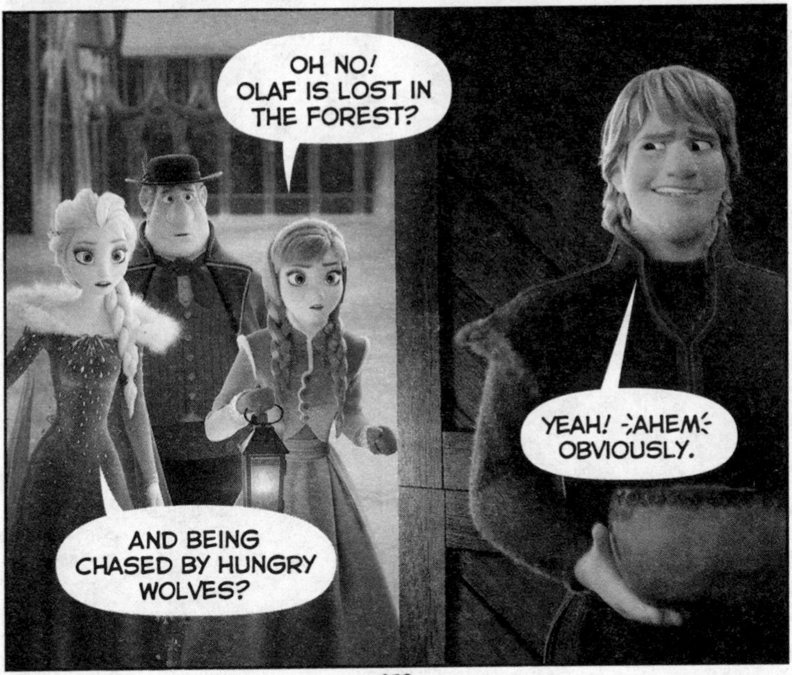
OH NO! OLAF IS LOST IN THE FOREST?
AND BEING CHASED BY HUNGRY WOLVES?
YEAH! AHEM OBVIOUSLY.

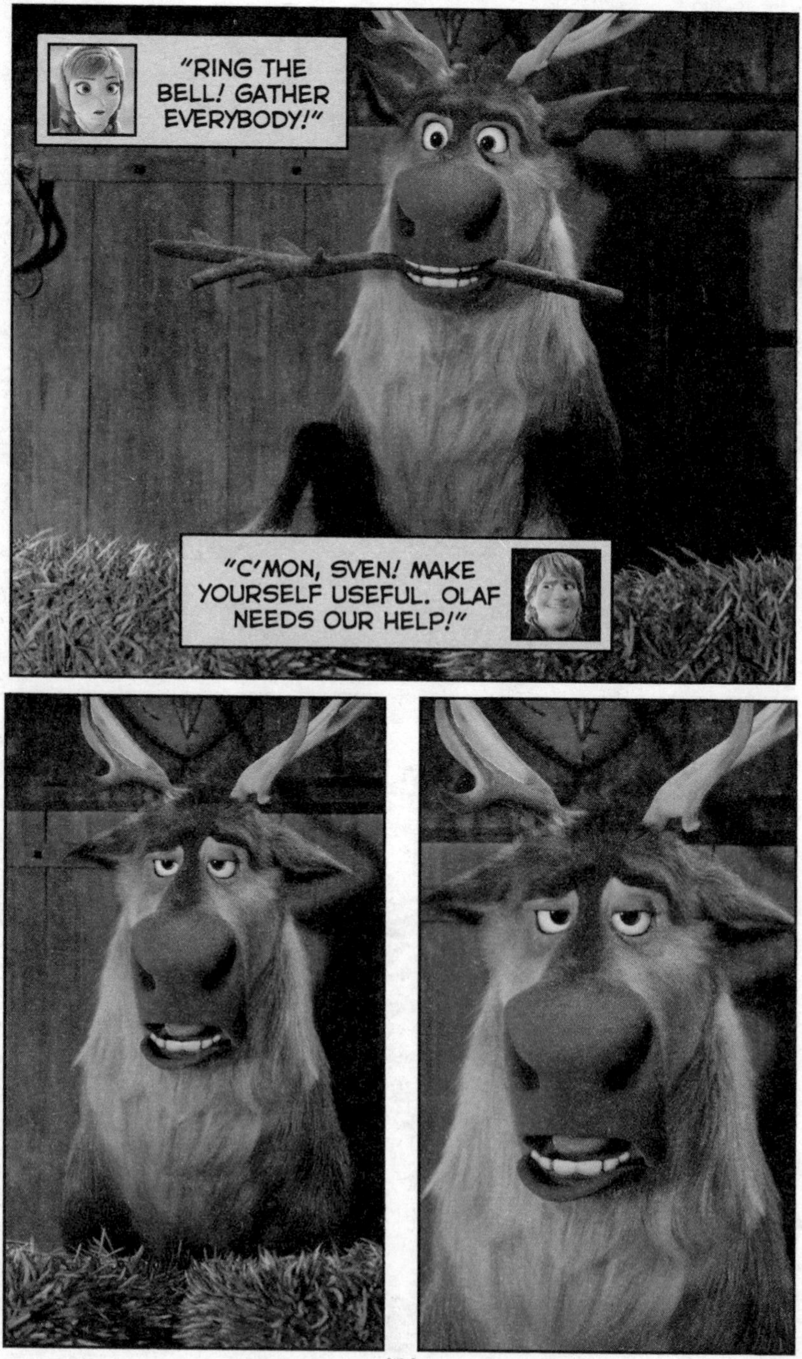
"RING THE BELL! GATHER EVERYBODY!"
"C'MON, SVEN! MAKE YOURSELF USEFUL. OLAF NEEDS OUR HELP!"

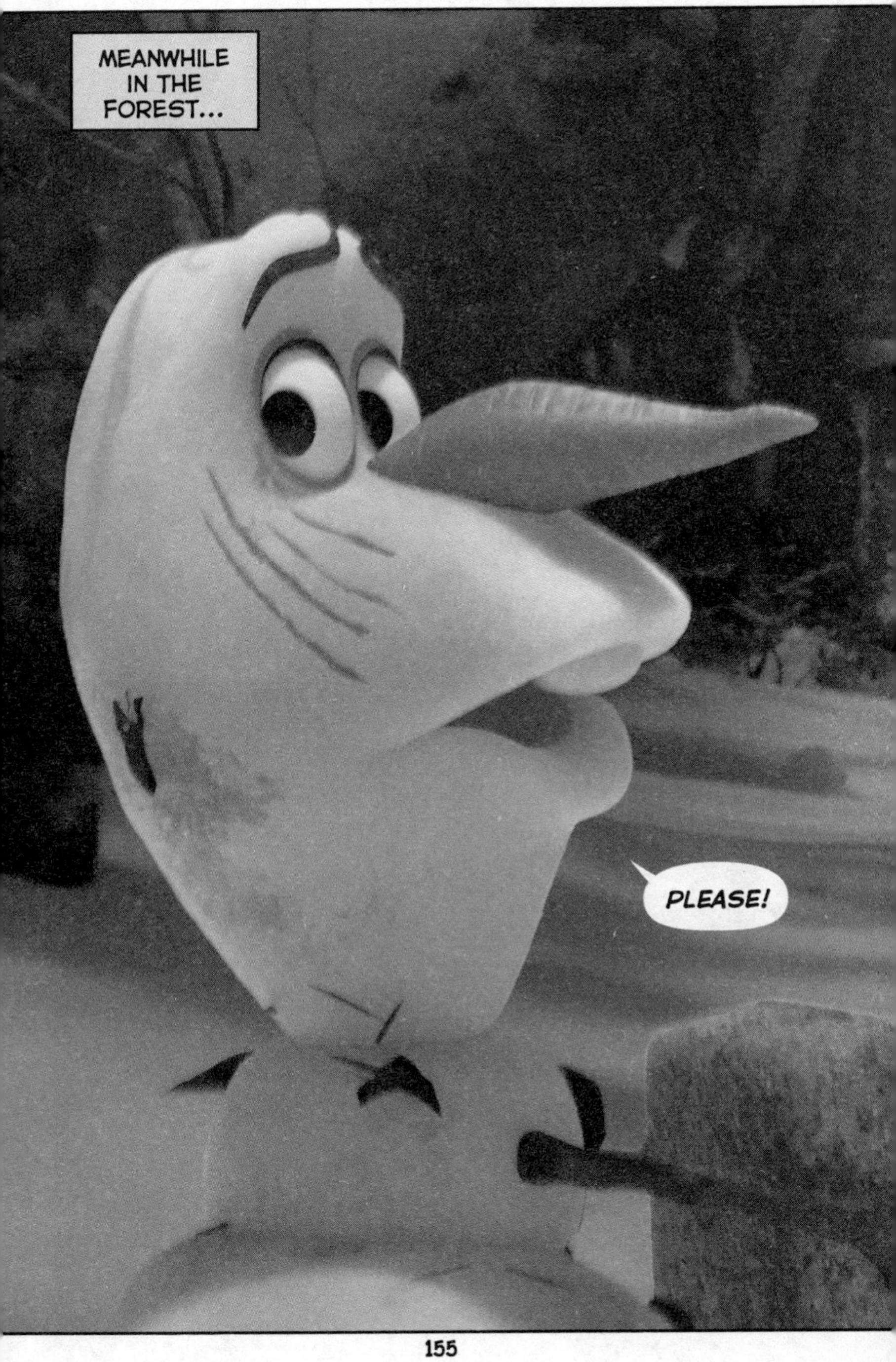
MEANWHILE IN THE FOREST...
PLEASE!

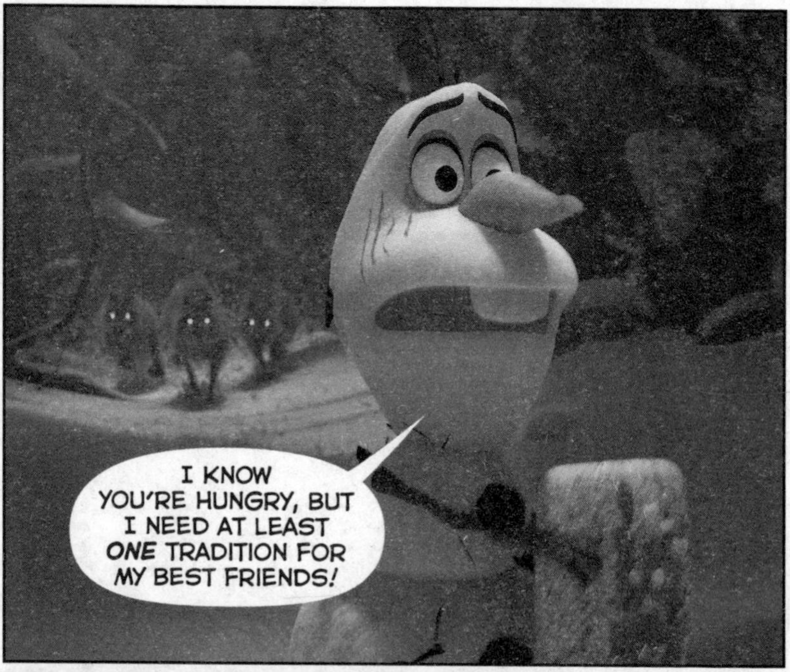
I KNOW YOU'RE HUNGRY, BUT I NEED AT LEAST *ONE* TRADITION FOR MY BEST FRIENDS!

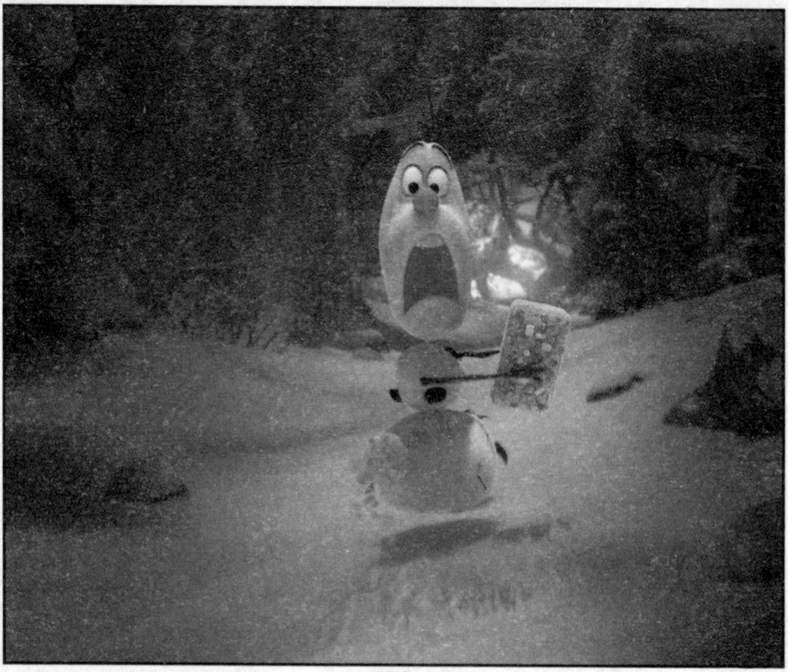

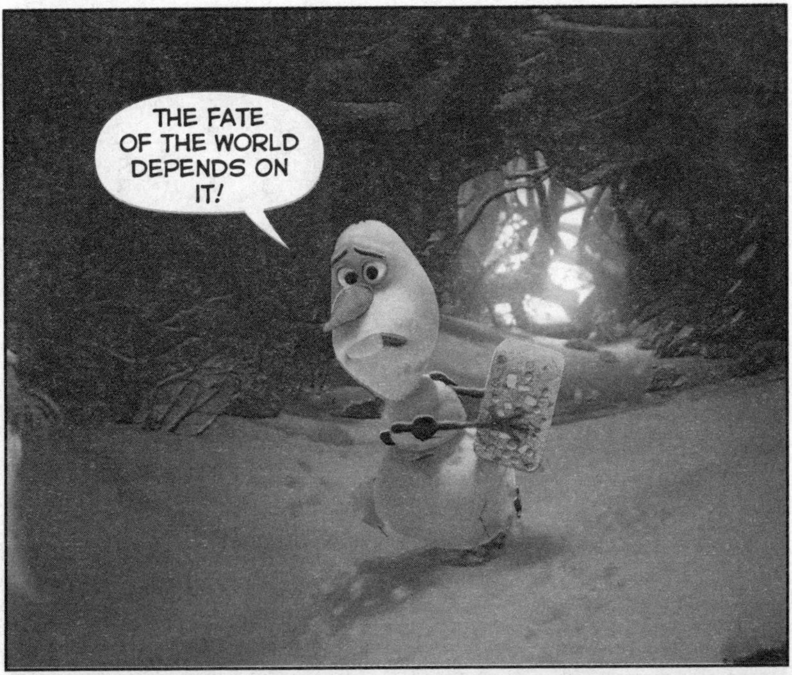
THE FATE OF THE WORLD DEPENDS ON IT!

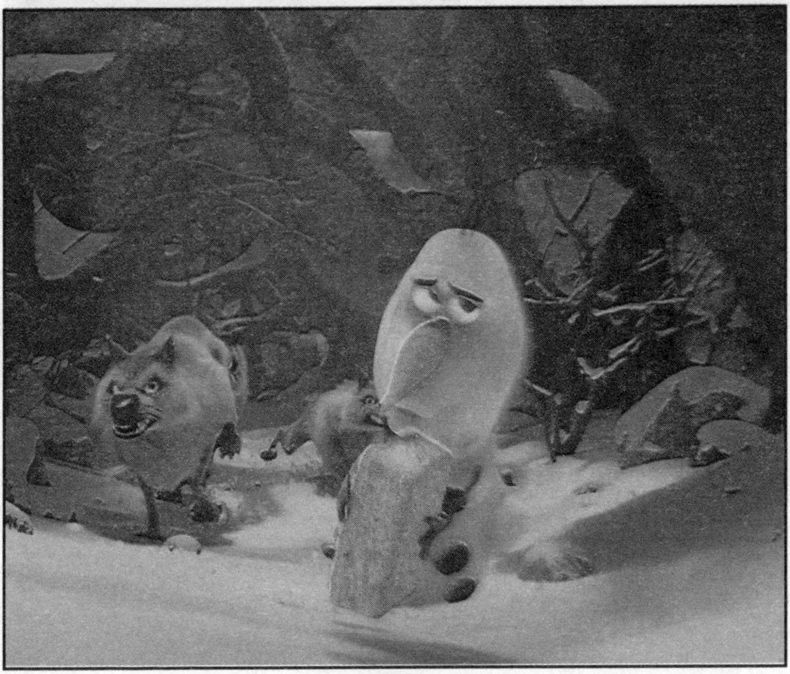

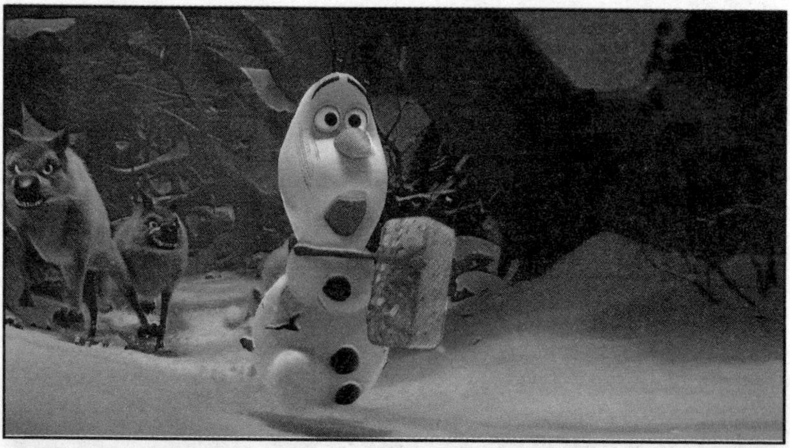

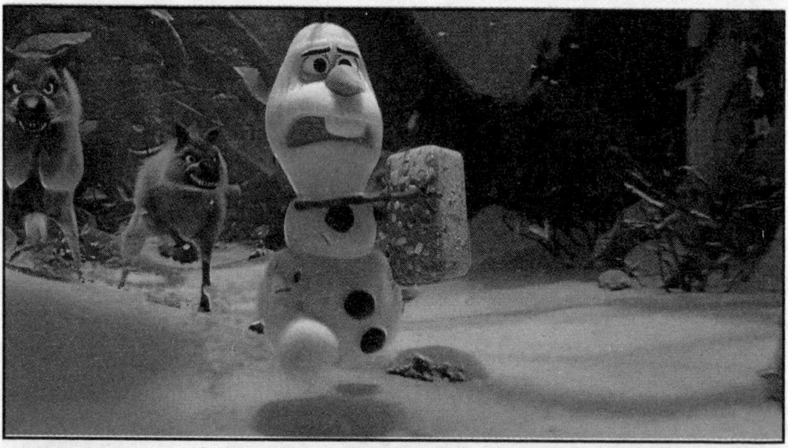

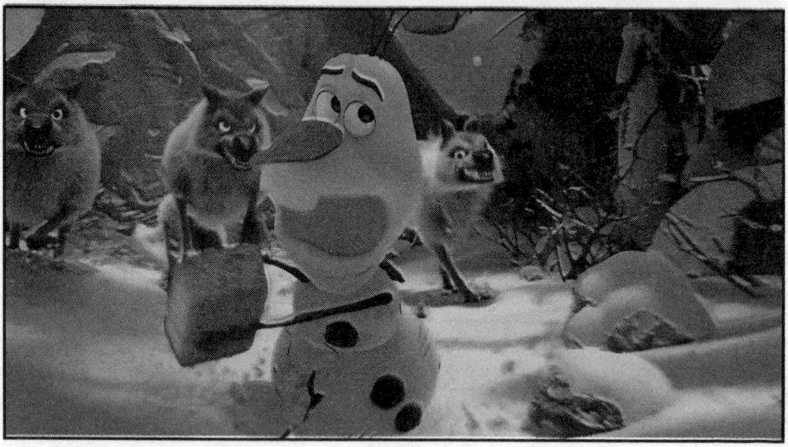

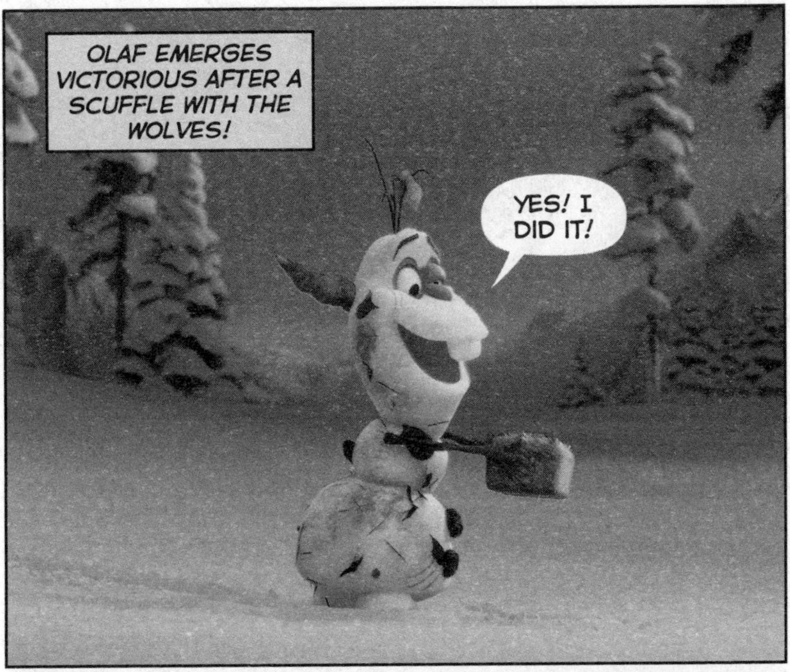
OLAF EMERGES VICTORIOUS AFTER A SCUFFLE WITH THE WOLVES!
YES! I DID IT!

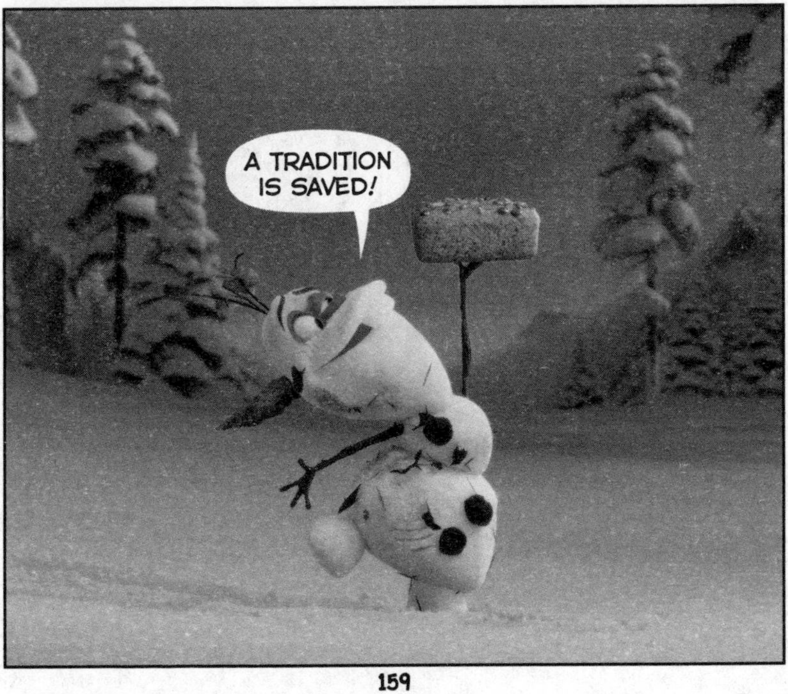
A TRADITION IS SAVED!

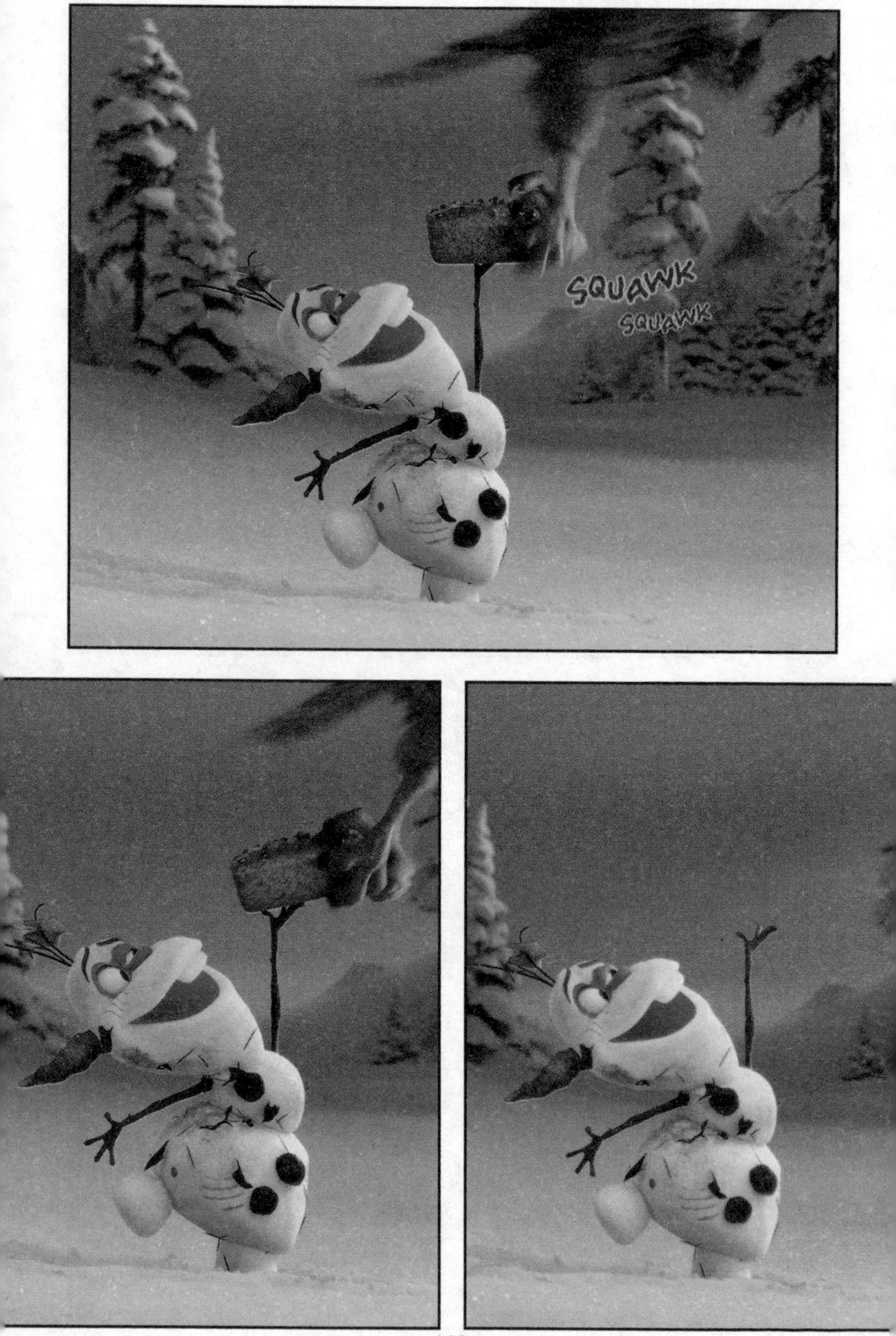
SQUAWK
SQUAWK

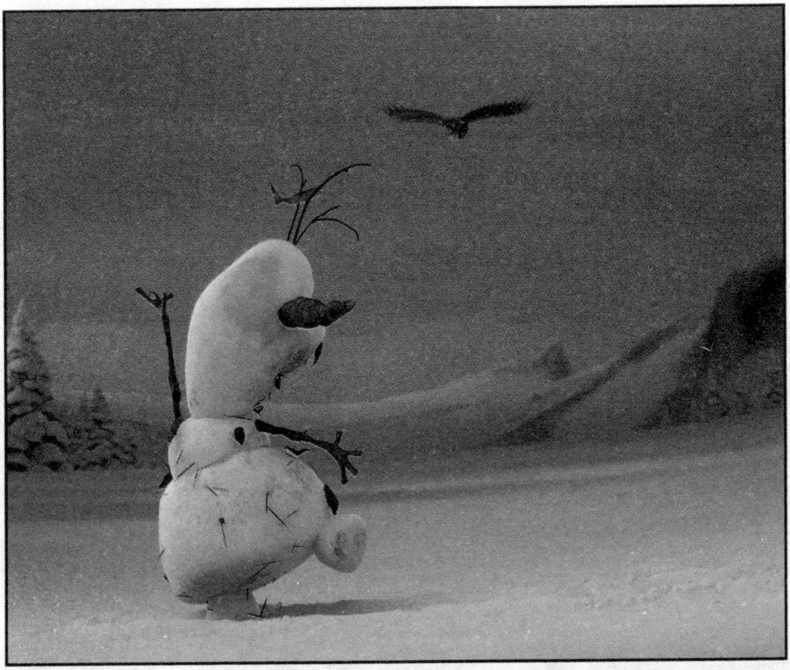

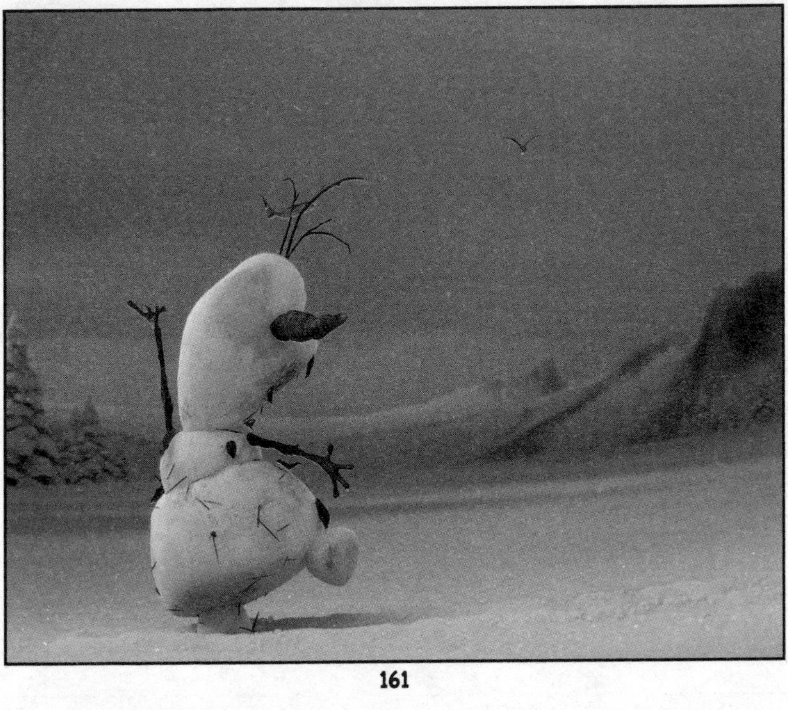

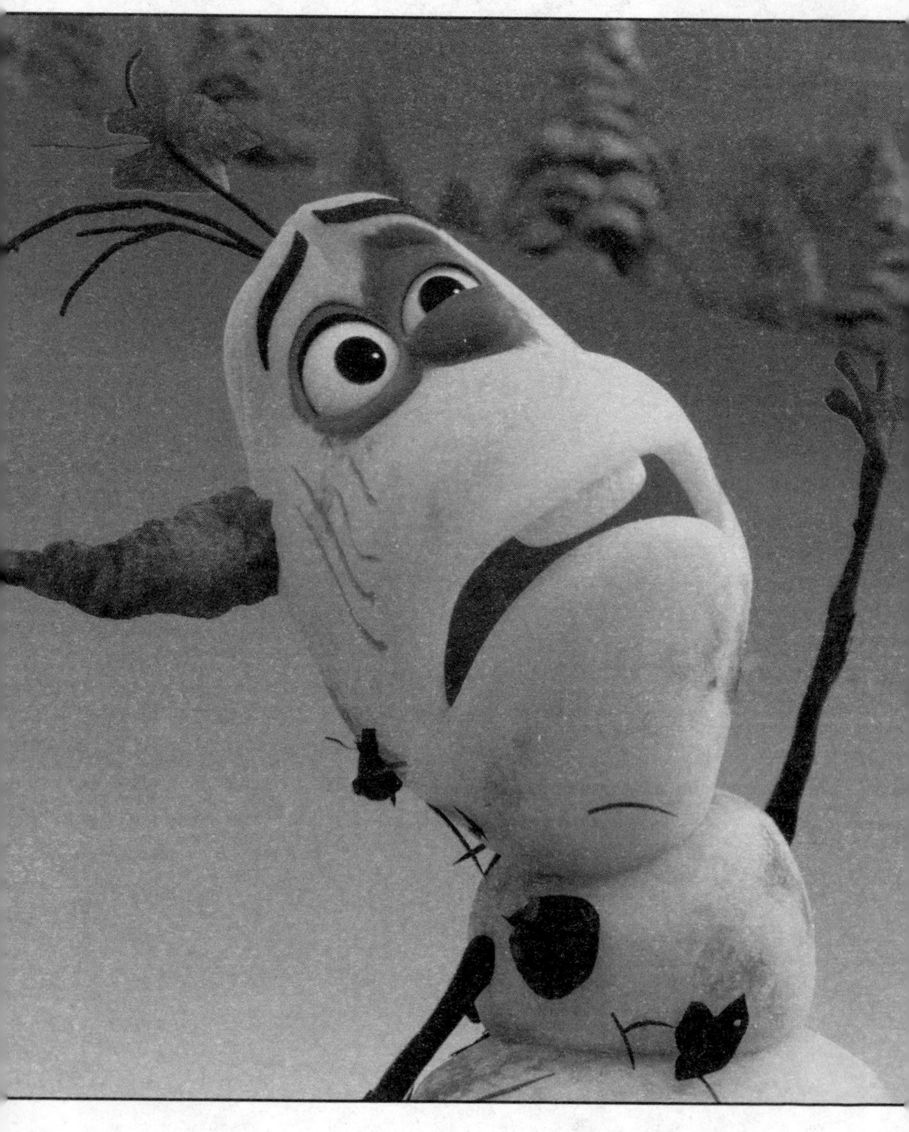

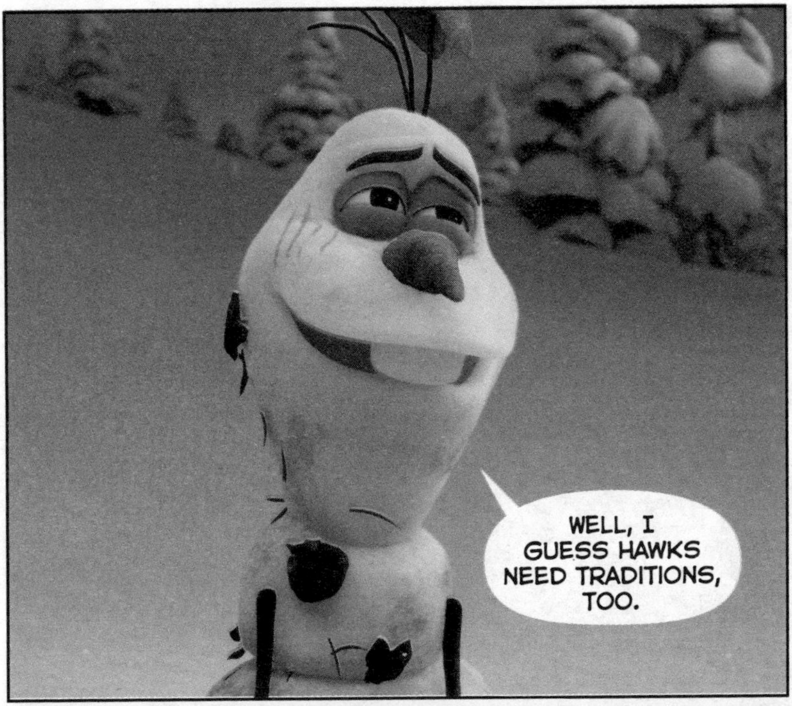
WELL, I GUESS HAWKS NEED TRADITIONS, TOO.

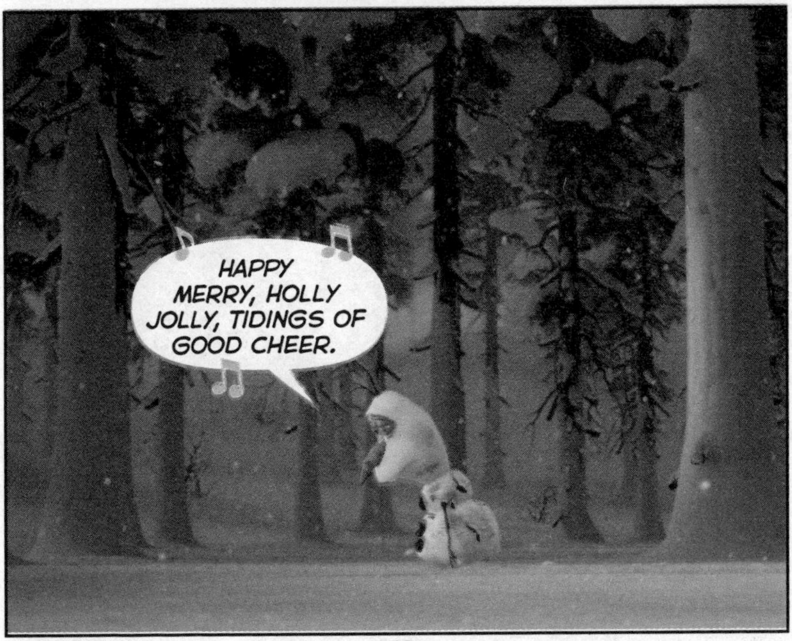
HAPPY MERRY, HOLLY JOLLY, TIDINGS OF GOOD CHEER.

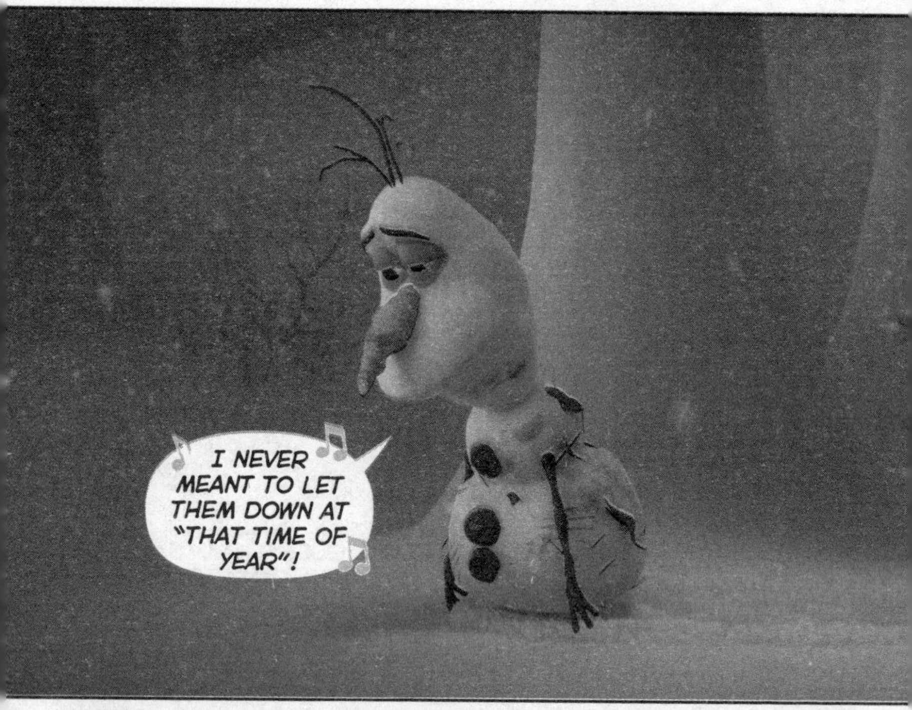
I NEVER MEANT TO LET THEM DOWN AT "THAT TIME OF YEAR"!

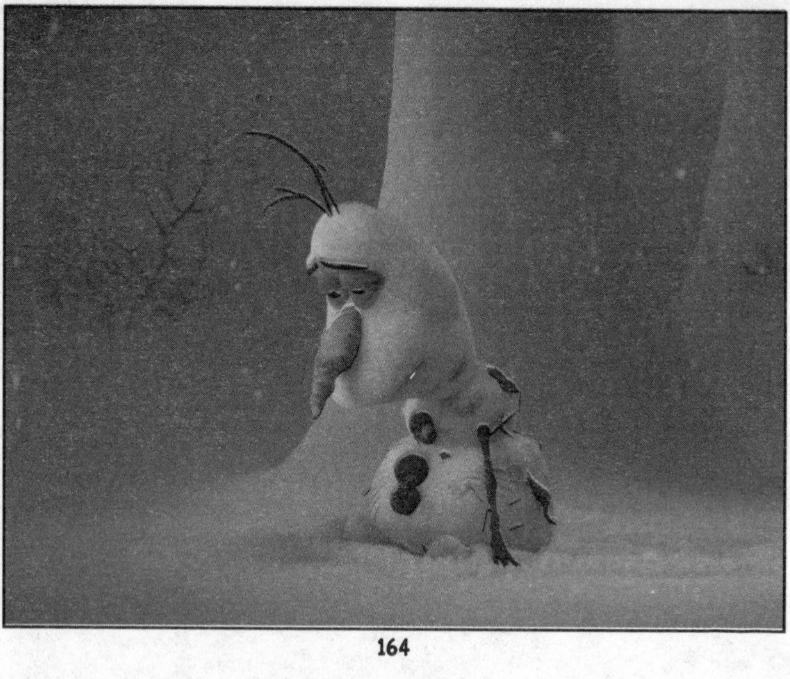

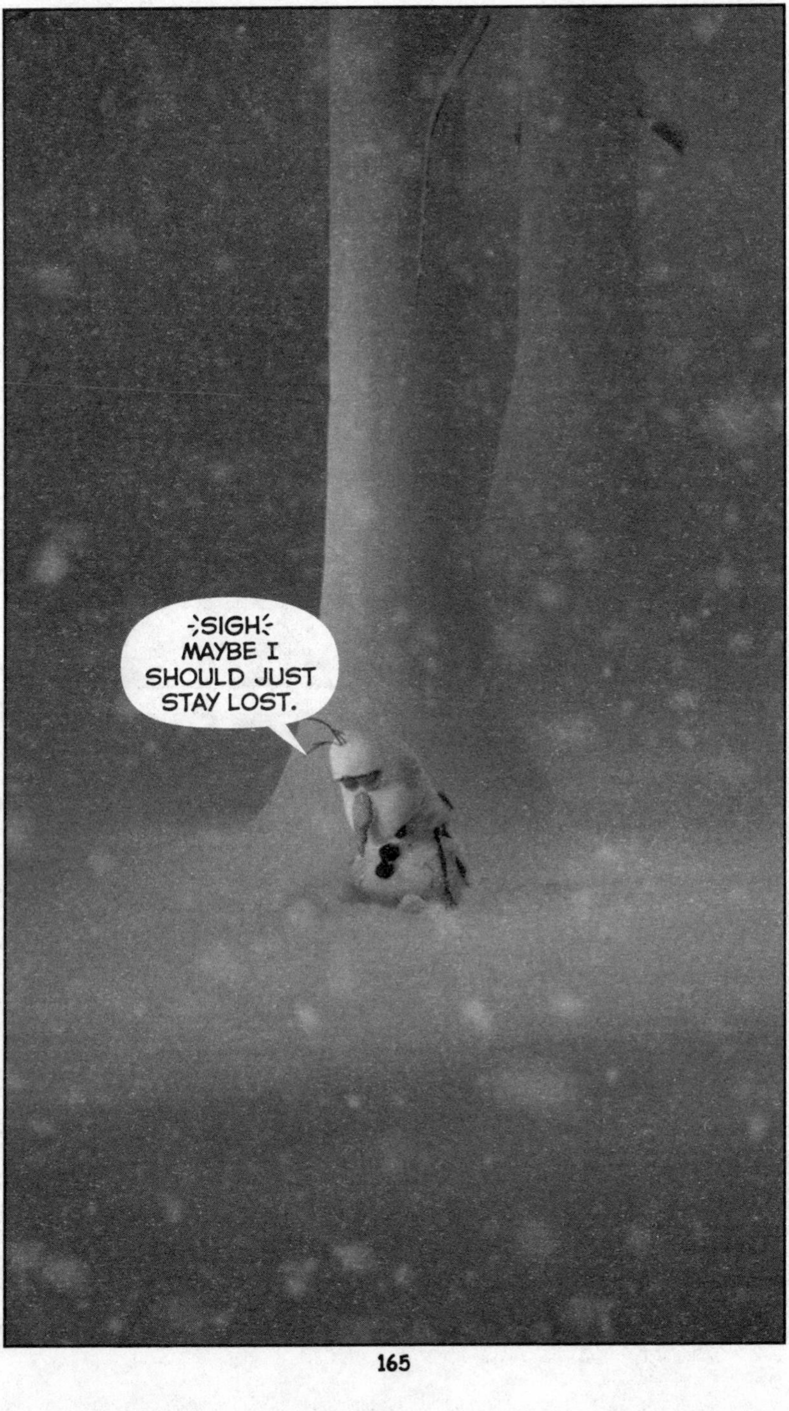
SIGH
MAYBE I SHOULD JUST STAY LOST.

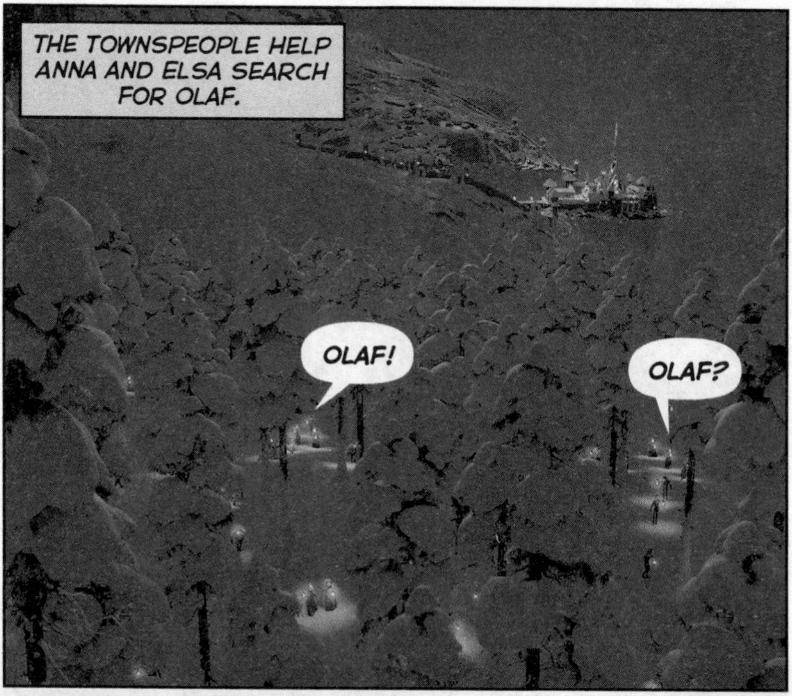
THE TOWNSPEOPLE HELP ANNA AND ELSA SEARCH FOR OLAF.
OLAF!
OLAF?

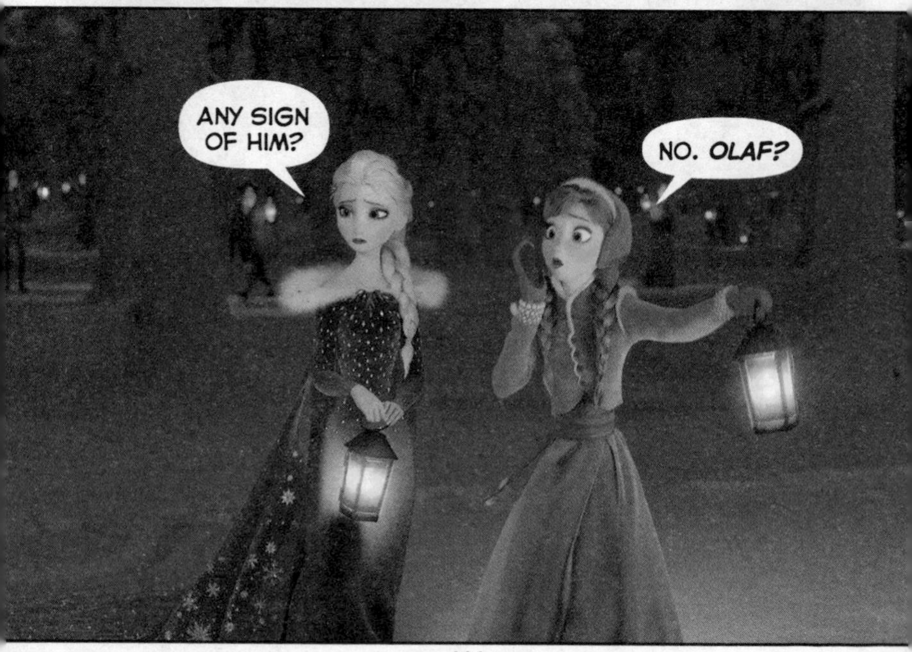
ANY SIGN OF HIM?
NO. OLAF?

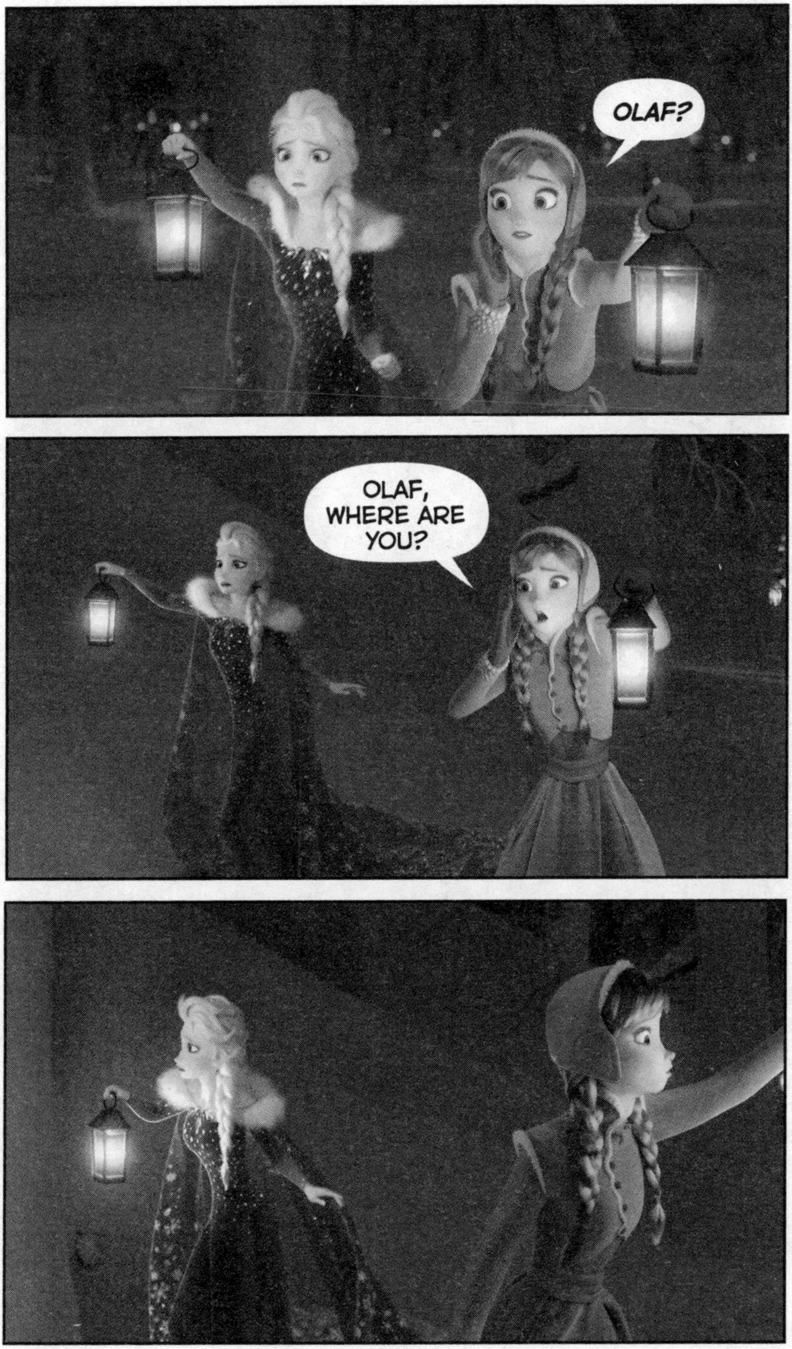
OLAF?
OLAF, WHERE ARE YOU?

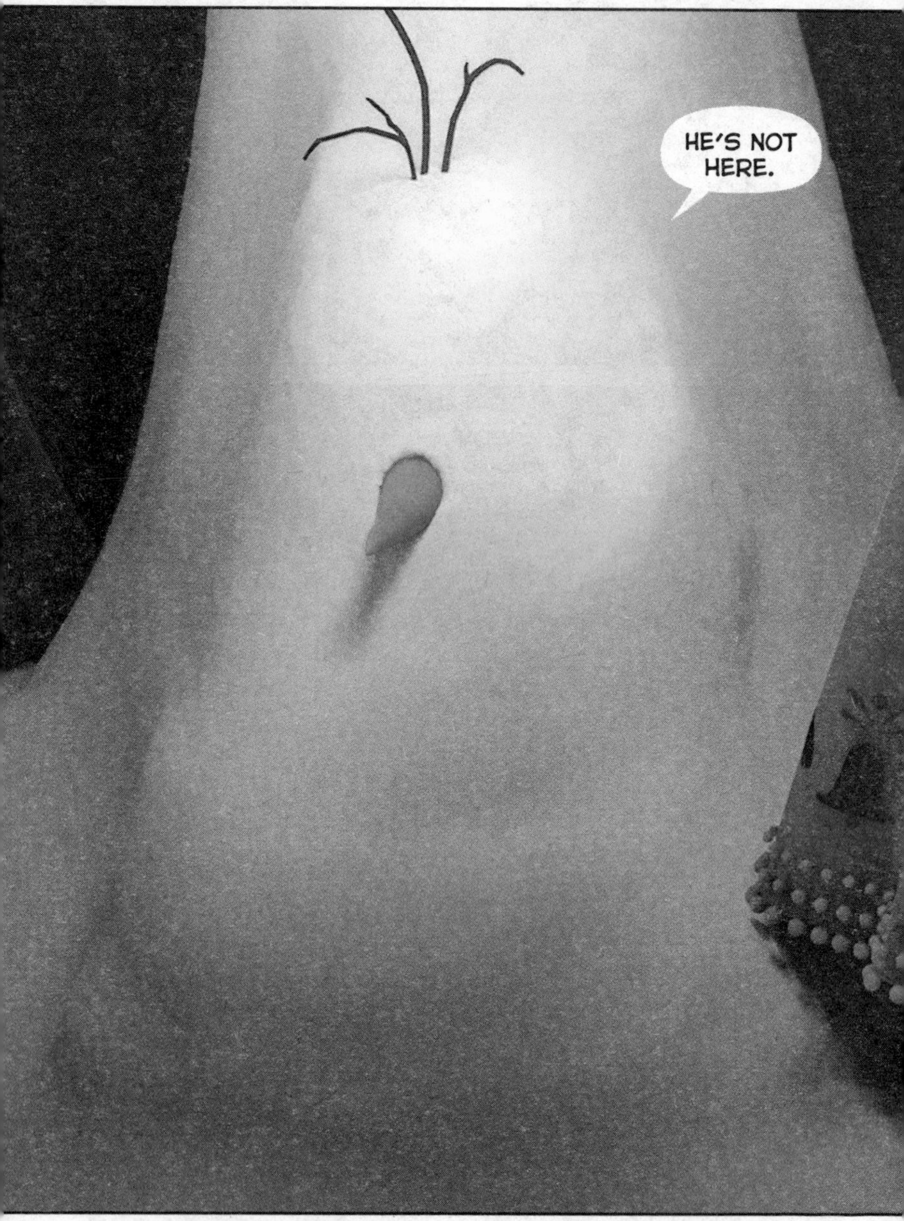
HE'S NOT HERE.

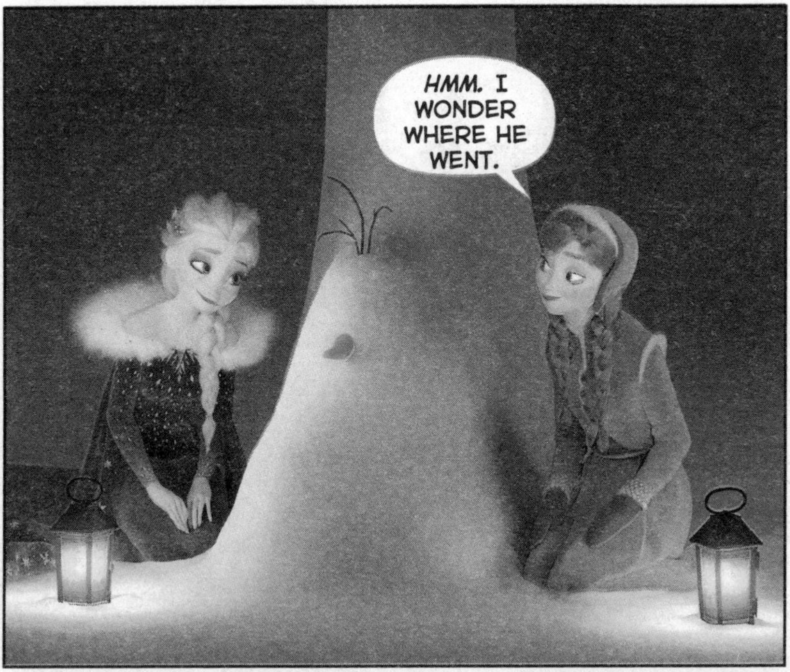
HMM. I WONDER WHERE HE WENT.

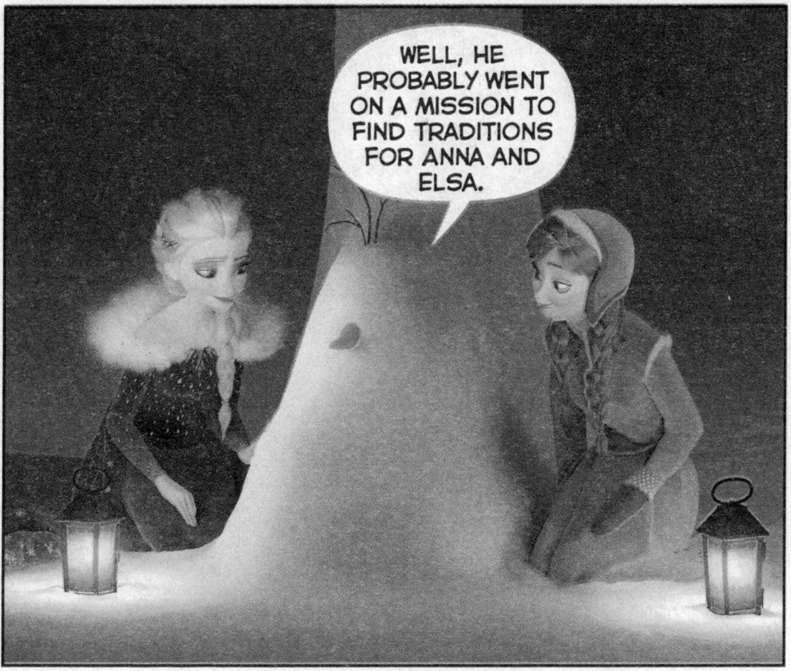
WELL, HE PROBABLY WENT ON A MISSION TO FIND TRADITIONS FOR ANNA AND ELSA.

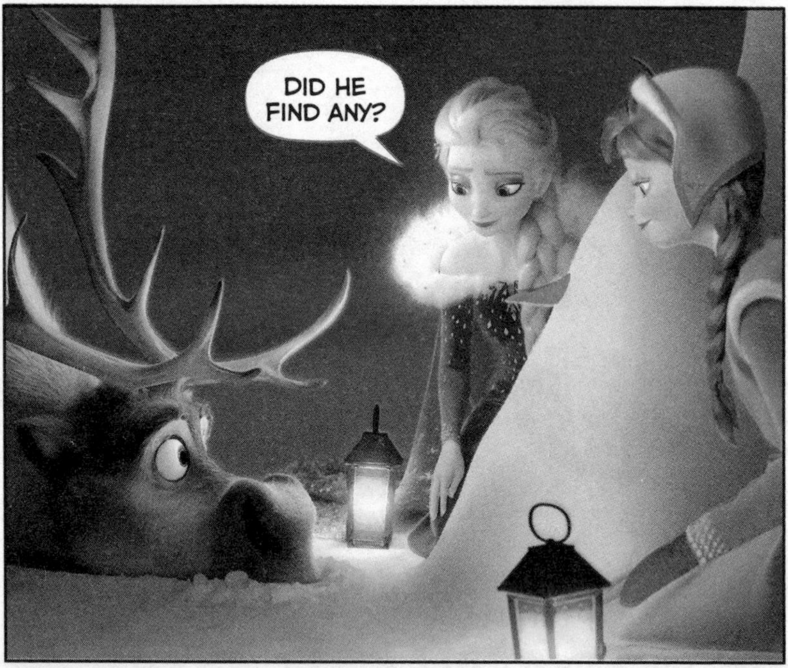
DID HE
FIND ANY?

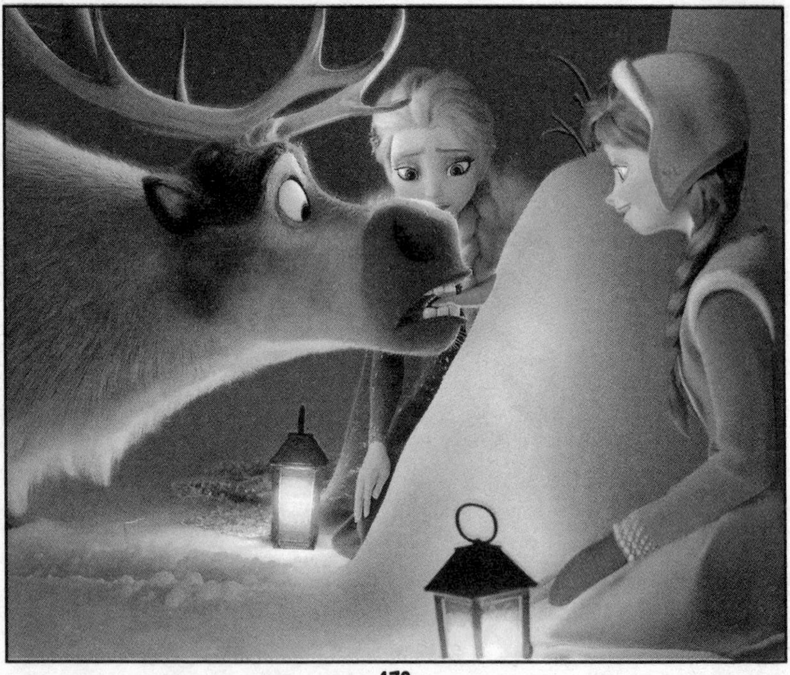

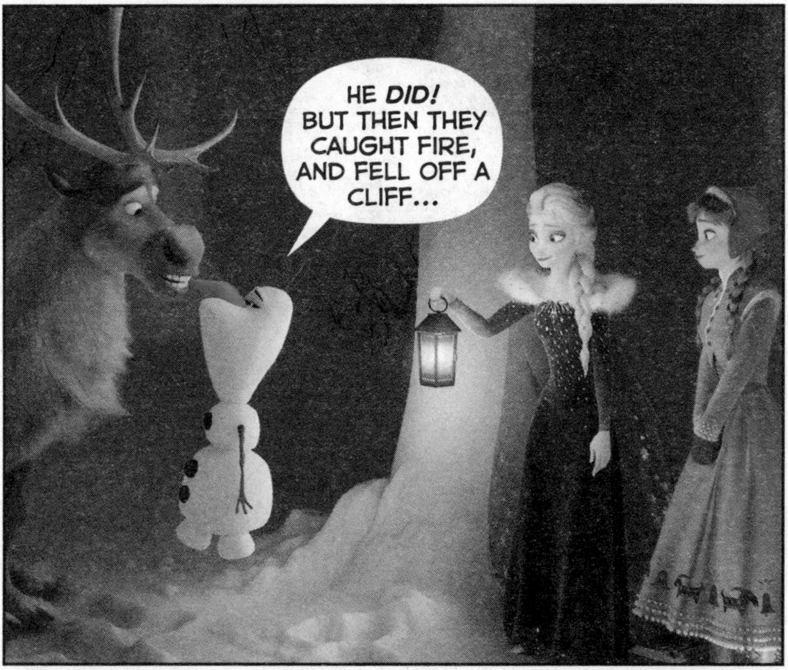
HE DID! BUT THEN THEY CAUGHT FIRE, AND FELL OFF A CLIFF...

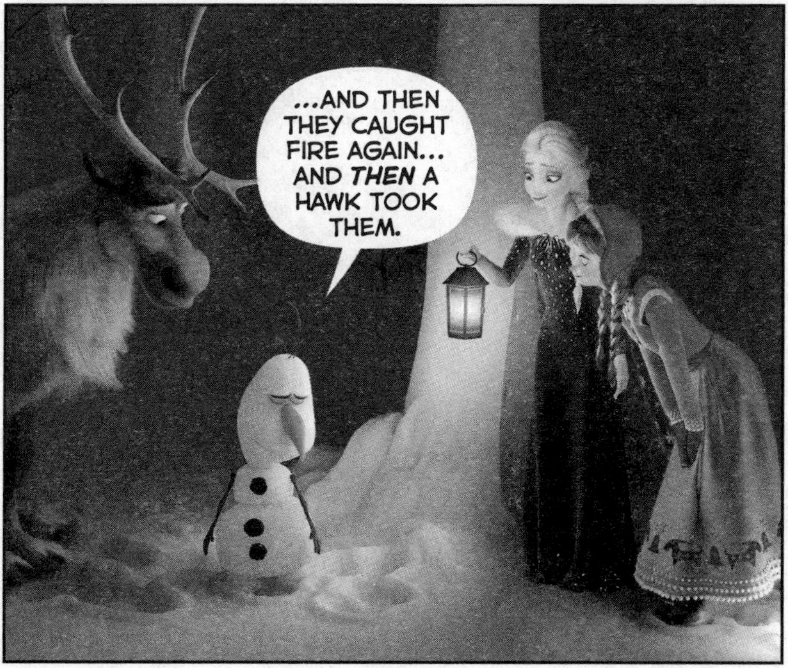
...AND THEN THEY CAUGHT FIRE AGAIN... AND THEN A HAWK TOOK THEM.

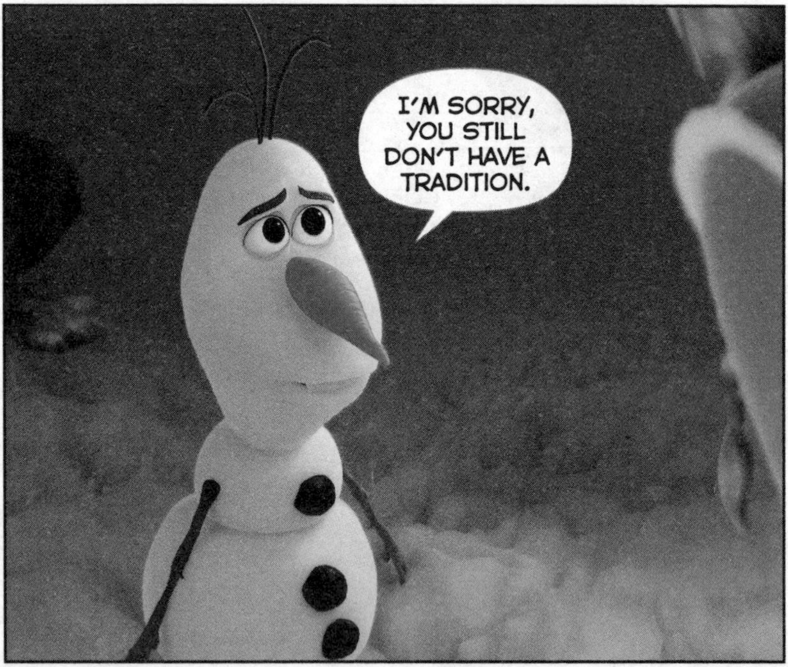
I'M SORRY, YOU STILL DON'T HAVE A TRADITION.

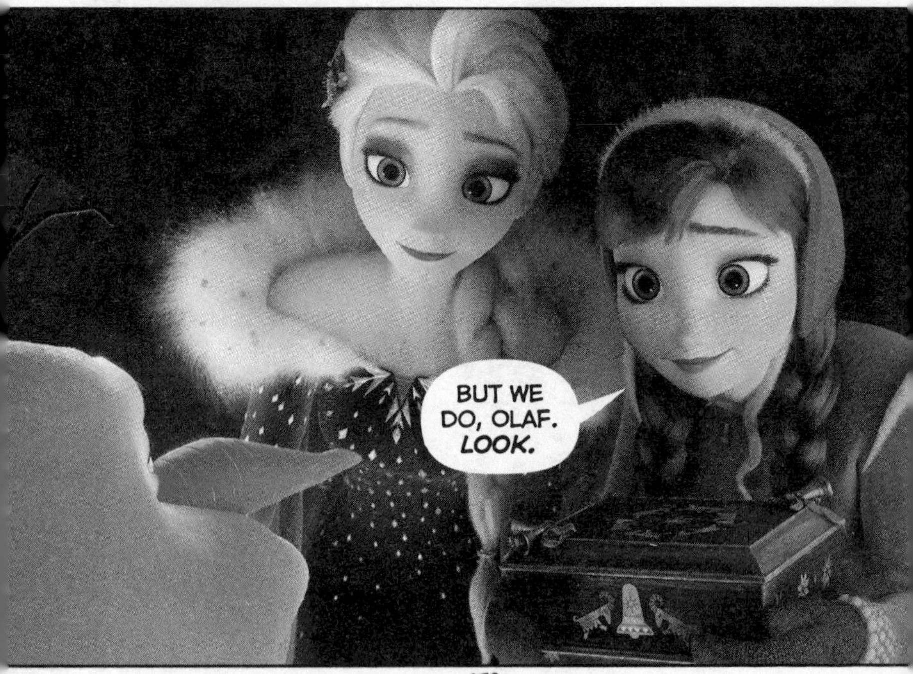
BUT WE DO, OLAF. *LOOK.*

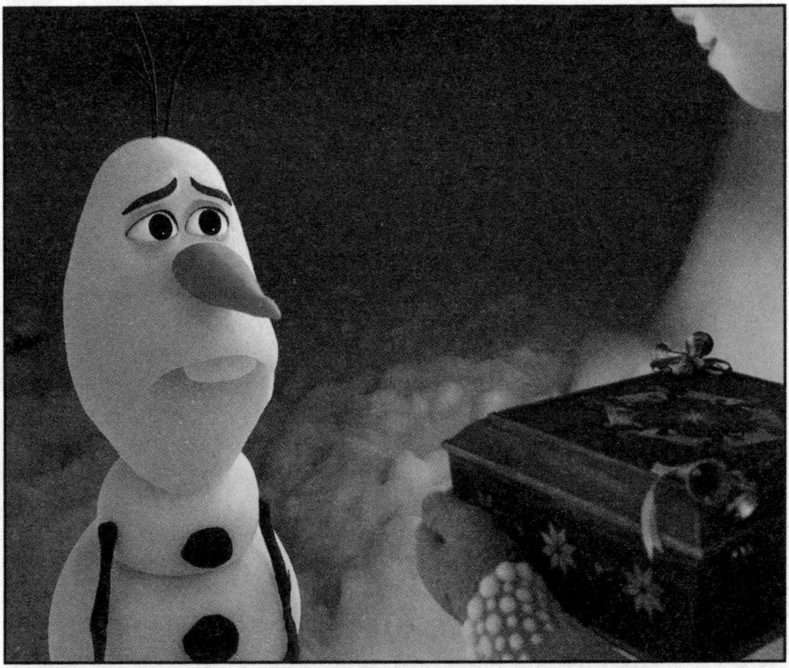

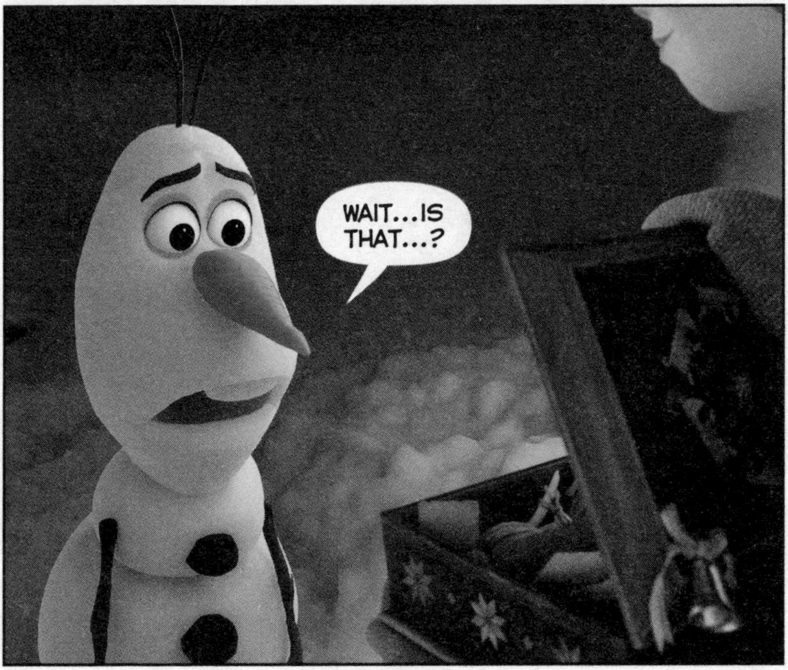
WAIT...IS THAT...?

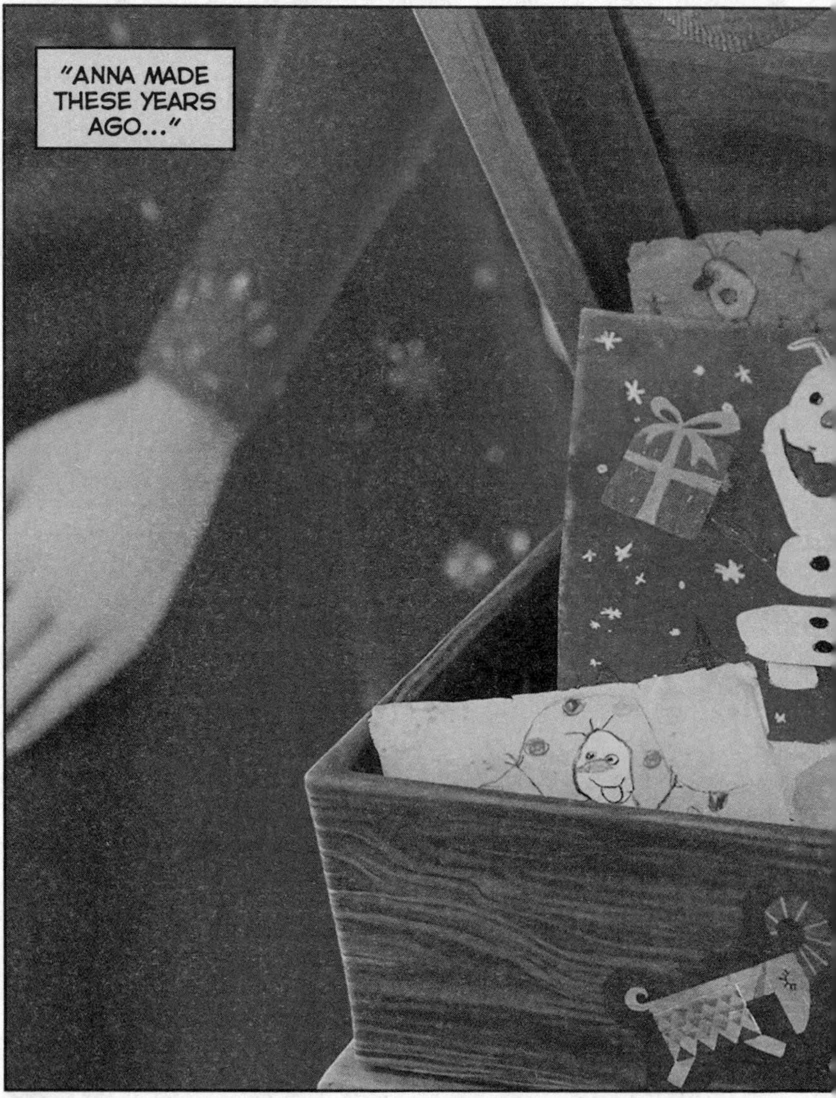
"ANNA MADE THESE YEARS AGO..."

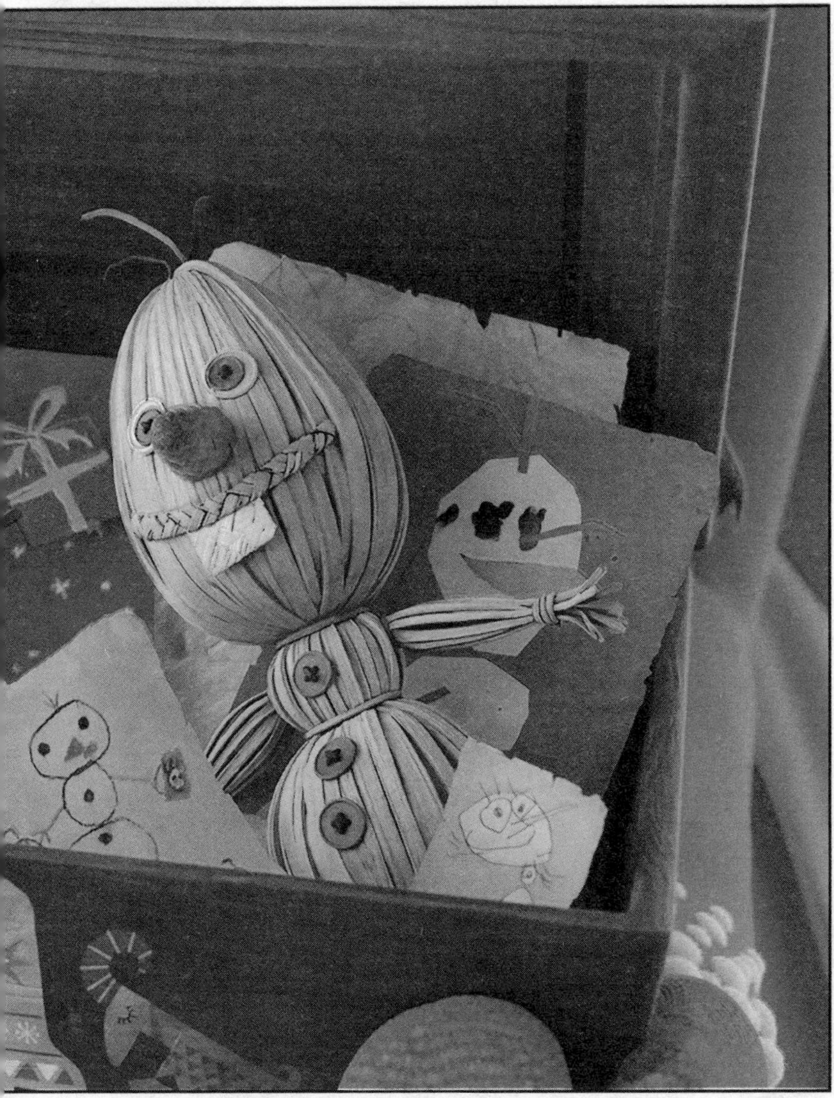

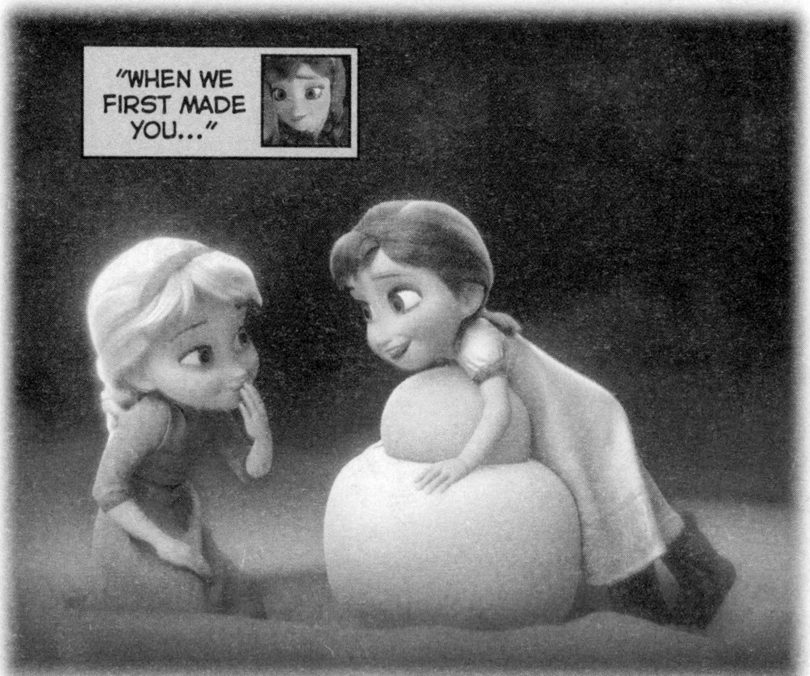
"WHEN WE FIRST MADE YOU..."

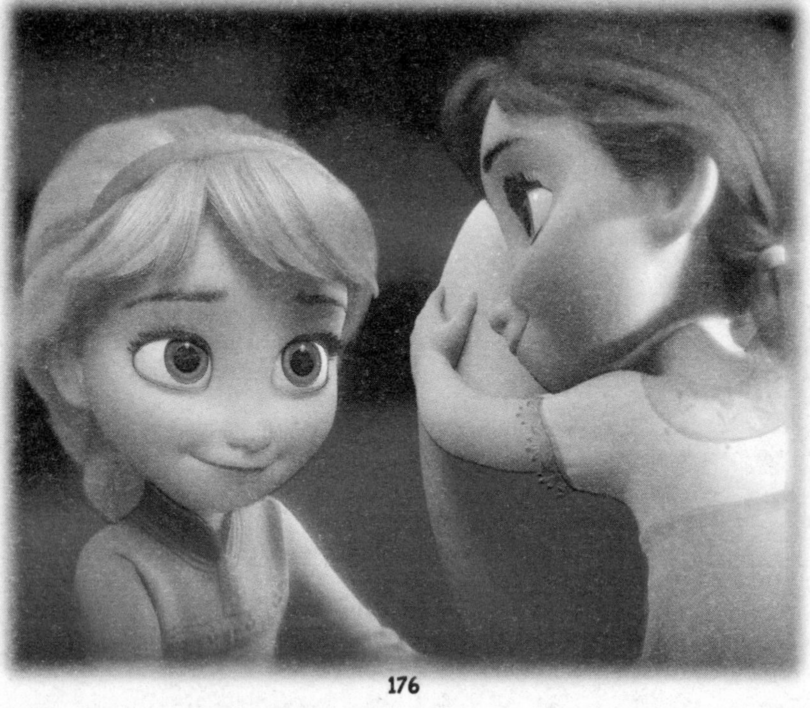

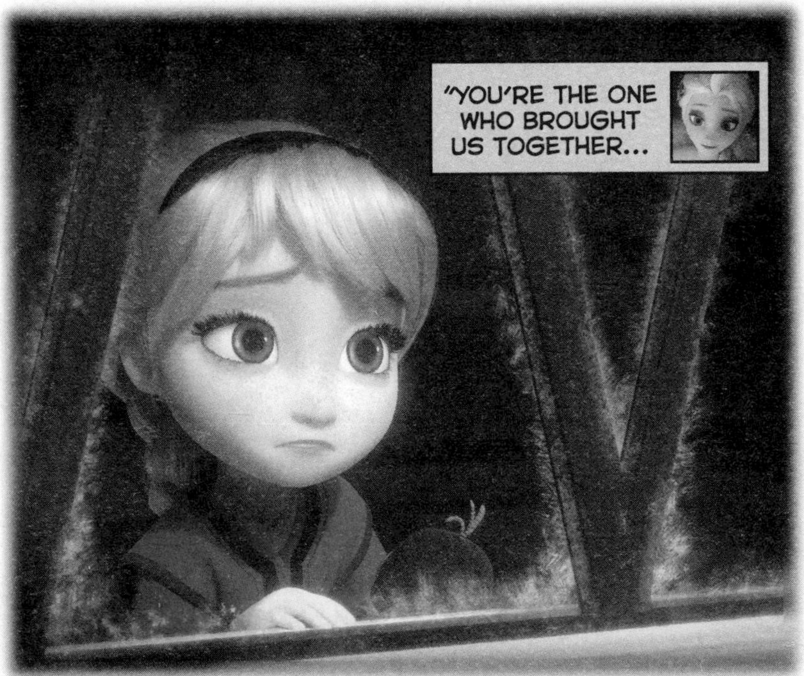
"YOU'RE THE ONE WHO BROUGHT US TOGETHER...

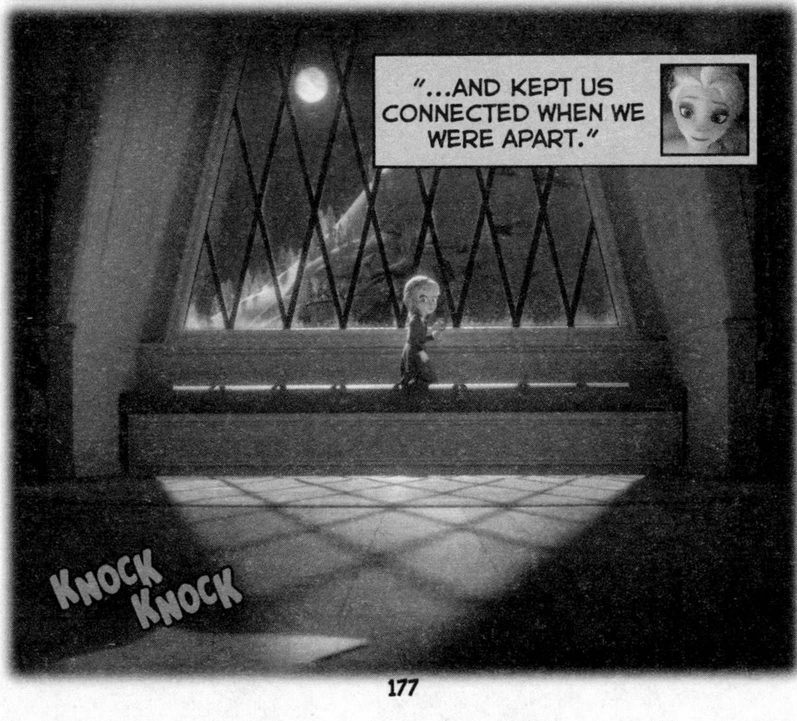
"...AND KEPT US CONNECTED WHEN WE WERE APART."
KNOCK KNOCK

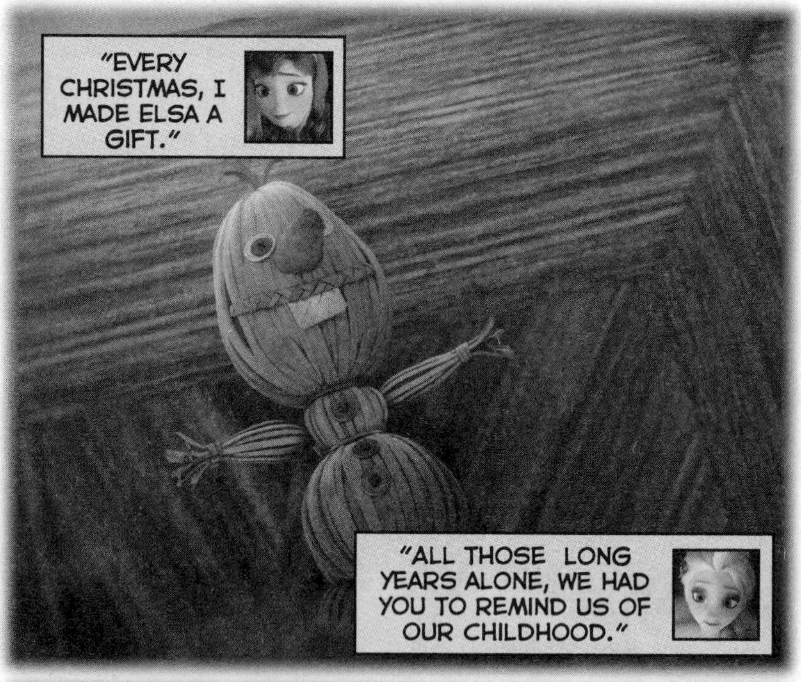
"EVERY CHRISTMAS, I MADE ELSA A GIFT."
"ALL THOSE LONG YEARS ALONE, WE HAD YOU TO REMIND US OF OUR CHILDHOOD."

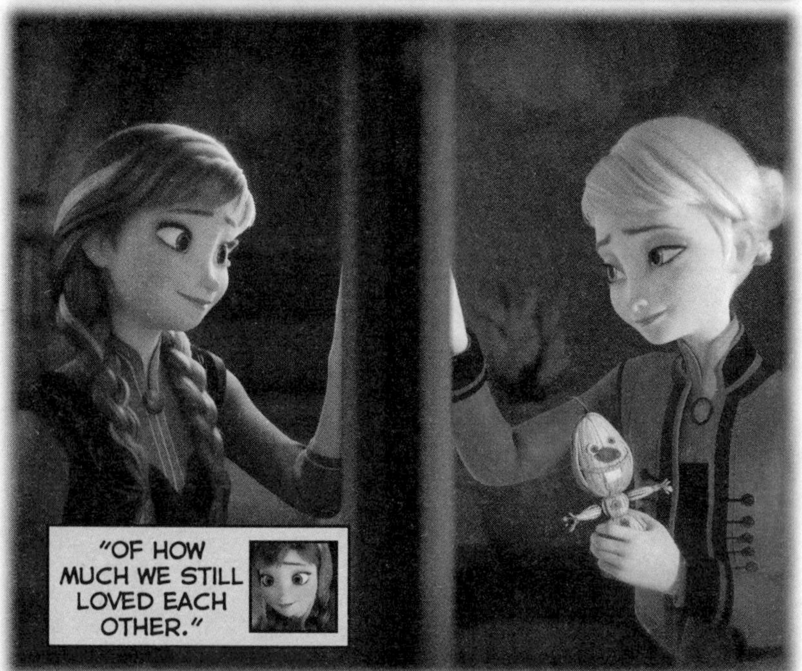
"OF HOW MUCH WE STILL LOVED EACH OTHER."

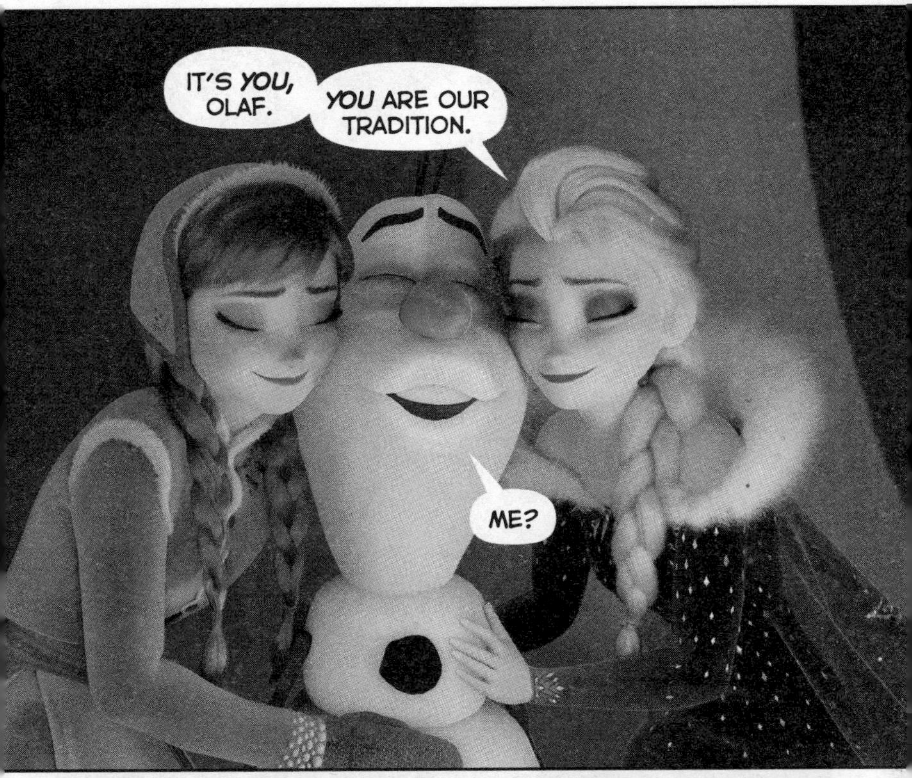
IT'S *YOU*, OLAF.
YOU ARE OUR TRADITION.
ME?

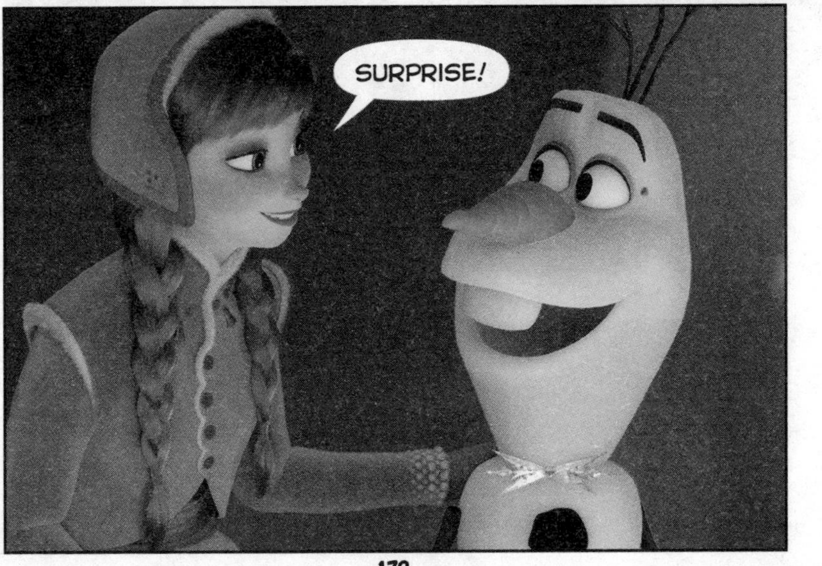
SURPRISE!

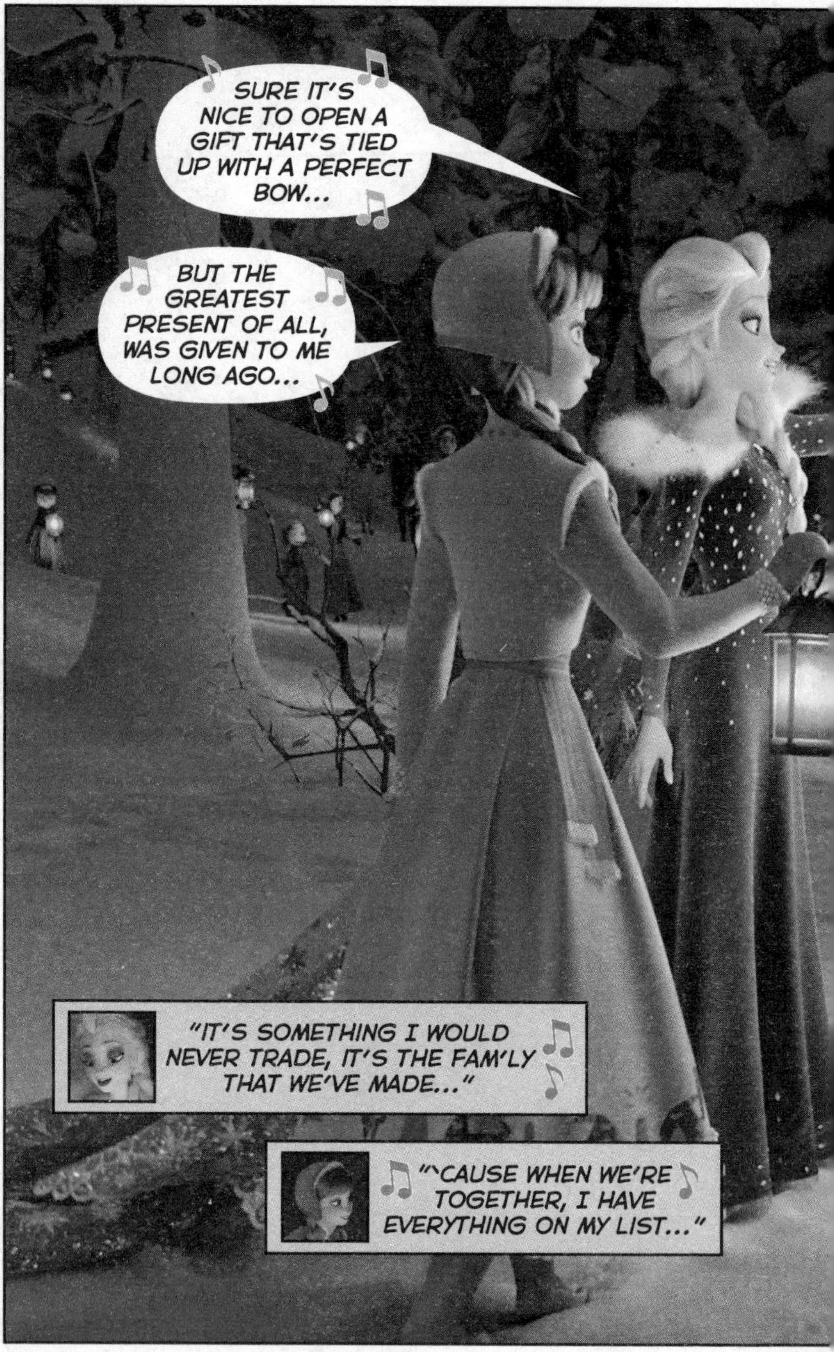
SURE IT'S NICE TO OPEN A GIFT THAT'S TIED UP WITH A PERFECT BOW...
BUT THE GREATEST PRESENT OF ALL, WAS GIVEN TO ME LONG AGO...
"IT'S SOMETHING I WOULD NEVER TRADE, IT'S THE FAM'LY THAT WE'VE MADE..."
"'CAUSE WHEN WE'RE TOGETHER, I HAVE EVERYTHING ON MY LIST..."

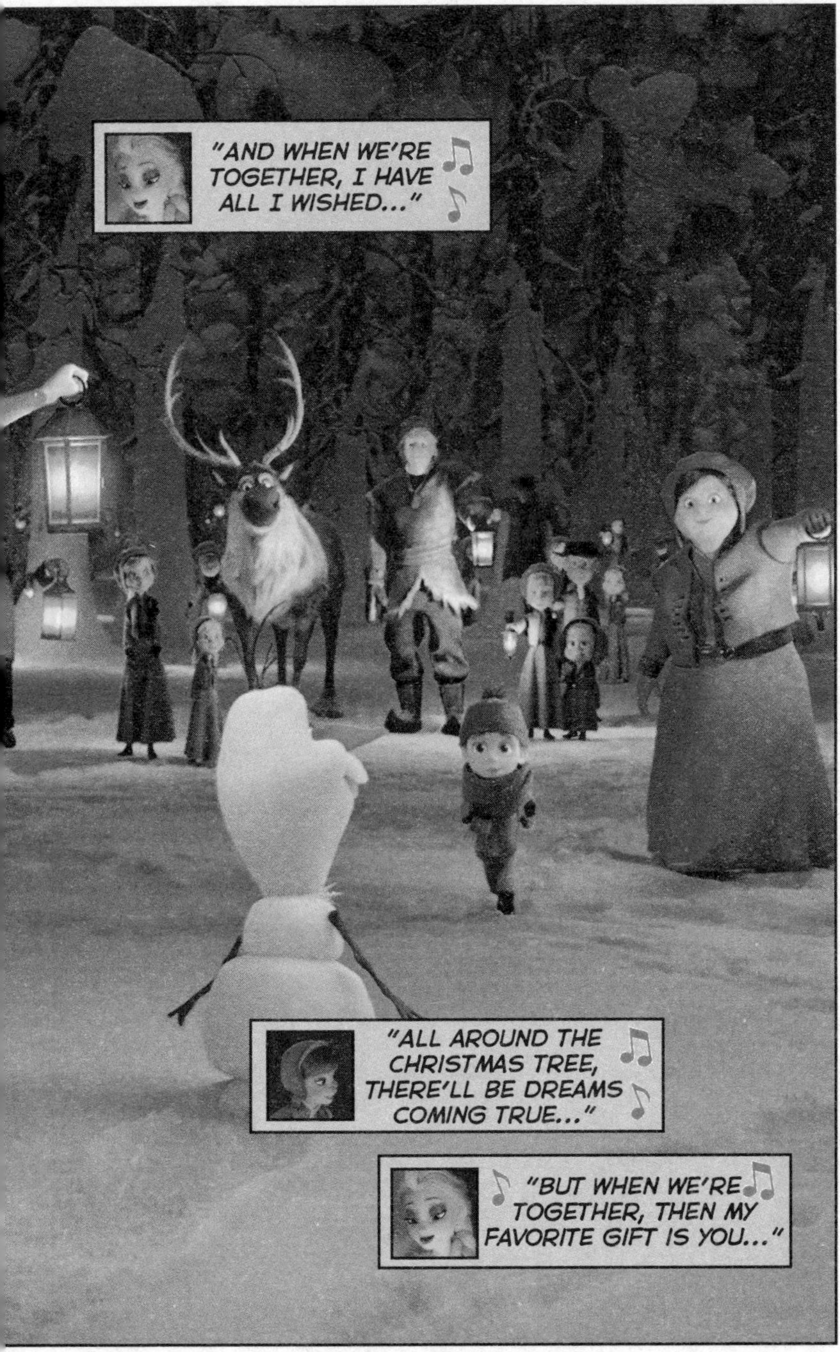
"AND WHEN WE'RE TOGETHER, I HAVE ALL I WISHED..."
"ALL AROUND THE CHRISTMAS TREE, THERE'LL BE DREAMS COMING TRUE..."
"BUT WHEN WE'RE TOGETHER, THEN MY FAVORITE GIFT IS YOU..."

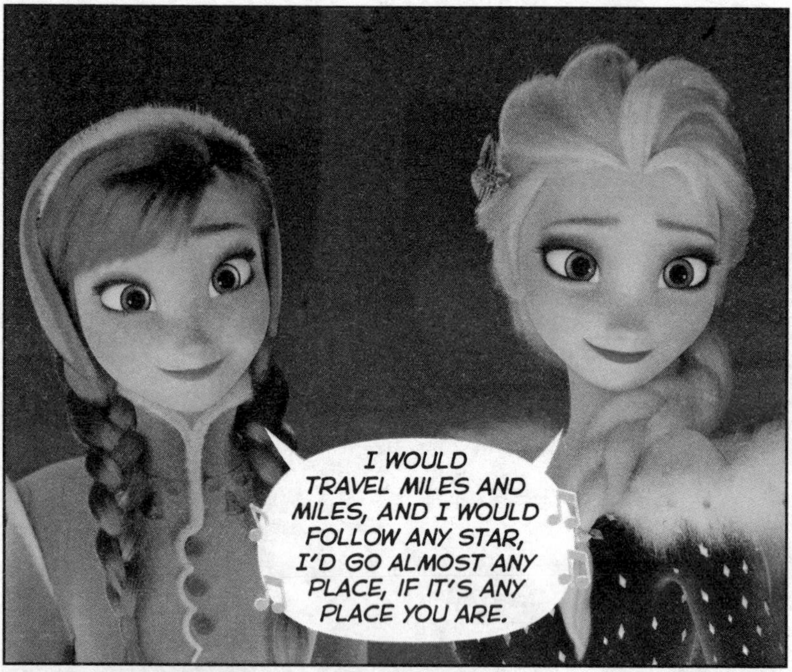
I WOULD TRAVEL MILES AND MILES, AND I WOULD FOLLOW ANY STAR, I'D GO ALMOST ANY PLACE, IF IT'S ANY PLACE YOU ARE.

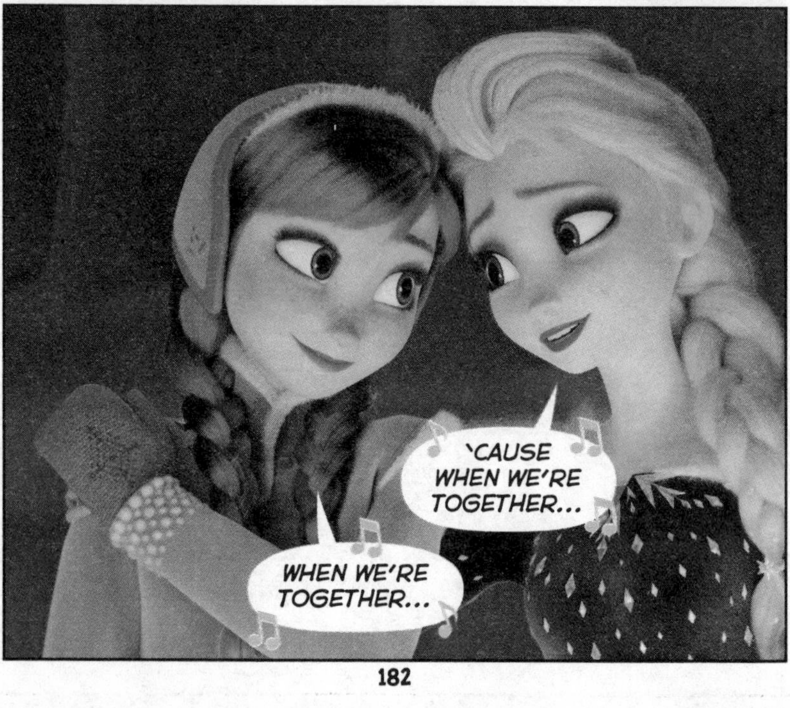
'CAUSE WHEN WE'RE TOGETHER...
WHEN WE'RE TOGETHER...

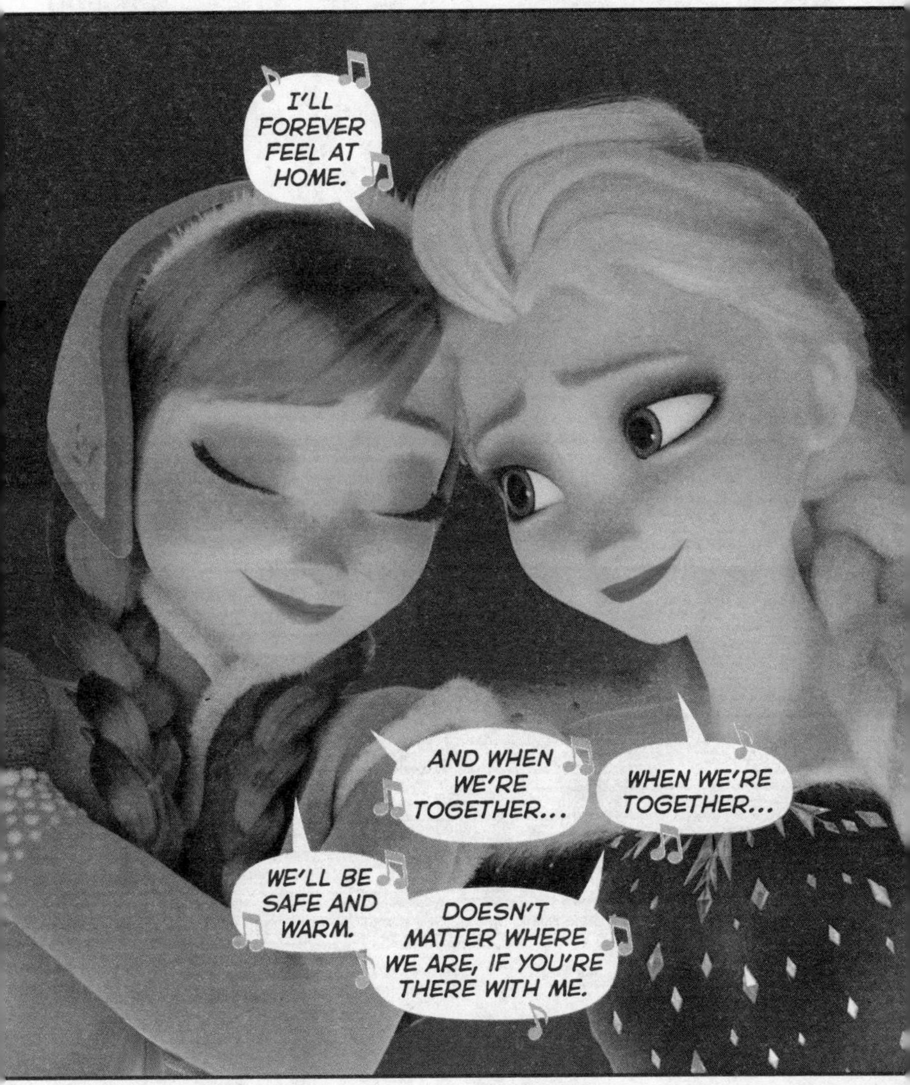
I'LL FOREVER FEEL AT HOME.
AND WHEN WE'RE TOGETHER...
WHEN WE'RE TOGETHER...
WE'LL BE SAFE AND WARM.
DOESN'T MATTER WHERE WE ARE, IF YOU'RE THERE WITH ME.

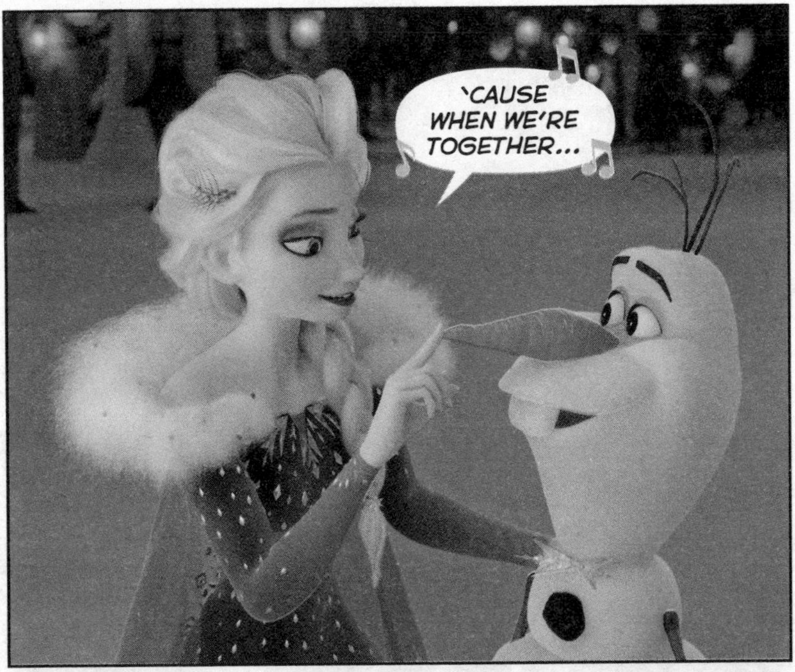
'CAUSE WHEN WE'RE TOGETHER...

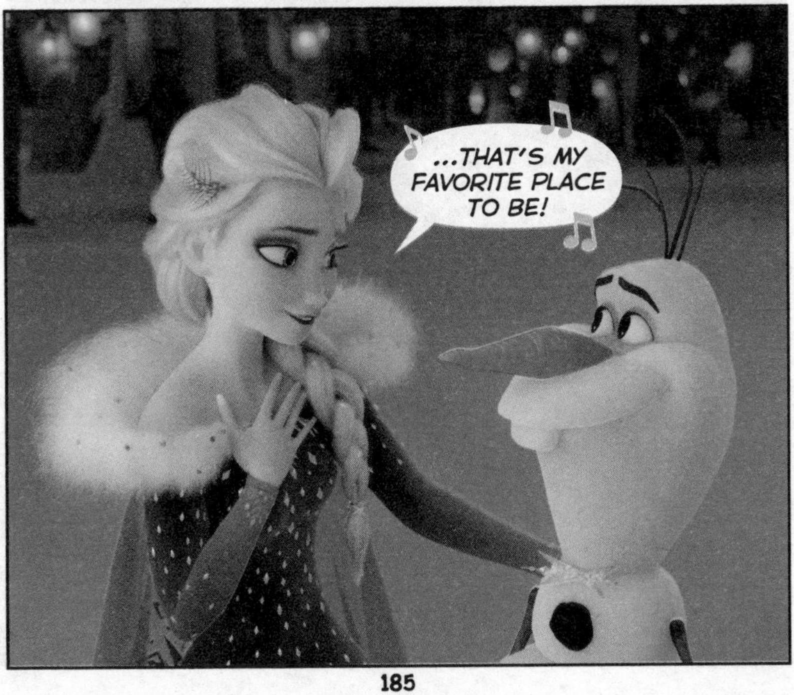
...THAT'S MY FAVORITE PLACE TO BE!

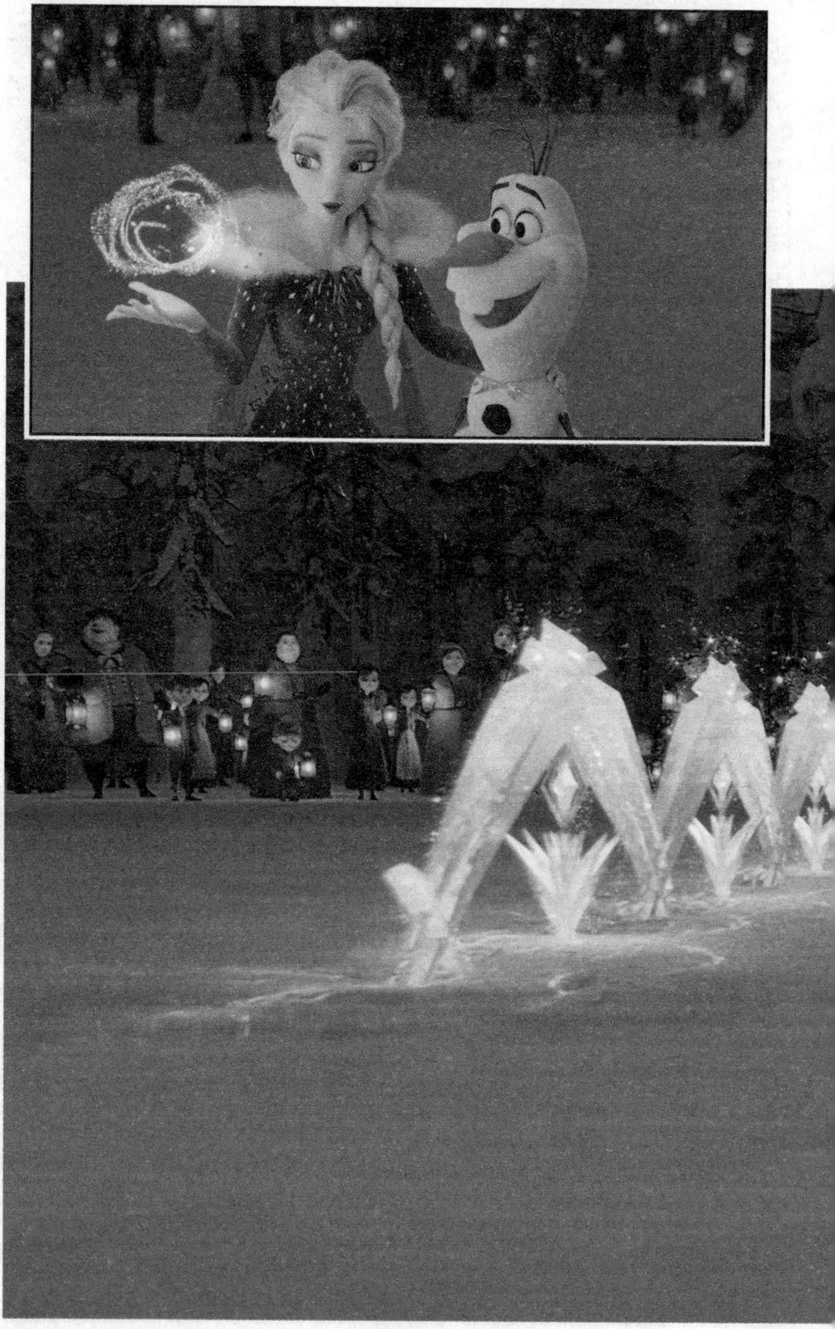

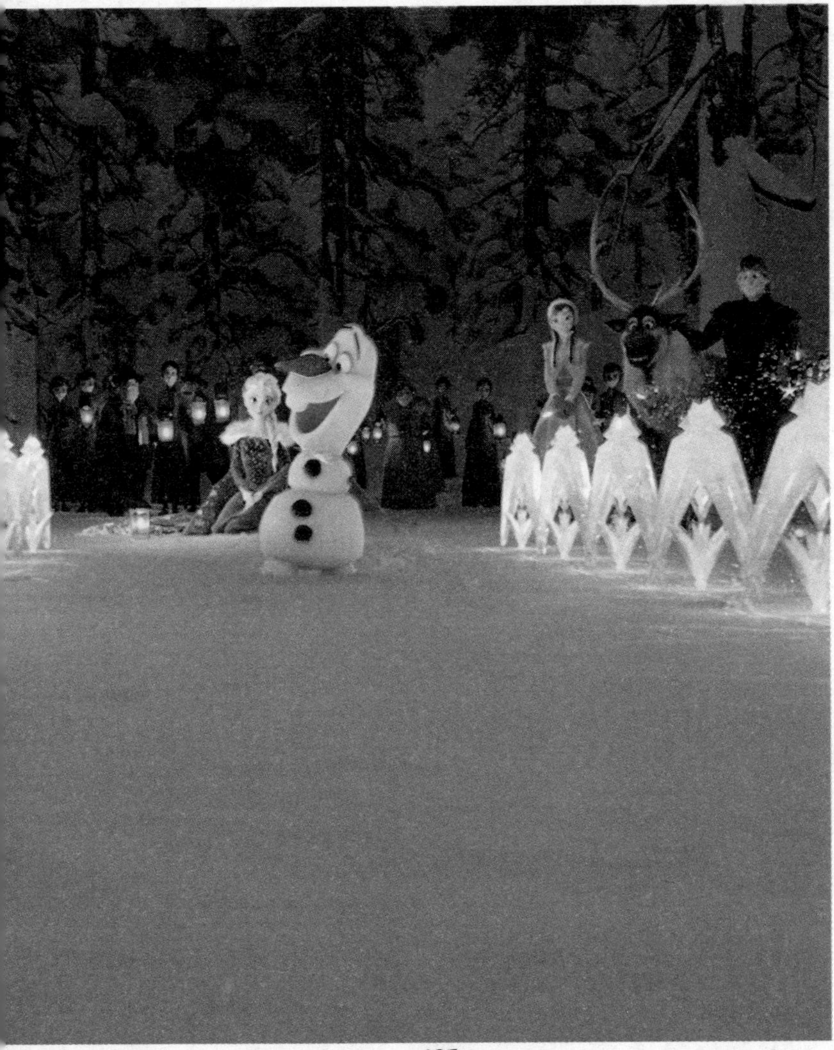

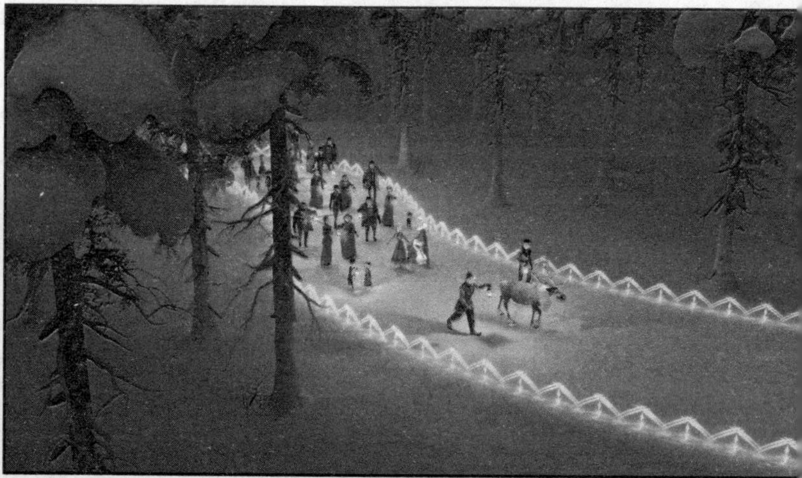

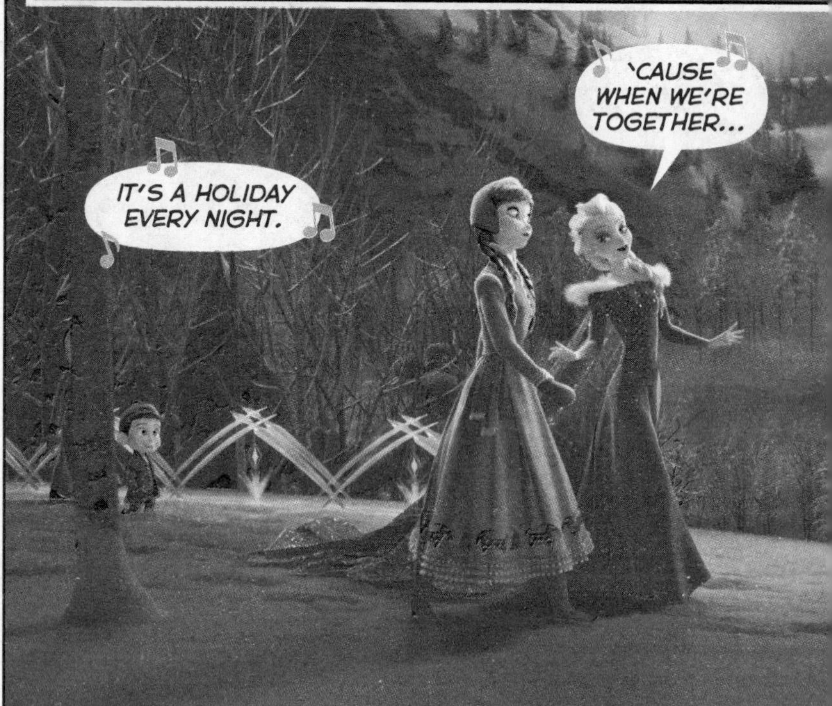
IT'S A HOLIDAY EVERY NIGHT.
'CAUSE WHEN WE'RE TOGETHER...

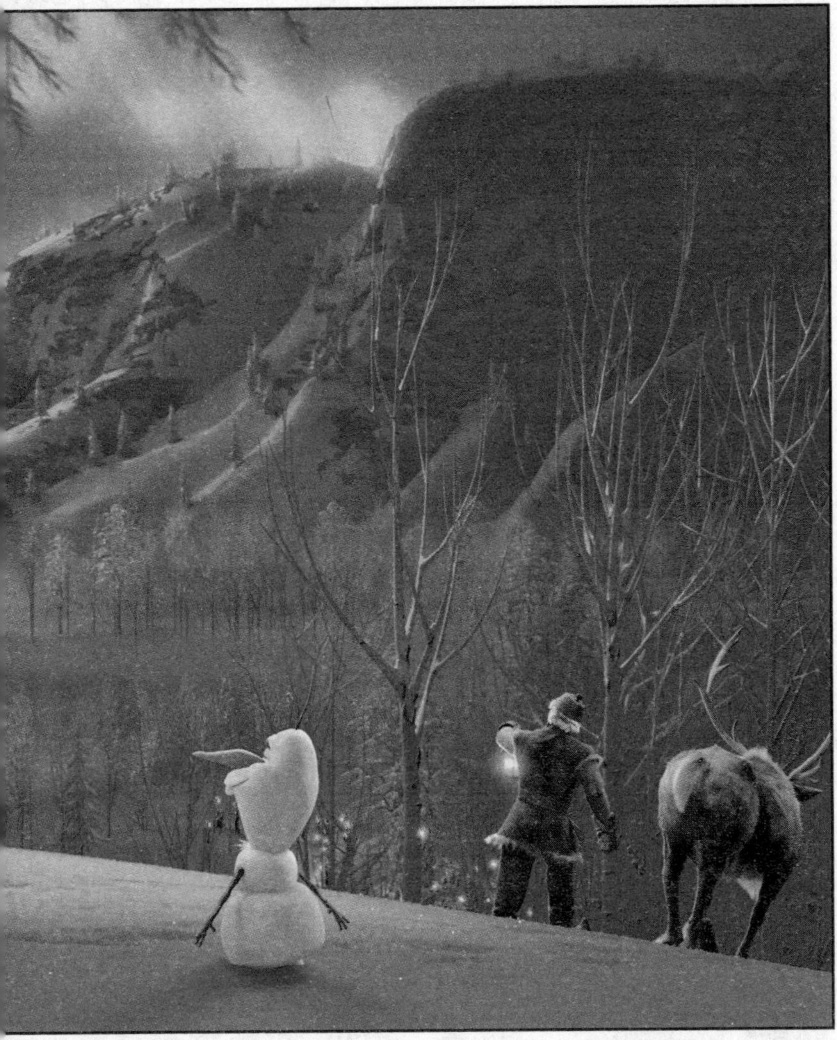

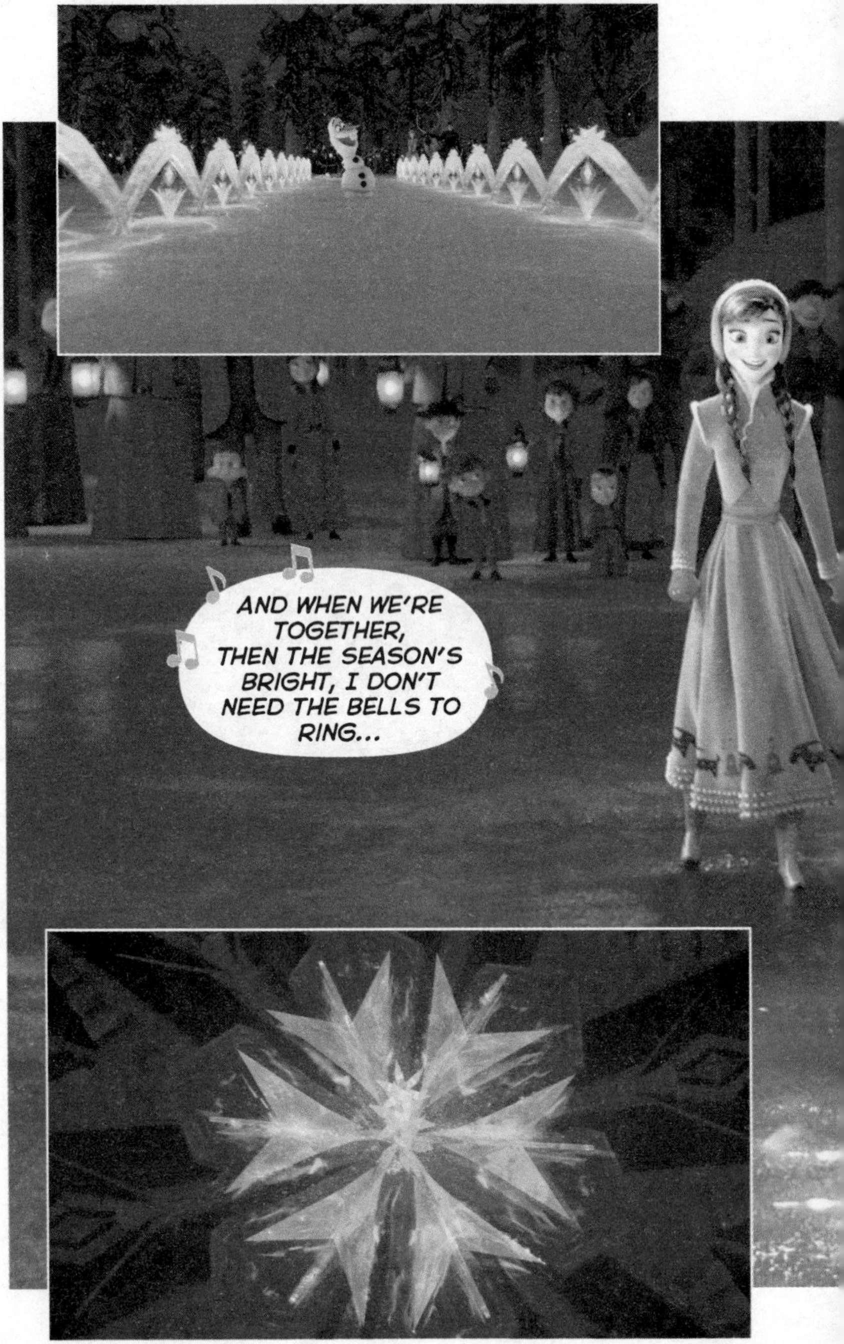
AND WHEN WE'RE TOGETHER, THEN THE SEASON'S BRIGHT, I DON'T NEED THE BELLS TO RING...

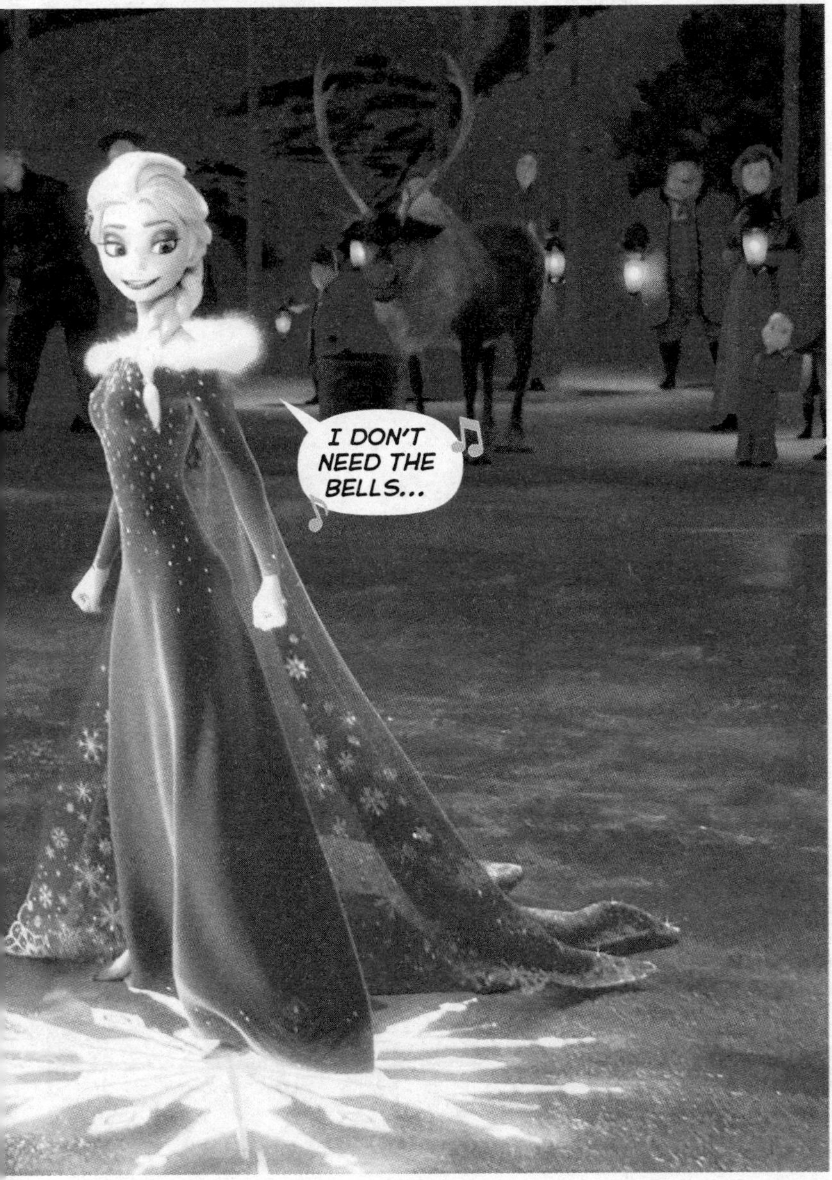
I DON'T NEED THE BELLS...

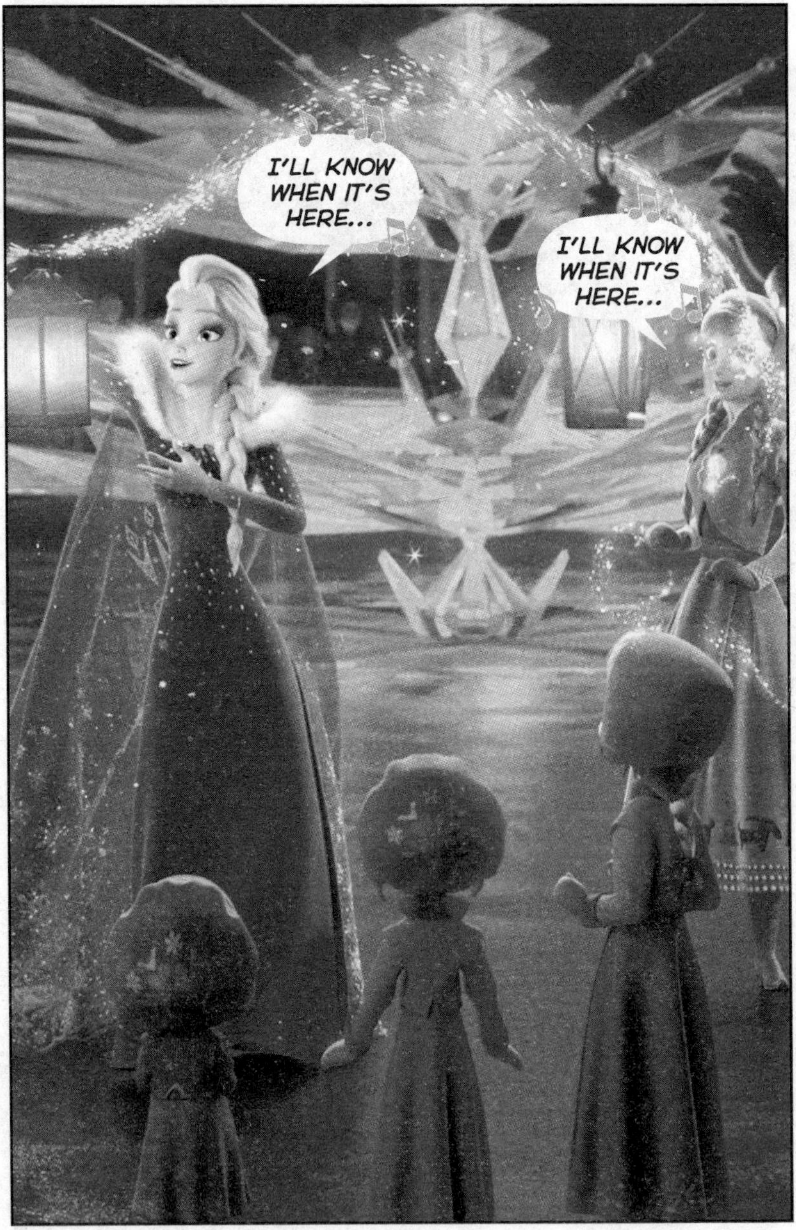
I'LL KNOW WHEN IT'S HERE...
I'LL KNOW WHEN IT'S HERE...

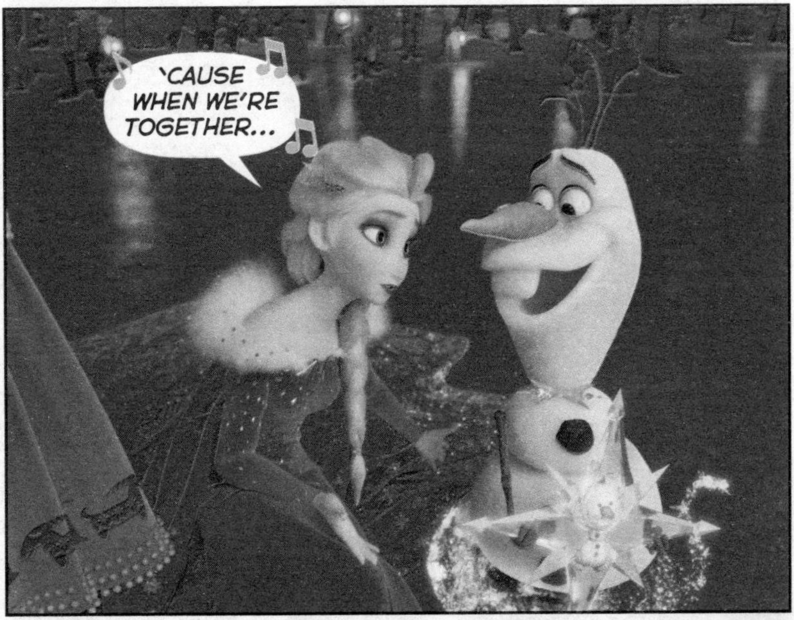
'CAUSE WHEN WE'RE TOGETHER...

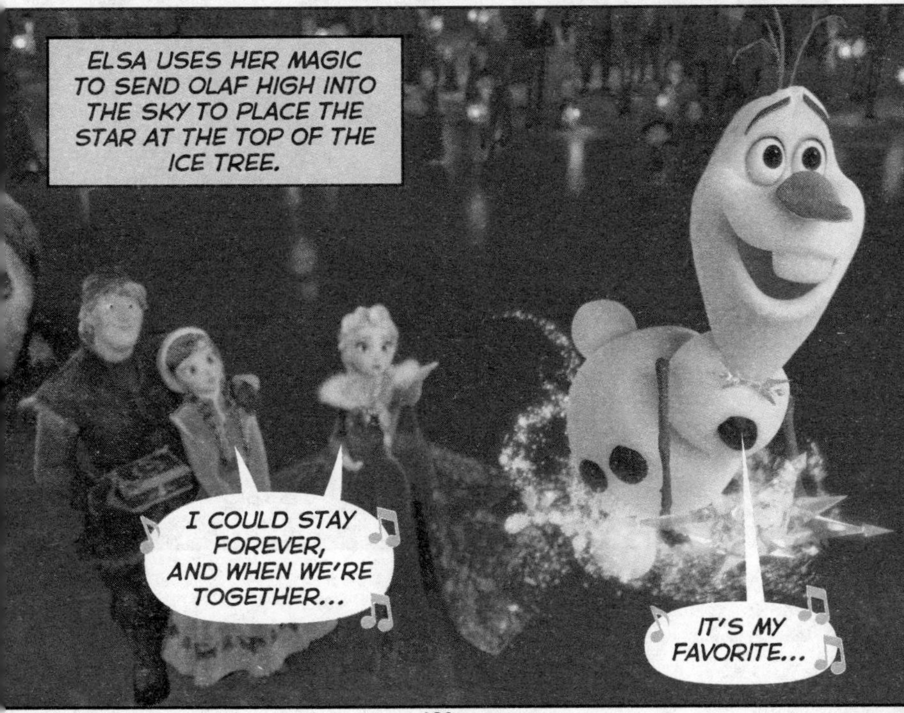
ELSA USES HER MAGIC TO SEND OLAF HIGH INTO THE SKY TO PLACE THE STAR AT THE TOP OF THE ICE TREE.
I COULD STAY FOREVER, AND WHEN WE'RE TOGETHER...
IT'S MY FAVORITE...

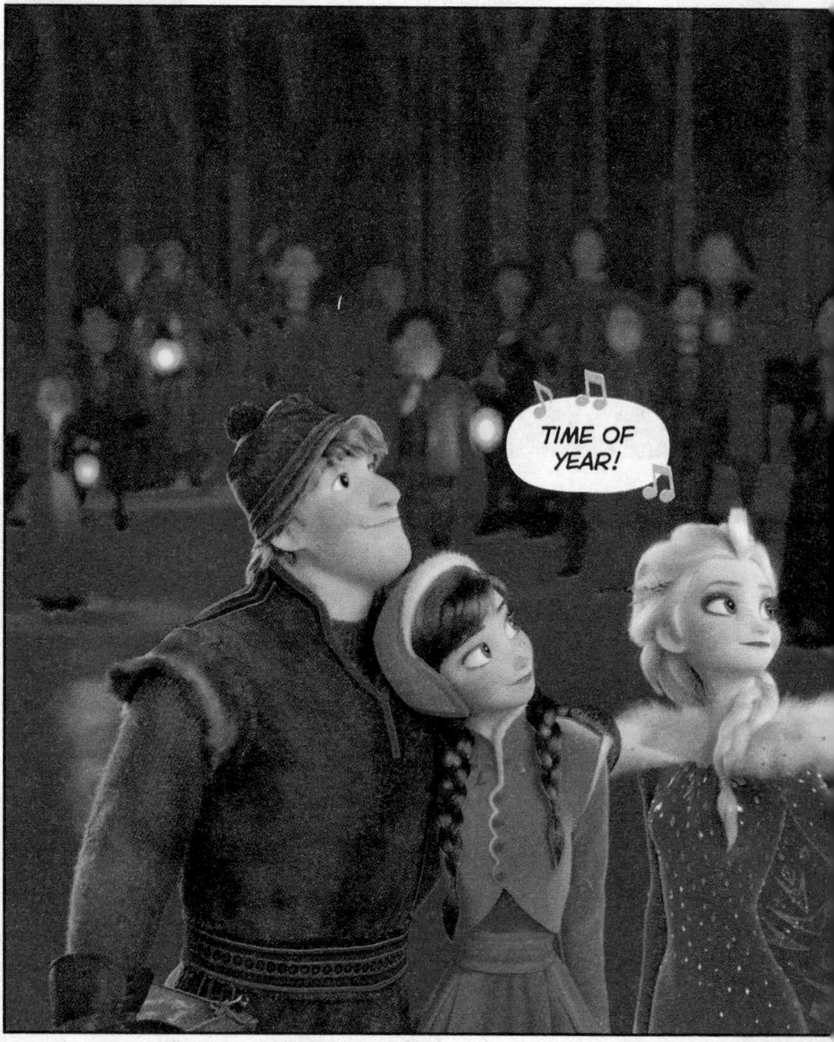
TIME OF YEAR!

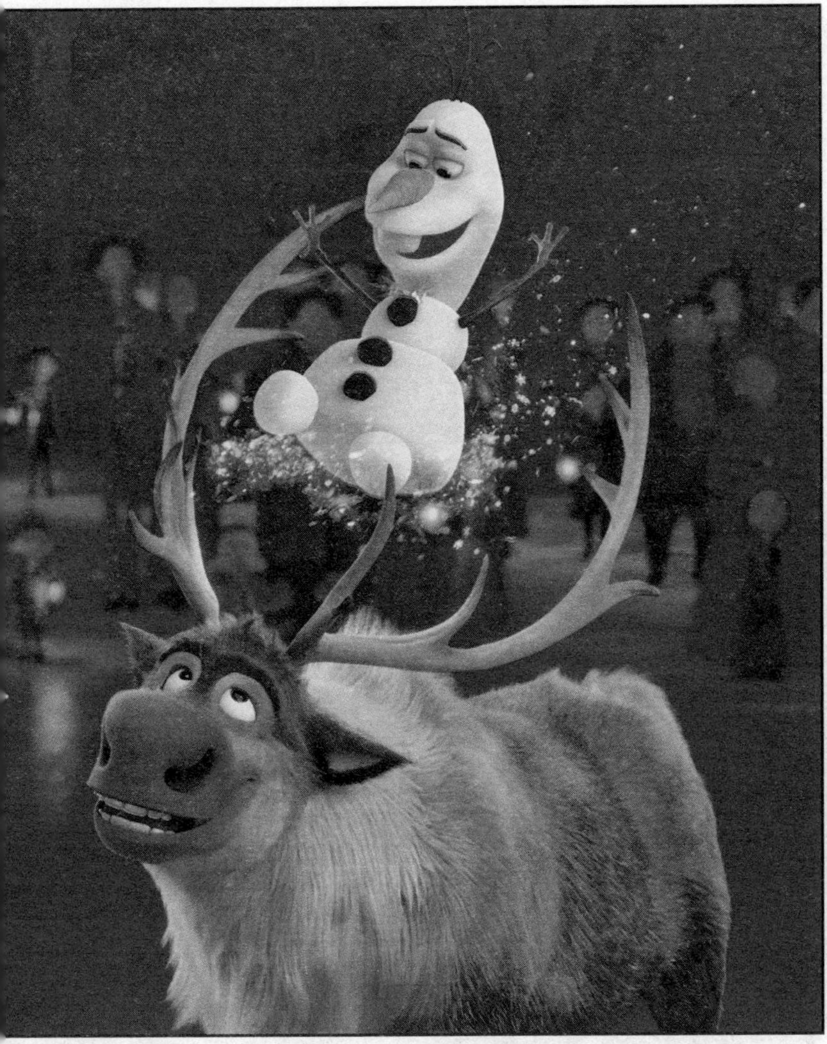

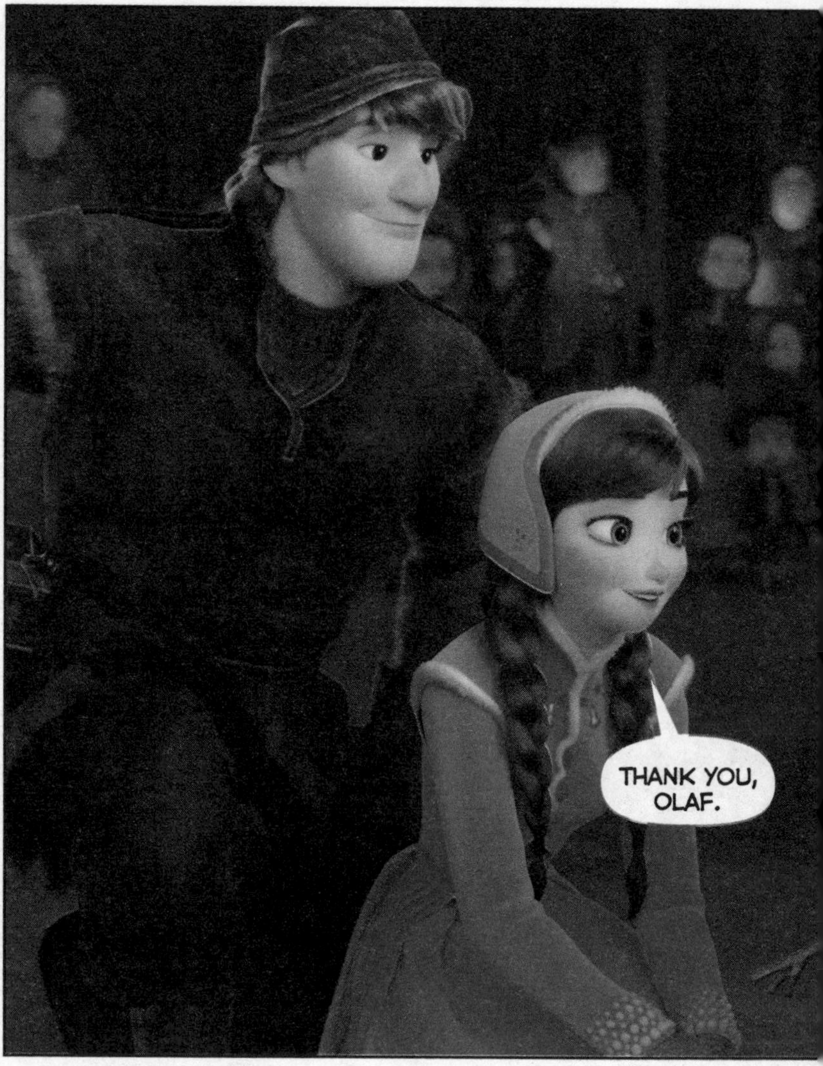
THANK YOU, OLAF.

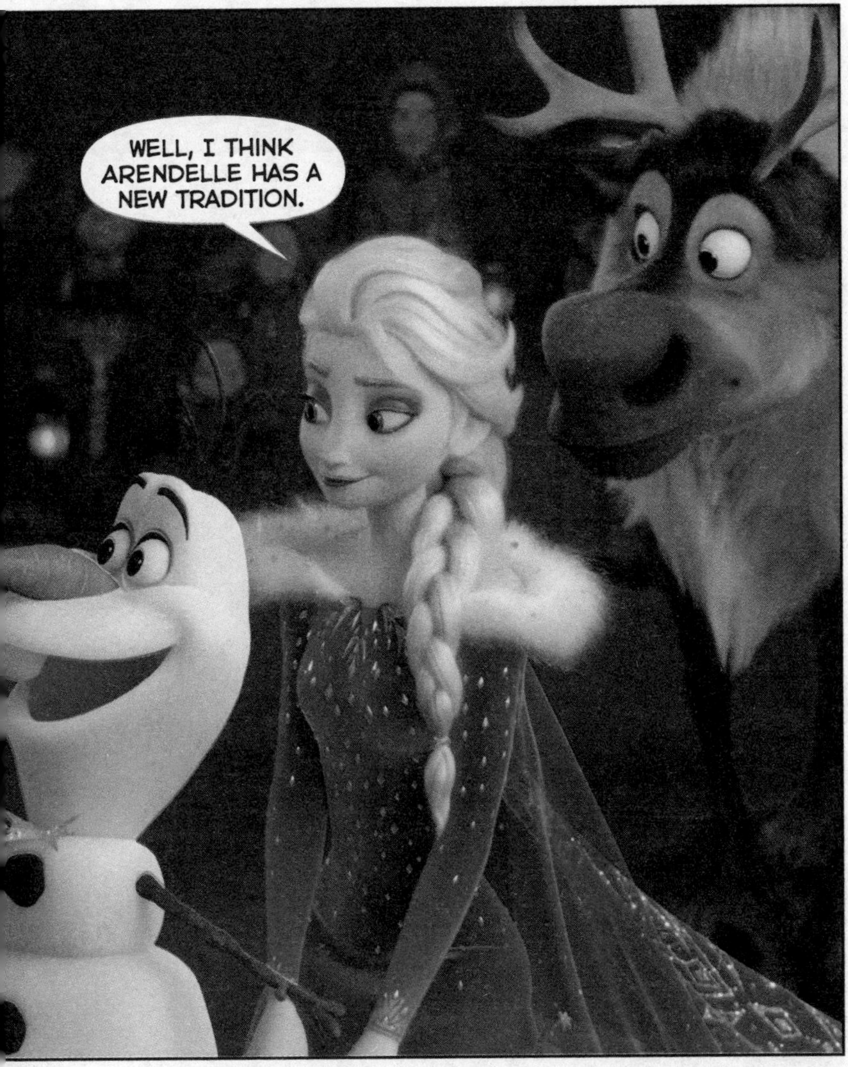
WELL, I THINK ARENDELLE HAS A NEW TRADITION.

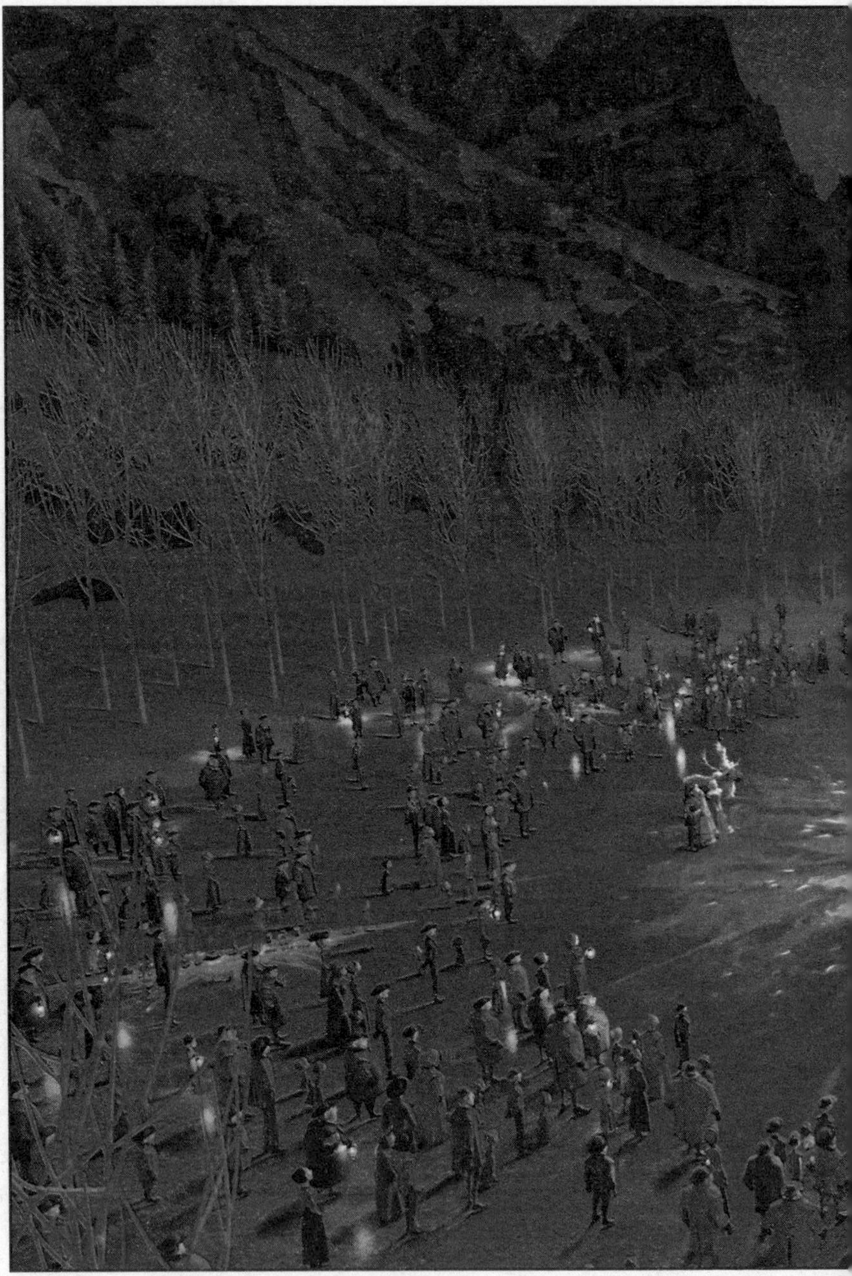

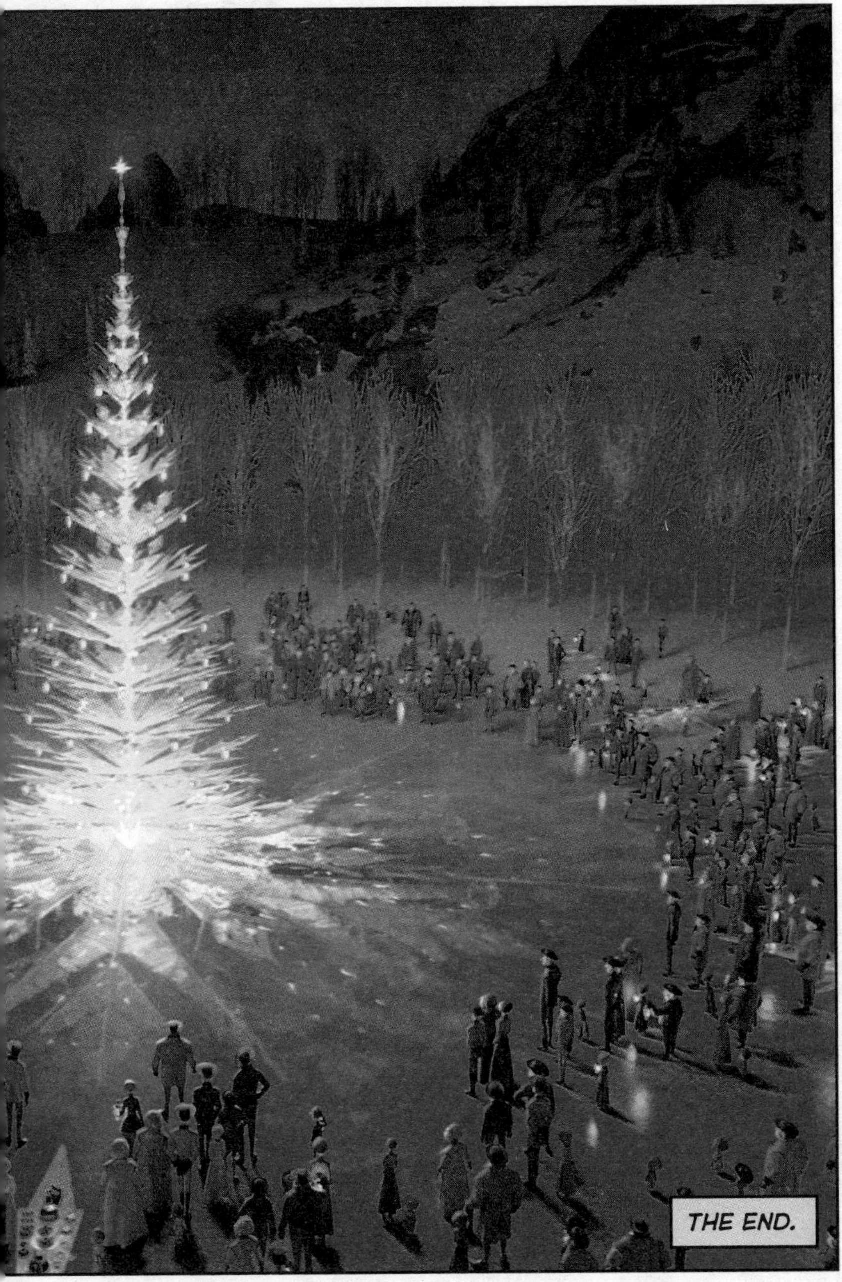
THE END.

Credits

Directed by:
Stevie Wermers-Skelton and Kevin Deters

Screenplay by:
Jac Schaeffer

Produced by:
Roy Conli

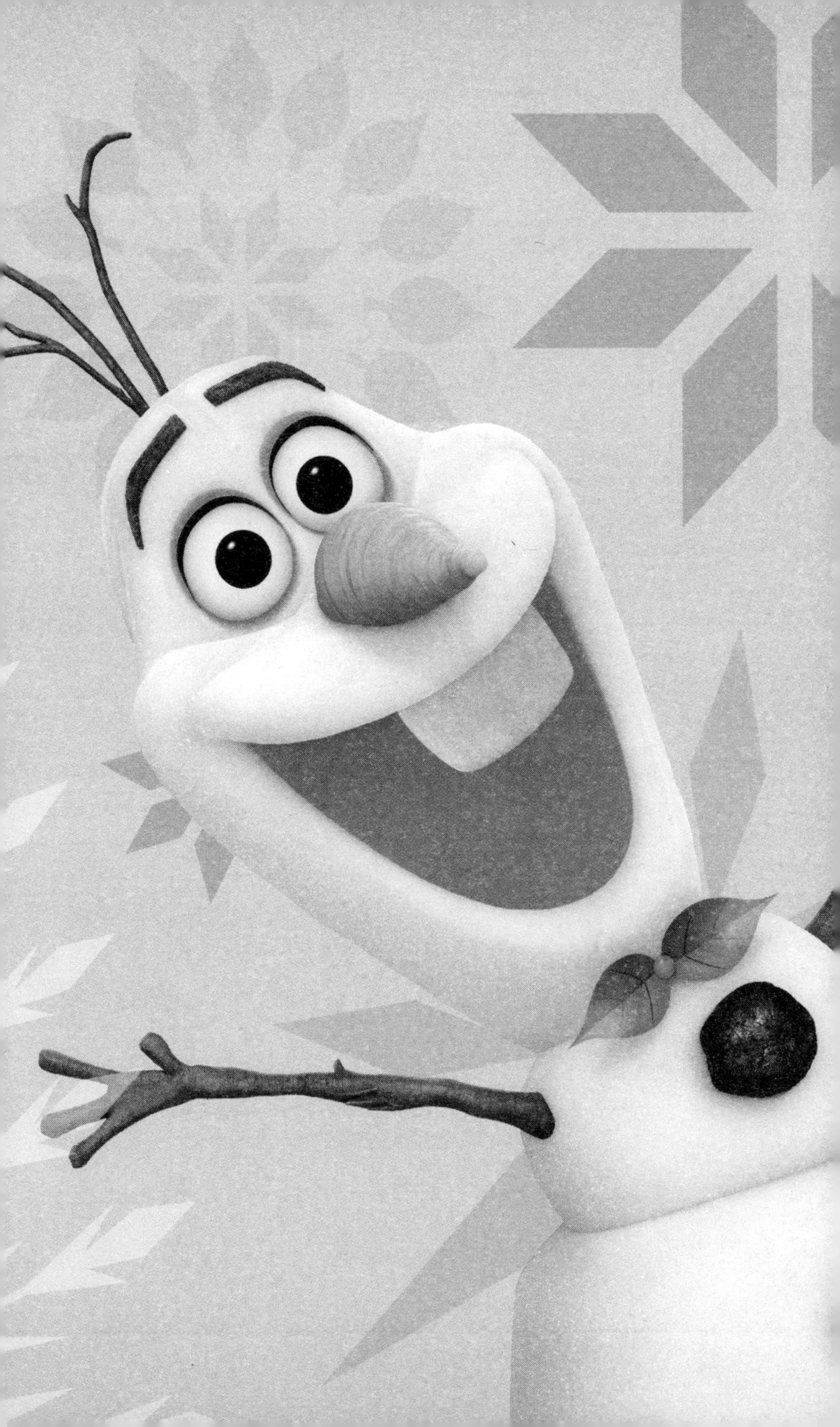